Hourglass

HOURGLASS

First edition. June 1, 2021.

Written by Elizabeth Means.

For my number one fan and ride or die bitch, Cassie

A Brief Timeline:

2080 – Fueled by dense population centers around the world, the second pandemic of the millennium starts. Scarcity of resources and disbelief in science add fuel to the wildfire-like spread. Death toll is higher than the pandemic of 2019 by a hundredfold.

2085 – After the deaths of half the world's population, an effective vaccine is created to counter the rapidly mutating virus. Annual reformulation and distribution of vaccines mandatory for all citizens of the United States.

2100 – Chief Science Officer of the United States government declares victory over disease at the fifteen-year anniversary of the end of the pandemic. Death from anything but old age and the body's natural decline has dwindled to the lowest levels in human history. Human population growth is on an upward trend, looking to reach pre-pandemic levels within a century.

Chapter 1

LUCY'S EYES OPENED slowly, fluttering and squinting at the daylight streaming through the window. Her brain brightened, neurons firing at half speed while her thoughts shifted into place, still slow from last night's sleep aid. The alarm hadn't gone off—though she didn't need one today, or ever again for that matter.

Today she was going to die.

She stood up, her feet crunching on the pages of a discarded magazine, and walked to the mirror next to the wooden dresser. Her olive skin was still dewy from sleep, only marred by a pillow mark on her left cheek. She gently rubbed the crease with a slim fingertip, willing it to smooth. A slew of image professionals were due to arrive in a matter of hours, descending on the Hanson household to buff and polish Lucy and her family. She would look perfect when the clock stopped and death came to collect her.

Her floor-length eggplant dress—selected weeks ago by her teary-eyed mother—hung on the back of the white closet door. The silver high heels with complicated straps were lined up precisely underneath the dress, waiting to pinch her toes and add enough height to let her tower over her stout father. Pointing out that nobody would see the shoes under the length of her dress—couldn't she just wear sneakers?—fell on deaf ears. While Nadine Hanson loved her daughter, Lucy knew her mother had always longed for a bigger family. Maybe the next time around she'd get it; twins and triplets were more common than a single birth, especially with second-chance mothers. Lucy hoped the bittersweet irony of losing one child for a chance at another would wane if the next had enough Lifetime Potential to outlive their parents. Lucy's hadn't been enough.

Glancing at her bedside clock, she noted the time—her sixteen years were almost up, and all that remained of the rest of her life could be counted in hours.

She grabbed her flannel robe and wrapped it around herself, pulling her thick, dark hair out from underneath the collar to flow down her back. The hall closet door stood ajar, cardboard boxes stacked behind it. Opening the door to peek, Lucy saw they were empty, ready to be filled with her belongings after she was gone. Her parents would be allowed to prepare for another pregnancy soon. At least they had something to look forward to.

Her mother, Nadine, was supposed to outlive both Lucy and her father. The itch to replace Lucy with a new child who would still be alive at Nadine's wake was unsurprising. Lucy had not won the genetic lottery, forcing her parents to learn to accept that she would only get a little more than sixteen years instead of the longer life they had been hoping for. Neither did her parents meet the requirements to try and conceive a second child during Lucy's lifetime—they had missed this window by six years, and Lucy had felt their resentment over this fact her entire life. Once she passed, they were free to pursue parenthood again, though Nadine would only have a year to get pregnant before she became a "high-risk" mother and was disqualified again.

Lucy started to get ready, savoring the heat of the shower on her skin as she scrubbed. The rosy scent of her shampoo filled her nostrils as she focused on doing everything one final time. Rinsing her hair, applying the conditioner and then the shaving cream, feeling the sting of her razor nicking the skin of her ankle. Would this be the last time she felt pain? She watched the faint trail of blood run down her ankle, turning pink in the water of the shower and disappearing down the drain.

Her fingers brushed against the scabs on her upper thigh, scratching absently, taking pleasure in knowing their existence on her body would remain her secret. The scars were sacred to her—the pain of losing her boyfriend, Colton, months prior, projected physically on her body with the help of a pair of sewing scissors. After tonight, she wouldn't feel anything anymore. Everyone said it wouldn't hurt, probably. She hoped this was true.

After the shower, she brushed her teeth, wiping the steam away from the bathroom mirror with one hand. With an index finger, she drew hearts and wrote her name on the surface of the glass, knowing that her father might find it after his early morning shower tomorrow. She thought it would make him smile.

Lucy dressed in her most comfortable lounge pants and a button-down top, which according to her mother, was easiest to remove without smudging the makeup artistry. They were paying for it to be perfect, after all. She made a face at herself in the mirror, sticking her tongue out playfully and widening her eyes, remembering a similar expression Colton had worn trying to make her laugh. He'd worn it better, though. Lucy was glad he had died only six months before. Any longer and she might not be able to recall his face and the way he had looked at her. The faces of those she had known growing up who had passed years before her, including both sets of grandparents and half of her friends, had already become blurry. This was the last day of her existing memory, and she could say with certainty that Colton would never fade—and for that she was grateful.

Chapter 2

Six Months Earlier

THERE WAS AN AWKWARD three-hour gap between Evergreen Mason's last panel interview at Virionics and the next scheduled meeting, one with a director who would decide—hopefully favorably—her fate with the company she had worked so hard to become a part of. There was enough time to take the thirty-minute ride back to the apartment she shared with her boyfriend, Zane, and shower off the nervous sheen of sweat. Evergreen dug into her purse for the familiar feel of keys adorned with a microscope keychain. Conscious of whoever might be walking by the deserted hallway, she snuck a whiff under the arm of her previously crisp white shirt.

"Rough," she declared. She vowed not only to shower but to take deodorant to go.

Finally locating her keys, Evergreen unlocked the door to the apartment. The inside of the apartment was untidy, with empty glasses littering the coffee table across from the doorway where she stood. She sighed, hating to come back to a cluttered home, and began to collect the glassware destined for the dishwasher. Her boyfriend's complacency was a source of frustration she convinced herself to swallow in order to maintain peace, telling herself that if she wanted things a certain way it was on her to make them so. Evergreen chocked it up to a learning curve; they had only lived together for a few months and were still adjusting.

"Zane?" she called. He must be home—his wool peacoat was draped over one arm of the sofa. Faint music drifted down the hallway from the single bedroom they shared. She closed the door of the dishwasher, her tidying complete, and pulled her heels off her sore feet, feeling immediate relief. She rocked back and forth on the balls of her feet, the sudden freedom so pleasurable.

Shoes in hand, she strode down the short hallway and called again. "Zane?" Reaching the doorknob, she turned it and pushed open the door, its hinges creaking.

"What are you—" She stopped mid-sentence as the door bumped lightly against the wall behind it. Clothing was scattered across the floor she had just tidied up that morning, including two pieces of sparse magenta lace she didn't recognize. Convinced her mind was playing tricks—she didn't own underwear that slutty—Evergreen's survey of the room was so contrary to what she expected to find, she had to blink several times to be sure. What she expected to find was Zane lying in bed playing a game on his tablet, smoking a joint, or sleeping, all of which would have been within the norm for him at this time of day. Rather, upon *her* pouf chair—the only piece of furniture Evergreen had contributed to their humble abode—the porcelain-skinned Silver Bennett sat astride her boyfriend of thirteen months, in completely stitchless glory.

Evergreen couldn't get out of the apartment fast enough. She rage-marched for blocks before realizing her shoes were still clutched tightly in one hand, her bare feet gritty with the filth of the sidewalk. Since Zane had nixed any chance of a relaxing shower, she opted for second best: drugstore deodorant and baby wipes. Willing herself not to fall apart before sealing the deal on her very last interview, she took deep breaths while staring into the water-stained mirror in the pharmacy bathroom. She had purchased makeup-removing wipes only as a desperate last resort—one she wasn't willing to use just yet. This mascara sample was supposed to guarantee elongation of her lashes by a minimum of a quarter inch. Why should she ruin that over a stupid *boy*? That thought alone brought a sting to her eyes.

"No," she insisted. "You earned this. You deserve this. You *will* get this job."

Two hours later, Evergreen returned for the final round of questioning. *You're ready. You have to be ready.* She felt unconvinced. The heavy doors opened, emitting a cool breeze that blew her blond hair into her mouth, sticking to her lip gloss. She batted it out of her face and stepped through the entrance, arranging the long ponytail tied low on the nape of her neck and secured tidily with a red ribbon.

Gleaming wax coated the floors, their pristine white making the lobby of the Virionics Institute appear bright enough to give the illusion of being outside. Though this was not Evergreen Mason's first trip across the threshold, the sparkle of the entryway was still enough to dazzle, reinforcing her desire to nail this final interview and finally join the ranks of Virionics scientists. The click of her "nail it" patent leather heels, so named by her best friend and biggest cheerleader, Arizona Janski, reverberated against the sparsely decorated stone walls and tall ceilings. Arizona would be livid when she found out what Zane had been up to this afternoon, and Evergreen vowed to call her afterwards. *Screw him, you've got this.* She set her inner monologue to repeat as she clicked past the marble Virionics logo, life-sized and shiny, its black surface flecked with gold. The large "V" dominated the center of the room, the twisting double-helix of DNA forming one side of the letter. It was impossible to tell whether or not the DNA represented was actually NNA, neuro-nucleic acid, the official name for what used to be called "junk DNA." NNA had turned out to be the key to unlocking the vault on how organisms think, evolve, and develop over time. It could even predict the moment of death.

Evergreen had always dreamed of following in her father's footsteps by working with the Scientific Operations Division at Virionics, and a cheating boyfriend was not going to be the reason she didn't succeed. Thus far, she had checked all of the necessary boxes: completing her High Lifetime Potential education near the top of her class, excelling at her year-long research fellowship in the small laboratory specializing in STDs, and impressing the previous three interviewers. Gerald Mason, Evergreen's father ranked high at Virionics, which had certainly helped get her foot in the door, but as he'd assured Evergreen, the accomplishments to make it this far were all hers.

Evergreen bit her lip and knocked politely on the door whose gold nameplate read *Susanne Abdul*. Gerald had warned Evergreen over coffee in their pre-interview prep session that, while he didn't know Susanne Abdul personally, her reputation as a hard-lined, goal-oriented woman and detester of time wasters preceded her. He'd coached her to get straight to the point and avoid long drawn-out explanations.

"Come in," a sharp voice called from the other side of the door. The small black panel meant for card reader access glowed faintly green to indicate it was open.

She entered cautiously, trying to conceal her struggle with the unanticipated weight of the door. Although Evergreen was expected, the fluttering nervousness in her belly betrayed her doubt that she was in the right place, despite the door's nameplate. "Susanne Abdul?" She sought confirmation using the most confident smile she could muster.

"It's pronounced '*Sus-ahn*,'" the dark-haired woman said firmly, yet not unkindly. It was obvious she had to make this correction with some frequency.

Crap. Her father had only ever referred to her as Abdul. Frustration joined the existing pile of emotional strife, and tears threatened her eyes. She took a deep diaphragmatic breath, hoping to calm her nervous system. Susanne had yet to look up from her keyboard where her manicured fingers typed furiously. Evergreen stood anxious and unsure in the doorway.

"Can I help you?" Raising her dark brown eyes from the computer screen, Susanne's long lashes blinked several times as she settled her gaze on Evergreen, and Evergreen hoped her face expressed something near professional nonchalance instead of the manic wide-eyed anxiety she felt.

"Sorry—Sus*anne*. I'm Evergreen Mason," she began, clearing her throat. "We exchanged emails?"

"Oh right," Susanne said, her expression softening by a fraction. "You're my two o'clock." She glanced at her bio-watch and sighed. "I totally forgot. It's just been one of those days." A small smile appeared on her lips, and she gestured with a hand at the chair in front of her desk. "Have a seat while I get myself organized here."

Evergreen pulled out the chair, placing her leather briefcase on her lap, and began to sift through documents as Susanne busied herself with clearing paperwork on the desk and removing the remains of what had obviously been a working lunch.

"I have my resume here, my transcripts, letters of recommendation, and the two papers I've published, or rather, co-published." Evergreen placed the manila folder with her credentials delicately on the desk in front of Susanne.

"That won't be necessary. I've already received copies of all those things," Susanne said with a casual wave of her hand. "Top grades, competitive education program, a year-long research internship—Your resume is very impressive, Evergreen."

"Thank you, I—"

Susanne waved a dismissive hand, cutting her off.

"Don't worry, you can relax," she said authoritatively.

Evergreen managed to sit back further in her chair and adjust her posture in a way she hoped showed ease and respect. *Relax, goddammit,* she chided.

"The Virionics Institute has already put you through the interview ringer. If a candidate gets to me, they are fairly serious about finding you a position within our organization. I just wanted to meet with you and see if you might be a good fit for this assignment."

Susanne continued, but Evergreen realized she had missed something Susanne had said. Willing her hands into a neutral position on her lap instead of fidgeting, another coaching tip of her father's, Evergreen willed Zane's cheating face from the forefront of her brain and focused.

"That's good news." Evergreen could feel the tangled knots in her stomach and the sweat returning to her armpits.

"What interests you most about the role?" Susanne asked, her pen poised on the notepad in front of her.

The interview process had been exhausting and intimidating. Getting hired into the division of Virionics that was consistently innovating would jump-start her career faster than any other first job. So when Susanne began to ask her why she wanted to work on her team, Evergreen easily gushed about what an honor it would be to work alongside the scientists whose work she most admired, totally forgetting the horrifying details of her afternoon.

"The Virionics Institute is a large company, and so is the Scientific Operations division I oversee," Susanne said after a minute raise of her hand, indicating she had heard enough of Evergreen prattling on about her scientific experience and her desire to work with one of the teams Susanne was in charge of. "The Department of Pharmacological Development, where this job opportunity exists, has broad responsibilities. Not only do we have teams which develop the yearly vaccinations with any updates discovered from emerging pathogens, but we also create antibiotics and cell-targeting formulas for people identified as being prone to cancerous cell mutations. As the health arm of the government, we exist to protect our population against disease and prevent early death. Everyone should get to live life to the fullest extent of their Lifetime Potential."

That last was a line Evergreen had heard many times throughout the interview process. Virionics was big on reiterating their company's mission and strategic principles whenever possible. Her father suggested it was to show how well-aligned they were with the objectives shareholders and government higher-ups supported. Linking their mission into the interview process hadn't surprised him when Evergreen shared similar comments made by other employees—all incoming staff should be well-versed in what Virionics stood for and keep their overarching goals in mind whenever approaching a new project or solving a problem.

Evergreen nodded her head with hopeful enthusiasm. She desperately wanted to strike the right balance between highlighting her experience and not making herself appear naïve to think it was more impressive than it really was.

"Now, I know people like you, Evergreen," Susanne said pointedly, waving a knowing finger at her. "You're obviously smart, driven, and innovative. I also know that you're applying for an entry-level position as a Junior Researcher where you will mostly be responsible for assisting senior-level scientists with their experiments. What I'm getting at is, I know this isn't the end point for a girl like you. Tell me, where do you want to go with this job? What's your career trajectory?"

Evergreen hesitated, unsure if this question was meant to be as straightforward as it sounded or if, in fact, Susanne was attempting to get her to talk herself out of the job.

"My father started as a Junior Researcher." She took a breath. "He always instilled the idea that one should work from the bottom up and learn the ropes on every level before jumping to the very top—or whichever way you intended to go," she added, reminding herself to tone down the ambition. "What I've always wanted to do was work with the Disease Prevention and Monitoring Department. I want to wear the 'space suit' and work directly with infectious diseases. I want to be the one responsible for discovering what a virus like Ebola is going to do next. I know that would be a long way off in the future for me, but I believe this is the right place to start. I want to learn, and I want to earn my position in the field," she finished, trying to sound as confident as she had practicing in the mirror this morning.

Susanne nodded, pressing her fingertips together. "Good. That is a common aspiration of those working in this area of the Institute. This is quite a competitive track you have in mind, as I'm sure you realize."

"Yes, absolutely," Evergreen said, straightening her back against the chair. "I'm a hard worker, and I'm eager to find ways to distinguish myself among my peers. While still being a team player, of course."

"Of course," Susanne said matter-of-factly. "There are certainly ways you can distinguish yourself here, Evergreen. This can be a challenging place to work—some people burn out and decide to transition to a more comfortable position. If you really want to work in such an elite department of the company, you'll need to be consistently publishing and keeping up with current literature. The more innovative the publications, the better. I see that you have been published already, which is a great step in the right direction. What the hiring committee for the Prevention Department would be looking for is scientific initiative. Aside from your regular duties, it will be looked upon positively if you have other independent projects related to the work we do here."

"I can do that. Thank you for the advice." Evergreen bobbed her head with a smile.

Susanne stood. "I believe you would be a great asset to our team here, and I would like to move forward with the hiring process."

"Really?" Evergreen felt a wave of relief followed by an overpowering urge to jump up and down or maybe cry. She managed to restrain herself by clutching the armrest of the chair, her manicured fingernails digging into the squishy material.

"You should expect to receive documents later today with your official offer." Susanne reached across the table to clasp Evergreen's hand in a firm shake. "Welcome to Virionics."

"Thank you! Oh, thank you so much. I look forward to starting work with you." Evergreen beamed as she grabbed her bag and began to back her way out of the office.

"Have a nice afternoon."

"Thank you." She bumped into her chair as she shuffled toward the door. "You too!" she exclaimed, fighting the urge to hug her new boss.

She barely made it to the bathroom at the end of the hall, heaving the contents of her stomach into the toilet. The culmination of the last few weeks' stress was gradually leaving her body and the nausea was already passing. One problem down, now the next to consider. It never seemed to end.

What had Zane been thinking? She wiped her watery eyes with a clump of toilet paper and pushed herself off the floor, knees aching. Evergreen didn't want to think about what to do next just yet. Her mind was done making decisions and making sense. She gathered her briefcase, washed her hands, and made her way out of the building.

The afternoon sun glared down, and she shielded her eyes with an unsteady hand. Evergreen's wrist vibrated and she looked down. Arizona was calling.

"Hey," she answered flatly.

"Hey? Wait, is that the 'hey' of someone who got the job or the 'hey' of someone who will definitely find someplace better to use her myriad of talents?"

"Huh? Yeah. I got it."

Arizona shrieked into her ear implant. "I'm *so* excited for you!"

Evergreen crossed the street, jogging the last few steps as the light changed. Her shoes pinched at the toes, and she felt blank, her mind struggling to transition between the success of landing the job she wanted and the obvious failure of her relationship.

"Yeah. It's pretty global," she said tonelessly while rounding the corner away from Virionics, passing the entrance to the train station. She didn't really know where she was going, only that her feet wouldn't be lasting too much longer.

"Wait. What the hell is wrong with you? You got the job, right?" Arizona asked, her tone a mix of confusion and concern.

"I got the job," Evergreen confirmed.

"So why do you sound like you were in Marian Markus's blast radius?" Arizona asked, citing the mean graduate student who ran their chemistry lab and her infamous temper.

"I . . ." Evergreen tried to find the words to describe what she had seen that afternoon, and her face flooded with the precursory pain of incoming tears. "Zane . . . he—I saw him with . . ." She struggled to say the name of the golden whore who had taken her boyfriend by storm. "Silver Bennett," she spat. "They were together. *Together, together*," she clarified, knowing Arizona would understand. "In *our* apartment. Today."

Arizona was silent for a moment, but Evergreen knew the phone hadn't disconnected. She heard some faint cursing and imagined her friend slamming her forehead into a hand with exasperation. "Where are you?"

Evergreen looked up, spotting a neon sign, and decisively pushed through the doorway below it. "I'll send you a pin."

"Be right there."

Arizona was the best.

Chapter 3

LUCY COULD HEAR HER parents outside her bedroom door, talking in low voices just out of earshot. It was a safe assumption that she was the topic under discussion. Her parents were undoubtedly worried about her and how she was coping with the imminent loss of her best friend—and, though they didn't totally approve, her boyfriend—Colton. In less than a week, his biological clock would be up and he'd leave Lucy alone in the interim months until her own wake.

"It's not healthy to become so attached in your age group," her mother, Nadine, had warned on numerous occasions. But like the literature Lucy loved to devour told her over and over again, there was no stopping teenage love, especially when adults tried to place barriers in your way.

As Lucy stared at the blank sheet of paper meant to record her feelings on the matter, she couldn't help but realize her parents may have had a point. This was so hard. Maybe if she and Colton had never gotten together, she'd be out enjoying her remaining months, like so many of her peers with short lives. About half of Lucy's friend group would outlive her, though only by mere months, having banded together at school early on based on their designated lifespan. A few planned deaths were interspersed between Colton's and her own wake, which meant parties to look forward to as she counted down the days.

No, she decided, he was worth the trouble. None of her friends really understood or would ever get to experience love like theirs. If only they knew what it felt like, maybe they'd be less eager to die.

Lucy's Wake Counselor, Tess, had proposed the currently incomplete assignment in front of her as a way to compose her thoughts. It was meant to allow her mind to process how life might change after Colton passed. His Lifetime Potential, or LP for short, was almost up. Tess, always one to enthusiastically embrace new trends in psychology, had insisted that Lucy write down her feelings *by hand*, because somehow that made this all easier to swallow. Handwriting, Lucy pointed out, was archaic and tedious. Why couldn't she just type it? Arguing had been a mistake. Tess had droned on about the importance of embracing her fate, honoring the past, and looking forward to the future for what seemed like hours. Lucy could practically feel herself getting older, Colton's death getting closer. While Tess emphasized the importance of allowing Colton to die without having any regrets between them, Lucy bit back her numerous retorts and agreed to do things Tess's way, if only to get her to shut up.

Lucy was pretty sure her counselor gave this particular assignment to all the other low-LP kids she met with while revealing her coping strategy as an epiphany every time—as if it were specialized treatment for that kid's specific relationships and family situations. This chore was total bullshit. Lucy and her friends regularly compared notes and mocked their counselors' suggestions, all of them too cool for mandated therapy.

She imagined how her remaining friends might be asked to complete this same exercise to deal with her death, six months from now. It was meant to give meaning to the last days of someone's life in some existential way, transforming it into something more special than it was. Or at least that was the argument. Well, not everyone *was* special. The only thing that ever made *her* special was Colton. He was the global, awesome one. Not her. Never her.

Lucy grunted at the cliché of it all, the pen poised awkwardly in her fingers, struggling with the decision on what to write. Whether she should spill all of her secrets and feelings or keep them inside, preserving them just for her. She jotted down the date, October 16, 2315 and felt mild satisfaction that at least something was written.

Where to begin? Putting their story into words from the beginning seemed like the best place to start. Lucy retraced her memory to the first moment she laid eyes on his face. Colton had star quality; that was certain. It was in the way he smiled, warm and a little lopsided, and how his eyes locked with hers as if she were the most interesting person in the world. They had reached for the same book, *History of Music: From The Beatles to The Anti-Bodies*, and she'd immediately blushed, averting her brown eyes.

"It's yours," she'd muttered, trying hard not to disturb the quiet of the library.

"You saw it first. I insist." Colton had thrust the book toward her hands. "I'm new here, wouldn't want to step on anyone's toes."

She'd nodded, averting her eyes again.

"I've seen you in here before, haven't I? I just moved here last week. I'm Colton Goodman, AKA 'the new kid.'" He'd chuckled at his own jest and reached a hand out to shake hers.

What kind of twelve-year-old shook hands? Lucy had made eye contact, her blush deepening, and shook his hand. "Lucy Hanson, the old kid." She'd immediately regretted her halfhearted attempt to joke back with him, but his smile had merely widened.

They became friends that day, and every day since their bond had strengthened. Lucy had been quiet, introverted, and lacking any close friends before she met him. Colton couldn't have been more different. The rest of the school had noticed his gregarious personality and agreed that between his height, his blue eyes, and the loss of an adolescent crack to his voice despite his twelve years, he was good looking. His other twelve-year-old peers were eager to place him on the ladder of their social hierarchy, though after their first pleasant encounter Lucy had doubted that there would be many more, as he was likely to rise to the top. The so-called 'popular' crowd had never been very friendly toward her, and she didn't find it likely that Colton Goodman with his shining aura of possibility would waste any time with *her*.

She had accepted her role on the lower rungs of her social ladder and hadn't intended to alter her position. Despite that, Colton stuck to her like a magnet and refused to admit himself to higher circles without her inclusion. The other girls had never really warmed to Lucy prior to his arrival, much less paid attention to her at all. Yet as the adopted bestie of the handsome and charming new guy, she was taken into the fold without much argument. Lucy had been the price to pay to be friends with the enigmatic new kid. She soon became inaugurated into the world of the social clique, learning to navigate their complicated communications—like whether or not someone *really* liked your new shoes based on how they said the compliment. Classmates would pass, and the girls of the group would attend the wakes and compete against each other in various ways: who dressed best, who drank the most without vomiting, and whose show of emotion looked the most authentic. It was hard to discern where Lucy would rank after Colton was gone.

Though the library continued to be a respite for Lucy, and oftentimes a place Colton and she would go together, her new group of friends and their habits became part of her daily routine. They could spend hours talking about boys, the others in the group always speculating on which boys had crushes on which of them. Inevitably, the girls had suspected romance between Colton and Lucy, but she had always shrugged it off, insisting they were only friends. This had been true up until a little over a year ago, just after they had both turned fifteen. Colton had caught her off guard with a kiss during a schoolwide game in the Forest Dome, a version of capture the flag he had invented and proudly called *Coltynomite*. They had been hiding in a tree, only a few feet above some passing opponents. Lucy had been out of her comfort zone in the height of the branches, but Colton had helped her up *and* promised to help her down when their opportunity in the game was right. Nearly on top of each other trying to maintain their footing in the tree limbs, they had held their breath as the other team walked past without looking upwards. Colton had exhaled loudly once the coast was clear.

"That was close," he had said with relief.

"Can we get down now? I'm afraid I'm going to fall and break my neck."

"Man, Nadine would be so disappointed if you didn't make it to your LP," Colton had joked. "They could come back though, so we should stay up here." He'd looked at her, and she had suddenly realized how close their faces were. There had been a few occasions when Lucy had felt Colton might try to kiss her, but they were always interrupted—usually by someone walking into the room unexpectedly, making them jump apart like they had been physically pushed. Once, the sound of the screaming fire alarm had broken the spell. But this time there had been no interruptions. Colton had leaned in and pressed his lips against hers, making her forget any fear of tall places and the need to get back onto solid ground. Instead, she'd felt practically dizzy with happiness.

Lucy closed her eyes for a moment and smiled at the memory. She began to sketch little hearts, letting her mind wander, imagining Colton kissing her, his warm hand on the back of her neck as he pulled her close. His tongue lightly touching the inside of her lower lip as she kissed him back. She pictured herself pushing him down onto the couch in the hidden back nook of the library, their favorite spot.

Lucy jolted upright from her slouch at the sound of the knock on her door, a guilty blush spreading quickly across her cheeks. She grabbed hastily at the papers she had been scribbling on, shoving them into the desk drawer. "Yes?"

"Luce, it's me," the familiar voice said on the other side of her bedroom door.

"Oh." She smiled, recognizing his voice. "You can come in!"

Colton pushed open the door and smiled at her. The light from the hallway illuminated him from behind, making him radiate like a star. She sometimes still couldn't believe he had chosen her. Just like she still had trouble with the idea that soon he would be gone from her life, his light extinguished forever.

"Your dad let me in," he said, closing the door behind him and returning her bedroom to its usual state of dimness. He strode the few steps to her desk, leaning down to kiss her lips, his hand on her shoulder as she looked up at him.

"Hi." She grinned conspiratorially.

"Hi." He pulled up the only other chair in the room to sit next to her. "What are you up to with that look on your face?"

"Wouldn't you like to know?"

"I asked, didn't I?" He sat down with the back of the chair facing his chest, his legs straddling the cushion.

"Nothing. I was just . . ." She trailed off, slightly embarrassed and feeling exposed, like he could read her mind. She began to fumble with the stapler on her desk, pulling the staples out and lining them up evenly in front of her.

"Just . . . ?" he teased.

"Just thinking." She smirked at him.

"Oh? About me?" He always knew. Colton feigned surprise and gestured to himself, his blue eyes sparkling with mischief and teenage hormones.

"Something like that . . ."

"I see." He brushed Lucy's dark hair over her shoulder, revealing her neck, touching her lightly with his fingertips. "Want to tell me about it?" He spoke as gently as he touched her, flushing her neck and chest an excited pink.

Not wanting to spoil the moment by bringing up her morbid assignment, she turned toward him. "I can show you . . . Lock the door," she instructed. He chuckled quietly and obeyed.

Afterwards, Lucy lay comfortably against Colton's shoulder, breathing softly against his chest and watching his rib cage move up and down in time with his inhales and exhales. Would this be the last time? Surely, they would be alone a few more times before Sunday night? She could feel the sting of tears building in her throat and struggled to keep it under control. She would lose him soon, and then what would she do? How would she spend her last six months? Four years of Colton's attention, his arms around her, his laugh—it wasn't enough. And all of it would be gone soon. Despite her best efforts, a choked cry escaped her throat, and she pressed herself as close to him as possible.

"It's going to be okay, you know," Colton said, stroking her arm as it tightened across his stomach. He kissed her forehead, holding his lips there for several beats. Tears leaked from her eyes, and she turned her head into his armpit to hide her face. "It's only Tuesday. We still have almost five whole days together."

"Please," she muttered into his skin. She brought her head up and looked at him. "Your mother is going to make you do all kinds of family stuff the next few days, and Sunday you will spend most of the day helping her set up for your own wake. She's so goddamned selfish." He made to reply but she cut him off. "And don't say 'I can get out of it,' because no, you can't. She's been planning this for a year now, and you know the Marianne train cannot be stopped once she builds up steam." She paused. "I mean, I knew the deal. I knew how much time we had, but it doesn't seem like enough." She choked out the last word, trying and failing to suppress a sob. "You're sixteen, goddammit! This isn't fair!"

"It *is* fair, babe. Everyone knew all along. Isn't that better than having it be a surprise—boom, you're dead!" He pointed with a finger gun for dramatic effect. "At least we can prepare, throw a totally global party and get the chance to do what we love one more time," he emphasized with a squeeze of her shoulders. Colton stroked her cheek and brushed away a tear, flashing his brilliant smile. "You, for example, are something I love to do." Lucy gave a false laugh. "I mean, I love you," he added.

They lay silently for several minutes. The room felt cold against Lucy's skin, and she shivered involuntarily, pulling a blanket over their bodies.

"You won't have long without me," he whispered.

"Lucy! Colton! Dinnertime!" Lucy's father had learned the hard way what he might find if he barged into her room without knocking, and had since overcorrected the mistake by hollering instead.

Lucy sighed and disentangled herself from Colton, pausing by the door. "Coming?"

Chapter 4

THE RINGING OF HIS phone jolted Axon from a heavy sleep. He groaned and reached blindly for the source of the disruption, his hand brushing something warm and solid as he stretched for the bedside table. He opened his eyes a fraction and remembered the woman he had brought back with him the night before. At the second ring, she rolled onto her stomach, the pillow pressed over her head, obscuring her face. Axon had been trying his luck with two girls the previous night, cousins in a clear rivalry with each other. His brain was fuzzy, and he couldn't recall if he had been successful with the one with the nose ring and the plum lipstick or the one with the pointed chin and cat eyes. His fingertips finally found the phone and he answered groggily, halfway through the next ring before the call could go to voicemail. "What?"

"Is that how you answer the phone for your boss, Davis?"

He rubbed his eyes with the tips of his fingers and muttered a hasty, "Sorry."

"Bad time?" she asked without missing a beat.

"Last night's LP didn't go out until 4:25 a.m.," he grumbled.

"And you didn't want to miss a single minute of the after-party, I'm guessing?" she chided acidly.

"Veronica, is there something you need? I'm exhausted. I'll get the story in by noon, okay?" He attempted to contain a yawn but failed.

"It's twenty to two," she pointed out.

Axon pushed himself up and sat on the edge of the bed, hunched over his knees. Had he forgotten to set an alarm? *Shit*. "Okay, I'm on it. It'll be there by three o'clock." He ended the conversation with a click before she was able to respond. He'd pay for that one later, surely.

He'd taken the job at the *Times* three years ago, and it continued to be the easiest way to get a high-caliber meal, take advantage of an open bar, and enjoy an endless supply of mourning women eager to throw themselves at the first person willing to listen. He would make himself readily available to provide a consoling shoulder for their tears, an ear to hear stories of their dying friend, cousin, brother, whomever, and a body to touch in the darkness as they tried to forget their grief.

The job itself was relatively easy, mostly requiring video taken from the party the night before to be edited and pasted together into a montage. Prior to the wake, he would usually spend some time with the subject, getting to know them and taking video. Clips from interviews would be pasted together along with family moments set to the background of a pre-selected musical score of the subject's favorite tunes. The final product would be given to the family and posted on the *Times'* website along with a short obituary Axon would write. Though he had moderate talent when it came to writing, the accompanying blurb was hardly enough to make him break a sweat. Despite this, he was able to make ample use of his extensive vocabulary of death euphemisms—passing on, sudden departure, moved to another world, went the way of the wind, went belly-up, danced the last dance, and kicked the bucket were some of his go-to expressions.

Nose Ring or Pointed Chin shifted, pulling the loose covers over from the space Axon had slept in. He scratched the back of his head absently, dreading having to wake and awkwardly dismiss her. Unfortunately, it had been a bit of a wild night and Mystery Girl was still solidly asleep, or at least pretending to be. Reluctantly, he nudged the girl and removed the pillow covering her head. Nose Ring had won, he noted. Realizing he couldn't quite remember her name, though he was relatively sure it started with a K, he improvised.

"Hey sweetheart, I've gotta get to work."

"Huh?" She opened her eyes and then immediately squeezed them shut and brought her hands to her head in a gesture of pain. "I'll get out of your way. Can I get some water?"

He tried not to sigh in annoyance, the clock ticking away the seconds to his deadline. He handed her a glass of water, which she drank down gratefully, having sat up in his cover-mussed bed. Her complicated updo, held in place with an abundance of hair product, hadn't fared well overnight—parts of it were still held down by a series of pins, and others had pulled free, her light brown strands falling flat against the back of her neck. She looked remarkably plainer without the aura of twinkly lights and intoxication. Her eye makeup was smudged and crusted slightly in the corners of her eyes, and the dark lipstick rubbed away by the night's endeavors revealed a thin, small mouth. Trying not to let his distaste show, he handed her the discarded dress from the floor. She yanked it over her head, wiggling her hips into the skirt quickly.

He judged from how quickly she gathered her things and slipped back into her high heels, her embarrassment obvious, that she wouldn't require any help finding the way out—lucky for him.

He turned to busy himself with the laptop on his desk and began uploading the videos he had taken of noteworthy party guests, namely the family and a few close friends of the recently deceased. Setting about compiling the short video clips into a manageable chunk, he quickly patched the stream together using one of his templates. After a slideshow of family-provided photos, he was always sure to show the final minutes of the subject's life set to the selected goodbye song. His boss, Veronica, always referred to it as the "tearjerker moment," meant to send viewers into a frenzy of sadness and—hopefully—gratitude for the emotional and thoughtful *Times* tribute. Associates of the deceased frequently sent in messages after the clip aired, praising the news source for the heartfelt tribute to their loved one's life.

The final product was not his best work—he had waited too long to prompt the dying man to give a speech and subsequently missed the window when he was most sober. Instead, much of his final goodbye was an unflattering compilation of slurred words and watery eyes that lingered too long on nearby cleavage. It was four minutes until Axon had promised to submit, and there wasn't time to carefully remove the woman with the breasts from the clip without making it look too unfinished. He hastily wrote up his final words on the man, Yeaton Herman, LP of forty-two, a generous, loving and dignified man—or so said his fingers on the keypad.

Reaching for his phone, he dialed Veronica while simultaneously hitting submit on the obituary, just as the seconds hit "59" and the clock changed to 3:01. Just in time.

"Did you get it?" He could hear the dead air indicating she had picked up the phone.

"You're late," she said, her displeasure apparent.

"It's three o'clock!" he protested, trying hard to sound innocent.

"Not what the timestamp says."

"Oh, one minute, boo-hoo," he joked, trying to keep the conversation upbeat, though he sensed she was about to bring down the hammer.

"No, Axon, three *hours* and one minute," she said. "You are aware that these pieces are due by noon, regardless of when the LP went out the night before. That's the job. And if you can't make it work, there are a lot of other people who would love to take on the role."

He knew this was true—the friends he'd kept from school who were still alive constantly told him how envious they were of his "sweet deal."

"I took a risk on you," she continued, "hiring someone with such a low LP You only just made the cut-off for a position here, and I made the decision to take you on because I liked you. Now you've had a lot of fun, but lately you're missing deadlines and your pieces have become dull and lifeless." There was no irony in her tone, despite the essence of the subject matter.

His body twitched in anger at her mention of his LP. He had always been sensitive about his age, or lack of expected aging. While some people held this romantic notion of dying young, Axon had always wanted to pursue something more but was limited by his determined age of death. At twenty-four, he had slightly less than two years remaining, which meant that most professions which required any sort of training would likely be barred to him. He had long ago given up on the idea that he would be able to do anything more than live in the pursuit of pleasure, and without this job he would likely end up unemployed for the remainder of his short life. While that would allow him more consistent free time, anyone out in public during the day without a job at his age was assumed to be branded for imminent death. This usually coincided with a knowing look he loathed, a mixture of pity and irritation at his inability to contribute meaningfully to the society that supported him.

"I know, V," he said after she railed on him a little more. "I've been slipping. I admit it."

"I'm glad," she said, still sounding not at all pleased, but he could hear her resolve cracking.

"You've been such a great mentor to me, and I really do appreciate you giving me this job. I really love what I do, but I know what you're saying. I need to better balance the fun with the work. I own it, and I promise I'll heed your criticism and do better." While he knew she was serious, he also knew an admission of wrongdoing would be the ticket to calming her down. Veronica had always been tough as nails, but she had a soft spot for him. Not only did it look good to the higher-ups that she had taken on a twenty-something LP, but he had a knack for getting people to give memorable quotes, another incentive to keep him on. "I will be more consistent with deadlines and work on my editing."

"I think you would do well to make a more intimate connection with the soon-to-be deceased. And when I say 'intimate,' I don't mean you should take the girls to bed," she insisted before he could interject. "If you bond with them, the subject will be more likely to open up on camera and help you catch those superior last words for a better—"

"'Tearjerker moment,' I know," he interrupted. "The better the bit, the more comments and views. I got it. I'll work on it, I swear."

"You'd better because I *don't* want to have to repeat myself. This is a one-time conversation, Davis," she said seriously.

"Understood." He nodded and exhaled quietly, releasing the tension in his shoulders.

"Good. Now, I see you don't have an event tonight?" she asked, though she was well aware of his schedule, seeing as she was the one to give out the assignments.

He was relieved to hear her businesslike tone had relaxed considerably. "Nope, I'm free," he said casually, smirking.

"My place at seven, then. And *please* don't wear the glow-in-the-dark boxers again. They give me the creeps." She ended the call abruptly.

Tossing his phone onto his desk, Axon leaned back in his chair, lacing his hands together behind his head, and said self-assuredly, "Yes ma'am."

Chapter 5

TODAY SHOULD ARGUABLY have been the best day of her life. Years of hard work finally culminating in the reward she sought, working for the company of her dreams, doing the job she was meant for.

Instead, Evergreen Mason was staring at the bottom of a pint of beer. She should be celebrating, but she needed to wallow. Though she preferred cocktails, liquor was too quick to soothe this pain, which was both visceral and confusing. No, this ache would only be dulled by consistent alcohol intake, and if she was drinking anything but beer, she would never make it more than ten minutes past when her best friend Arizona Janski finally showed up to the bar to share in her misery.

Arizona Janski had been like a sister to her since they were kids, having met in their accelerated High Lifetime Potential school when they were nine. While most of her other peers were in constant competition for the best positions, Arizona had never wanted the same things professionally as Evergreen, which made them natural allies in a school where teamwork was encouraged but duplicity was common.

The door opened and in swept Arizona, her curly red hair pinned elegantly back into a unique twisted hairstyle. Her job developing smart makeup—whose microtechnology adapted to any skin tone and face shape for the perpetually perfect look—ensured she always looked fierce. Noticing Evergreen, she smiled brightly behind expertly applied red lipstick.

"Sorry to pull you from work." Evergreen set her empty pint glass down delicately on the tabletop.

"Nah, I got done early. The trial results came through for the new product line I've been working on. *RedStick* is going to dominate the market, I already know it." Arizona made a sweeping motion around her painted mouth, drawing attention to the product Evergreen had already noticed.

Arizona's job was at a cosmetic design company whose specialty was formulating new products that personalized themselves for each individual wearer's unique biochemistry. Though, like Evergreen, this was her first real job outside school after completing her education, Arizona had already been promoted twice and was working on a lipstick line which she deemed "way more lunar than lotions and hair removal cream."

"You've gotta try this stuff. You will *love* it. Red is totally your color, and this lipstick will know precisely the shade that will look best on you. It's perfection."

Evergreen tapped on the empty pint glass she'd reserved for Arizona, who complied and filled it from the full pitcher between them.

"Hm, that sounds good. When are you gonna give me my free sample? Now that you know it didn't give any of your trial patients giant blisters or swollen eyes like that last product."

Arizona made a breezy, noncommittal noise. "No unusual side effects on this one, I promise!" she said with her typical sassiness. "I'm going to go see Seth on Friday. Maybe it will cheer you up to come along."

Evergreen stared blankly at her friend.

"You know, Seth Rivers, lead singer of *The Bionic Breezers*?"

"Literally never heard you talk about him before," Evergreen said sarcastically. Concerts weren't usually her thing, but she reluctantly agreed, knowing that if Arizona went alone, there was no telling what kind of trouble she might get herself into.

Once school had officially ended, Arizona had wasted no time in dedicating her former study nights to discovering her wild side. Not that she was unfamiliar with her wild side to begin with. Arizona never quite toed the line when it came to doing what was expected of her. She did well enough in school that her parents rarely put restrictions on her, though Evergreen suspected her brilliant friend could have done better than designing cosmetics had she focused less on male attention, drinking on Wednesdays, and fashion. Arizona had forged a path for herself, balancing the expectations of having a high Lifetime Potential with all the fun of a low LP, seemingly without having to try too hard. Arizona had been the alleged "bad influence" who had at various times convinced her to try cutting her own hair, get a tattoo, and sneak out after dorm hours to attend events typically restricted for those who were underage.

"Oh hush. It's a small venue. Maybe I'll catch his eye. It could happen."

"I love the optimism." Evergreen shook her head, smiling.

Arizona sighed heavily and shifted gears. "I always knew Zane was a prick." She tipped her head back to finish the amber liquid in the bottom of her glass. "There, now I'm caught up." She lifted the mostly-full pitcher and sloshed more beer into her empty glass. "That asshole belongs in Leydig," Arizona muttered, referring to the high-security prison only the worst criminals were sent to.

Evergreen thought back to Zane's look of surprise and confusion at her interruption of his sexual venture with Silver Bennett. That had nearly snapped her self-control. It was as if a curtain of rage had closed around her entire being, and it had taken all her better instincts to turn on her heel and slam the bedroom door behind her. The anger had wound itself around her body, roping so tightly she'd practically seen red. Frankly, she was lucky she hadn't done something violent and ended up in Leydig herself, she was that angry.

"Are you going to tell me what happened, or what?" Arizona nudged.

Evergreen exhaled and spat out the story. She was barely able to get the words out, the fury and creeping sensation of shame that her boyfriend had been caught with another woman overpowering her.

Shame, of all things! He had cheated on *her*. Why should she feel ashamed at all?

"I got my first job today! He practiced with me on my interview questions this morning!" she said incredulously. "And then I turn my back for *one second* and he stabs it . . . with his dick!"

Arizona grasped the pint glass and slouched in her seat, shaking with mirth. "I'm sorry." She laughed. "It's just, I'm picturing a dick . . ." Her sentence trailed off, ending with a crude hand motion and a fit of giggles. She had always been a cheap drunk.

"I just feel like such an idiot. I mean, what the fuck is wrong with me that I attracted this asshole in the first place?" Evergreen swallowed more beer and gestured toward Arizona, waiting for an answer.

Mid-sip, Arizona put down her glass. "Oh, that was an actual question?" She cleared her throat. "There isn't anything wrong with you, Ev. He's just a jerk."

"You're supposed to say that, though. What if there *is* something wrong with me? You'd tell me, right? Do I have some fatal flaw I'm completely oblivious to?"

Arizona clasped Evergreen's hand reassuringly. "You are a sublime, global, and independent woman. This is not the moment you start questioning yourself."

Evergreen smirked. "You didn't answer my question though. What's the flaw? What can I fix?" It was easy for Evergreen to be competitive, even with herself. She constantly sought ways to improve, to better herself, so why should her approach to dating be any different than academics, in which she so excelled?

Arizona pretended to take the question seriously, a mock thoughtful expression on her face, one finger resting lightly on her chin.

"I'm serious! Tell me!" Evergreen gave her a small kick under the table, her toe barely making contact with her friend's shin.

"Oww," Arizona exaggerated, throwing Evergreen a pouty look and rubbing her shin. "Fine. Now that you've maimed me, you're a little less sparkly. You really want to know?"

Evergreen nodded.

"I guess . . ." She paused dramatically. "I guess . . . You're pretty serious. Maybe you could be more fun?" It came out like a question, carefully, as if expecting a rebuke.

Evergreen cocked an eyebrow. "Like Silver Bennett?"

"Yes?"

Evergreen mock-gasped and slapped her friend's hand.

"I mean, she's a total nasty woman whose guts I hate with a frenzy," Arizona raised her hands, admonishing Evergreen not to overreact, "but she *is* fun."

Evergreen glared as she tilted the drink in her hand toward her open mouth.

"Remember the party Silver threw after we all graduated from High LP school?"

Evergreen shuddered. "Can we just call her 'that bitch'? I can't even hear her name right now."

"Sure," Arizona said. "That bitch hired a live band, served actual hard cocktails, and then she got all the boys to strip naked and run a circle around the outside of the house on a dare while she flash-froze their underwear in her dad's food preserver. It was hilarious. That was a *wicked* night." She laughed at the memory, jostling Evergreen, whose beer sloshed onto the tabletop.

"But she's still a bitch," Evergreen said into her glass.

Arizona nodded enthusiastically. "Absolutely! What kind of girl sleeps with the boyfriend of someone she knows? The least she could do is find a low LP guy she doesn't know from an atom."

"It's 'from Adam,' as in, a man named Adam," Evergreen corrected.

Arizona shrugged. "Still works."

"I guess."

"Anyway, I never saw the appeal of Zane anyhow. Sorry, Ev. You could do so much better than him, you know."

"Oh great, here it comes," Evergreen said under her breath while she sipped her drink.

"I heard that." Arizona cleared her throat, preparing for a speech. "Let me do my job, dammit! As your best friend, I am obliged to tell you that you could do better than him. But honestly, I don't think you should aim to be in a relationship right now, anyway. If you think about it, he kind of did you a favor."

Evergreen glared at her friend again.

"You know what I mean. You are just about to start your first real job! It's time to focus and put those mighty brain cells to work. There's no need to waste time on a relationship that will frankly cost you more emotional energy than you're going to have during your first year at Virionics. They'll work you to the bone over there, but you already know that. This will honestly make it so much easier." She gave Evergreen an encouraging look. "Seriously! Now you can just find boys to have fun with instead of boys that you need to comfort or clean up after."

"So, basically what I'm hearing is that, one, I'm not fun, and two, I need to find a fun boy to complete me."

Arizona mock-punched Evergreen in the shoulder. "That's not what I'm saying, and you know it."

Evergreen grinned.

"I just want you to enjoy yourself when you have time away from the lab. There might be hard work ahead of you at Virionics, but the beauty of the job is that you don't have to take it home with you. Once you're done for the day, you go home. And why go home to an empty bed?" She nodded flirtatiously toward the bartender who winked in return.

"I thought I wasn't supposed to be in a relationship, thus should expect to come home to an empty bed?"

Arizona groaned in exasperation. "Evergreen!"

"I know, I know. So I should expand my extracurriculars to allow me to have both my freedom and fulfill the needs of my lady parts."

"Now you're hearing me." Arizona slapped the table with the palm of her hand and poured them both another drink, setting the empty pitcher on the table. "On that note, I think you should go find your next fling."

Evergreen scoffed. "I don't think so."

"Come on, you need to celebrate! Forget about Zane, and focus on your triumph today!" She clinked her glass to Evergreen's and sipped. "Bathroom!" She motioned and scooted off to the other side of the room, leaving Evergreen alone.

The beer had helped, and Evergreen realized that her anger had dissipated dramatically. Arizona was right, of course. Her new job deserved recognition. She had *only* been working toward the position with Virionics for years, decades even, if you counted her years of schooling before High LP school. Evergreen began imagining where her career might be propelled from this first big step, letting her mind wander. Arizona came out of the bathroom, and Evergreen watched as her friend leaned up against the bar, one ankle twisting in the air behind her while she flirted shamelessly with the man behind the counter.

Evergreen knew from the start that Zane wasn't a good match for her, but his looks were atomic enough that she'd dismissed the red flags. Their personalities and ambitions weren't compatible at all, a fact that Arizona had pointed out on many occasions when Evergreen griped about her relationship. He never could figure out the right balance of fun to work, always leaning toward fun while she toiled away at her studies. He had opted not to reach for what was expected of most other high LPs and go into some sort of science or engineering. Instead, he chose to play at advertising, a respectable profession but usually a mid to low-level LP game due to the industry's tendency to prefer the youthful perspective. His executive father had pulled strings and greased wheels with the claim that his son had a "young soul," and thus would thrive in the industry meant to keep the fresh ideas and energy the expected LP level brought to the table. "Revolutionize" was the word she remembered Zane using, his small pouty mouth spreading into an arrogant grin as he bragged about how he would be the highest LP there, guaranteeing him a high position in the company by the time he was thirty-five. "Yeah, because the rest of your peers would be dead," Evergreen had replied tartly. That comment had sparked the biggest fight she could remember them having, ending with him storming out of his own living room and slamming his bedroom door.

Despite all the evidence he had been the wrong choice, she'd ignored the advice to break up with him—up until now, that is. There was no going back after what she had walked in on today.

Arizona returned to the table, smiling back at the bartender, and reached into her purse for her lipstick. Evergreen rolled her eyes as Arizona reapplied her makeup with the help of her rhinestone-covered compact. "I thought we were celebrating?"

Arizona looked up from her mirror, puckered her lips in an air-kiss to Evergreen, and snapped the sparkly compact shut. "We are. But I'm not going to take *you* to bed with me tonight. You're only part of my plans this evening, my friend. And since my night won't end with you, your night shouldn't end with me," she said, her smile suggestive.

"Is there someone you had in mind?" Evergreen looked around the bar in mock ignorance. She glanced purposefully over at the man behind the bar, his blond hair streaked with purple highlights hanging asymmetrically over his left ear, where a triangular silver earring dangled. "Good choice." She chuckled.

"What? He looks like he might know his way around the kitchen, if you know what I mean . . ." Arizona wiggled her light eyebrows suggestively and displayed a naughty grin.

"Yeah, the way he's drying that glass with a towel really is the epitome of seduction."

"I think it's more the way he squeezes that lime wedge into the drink. Just look at those agile fingers." Arizona mimed crustacean pincers with her fingertips, laughing. "Anyway, I already have his number. He gets off at 1 a.m.," she said knowingly.

"Okay, so your vagina is booked for the night. What am I supposed to do when you ditch me?"

"Hmm." Arizona tapped her chin thoughtfully, scanning the room with her sharp blue eyes, zeroing in on her target. "Him." She gestured minutely at a man sitting at a tall table on the other side of the bar.

The man had smooth, chestnut skin and dark hair, his eyes gazing into the drink in his hand as if deep in thought. She found herself immediately intrigued, wanting to know what he was thinking about—a girl? Work? His mother? He twitched slightly and reached for his pocket to retrieve a phone, half-smiling at whatever message had appeared on the tiny screen. Replacing the device in his pocket without thumbing out a response, he returned to staring at his drink.

"What do you think?" Arizona asked.

Evergreen kept her eyes on the man, who she had to admit was fairly good-looking. "Well, you know how I like them. Tall, dark, and handsome," she said, just as the song playing from the speakers came to an abrupt end, leaving them in a reverberating silence. The absence of sound amplified her comment so that many of the patrons sitting on the barstools turned to look at her, and the dark-haired man glanced up, meeting her eyes. He grinned with a white-toothed smile and held her gaze until she looked away, her cheeks aflame with embarrassment.

The music picked up again as adrenaline accelerated her heartbeat. She chanced a glance back at the man, who was sipping his drink, still looking at her. Arizona tittered next to her with girlish laughter.

"Shut up!" Evergreen snapped, knocking her knee sharply against her friend's leg.

"Shh! He's coming over here!"

Not wanting to scare him away with their beer-induced immaturity, she fought the lingering teenage reflex to giggle at the approaching man.

"Hey," he said simply.

Evergreen looked up toward the voice, unsurprised to meet the gaze of dark chocolate eyes. Her blush deepened. "Hi."

Arizona shook with suppressed mirth. Beer always had the propensity to keep her in a near-constant state of giggles. "Hey," she said in a mockingly deep voice before bursting into hysterical laughter.

"Don't mind her, she's drunk." Evergreen glared in Arizona's direction.

"I also answer to Axon. But if you prefer 'Hey,' that's okay by me."

"Evergreen." Her cheeks burned as she reached to shake his outstretched hand. His hand was warm as she shook it using what Arizona called her 'interview grasp.'

"Like the tree?" Axon asked.

She shrugged. "My parents are into forests."

Arizona let out another loud guffaw. "Sorry. I'm leaving," she said breathlessly, dabbing a tear from her eye. "I've got things to do." She slid out from behind their table with her half-empty glass in hand and scooted over to one of the tall barstools.

"She means the bartender." Evergreen said, rolling her eyes.

Axon chuckled low, glancing in the direction of the bartender whose attention Arizona had managed to capture again in record time, aided by her cleavage pushed together by her upper arms. "I see." Axon gestured toward the empty chair across from her.

"All yours." Evergreen waved her hand in what she hoped was a casual and not-too-enthusiastic gesture. She smiled at Axon as he gestured for another round from the waitress. He was pretty cute, and she could really use cute right about now. She just had to think like Arizona and live in the moment—she could totally forget about Zane. He wasn't worth another second of her time. Silver Bennett could have him, and good riddance. Evergreen tried to channel Arizona's enthusiasm and tried telling herself that she was brilliant and global and definitely someone worth knowing.

". . . your friend." Axon gestured toward Arizona with his thumb.

The positive self-talk cloud that had temporarily arranged itself over Evergreen's ears cleared, and she realized Axon had been speaking to her. "Huh? What did you say?"

"I just asked how you knew your friend," he said louder, mistakenly thinking that Evergreen's hearing had been the cause of her lapse of attention.

"Oh. We went to school together."

"High, low or mid?" he asked casually, concealing any bias he might have had.

This question had always caused Evergreen some trepidation when she met new people. Those in lower LP groups than her own were often jealous of her prospective long lifespan, while people in her own LP group tended to compete subtly—or in some cases not so subtly—regarding who would lead the more charmed life. Evergreen could remember meeting a girl named Claire around her age, and how once she gleaned that Evergreen's LP was twenty years higher than her own, she had attempted to one-up everything Evergreen would say with something more impressive. If Evergreen mentioned that her ambition was to work at Virionics, Claire would reply in a falsely congratulatory tone with something like, "I wish I could give up *my* best researching years, just to find out I wasn't cut out for something. That's so brave of you to try!" As if the same thing couldn't be said about Claire's own uncertain career trajectory—her goals included becoming the next female prime minister. Evergreen hadn't risen to the bait, however. Her father had taught her it was best not to boast about lifespan; it was tacky. Having the privilege of longevity with the hours to achieve all of her career aspirations should be satisfying enough.

Axon appeared to be in his mid-to-late twenties and didn't have the manic look of someone who only had a month to live. Other than that, she couldn't guess.

"Mid," she lied, not really knowing why. "You?"

"Same," he said shortly, with a subtle hint of discomfort, though he had suggested the topic. "So, what do you do?" he asked as he absently swirled his finger in the condensation left by his glass on the tabletop.

"Research assistant," she said, still unsure why she was downplaying herself.

"I work in the media," he said vaguely.

"Ever meet any interesting celebrities?" Evergreen asked between swallows of her drink.

"I prefer real people," he said, leaning his body toward her confidentially.

The circulating waitress set a heavy pitcher full of beer on the table between them. "From the girl over there making eyes at Hank." She pointed toward Arizona, whose upper body was leaning over the bar top in the direction of the bartender, arms still pressing her breasts together in a way that Evergreen knew was purposeful. Arizona looked their way and winked.

Evergreen gulped down the remaining third of her glass, and Axon poured her a refill. His eyes were really nice up-close, almond shaped and chocolate brown, framed with dark lashes.

Evergreen giggled softly to herself. Zane the furthest thing from her mind.

Chapter 6

". . . AND I AM SO PROUD to have lived the past sixteen-and-a-half years of my life watching her grow into the woman she has become." Lucy watched tears glaze Ed Hanson's brown eyes, and his voice cracked slightly. Ed toasted Lucy in the last hours of her life while a roomful of people politely listened, sipping drinks from crystal-stemmed goblets and munching on canapés provided by the circling waiters. Nadine had made sure the event was as elegant as they could afford. There would be no other party like it in their daughter's short life—no graduation from a prestigious university, no celebration of marriage, no birth of a grandchild, so Nadine, like most mothers, had insisted it be perfect.

Ed continued in this vein for a few more minutes while Lucy stared on, a half-smile plastered to her face, eyes unfocused, hardly hearing his emotional words. She knew she should feel guilty for not paying attention, but she couldn't force a spark of interest. It had struck her hours before just how pleasant and calming the act of breathing was. Inhaling oxygen to fill her lungs, exhaling carbon dioxide her body didn't need. She had studied it once, curious about the biological necessity. Now there was so little of this left in her life, maybe a couple thousand breaths. So, she savored it, focused in a dream-like haze on the simplicity of the act.

She thought back to earlier in the day, when she'd had more hours left. While she prepared for the party, a silently working woman with tiny hands buffed her nails while Axon Davis sat nearby, one leg crossed over the other. "What has been the best part of your life?" He asked while Lucy looked on with passive interest. He was just doing his job.

She knew how she was expected to respond. Most people her age embraced their death, expressing that to die young meant you got to experience the best of life—first love, adventure, childhood,

while avoiding the worst—loss of parents, financial struggle, disso-
lution of a marriage, career burdens. *Go out in a blaze of glory*, declared many of her peers. To dream of a life otherwise was just a waste
of time. Colton would indulge her those conversations only on occasions where she was feeling particularly contemplative. Mostly he
had been accepting of his own time clock, his unbridled enthusiasm
for all that the world had to offer infectiously propelling the two of
them forward through their short lives.

When he was gone, everything stopped. Lucy could find no joy
in things she used to find amusing. Colton had been the center of
her life for so long, she couldn't figure out how to move on with the
gaping hole he left behind. In the weeks that followed his death, she
became more or less a social pariah. Girls who had been part of her
group had re-formed around a new leader now that Colton wasn't
there, leaving her on the outs. Whispers would break out behind her
as she walked the halls of the school, and the regular phone calls between her and others in her social group evaporated overnight.

She came to realize that Colton had protected her from gossip
and the cattiness that could easily overcome a group of teenagers. He
had been the best of them, and in his absence, the well was poisoned
against her. She suspected they had always been jealous of his affection and tolerated her only because doing otherwise would render
limited access to Colton, and he was like a star with his own gravita-
tional pull. She imagined the conversations they must have been having all along. *He will get bored and break up with her someday.* After
his wake it publicly became, *What a waste.*

It was hard to see the point in continuing until her last heartbeat
when she couldn't even live life the way she wanted, with Colton by
her side. It wasn't as if she had years to move past his loss and start
fresh pursuits in the world—she only had less than six months until
the end of her own story. No, it hadn't been worth it to snap out of

it, even if she had really wanted to. Books, television, and sleep were the only respite she had since he'd left her.

It wasn't fair. If only she could have died at the same time as him. There were permits for that. Unfortunately, those were reserved for older couples who had spent decades together and didn't want to live without one another. Lucy fantasized about the kind of ending she and Colton could have had, if only the stupid law permitted it. She pictured them holding hands as the countdown began, gazing into one another's eyes, a silent tear streaking down his cheek. She'd crunch down on the government-issued tablet at precisely the right moment and they'd fall to the floor together, perfect in death.

That was unrealistic, however. Only really old people qualified for the tablet via a lengthy application process. She would only be allowed to die naturally, like most people did where at the determined moment of her death, her cells would naturally undergo an accelerated full-body apoptosis.

The fate that awaited her parents if she broke the law and took her death into her own hands (better known among her peers as a "Code Preterm"), was the only thing stopping her from speeding up the clock. Not that others hadn't tried this. For the most part, choosing the quicker way out only happened for those whose remaining relatives were gone, diminishing the possibility of retribution. Mostly, individuals who had lost siblings, friends, parents, and significant others continued their existence in much the same way Lucy had for the last six months: waiting until their time ran out naturally to avoid financial and judicial consequences placed upon any surviving family members. It was her only comfort that her time was coming soon.

When she didn't answer the reporter right away, he prompted, "Now that you're at the end and have the ability to look back and reflect, what everyone wants to know is if you lived happily?"

"And *everyone* wants to know this?" she said, not caring to be polite. What would be the point? She should speak her mind now or never.

"Everyone who reads the reverse wake coverage does."

"Right, so I should say I 'lived the best existence I could imagine' so they can go on with their morning coffee, knowing that the world is working like it should? It's been totally global!" Lucy knew that mocking wouldn't change the fact that she was meant to die today, but she didn't care to filter her thoughts. "That's what you want to hear, right? How am I going to know what you publish, anyway?"

Axon sighed. "Oh I see, you're one of *those* kids. The ones who haven't figured out how to be happy with what life they had and enjoy the privilege of being able to stay a kid forever."

"Yes, what a *privilege* it is to watch your best friend and lover die in your arms and then have to wait *months* until it's your turn. It was just great to find out who my true friends were too," she had told the reporter acidly.

He was irritatingly unperturbed by her attitude, Lucy noticed, and hot anger began to rise in her chest. "The way I see it," he said, "low LPs have it pretty great. You get to live out your life doing only the things you want to do, learning the things you want to learn and not ever having to worry about competing in the real world. Mids like myself have to switch gears at some point and learn a skill so we can actually contribute to society. You've been cherished by your family, by your community, for your whole life."

"Lower-mid, if I remember correctly," Lucy snapped, remembering their conversation from Colton's reverse wake. Axon's face soured, and she felt a tinge of regret for pointing it out. "Sorry," she muttered.

Axon shrugged. "I might be lower-mid, but I'm not dying today. You are," he said matter-of-factly. "Ready or not."

They sat in silence for a minute as Lucy picked at the cuticles her manicurist had just softened. She wanted him to ask something else, but he didn't.

"I am ready to die," she said finally, her voice cracking. "The love of my life is gone. I suppose I was fortunate enough to *have* a 'love of my life' to begin with." Most people didn't get to experience love like hers and Colton's. She should feel bad for them, really. Lucy put her hands back on the table so the first coat of soft pink polish could be applied. "Anyway," she said, but didn't continue.

"You don't *seem* ready to die," Axon commented.

Lucy sighed dramatically. "What choice do I have, exactly? So, I am. Ready, that is."

Axon uncrossed his legs and scooted the rolling chair he was perched on closer. "That's the spirit," he said with false enthusiasm.

"Can I ask you something?" she said.

He shrugged.

She contemplated for a moment, then said, "Do you think you'll be ready? You know . . . in a few years from now?"

"Absolutely," he said without hesitation. "I know how much time I have, and I plan to live accordingly. I'll know death is coming, and I'll be ready."

Lucy sensed by his quick and politically correct response that she hadn't been the first person to ask him this. "And in what way will you 'live accordingly'?" she prompted.

"That isn't what we're here to talk about, is it?" he charmingly deflected, flashing his brilliant white smile.

"Come on. I'm kicking the bucket in approximately . . ." She glanced at her watch. ". . . seven hours, twenty-eight minutes. You can give me a *real* answer. Who would I even tell?"

His long fingers picked up a bottle of polish from the table, examining it. "I like my life. I'm not ready to give it up."

"See. That wasn't so hard."

"Sure, but I'm not the one who dies today, am I?"

"Nope. That lucky winner would be me," Lucy said sardonically.

"I'm saying that when it comes closer to my time, I'll be prepared."

She nodded, unconvinced.

Lucy had always wanted to be more, but confined to her Lifetime Potential, she never dared but dream and divert her interest into reading. Wouldn't it be great to live as long as the high LPs? They were able to experience life like the characters in her books. They loved, they lost, they loved again. Lucy would only remember love and loss, nothing else. But her memory was fallible and limited. It was worthless after this day anyhow. It only mattered to her and her alone. Her existence was to simply live and enjoy—she understood that there were probably some people who wished they could be this way too.

She hesitated to share the thought, but decided life was literally in too short supply not to speak her mind. "In a perfect world, Colton wouldn't have died, and I wouldn't be dying today. We would be able to pursue our passions. Maybe he'd be an architect, maybe I'd be an engineer. We would build bridges and skyscrapers and libraries." She paused thoughtfully. "But that isn't what happened. What's *happening*," Lucy corrected, "and I can be okay with that."

"If you weren't dying today, when would you rather?" Axon asked.

"I don't know. Maybe not knowing when I'm going to die would be a better way of living."

He set down the bottle of polish whose label he had peeled off with a thumbnail. "A radical notion, most would say."

"It's how humans used to live for thousands of years," she argued.

"I don't think you mean to live like people did thousands of years ago. They didn't even have WiFi then."

She chortled, though his attempt to lighten the mood annoyed her.

"Besides, the way humans used to live was in fear of death, in fear of the uncertainty of it. Now that we know when we will die, we can adjust accordingly. No more keeling over at 35, after expecting to live until at least 60, and leaving your wife with a horde of children to take care of on her own. Death might be inevitable, but now people can plan for it."

"Inevitability made predictable," Lucy said, hoping it sounded as profound out loud as it did inside her head.

"Made *exact*," he corrected, referring to the differentiator technology that fueled the Lifetime Potential calculations. "You have to admit, the manner in which society has conquered death is comforting."

"Predicted death. Not conquered. If it was conquered, I wouldn't be dying today."

The round of applause jostled her attention back to the present where Ed's toast had concluded in a predictable fashion, with the linen napkins blotting the cheeks of tearful guests. She felt empathy toward her sorrowful father, who hugged her tightly while the applause rang loudly in her ears. Vaguely, she considered the idea that she would never live long enough for her life to matter to the world outside of her parents and other low LPs like Colton. Their sole purpose was the same as hers, to bring joy and to experience childhood in a protected and predictable bubble.

Nadine approached and stroked her cheek lovingly before holding her close. Wasn't she happy that her mother would get what she wanted, another child? A chance to be outlived by her own flesh and blood? Or maybe she should be sad for her father, who had always loved her best and whose grief would be more severe. She assured herself that a new child would soothe this sadness, that he would be okay.

She caught her reflection in the decorative mirror across from the dance floor and noticed how truly beautiful she looked tonight and appreciated it for one last moment. Her dark hair was piled flawlessly on top of her head, her eyes painted with a smoky hue complementing her dark purple dress. Lucy turned away from the mirror. She would never look at herself again.

How had the world seen her? She pondered distractedly while politely making her expected rounds, receiving hugs and the familiar, "Do you remember when . . . ?" from many of the people she checked in with. Would they remember her as a young woman whose potential had not been met? One whose lover had died young like herself, immortalizing their affection for all time? Or just another ordinary low LP, destined to live a brief existence and depart this world with hardly a footprint left upon the planet? Would they even remember her a year from now? The impression she'd made on some of their lives was small in proportion to the number of years many guests had remaining.

Lucy looked around the room, willing herself to take it all in. Everyone was dressed glamorously. Hair in place, manicured nails on the women, bow ties on the men. The room was dimly lit, fuchsia uplighting on the walls giving the room a chic glow. Candles studded the tables spread around the dance floor where a DJ played songs from Lucy's childhood, along with a few favorites she had put on the list her mother forced her to fill out. When they'd been planning, she hadn't cared much what was played, or what the room looked like, but now she felt grateful for the time Nadine had put into the party. Everything looked perfect.

Growing up, Lucy had always envisioned her reverse wake to be somewhat like tonight, but when it came time to make it a reality, she'd felt largely disconnected, leaving the finer details to her mother. The simple truth that reverse wakes were more for the living than the soon-to-be dead dawned on her in the weeks leading up to the soiree.

However the party looked, whether the food was elegant or the colors complementary, at the end of the night she would be dead, and none of it would have really mattered anyway.

She made eye contact with Axon Davis, nodding minutely. He gave a brief smile and then returned his attention to the girl he had been chatting with, whose hand was flirtatiously touching his forearm. Lucy placed his companion as an older sister of a classmate who had departed nearly eight months ago. There had been so many wakes since then, she could hardly remember the music, decorations, or whether or not she had enjoyed the party.

She recounted the times she'd thoroughly relished and looked forward to these kinds of parties. It was always a good time to have fun with your friends, cry a little, reminisce a little, and laugh a lot. The first time she had gotten drunk had been at the reverse wake of a classmate whom she hardly knew. Colton had managed to acquire a bottle of liquor from an older cousin, which he had shared with Lucy and a few of their friends, sneaking splashes into their orders of soda over ice in the back of the crowd. It was common knowledge that teenagers experimented with things like alcohol, cigarettes, and the occasional recreational drug at reverse wakes, a fact which was mostly ignored by parents, and the authorities usually looked the other way. Lucy wondered vaguely how many kids were spiking their drinks or inhaling flavored smoke in an effort to feel something different and new at her own party.

She glanced upwards at the wall behind the dance floor, with its display in large letters—her name and LP along with three clocks: one showing the present time, another showing the time of her impending death at exactly 22:08:27, and finally a countdown of the hours, minutes and seconds remaining before the present time and the death time were identical.

With only a few minutes left before Lucy's last, the party guests began to gather around her, forming a loose circle with her and her parents in the center. Her mother wrapped her arms around Lucy tightly, resting her chin on her daughter's shoulder for a moment and breathing in. Nadine had been preparing for this moment, this pain, since the day her child was born. Their time having been realized made her face appear drawn and older than she had earlier this morning. Exchanging words of love with her parents while onlookers shouted "We love you, Lucy!" and "We'll miss you!" at irregular intervals, Lucy prepared to see the world one last time.

She looked around at the guests, some smiling, others pleasantly chatting with their neighbors while sipping drinks, nonchalance radiating from their bodies. A few of the other students from her LP school had congregated on one side of the inner circle of people, wiping tears from their eyes and smiling over at her as she scanned the crowd. One of the girls she had hardly spoken three words to in the past months waved timidly and gave a final thumbs-up before Lucy looked away.

The guests began to count down with the red numerals on the wall clock. Lucy savored every inhale and exhale—breathing had never been so pleasant as it suddenly was in this moment.

Feeling like a small child, a wave of anxiety crashed through her chest as she wondered if it would hurt in the end.

She closed her eyes in preparation while the crowd counted down merrily, her father's arm wrapped protectively around her waist, ready to catch her lifeless body in a moment's time.

"*Two . . .*"

Colton's face flashed through her mind, and she took a deep and final breath.

"*One!*"

She felt the confetti rain down over her head, knowing the effect of little rainbows it would cast over the tastefully lit ballroom without having to see it. Hearing the exalted cries and chorus of voices as they began the happy song of departure, she let the oxygen slowly leave her chest as her heart pounded in anticipation. Lucy could smell her father's musky cologne, the one he only wore on special occasions.

She took another breath.

Her heart skipped a beat as she realized she was still able to inhale. Was this what dying was supposed to feel like? Would she just start to float above her body, her natural reflexes—like breathing and blinking her eyes—still intact without being connected to her physical form? She opened her eyes and fluttered her eyelashes a few times just to make sure the feeling was still there.

Her mother was standing in front of her, next to the emergency technician who had been ready to pronounce her deceased at the exact moment of death. Nadine's eyebrows furrowed together, and she shared a look of confusion first with her husband, who was still standing behind Lucy, supporting her waist, and next with the technician. People nearby were murmuring to each other and checking their watches and comparing the exact time to that on the display wall behind where Lucy still stood. Lucy glanced down at her father's wrist, noting the time she knew would be exact.

22:09:05

Thirty-three seconds had passed after the clock counting down her life had zeroed out.

"But why isn't she dead?!" an angry voice shouted through the crowd.

"What's going on?" questioned others as the volume of the crowd rose with confusion and disbelief.

Lucy barely remembered being whisked away from the ballroom by her parents, her feet feeling like they hardly touched the floor. She was still alive. How was this possible?

Chapter 7

EVERGREEN ARRIVED EARLY at the Virionics Institute, just like she had for the last several weeks. And like the past several weeks, she planned to work late as well. It was the price to pay for her newbie status. Most days she spent her time performing menial tasks for other scientists' projects. Between extracting DNA from bacterial colonies, making gel agar for electrophoresis, or monitoring the progress of data collection from analysts working in the field, she managed to stay very busy. What little time remained after her primary duties were complete was devoted to pursuing her own research project—an idea which hadn't completely solidified in her mind yet. Creating a unique research proposal that Virionics would approve and support was a challenge, to say the least. Approved projects usually had some sort of expected financial return for the company, not merely satisfaction for the researcher's own curiosity. If she was able to come up with something solid, be granted approval and achieve usable results, it would almost guarantee recognition from higher-ranking members of the company and an eventual promotion. Recognition was the key to the career trajectory she dreamed of. Having talent only got you so far. Hard work, a little bit of luck, and timing were the rest, her father had always said.

Usually, the only time she had to engage her own interests was after the other scientists in her lab had gone for the day. She spent most evenings scouring journals and performing searches, trying to find something that struck her. Something that would make her brain itch for more.

Gregor Petrov, an LP graduate from Evergreen's school two years prior, was usually the only other person remaining in the lab when she would finally shut down her computer and retire for the evening. His study of the nocturnal hormone cycle on male birth control recipients kept him working odd hours, often late into the night.

Having never been very friendly with one another in school, Gregor quickly established himself as the alpha scientist despite Evergreen being the only person in the lab he had seniority over. She had been the first new hire in two years, and his transition from being the lowest ranking member of the team to the second-lowest was met with an enormous boost in ego, or at least it appeared that way to Evergreen. Toward their other coworkers he was nothing but polite, offering his assistance on anything from washing glassware or organizing complicated data after hours to dog-sitting when someone would go on vacation. The staff ate it up. In the meantime, with Evergreen, he expressed nothing but derision. In his opinion, her every move demonstrated inexperience, and she was subjected to mockery when nobody else was listening. Mistakes that he made would often get blamed on her. If the inventory didn't arrive on time, it was Evergreen's doing. The incubator temperature wasn't lowered at the designated hour—Evergreen forgot it. Even when the Zone 2 research lab door was left ajar, it was her fault despite the fact that she didn't even have access to that area yet. If the other scientists noticed, they said and did nothing. She supposed it was a form of hazing they had all gone through and resolved to grin and bear it for as long as it took to get her footing.

Whenever she called, nearly in tears at the end of a particularly grueling day, Arizona would reassure Evergreen. "You wouldn't be there if you didn't deserve to be. Let Gregor be a bully. Just ignore it and do your own work. He's just jealous your LP is higher and that you're a Virionics legacy—meaning you not only have more to live up to, but you have more opportunities to get your work noticed. That's the part I'm sure he wishes *he* had."

Though he was winding closer to retirement, Evergreen's father, Gerald Mason, was still active on a couple projects, and—most importantly—kept his coveted seat on the Virionics Scientific Advisory Board. His accomplishments in the study of virology were well known, and his many publications created a high bar for his only daughter to live up to. If she could find a worthwhile project, she would have the double-edged benefit of name recognition which would expedite the approval process while also ensuring that any proposal of hers would be held to higher scrutiny. They expected great things from Gerald Mason's daughter, and she didn't intend to disappoint.

Thus far, she hadn't had much luck in nailing down an appropriate research proposal the board would support. Her primary job was to help the production of new antibiotics and vaccinations for the annual booster. Since viruses and bacteria constantly mutated, it was Virionics' job to stay one step ahead. Gregor had managed to find a way to pursue his own ventures and was quick to point out how hard he worked and how many important committees he had partaken in to be able to spend time on his own independent project.

"Packing up for the day, Greenie?" Gregor said, using the nickname he had come up with for Evergreen, which thankfully hadn't caught on with the rest of the lab. "Get it, because you're such an Ever-*green* newbie?" he had said during her first week, laughing at his own joke and proudly patting himself on the back for his profound wit and creativity.

"Just taking a break," Evergreen replied lightly, ignoring his provocation while she got up to grab more coffee, the effect of which had diminished steadily over weeks full of late nights. Coffee breaks were merely something to do to break the monotony of shuffling through endless piles of published papers, her eyes growing heavier as the hours ticked by. Evergreen let her mind wander to a time in the future when another newbie would be doing the same thing, except the articles the nameless researcher would be looking through would include Evergreen's name as an author. Whenever these daydreams would cloud her ability to keep reading, she would force herself to take a break so she could reset and focus. Eyes on the prize.

Gregor followed her into the break room, snapping his gloves into the trash outside the doorway like a slingshot. The abrupt sound startled her, and she involuntarily jolted in surprise.

"Jumpy, aren't we?" he said mockingly.

"No. Just too much caffeine and not enough sleep." Her energy level was too low to bother inventing a witty response. Evergreen reached for her favorite gray porcelain mug, depicting a cartoon of two red blood cells, one smiling type B-positive cell telling the other sad-looking B-negative cell to "Be Positive!"

Gregor watched her pour the black liquid into her cup and cocked an eyebrow. "You know, that's neither decaffeinated nor a cure for sleep deprivation." He pronounced neither with a strong "eye" sound. Evergreen hated that.

"I don't care." She sighed and sat down on the leather couch in front of the flat-screen television. Picking up the remote, she flipped on the channel for the local news and blew over her hot coffee. There was a strict no food or drinks policy inside the lab, and with Gregor's ever-judging eye on her, she didn't want to risk breaking the rules by enjoying her beverage from the comfort of her desk. Besides, it was a pleasant change for her eyes to fixate on something other than the computer monitor for a few minutes.

"Have you found your Big Bang yet?" Gregor asked as he slid onto the opposite side of the couch.

"My what?" Evergreen asked, exasperated that he was *still* talking and trying her best to keep her tone pleasant.

"Your Big Bang," he replied with false reverence. "The project that will grant you access to the big kids club, where the published scientists live and the unpublished ones only wish they could be."

"Aren't you a third author?" she said, referring to his name being third on the list of authors, in order of importance, on the last paper he contributed to.

"Yes. On *two* papers," he corrected haughtily and without a trace of humility. "And once I'm done with what I'm working on, it'll be *my* name that comes first on the next one."

"Right."

Gregor leaned back into the couch and put his feet up on the table in front of them. "Guess you can't say the same?"

His presence was grating on her nerves, and she could feel a headache coming on. "Why are you asking me a question you already know the answer to?"

He put up his hands defensively. "Just making conversation. You know, words. Talking."

"Thanks, I'm good right now." She pulled her knees up onto the couch to sit cross-legged, her attention on the screen ahead.

"Sixteen-year-old Lucy Hanson of Middlebury County was enjoying her final hours of life at her reverse wake tonight before her departure at 10:08 p.m., when something unexpected happened. Here is a video post by reverse-wake writer Axon Davis from the scene," a female reporter proclaimed from behind a mahogany desk, her neatly-trimmed blond hair framing her prominent cheekbones.

The video showed a roomful of people gathered in a circle around three others, the older two with their arms around the younger girl with long dark hair and olive skin. Presumably, these were the girl's parents and this was the moment of her determined death. The people surrounding them were chanting a countdown from ten as the girl closed her eyes in preparation.

"Seven!"

"Six!"

When the counting stopped at *"One!"* the girl remained standing and opened her eyes with a hesitant and confused expression. A uniformed woman approached, clearly a medic, and glanced between the clock and the girl in the long dress, trying to make sense of what she saw. The crowd began to make noise, a jumbled mix of singing, bewildered shouts, and general uproar, while the space between the girl's family and the crowd began to narrow. The commotion of the crowd made it difficult to see what was going on, the camera obviously hand-held and slightly shaky as others bumped against the reporter. Soon the three people emerged from the center of the circle, having elbowed their way through, parents shepherding their daughter over the ballroom floor to the exit.

The camera flipped back to the perspective of its operator, a handsome, dark-skinned man with black hair and a pouty, attractive mouth who began to speak hurriedly. *"This is Axon Davis, and I have just witnessed that a person's LP could be wrong."*

Evergreen inhaled sharply and proceeded to choke on her sip of coffee. She knew that face. The last time she had seen it was several weeks ago, first thing in the morning, while she quietly collected her clothes from his bedroom floor. The night she spent with Axon Davis had been a blur—her last complete memory was the delivery of a second pitcher of beer to their table at the bar, and the rest was hazy. She vaguely remembered thinking his lips were softer than she'd expected while his hands were knowing and warm, touching her body in all the right places. It had been weeks, and neither of them had attempted to contact the other, though she couldn't be sure they had actually exchanged information. All she knew at the time was that he worked with the media, but in what capacity he hadn't disclosed. Obviously, he had exaggerated his LP, having told her he was a Mid when she knew reverse wake reporters were typically lower than the average Mid. Remembering she had also fudged her LP, she could hardly hold it against him.

"I repeat, Lucy Hanson was supposed to die today at exactly 22:08:27, but it's currently," he glanced behind the camera at what *must be the countdown clock, "22:10:09."* The camera perspective *flipped again to show the clocks, verifying what he said. "As the reporter covering Lucy's event, I spoke to her this morning. She expressed dissat-*

isfaction about her impending death and mentioned how difficult the past months had been since she lost her boyfriend, Colton Goodman, when he departed. The tone of the room is that of confusion—I certainly feel that way. To my knowledge, nobody has ever witnessed an incorrect LP. This is certainly a moment that won't be forgotten anytime soon. As the wake reporter, I am entitled access to any medical proceedings following her death, or in this case her unexpected extension of life, and will be following up with the story as it progresses."

The video cut out and the blond reporter was back front and center. *"In this curious twist of fate, sixteen-year-old Lucy Hanson has just become the first ever person in known history not to die at her designated LP. Will the timing be off by mere minutes, or will she continue to exist long past tonight? More from Axon Davis in a few minutes."*

The segment ended, and the silence that swallowed the breakroom reverberated in Evergreen's ears.

"Holy shit," Gregor said finally.

All she could do was nod in response, her mind going a thousand miles per second, a concept taking form. Suddenly, she knew exactly what it felt like to come up with her own Big Bang idea. Nobody would be able to resist the research potential Lucy Hanson had just offered. But as Axon implied, few were granted access to the family after a wake. Luckily for Evergreen, she knew just the person to help her get ahead of the competition.

She fumbled for the phone in her pocket and quickly scrolled through the contacts starting with "A."

Amanda Germain
Alicia Headway
Antoine Duncan
Avalon Armond
Axe on Damien

"Precision," she said, recognizing her autocorrected drunken text. Abruptly, she stood up, nearly bashing into Gregor's shins while she attempted to step over him.

"Where are you going?" he asked incredulously.

She barely heard him as her mind continued to twist and turn through the possibilities. Ignoring him as he loudly repeated himself, she collected her things and left the lab.

Chapter 8

THE NEWS CAMERA CAUGHT the headlights of a car through the early morning gloom, approaching the milling crowd of reporters. *"There she is!"* they exclaimed, clearly excited that the climax of their hours-long wait for Lucy Hanson's return had finally arrived.

The car crept cautiously toward the group as they shuffled sideways to allow the vehicle to pull into the driveway. The house had remained unlit all night while they waited for Lucy to be released from the hospital. The reporting stations, which had flipped the coin in favor of Lucy dying en route to the hospital or during her stay, remained camped in front of the emergency room's neon sign until the Hansons left and now barreled down the street, trying to catch up to the action. Lucy Hanson was alive and on the move.

The silver sedan pulled into the detached garage, and the driver, Lucy's father, stepped out from behind the wheel, avoiding eye contact with the cameras at the end of the drive. Axon swung open the front passenger door and stretched out the kinks in his back. Lucy's mother stepped out after her husband opened the door, shielding her body from view with his own. Lucy came next, tucked protectively under her mother's arm. The crowd surged as the reporters all began asking questions simultaneously, their microphones held out at arms-length toward Axon and the Hansons.

"Lucy! How does it feel to escape death?!"

"Lucy! How long will you live for?"

"Lucy! Why do you think your LP was wrong?"

The family ignored the wave of sound and commotion at the edge of their property and shuffled awkwardly toward the back door of the house.

A blond woman with a petite upturned nose and bright pink lipstick shouted above the noise into her microphone, *"I'm standing here at the residence of Lucy Hanson, a sixteen-year-old girl whose LP was sixteen. Her exact moment of death was due to occur yesterday evening at 22:08 during her reverse wake celebration. However, she is miraculously still alive. The teenager was rushed to the hospital, where our sources indicate that a series of medical tests were performed and determined that the girl is in perfect health. Her LP remains unchanged, yet she is still alive and well. No word yet on whether it has been determined if Lucy will perish at a time in the near future. We can only wait and see. I'm Cindy Grundwaldt with EverChange News. Back to you, Ted."*

A smug smile crossed Axon's face. For once, his story was in the headlines.

"Dad, can you turn it off?" Lucy sighed, her chin resting heavily in her palms, elbows on the kitchen table. It had been an exceptionally long night with little rest and a blur of activity, questions, and medical tests. Lucy's parents had attempted to convince their daughter to go to bed, but she resisted, claiming to feel too tightly wound for sleep. Instead, she had been staring at the television for the last two hours as the news played the same loop of footage every fifteen minutes. Word that someone had passed their designated death time and survived spread like wildfire. Axon's phone had been exploding with messages from friends and coworkers who had witnessed his online report of Lucy's wake.

Lucy had been receiving messages nonstop. For the first few hours, she'd read each message aloud, but had since grown annoyed as more and more unknown contacts reached out looking for a response they could broadcast.

Ed, in a grunt of frustration, had swiped the device, declaring, "Enough. I'm drawing the line." It remained off, perched on top of the refrigerator.

Axon's presence seemed to irritate the Hanson parents greatly, but as the *Times'* corporate contract lawyer had told them, they'd signed a contract and were obligated to allow him to remain in

Lucy's presence for the foreseeable future. Axon was, in fact, under strict orders from his editor not to leave her side under any circumstances for the next seventy-two hours at least. "She could die at any moment. We . . . You are *not* going to miss that," Veronica demanded. Lucky him.

"I'm making some eggs, honey, do you want some?" Ed asked his daughter hesitantly.

"I'm not hungry," Lucy responded monotonously, her eyes glued to the television screen.

Ed nodded. "Axon," he began, an edginess to his tone, the internal struggle over his obvious dislike and normal polite behavior demonstrable. "Would you like some eggs?" he asked, politeness winning out. Ed was still visibly defeated after his row with the corporate lawyer over the appropriateness of a reporter being around during "an emotional family experience." The lawyer had responded with a string of complicated legal jargon clearly going far over Ed Hanson's proud head, embarrassing him and infuriating his wife. After much discussion and a reminder of the consequences defying the fine print would lead to, including exorbitant fines and possible jail time if a court sided with the network—*which they likely would,* the lawyer added for good measure—the Hansons backed off.

"Sure thing, scrambled for me, please," Axon beamed, pretending not to sense the tension, and Ed's face turned pink.

Ed began cooking, grumbling to himself, Axon catching the words "*capitalizing on my daughter's life*" while he cracked an eggshell onto the skillet.

"Lucy, go ask your mother if she wants any breakfast," he said gruffly, his back to the kitchen table as he prepared the ingredients.

"I'll go," Axon offered, grabbing his phone from the tabletop as he stood to find Nadine. He wandered around the ground floor of the house in search of Lucy's mother, scrolling through the media updates on his phone. The sixteen-year-old's survival story was a "miracle," "anomaly," or "an example of the collapse of our world"—the reactions on his feed were varied. Light caught Axon's eye as he passed the living room, the mantel adorned with framed photographs reflecting the late morning sunshine coming through sheer curtains. Lucy's parents had attempted to block the journalists' view, but the decorative window cover did nothing to hinder the journalists' ability to see into the family's private space from the crowded front walkway. Ignoring the murmur of muted voices outside, Axon examined the printed memories, all the bright and smiling faces in their decorative frames. A progression of Lucy as she grew up began on one end and ran to the other: first breath through first steps, family vacations, and portrait shots from school, pictures of her looking prepubescent—her face more rounded, less made-up—and finally some more recent shots which had been included in the wake announcement Axon had written. Picking up a frame, he examined it more closely. Lucy's expression was determined, jaw set, eyes looking slightly away from the camera as if seeing someone behind the photographer. *Perhaps it was death she saw,* Axon thought grimly before reminding himself that the future she must have envisioned had not come true; she was very much alive. Still alive. For how much longer was unclear.

Axon's own mortality crossed his mind, his numbered years haunting him like a shadow, always lurking nearby. His own parents had died young, and he only remembered them in snippets. The way his mother smelled of sandalwood and citrus, his father's baritone laugh. Then there was the black hand-me-down suit he had worn for the first time when visiting the grave of his older brother. The jacket was slightly too big in the shoulders and long in the sleeves, covering the tops of his hands as he held a drooping bunch of hand-picked daisies from his mother's garden. This particular image stood out above other childhood memories. The knowledge that he was a replacement for his brother, whom he'd never met, was not yet made clear as he and his mother had stood above the small headstone and she'd openly wept. Not really understanding the reason for her sadness, he'd attempted to comfort her by wrapping his small arms around her calves and hugging his face to her knees.

He set Lucy's photograph back on the mantle, carefully aligning it with the other silver frames, and continued his search for Nadine. Mounting the stairs at the front of the house, he heard a shuffling of heavy objects on the floor above and slowed his pace, listening. Treading lightly, he reached the landing at the top of the stairs and leaned into the wall, trying to see around the corner and down the long hallway without being detected. Nadine stood underneath the exposed entryway to the attic. The wooden steps pulled from the ceiling rested on the floor by her feet, which were surrounded with boxes labeled "Baby." Baby clothes, baby dishes, baby toys. All neatly printed in careful black marker on the outside of the brown cardboard boxes. Her back was to him as she held a yellow terry cloth onesie with small floral embroidery on the left lapel. Nadine sighed audibly, delicately cradling the fabric as if it covered an actual infant. A small sound escaped her, a whimpering noise, and Axon knew she must be crying. Her thumb brushed lovingly over the textured flowers. He watched as she carefully folded the clothing and set it atop the items in the nearest box. Securing the lid, she stood and brought both hands up to cover her face, taking several loud sniffling breaths. Wiping her face with the sleeves of her sweater, she bent down, lifted the box at her feet, and began climbing the steep, narrow steps, consigning the boxes to storage once again.

Muffled noises floated down the stairs as Nadine moved items around overhead. Axon debated his position. He heard the characteristic creak of her weight settling on the ladder rungs again just as his phone chimed with an incoming message.

"Shit," Axon said under his breath as her footsteps paused.

"Hello?" Nadine called, stepping further down and craning her neck awkwardly around to find the source of the noise.

"Oh hey, Nadine," he said, trying to be nonchalant, rounding the corner so he was face-to-face with her coming down the steps. She wiped hastily at her eyes with the cuff of her cardigan sweater, hiding her tears.

"Dusty up there," she muttered with a half-smile.

"Yeah." Axon flushed, silently thanking his genes for a complexion that allowed this to go mostly unnoticed. "So, um," he started, unsure how to clear the air.

Nadine's gaze sharpened on him as he struggled to pretend he had just arrived upon the landing of the stairs while she was cleaning. Finally finding his excuse, he stammered, "Ed is making breakfast. Did you want some?"

"Oh. No. Thank you. I'm not hungry. Tell him I'm just picking up the hall," she said with a slightly dreamy quality, her puffy eyes gazing toward the boxes.

"Sure." He nodded, turning on his heel, and headed back to the kitchen.

"What do you mean, 'What are you supposed to do?'" Ed said gently, putting a hand on Lucy's shoulder, the hot skillet of eggs in his other. Axon tried to slink inconspicuously back to his chair, not wanting to interrupt.

"Dad . . . What am I supposed to do *now*? I didn't die. I'm still alive, still breathing. I grew up going to low LP school with—" She cleared her throat. "—Colton. I have no skills to take me in *any* career direction. Do I just stay in low LP school until everyone around me dies?" she demanded. "In a few months I'll be the only one left from my class."

Looking helpless, Ed stepped back to the kitchen counter and began to serve eggs onto plates. "You'll find something, honey."

"My whole life was structured around my LP," she continued. "I—" Noticing Axon back at the table, she paused.

"Nadine doesn't want breakfast. She's putting things away in the attic," Axon said tonelessly. Lucy looked at him, an unreadable emotion in her gaze.

"Thanks for the update," Ed said to Axon dismissively. "Honey, everything will be okay. We don't even know . . ."

"Don't even know how much longer I'm going to live?" Lucy offered. "That's what you were going to say, right?"

Ed was silent for a moment, as if choosing his words carefully before picking up the plates of cheesy eggs and bringing them to the table in front of his daughter. He put his arm around her shoulder. "Well, kiddo," he began. "The truth is, we *don't* know how much longer you're going to be around."

Lucy inhaled sharply at those words, as if the truth was somehow worse coming from her father's mouth. Ed squeezed her shoulder again.

"What exactly am I supposed to do?" Lucy whined.

"You're a medical anomaly, remember?" Axon said sardonically. "The future is limitless."

Chapter 9

WHILE EVERGREEN RELISHED any opportunity to puzzle Gregor, she realized after her hasty departure that it was past midnight, and Axon Davis would surely be inundated with activity surrounding Lucy Hanson at this time. This would likely be the most exciting story in his inherently short career. Unsurprisingly, he did not answer her calls. Though the lab offered the best resources to begin planning her study, Evergreen opted not to give Gregor any satisfaction by retracing her steps that night. Instead, she went home and worked out her plan, detailing the many questions her mind rapid-fired.

How did Lucy Hanson survive past her LP? How much longer would she live? What made her special, and could whatever made her special be the key to elongating others' undesirable LPs? And perhaps the question she imagined Lucy would be asking herself: Was she the only one?

Evergreen decided that the best way to start was to dive into learning everything she could about predictive technology, the history of its integration into society, and how it worked. Her scientific education offered some insight into all of these questions, but specific facts and figures would be paramount to any research proposal she'd make to her superiors at Virionics. Maybe she could even get *more* than one paper published on this? She started by going through several meta-analysis publications where authors had collected background and history on particular topics and brought them together into one article. While many scientists looked down on meta-analysis works for their unoriginal science and opportunity for bias in gathering background data, this was a good way to get a general feel of a topic and the current strides taken within the scientific community to understand it. Examining these papers, she discovered the usefulness of looking at the reference sections to find the original papers cited. This led her from one collection of interesting information to another.

For over a week, Evergreen scoured the Virionics database—containing millions of scientific publications, population demographics, government initiatives, and other official documents, all within easy access of her work station. Unfortunately, access to the plethora of knowledge contained within Virionics' workstation terminals was only available when she was on campus, so she found herself spending even more time at her desk. Evergreen called Axon Davis every chance she got, trying to get him to pick up the phone. Maybe by the time he finally picked up—if only to get her to stop calling—she would have something of substance. Something shiny enough to entice him to arrange a meeting with Lucy Hanson, where Evergreen could convince the teenager to work with her. Evergreen spent her time jumping from article to article by using references in major papers to map out the history and functionality of the technology. Sometimes she was unable to locate a listed source, which would slow her progress to a frustrating pace as she dug through the various searchable areas of the vast Virionics database. Most of the time, she was able to find a missing article but discovered she didn't have the appropriate access to read it. In those cases, she would add the titles to a list she intended to submit an access request for. These requests would get shunted up the chain of command and were usually approved quickly.

Project approval and experimentation would take time. Before she could submit a proposal to the review board, Evergreen would need to demonstrate her complete and thorough understanding of the subject. Others might be interested in pursuing the same questions she had, but if Evergreen could prove her competence and submit a proposal first, she'd be more likely to be granted approval for experimentation and further study. Knowing that there might be competition merely spurred her on to find *something*. Though Evergreen was never one to give much credit to emotions or so-called "gut feelings," she was certain that Lucy was special. And she was going to be the one to find out why.

Maybe she'd even get awarded a prize? Something prestigious that would propel her career and allow her to throw her success back in Gregor's smug face. *Subtly though, no need to be immodest*, she reminded herself. She'd be an award winner, after all, and nobody likes a braggart. But she was getting ahead of herself. Hours of research, inquiry, and possible experimentation lay ahead before she could claim any accolades.

Of course, during this period of intense research, where Evergreen practically dreamed in search engines and Times New Roman typeface, her job was no less demanding. Luckily for her, spending even *more* time in her little lab nook after her other duties were complete went virtually unnoticed among her coworkers, who were used to seeing new hires burning the candle at both ends. Nobody except Gregor ever bothered her to see what it was she so furiously spent hours on.

There had been some minor interest in the Hanson case from her fellow scientists after the news had initially broken. However, everyone was so absorbed in their own projects that talk was merely speculative, and never developed into a call to scientific action. Someone else was probably already looking into it, they assumed. Certainly, the case study would be interesting to read once it was published, the general consensus seemed to be. Evergreen was pleased to hear these comments and forced herself not to focus on her coworkers' conviction that others were probably doing exactly what she was right now.

"Doesn't look like your great idea was very fruitful," Gregor commented one day as she refilled her coffee mug for the fourth time that evening, her unsteady hands splashing some of the hot liquid onto the countertop.

She merely shrugged and said, "We'll see," before walking away, which pleasurably seemed to irritate him.

Only in moments of frustration, dead ends, and repeated ignored phone calls to Axon Davis would the doubt that she was still ahead creep into her mind like an unsettling fog. She tried not to let herself dwell and instead would immerse her mind in data such as that produced by the Census Bureau, which she found extremely educational. Not only did it provide statistics on the population as a whole, including gender, birth year, occupation, and LP, but it also provided the exact number of people meant to die in a given year. And the data correlation between predicted deaths and actual deaths was exact. No scientific data was this perfect for any other topic besides LP, which was fascinating to see. Imperfection was expected in science. Outliers were anticipated, and pure data was typically discounted, never making it past peer review into publication. The basis of science was for data to be replicable. If the study couldn't be repeated under similar conditions, it was invalid and viewed with suspicion. LP data was the exception.

Or was it?

Evergreen considered this thought carefully. Was there even a way census data *could* be biased? This data represented a real record of people's lives, deaths, ethnic background, occupation, and education. Information like that didn't change to please the scientific norm. The data in support of LP accuracy *must* be that damning. If years of schooling and hours of research on the topic had taught her nothing else, it was that LP was the epitome of perfect data, despite breaking norms. However, it was the years of scientific schooling that also prompted her to question this consensus. A scientist should always question the status quo—otherwise, how would new discoveries be made? Without questions and inquiry, poking and prodding of existing theories, science would never grow.

She rubbed her satin hair ribbon between her fingertips, a habit she engaged in whenever she was lost in thought. Evergreen's mother had given the ribbon to her when she was seven—the last gift she'd ever given.

She remembered the day of her mother's death clearly. Ilana, so tall and beautiful, her bronze hair braided intricately and interspersed with several golden ribbons, as was the style at the time, had gently combed Evergreen's tangled hair until it shone. Her mother had twisted that same red satin ribbon into Evergreen's braids with deft hands that morning, humming softly. She had insisted on having a more intimate wake, with few family and a handful of friends. Pomp and circumstance was never her style; she'd preferred to keep it simple, without stylists, a photographer, or a wake reporter present.

She'd passed in the afternoon, sitting in her favorite reading chair, a cooling cup of Earl Grey tea and chocolate cookies on the nearby end table. Evergreen had barely understood what happened—her mother only appeared to have fallen asleep. It wasn't until after the guests and paramedics departed, leaving only a lace tablecloth scattered with plates of half-eaten sweets and the delicate white china teacups patterned with tiny roses that Ilana had favored, that the absence of her mother in the house felt permanent. Evergreen's father had shuffled around the table, beginning to pick up the mess while Evergreen sat in silence in the chair her mother had so recently sat warm and alive in. She remembered feeling intense frustration at the silence of the house, of her father's wordless tidying and the emptiness that was starting to fill her.

Perhaps wanting to fill the quiet with something besides the small tinkling of porcelain being stacked, Evergreen had lashed out without really understanding why. She'd shoved the china plates and teapot from the table with all the force her small seven-year-old body could muster, the irreplaceable pieces tumbling to the wooden floor with a loud crash. Brown tea had begun to seep from the wreckage as her father walked back into the room from the kitchen. He'd found his small daughter standing in front of the disaster, breathing heavily with shoulders heaving and tears streaming down her freckled face. Wordlessly, he'd scooped her up and held her close, letting the tears roll into his shoulder. Afterwards, the surviving pieces of the tea set went on permanent display in the dining hutch with the colorful stained-glass door, never to be used again, a fragmented reminder of her mother.

Evergreen had been staring at her computer screen for hours when an idea occurred to her. She had been skimming various years of census data, just trying to get a feel for the numbers, oftentimes finding herself distracted with thoughts of the people's lives they represented. It hadn't yet occurred to her to check the math of the numbers. Taking out a calculator from the back of her desk drawer, Evergreen did some simple arithmetic. Data was collected to represent births, deaths, and predicted LP for all ages of the population. Evergreen compared the year-end population numbers with the expected number of deaths. Occasionally there were accidental deaths and a rare murder or suicide which were also noted in the census document. She made sure to take into account this small number. Like an accounting document, the two amounts should balance. Strangely, they were discrepant by two. Two people.

Evergreen opened a new search to find the following year's census document. Strangely, though she had been looking at these documents for a few days, it had never occurred to her that the data was only collected every third year. She remembered completing her own census documentation each of the past several years, but why wouldn't the data have been published if it was collected? Maybe there was some governmental regulation that mandated collection but only required compilation of population data every several years. Evergreen had little familiarity with policy and could only speculate.

Deciding to see if this pattern went back the entire history of the census, she decided to meticulously search publications starting as far back as two hundred years ago, close to when calculating LP had become mainstream. It was tedious work, as not all the censuses were filed using the same format for naming, requiring her to dig a little, searching by year instead of keyword. Her eyes were sore from staring at the blue light of her computer when, finally, she found what she was looking for: two years of data published in a row. The second year's data appeared to be named using a slightly misspelled version of the word "Census," as the word "Censes" was what it was filed under.

Whipping out her calculator once more, Evergreen repeated the same calculation she had made on the other document. Once again, she compared the expected deaths to the year-end total population. She typed the numbers in, each one representing people she had probably never met. The numbers did not match, this time by three. Three people.

She rubbed her tired eyes and repeated the work, carefully making sure to hit each key of the calculator precisely to get her result. The numbers still did not match. They might only be off by three, but with everything she knew about how LP worked, her calculated total should match the actual total precisely. Surely this was some sort of clerical error? If the person saving the data had misspelled the word "census," it was also very possible that some sort of numerical mistake had occurred.

She leaned back in her desk chair, gripping the arm rests and staring unfocused at the cubicle wall. How could this be? Could the three have been missed somehow in data collection? No, because all citizens were required to complete the census—in fact, your bio-watch would continue to glow red until any government mandated tasks were completed. The only other time your bio-watch would light up like that was a reminder to have an annual health screening, which included the most recently developed vaccination regimen from Virionics. It would be hard to ignore for an entire year. Perhaps accidental deaths were inflated? Or another category was reported incorrectly? Both were possible, but Evergreen considered them to be unlikely. What if the numbers represented people like Lucy? Others who survived past their LP? She had not found evidence of this happening before, despite the hours of search time she had put in for the past several days. The only thing she *did* know was that she needed more data.

Chapter 10

MAGNUS STRYKER APPEARED smooth, polished, and presentable as ever as he stood on the presidential podium. His dark pinstripe suit would look somber if it weren't so becoming on his bull-like physique. Grinning jovially, his white teeth stark against dark skin, he had a way of making others trust what he said. And while it was true that Magnus Stryker was his elected rather than his given name, his followers regularly commented ironically on just how striking he was. Magnus had been born Michael Stromwell to a mid-LP family and had decided early on to pursue a life in politics. While he could alter his name for political appeal, he couldn't do anything about his predicted lifespan. His LP was a modest sixty-four years, of which nineteen remained to serve in the political spectrum. As part of all major campaigns for office, he was required to publicly reveal his LP, lest the public elect someone who was about to drop dead, and Magnus was noted as one of the first politicians whose lifespan was below seventy. This required him to flaunt it with pride while secretly stewing in his disappointment with not being born with more time. He compensated for this perceived shortcoming by speaking loudly, dressing well, and keeping his facial hair closely trimmed.

It had been over a week since the failed death of Lucy Hanson. It was a week which was marked with a flurry of news, reports, and speculation. Everyone had different questions, but all with an underlying theme: *What does this mean?*

His booming voice prevented him from standing too close to the microphone in the press room. "... and we are grateful for the extension of life for this young daughter of our community. While unexpected, our scientific experts do believe that the prediction of LP is consistent for 99.99% of the population. Lucy Hanson may consider herself to be one in a million, though perhaps more accurately one

76

in a hundred-billion." His smile glittered with the perfect mixture of hope and skepticism. The reporters used his pause to shout out their questions all at once.

"Mr. President, do you know if Lucy Hanson's LP is far off the mark? Will she need to be re-categorized completely?"

"Will she be enrolled in high LP programs?"

"What is the government's plan if this turns out to be more common than a fluke?"

"Do we know why this happened?"

Easily speaking over the reporters, he stated, "Let us all hope that Lucy Hanson enjoys what extra life she has been given, though our scientific advisors do not believe this to be much." President Stryker stepped down from the podium amidst the flashes of cameras. His smile never faltered as he strode across the small stage and out of the reporters' view.

His cheerful smile dropped immediately once he was behind the curtain, and he strode confidently back toward his quarters.

"Mr. President, I have the report from Arnie Hamilton's office." A man in his early twenties handed Stryker the leather-bound folder. His brown suit jacket opened on a tight button-down shirt. The President looked at the young man, his eyes hovering over the overexerted buttons around the belly of the shirt, reading the story of early career stress and one too many morning donuts. The man followed Stryker's gaze and fiddled self-consciously with the button on his suit jacket, giving a false cough to hide his discomfort.

"Thank you." Stryker opened the folder to see the manila envelope marked "CONFIDENTIAL" and emblazoned with an hourglass seal, the mark of the Lifetime Potential Bureau. He grunted noncommittally.

A gray-haired politician who had kept up with Magnus's long strides took the opportunity to speak. "Mr. President, if I could just have a moment of your time to discuss the—"

"Not now, Jordan," the President said with a wave of his hand. He immediately recalculated, seeing the benefits of placating the party member, and added with finality, "Tomorrow."

Having reached his office, he brushed past Chereeza, the woman who brought his late morning half-milk no-sugar coffee. She was carrying the usual silver tray with his drink and a small bowl of almonds and raisins to his desk. He normally preferred cookies, but had switched to a healthier alternative recently in an effort to maintain his waistline. The public was always watching.

Gazing with admiration at Chereeza's backside, he settled behind his desk with the tray and waited for the door to click shut, leaving him alone. He flipped open the leather folder with a soft thump on the desktop and picked up his coffee. Taking a sip, he skimmed the documents, flipping the pages of the report slowly. His brow furrowed, and his eyes narrowed as he finished. Magnus leaned back in his chair, lacing his fingers behind his head, and stared at the opposite wall, letting his mind mull over the folder's information. This was his thinking pose. He did his best decision-making alone, contemplating all angles of the problem while staring at a piece of contemporary art he had hung a year prior, depicting a mixture of colors and shapes which suggested human forms. He found that each time he looked at the artwork while mulling over a problem, he saw something different in the acrylic colors. That was the beauty of modern art.

Picking up his desk phone, he dialed. "Get me Maletich," he barked at the female voice who answered.

A moment later, a deeper voice answered, "This is Maletich."

Magnus's half-consumed coffee had gone cold, forgotten on the desk. "I need you to do something."

Chapter 11

VERONICA BREATHED HEAVILY and bit just a little too hard on his earlobe. Axon made a surprised groan of pleasure in the back of his throat.

"Not yet," she insisted. Abruptly adjusting the rhythm of her hips, she pressed her lips to his neck, and he felt a tug that was sure to leave a lingering mark.

Axon gasped, his breath rapid as he leaned his damp forehead against the exposed skin of her neck.

She stopped the movement in frustration. "I said not *yet*," she complained as he caught his breath.

"Sorry," he apologized, trying to slow his heart rate. "You're just so . . ."

"Unbelievable?" she offered. Axon tapped his forehead against her pronounced clavicle, a product of Veronica's severely calorie-restrictive diet, before nipping at the area playfully. She rolled back into the driver's seat, knees tucked to avoid the gear shift. "Maybe you're just out of shape," she commented with a flip of the visor, glancing in the mirror to smooth her eyeliner with a fingertip. Her manicured fingernails gingerly tugged the hem of her slim pencil skirt, pulling it down and shifting back into professional mode.

The moment for sultry pillow talk had passed. Things usually ended abruptly and, as they both preferred, without much further complication. "Well, you *are* supposed to drop me off at the gym." Axon gestured to the bag at his feet. "At least these parking lot detours count as cardio. Besides, the risk of being caught is so stimulating . . ." He attempted to kiss her neck while she continued to inspect herself in the mirror.

She swatted him away, using the heel of her hand to push his head back in the direction of the passenger side of the car. "I think you should walk from here," she said with nonchalance.

"The gym's still a ways away," he countered, gesturing down the road.

Veronica rolled down the window. "Call it part of your workout." She shrugged, pursing her lips in mock sympathy.

"Ha-ha. Very funny," he said, still not really believing her, while adjusting the chair back to a more upright position. With his hand occupied with the lever, Veronica snatched his bag of athletic clothes from the floor near his feet and chucked it out the open window.

"Get. Out," she said, a definitive pause between each word. The car had been idling, but revved as she tapped the gas and reached for the steering wheel.

"Oh, come on," he said, exasperated.

She shifted the car into drive and tapped the accelerator lightly, moving the car forward several feet.

"Alright! Alright!" Axon said as he reached for the door handle. He exited as the car continued to creep forward slowly. After he slammed the door Veronica sped up, circling around to face him from her open window.

"Keep on the story," she said, popping a piece of mint gum into her mouth.

"I know. Emma is covering the Hansons while I attend to other . . . needs," he said, resting his hands on the top of the sedan.

She nodded once, her brown eyes looking sharply at him. Revving the engine again, she added with a raised eyebrow, "Your belt's undone," before peeling out of the parking lot.

Axon strode into the gym half an hour later, the bag slung over one shoulder still showing evidence of being tossed around the pavement. He nodded hello at the woman with a blond ponytail behind the front desk. She flashed a brilliantly white smile, showing teeth slightly too large for her mouth.

"Hey," Axon said, drumming the surface of her desk with his fingertips.

"How's it going today?" Her ponytail bounced from side to side, though she hardly moved.

His phone gave a sharp ring from the bottom of his pocket. Glancing at the screen, he quickly silenced the call. "Sorry," he muttered.

"I saw you on TV!" Ponytail blurted out as if she could barely contain the words.

"Oh. Yeah. It's been interesting." He ran a hand through his dark hair, working the modest-and-slightly-embarrassed look he had mastered.

"What's she like? Is she like, suicidal?" Ponytail asked excitedly. "I'd be totally freaking out."

"I don't know," he said coyly. "You'll just have to watch the exclusive when it airs to find out." Thus far there was no exclusive, though Veronica had been pushing pretty hard for him to make it happen. The Hanson family was reluctant to subject their daughter to an on-screen interview, but the final decision sat with Lucy, who had yet to be convinced it was in her best interest.

"Oh, I will!" She leaned closer to him and rested her chin in her palm, tapping her fingers delicately on her peachy cheek. "I'm Olivia, by the way."

"Axon." He smiled.

"Yeah," she giggled, "I know."

"Right. TV," he said, looking down at his feet before glancing up at her with a smirk.

"I'm off at seven." Her cheeks flushed. "Well, why don't you give me your number and maybe I'll call you after seven?" He had hardly been out of the Hanson's house in days and hadn't been able to use his newfound notoriety much. Not that he had ever experienced issues charming women, but this new media blitz around Lucy Hanson was likely to be a game changer. If things went his way, he'd be able to pick and choose which wakes he covered. Maybe he could even crack his way into tighter circles of the social elite. Bored, younger senators' wives with mid LP sounded like a challenge he was up for.

". . . Axon?" The girl at the front desk was pushing a slip of paper hopefully toward him over the countertop, her phone number typed neatly—writing by hand had mostly fallen into antiquity. She had been trying to catch his attention long enough for the blush to return and her toothy smile to waver with uncertainty.

He took the paper from her hand, skimming her fingertips with his in a gesture he knew would soften her. "Thanks. I'll call you." He gave Olivia his best smile. She pulled back from the counter, covering her mouth, hiding her smile and blushing deeper.

"I'd better get changed," he said softly as he took small steps backwards toward the locker rooms.

He was midway through his bench press sets, the implants in his ears blaring the energetic music without lyrics that he preferred. Sitting up between sets, he saw motion in the otherwise sparsely filled gym from the corner of his eye. Turning in the direction of the front desk he saw Olivia, arms outstretched, ponytail swinging violently, trying to actively block the path of someone who seemed determined to march in his direction. Tapping his wristband, he paused the music.

"You don't have a membership!" Olivia proclaimed loudly as the woman tried to push past her. Though Olivia worked at the gym, she was losing ground as the other woman muscled her way past toward Axon's bench. The newcomer was also blond, with long legs stretching out of her professional pencil skirt. Her hair was pulled back into a long braid that hung over her shoulder, interwoven with a piece of red ribbon. It was then that Axon realized he knew her.

"Emily?" he asked as she strode toward him, Olivia clawing at her arm to keep her from reaching his side.

"You know her?" Olivia interjected.

"Actually, it's Evergreen," she said, finally prying the front desk girl's glittery fingernails from her upper arm. "Told you I knew him," Evergreen quipped in Olivia's direction.

Axon snapped his fingers in recognition and nodded. "Evergreen. Right." Olivia scoffed and stepped away, defeated and mumbling something about a membership and common courtesy.

"I've been calling for days, but you've ignored me, so I had to track you down," she said matter-of-factly, clearly struggling to rein in her annoyance.

"I thought I was the journalist here?" he said, his charm hardly missing a beat.

"Anyone can use the internet," she retorted with a raised eyebrow.

"Ah, but some skill is required," he conceded while bending over to grab his water bottle. "Otherwise, my recent fan base would be upon me imminently." Tilting his head back, he took a swig and swallowed. "Must have been something important, to use that big scientific brain to find me."

"Remembered my profession but not my name, I see."

"Hey, give me some credit, *Evergreen*." He enunciated the syllables in her name to prove his point. "Why don't you tell me why you're here interrupting my workout and stressing out my poor gym cheerleader?" His hand waved in the direction of the front desk where Olivia had retreated. Olivia smiled back uncertainly.

"I need your help."

"Off to a great start with asking. No please, no preamble, some light stalking . . ."

"Remember how I said I was a research assistant?" she asked quickly.

Axon pressed his hand to his chest in mock surprise. "Are you saying you lied?"

"To be fair, you said you were 'in the media,' so you never specified either," she said. It was apparent that his antagonism was having an effect. "Anyway, I technically do assist with research, so it's not really a lie."

"Okay . . ."

"Anyway," she started again, "I saw you on the news reporting on that Hanson girl, and well, I've been looking for a project . . ."

Axon cut her off. "Do you know how many people want access to that girl? You're not alone, you know."

"Well, I figured. I just—"

"Thought you had special access?" he said thoughtfully, bending to pick up his towel and flipping it over his shoulder. "You're the fourth girl I've hooked up with who wanted to meet with Lucy Hanson. Since *yesterday*. Everyone has a friend, a sibling, a boyfriend, whatever who will die before them. They all want to know what makes her different, with the small hope that if they knew the secret, they could prevent their loss too. Believe it or not, I like my job and I intend to keep it. And right now, my job is to protect my company's exclusive right to unfettered access to the Hanson family. It was fun that night with you, and I know you spent all this energy you could have used toward creating brains in a jar or some scientific shit, but I'm sorry, I can't help you." He began walking in the direction of the locker rooms, turning his back to Evergreen.

"Look, I don't really care about a meet-and-greet with her. Just listen. I'm on a high-LP track to be a senior scientist at Virionics, and I've been doing some research."

"Cool, good for you. Still not interested."

He continued to walk away, causing her to practically shout across the nearly empty room, "She's not the only one this has happened to!"

Axon stopped and turned to face her again, suddenly much more interested in what his new stalker had to say.

Chapter 12

THE WATER RAN WARM from the tap, splashing against the porcelain basin of the bathroom sink. Lucy cupped her hands and scooped water, bending down to splash it on her face. She rubbed at her eyes, the residual black eyeliner from the night before trailing below her lashes, giving her a raccoon-like appearance. She reached for the makeup remover and wiped roughly at her eyes, eliminating the trailing blackness. Uncapping the plastic bottle beside the sink, she dragged a small white pill along the inside of the container, leaving her fingers with a residual watery whiteness. Lucy sucked the bitter residue from her fingertip and tossed the pill into the back of her mouth. She turned the tap cold and cupped the running water in her palms again, swallowing a mouthful with a backwards tilt of her head. The drug was supposed to help her cope with impending death, but her dose had been increased after she'd failed to die as prescribed. It made her a little dizzy; she was still getting used to it.

Thanks to the ever-present media outside her house, she hadn't been outdoors in over a week. Not that she had anywhere to go. Axon Davis had convinced her to make a small appearance for his news outlet the previous evening, which was thankfully from the comfort of the Hansons' living room. Rumors were circulating that Lucy had died while hiding out at home, and he'd hoped to placate the public, giving them some new footage to dissect. His suggestion to make intermittent appearances at the living room window managed to drive the news reporters still camped out at the end of her driveway into a frenzy, but it served the purpose he had explained. The reporters believed she was still alive. Not that it truly mattered to the media whether or not she still survived—they only wanted a good story to keep their ratings high. Axon was strategic, ensuring every contractual obligation she had to his advantage. Lucy respected it.

As her isolation continued, Lucy spent more and more time alone in her bedroom, staring at the ceiling and putting together scenarios of what her life could look like. If she went back to school, eventually the rest of her peers would die, leaving Lucy the sole survivor of her low-LP class. There was always the chance that at any moment she would join Colton and her other dead friends. *The anticipation is killing me*, she thought, then laughed out loud at her own dumb joke. Drying her face with a towel, she looked at herself in the silver-framed mirror. Her brown eyes stared back, an emptiness in their pupils, a dullness to their color. The slightly relaxed feeling that usually accompanied the medication started to take effect. Lucy rested her arms against the edge of the sink and continued to stare at her own reflection.

Most people who felt inclined to comment had insisted the extra time she had been given was a "true gift," but to Lucy it only seemed like a punishment. It was hard to believe that civilization had lived with the uncertainty of death for millennia. Lucy tried to imagine how people must have felt before technology could remove unpredictability and pinpoint the time of death for everyone—except her, that is. Constant anxiety? Being afraid to go outside? At least that's how *she* felt. People must have adjusted to the idea, it being a truth they were born into, but it was still hard to imagine. The eventuality of death was just as present today as it was back then, and like now, people simply continued living their lives.

In her own case, not having a known time of death created confusion, threw off plans, and created doubt. Not only was this clear on the internet—where Lucy had initially closely followed commentary before growing disinterested when it was made clear nobody could answer any of her questions—but it was true in her own home. Lucy knew how badly her mother wanted another child, and if she lived much longer, Nadine would be unable to legally conceive. The baby boxes standing ready on the morning of her wake had already been placed back into storage with no word or comment from either of her parents. Why hadn't they just started to decorate her room in blue or pink pastels and asked her to relocate to the couch? She didn't understand why they wouldn't just move on with their lives already. She could take a hint. Her LP couldn't be *that* far off. They should have just continued on with their plan like business as usual. Who was she to stop them? Besides, wasn't her birth as a low LP already a disappointment? So, what did they care whether she saw their preparations for her replacement? They certainly hadn't held back before. Supposedly this transparency was a part of moving on and accepting the normality of the situation: one where she would die knowing that her parents had a plan to cope and move forward with their lives. Maybe next time they'd get lucky and produce a mid or even high-LP child who'd outlive them both. *Something about family legacy and carrying on the name and history, blah, blah, blah,* Lucy thought, her eyes going in and out of focus.

She couldn't stay inside this house forever. At some point, she would need to face the world and decide what to do next. It hadn't exactly been comforting to hear the actual *president* weigh in on her situation. Even his experts thought she didn't have much time to live. In the long hours she spent laying on top of her bedspread with nothing to do but think and daydream about what could be, she had contemplated the idea of helping speed the process along. Wasn't she just going to be an emotional drain on her parents, whose conflicting emotions were apparent in the way they looked at her?

She thought about how she might do it, how best to end her life so everyone could just move on. It was frustrating enough that she even had to consider this. Why couldn't the technology have worked the way it was supposed to, so she died when she was predicted to? Everyone else got to have the ending they planned. It wasn't fair that choice had been taken away from her.

It would be easy. Lucy opened the cupboard above the sink to investigate its contents.

Tweezers, no.

Mouthwash, hardly.

Nail polish remover, gross. She never could stand the smell.

Nothing proved useful. She needed something sharp. She thought of the small pair of sewing scissors she'd found useful after Colton died. But the small, shallow cuts they were good for wouldn't suit this purpose.

She fingered the nail file, the dullness of the metal smooth against her finger, the periphery of her focus slightly foggy. What she really needed would be downstairs. The kitchen was full of tools with bite. She had once sliced the top of her knuckle with a potato peeler. Such a small device, and yet the blood had rolled down her hand, making the injury appear more serious than it was. The chunk of skin that it had caught was easily plucked from the blades with a pinch of her fingers.

She knew there would need to be more blood, a deeper cut.

Lucy fingered the satin of her bathrobe, twirling it around in a knot and letting it fall from her hand like a streamer. It felt smooth against her skin, almost like water.

Focus. She steeled herself for her next move. What she needed was downstairs in the kitchen where she knew her parents were sitting, having chosen the hard wooden chairs near the smaller television over the comfy couch in the living room, as if their physical discomfort could somehow compensate for their emotional turmoil.

Taking a breath, she braced a hand against the wall as a crutch as she left the bathroom, feeling as if her palm left a hot imprint on the wall behind her. Making her way downstairs, she could hear her parents murmuring, only slightly discernable from the noise of the TV.

The sound grew louder as she rounded the bottom of the staircase. Chanting. They were chanting. Chanting *her name*.

"Long live Lucy! Long live Lucy! Long live Lucy!"

Confused, she rounded the corner into the kitchen and realized that the voices almost blurred together, as if some of the voices were off-rhythm by a half-second. The screen showed a scene with people tromping down a street together, shouting the message.

"Honey, they're cheering for you," Ed Hanson said softly.

Walking slowly into the room, Lucy looked at her father, then back at the TV. The sound was definitely coming from more than one place. Suddenly, she recognized where they were.

Feeling almost like she was floating without touching the floor, she swept into the living room where the front windows stood covered by the white gauzy curtains her mother had chosen. Reaching out her hand, she brushed the fabric back to more clearly see the scene occurring in the street in front of her parent's house.

"Long live Lucy! Long live Lucy! Long live Lucy!" shouted at least fifteen people. They marched in a circle around the parked news vehicles that had become more or less a permanent fixture in front of the house. Everyone chanting held wooden pickets with clearly handmade signs adhered to the ends, which displayed several versions of the same message—that she should *live*.

Chapter 13

LISA MONTEZ EVALUATED risks for a living, but she was not a risk-taker. She spent her days working in a downtown office for a national firm that used various algorithms to assess potential investments, construction projects, and political policies for how well they would stand up over time. With a modest mid-level LP of fifty-five, she had been approved to acquire her actuarial education—she was a good investment.

Lisa enjoyed her job. Her team was responsible for evaluating the likelihood of serious injury or death from activities such as cliff-hanging and bungee-ballooning, once quite popular among the low-LP crowd. Through their number crunching, her firm had contributed to the overall effort to decrease these high-risk sources of "fun," achieving a solid 47% drop in high-risk activity. It had been a success her company celebrated by sponsoring their employees to become subscribers to the city orchestra, which performed monthly in the newly constructed, acoustically perfect theater. Her firm had been integral in evaluating the theater foundation, so it was a heavily discounted deal.

The gravel crunched beneath her black flats, which were thick-soled to provide cushion for her high arches and treaded to avoid slipping on smooth surfaces. She walked along the garden path running in front of her building twice a day, though sometimes four if she decided to go out for lunch. Whenever she passed beneath the metal archways, where in the spring, fragrant flowers grew up and over, she inhaled deeply, appreciating their scent. It was early in the season, but there were some buds releasing their genetically enhanced smell, so she paused to take it in, smiling. The small wrinkles which had started forming around her eyes several years back crinkled as she enjoyed the atmosphere.

She had purposely adopted this habit after attending a work-sponsored seminar on maintaining happiness and positivity. Even if diseases were generally cured, maintaining a healthy mood balance without resorting to prescription assistance was always preferable among her age group. The class suggested forming smile-inducing habits to follow regularly. Flossing your teeth was no longer sufficient to better oneself, though Lisa did this twice a day.

Crunching onward until she reached the street, Lisa walked in the direction she always did around this time, to catch the 5:12 train back to her neighborhood. The sky had already started to dim, just enough to be of notice through the gray clouds that persisted most of this time of year. Lisa zipped her waterproof jacket closed, pulling the hood over her dark curly hair before tucking her hands into the pockets, fidgeting with her train pass and house keys. Her wrist vibrated with a message. She chose to read it displayed as a projection above her arm instead of listening to the slightly nasal voice of her boss, mimicked by the computer to read out the message in her ear implant.

Beaterman Group wants to meet tomorrow at seven sharp. Can you come in early?

Always the prompt and dependable employee, she answered immediately that she would be there bright and early. Tomorrow would be Friday, and having an early start to the weekend would be a nice beginning to her days off.

The train station came into view as she rounded the corner past the bakery which served specialty sandwiches on warm bread during the week, catering to the business crowd. The lingering scent of fresh bread drifted past as she strode closer to the stairs leading to the platform. Maybe she would get in early enough to grab fresh donuts for everyone the next morning—she tried to be considerate in that way. All of the employees at her company loved donuts. They would probably go fast, most likely before the meeting with Beaterman Group ended, so she would have to make sure to grab her favorite before they disappeared. Cinnamon twists with sweet white icing were her weakness, though they were also a customer favorite and sometimes were sold out before she could get to the front of the line. *Early would work best*, she thought.

Grasping the handrail, she began her ascent of the stairs to the train platform. A man in a long wool coat and a sleek briefcase slung over one shoulder, brushed past her on the stairs as he had a conversation with the voice in his ear.

"I've just got to finish the analysis, and then I'll shoot it over to you. Should only take about thirty," he said breathily to the air in front of him as he huffed down the stairs.

She reached the top of the stairs just as the gray, low-hanging clouds released their first sprinkles. The cool raindrops tapped the top of her head, and she looked skywards again, allowing the water to fall across her nose. A droplet fell softly onto her eyelashes, and she resisted the urge to wipe the water away, lest she smudge her carefully applied mascara. Luckily the platform was mostly covered by a clear glass roof, meant to keep its station commuters dry while blocking minimal seasonal sunlight. She stood underneath the awning and noted that the electronic timetable indicated her train was still on time. It was 5:11—only one more minute until it arrived. Lisa had her work departure time down to a science. Without needing to leave early and be perceived by her coworkers as less dedicated, she was always able to make it to the station in time for her train, even if she stopped to literally smell the roses.

A faint rumbling began in the distance as the train cars approached on the tracks. Though some sections of the line were underground, most of Lisa's commute was raised above street level to allow for a view of the city from the train. She usually preferred to look out the window and watch the familiar sights go past rather than read or play on a device. The billboards with constantly rotating advertisements, the park with its modern art structures, the brick apartment building with the old-fashioned fire escape stairs on the side of the building. Of course this was only decorative, but its quaintness always made Lisa think of simpler times, before mitigating risk had been the norm. People had died in fires or suffered crippling injuries from jumping several stories because the building staircases were badly maintained. Not anymore. Hydraulic lifts were created to fit aesthetically next to the older modes of fire escape, seamlessly blending into the architecture of the building without taking away from their ultimate purpose. She hardly noticed them anymore.

The train came to a halt with a slight hiss and squeak of the brakes. The doors opened slowly, and a few people trickled out. The compartments appeared mostly full, meaning she likely would not get to sit on her preferred side of the car. Noting the few empty seats, Lisa walked into the second car of the train and sat down on the cushion-less bench, her purse swinging to rest in her lap. She would have the less-preferred view of the single-storied houses that populated the opposite side of the track, with only the shingles of the roof visible as the train sped by above them.

Not being able to see into the windows of apartment buildings was a little disappointing. Usually she made up stories about the people she saw through the windows, carrying on with their lives. Sometimes she witnessed mothers with small children she imagined to be playing a game of make-believe. Other times she saw couples who appeared to be talking or arguing—probably about the children, she thought.

Lisa had not pursued the role of mother. Patrick had been her boyfriend and lover while she was in school finishing her career training. Unfortunately, as they say, love is blind, and she'd found herself inseparable from a man destined to die in only two years. There was not enough time to check all the boxes and apply for parenthood before his death date, so the couple had opted to ignore the topic of children altogether and enjoy the time they had. Since then, she had never found another man who compared, and the possibility of having kids evaporated. This was okay, though. Lisa loved her job. She loved her hobbies outside of work, her friends and garden club, mimosas on Sundays. Everything had worked out for the best.

Looking across the aisle at the limited view of the landscape from the high vantage point of the train, Lisa's eyes became unfocused. The rain picked up as the train sped to the next downtown stop, splashing wide droplets sideways across the windows. Her mind relaxed as stops were made with decreasing frequency as people got off at their destinations. Her residence was located in a small subdivision about a twenty-five minute ride from work. She had settled into the townhome nearly a decade ago, and despite the drawbacks of sharing a wall with neighbors, she found it oddly comforting knowing that other humans were breathing just a few inches of insulated space away. Most of her peers either had families with one or two children, depending on their birth LP, or they lived with a roommate for company. Now that Patrick was gone, she preferred to live alone.

The train car was nearly empty, with only herself and a man in a tan suit and wispy hair remaining. Hers was one of the last stops, and usually few others rode with her to the end of the line. She smiled kindly at the man sitting across from her.

"Almost home," she said softly.

He nodded.

"Do you live in Stratsvold?" she asked.

"I have a work meeting scheduled there tonight," he replied with another nod, the bags underneath his eyes standing out starkly as the light continued to diminish outside and the fluorescence of the train took over.

"Ah," she commented for lack of something better to say.

"Government," he added, as if answering her unasked question about his profession.

It was her turn to nod.

They sat in silence for several minutes as the train sped by more houses below as they rounded a curve.

"Do you—" Her question was cut off by a sudden powerful rush of heat through the car, taking her breath away. A loud boom sounded, metal colliding with metal and twisting with the combination of explosive force and the speed of the train. Fire roared through the cars like the exhale of Hades, and the train tilted precariously. Gravity took its toll as the weight of the train pulled it toward the ground, seemingly in slow motion.

Train cars smoldered on the street below the tracks, with only the slight hiss of steam from the failed brakes and smoke escaping from pockets where the fire had raged.

The rest was silent.

Chapter 14

"BUT DON'T YOU THINK—" the woman on the larger half of the screen interrupted loudly, her wide mouth displaying an expression of outrage. "Don't you think," she repeated herself once it was clear she had bulldozed her way into the dominant position, "that it's unfair to the families whose children have followed their designated LP?" The dulled sound of protesters waving homemade picket signs with messages in support of Lucy Hanson's life continued behind her as she spoke.

"Well, I—" began a woman in a red suit jacket from her feed on the top-right corner of the screen.

"Just hear me out," Wide Mouth interjected again, holding the microphone firmly in her leather-gloved hand. "Everyone has to go through this if they have kids. I did it, you did it, and we all hoped for the same thing: for our children to have a long and happy life. Unfortunately, we know that not everyone is able to live until they're eighty-five. That's just not reality," she said matter-of-factly. "Sometimes children are born with the bittersweet news that while they will live a protected, extremely happy life, it will be tragically short. We as a society have come to terms with this. We expect this could happen to any of us who have children, though most people never think it will happen to them. Lucy Hanson was only supposed to live until she was sixteen years and eight months. What kind of example does this set for the rest of society if she is allowed to challenge our social norms by continuing the life she's been living despite her apparently false expiration date? Why is it that—" she began but was cut off abruptly by the mustached man in the gray suit on the bottom-right corner of the screen.

"But who said she will get to continue to live out her life in the same way she's been doing, if you're implying that she'll continue down the same low-LP track she's been on?" he interjected loudly.

"I'm not saying she should get to keep the cushy life she's had thus far. Lucy Hanson's life thus far has contributed relatively little to society. While she has served the function of providing a parent-child relationship and presumably friendships to others, this is merely a contribution on a minute personal level. Lucy Hanson's only skill at this point is being alive. But that doesn't mean she can't contribute now. There are plenty of low-skilled jobs she could qualify for if she were pushed from the comfortable nest of the school she's been enrolled in and forced to test her own wings. I think the main message of the protest group is that they are happy she is alive. It has given people hope that maybe the LP of ones they love could also prove to be false. The technology has been dependable for decades. Perhaps humans have found new ways to exist or adapt—"

"This isn't about evolutionary science here, Norm, we're talking about someone's life. One girl's life." Red Blazer spoke up adamantly, clearly hoping to spark some further controversy with the commentators.

"I know it isn't. I know it isn't," he said in quick succession. "I'm just saying, she's going to outgrow her school soon anyhow. What's the average lifespan of the students there? Twelve? With a maximum of seventeen? She's quickly approaching that limit anyway. I say, let her pick a career—something easy," he reiterated, "and have her live until her actual LP comes up. It can't be that far off the mark, otherwise we would have heard of these kinds of cases before."

"Well, if her LP is coming soon, what's the point of making her work in the first place? Consider the trauma of having prepared your whole life for the exact moment you know you will die and having it turn out not to be the case. I'm sure people can relate to this—everyone knows exactly their moment of death, people invariably plan their last moments of life down to the second. Imagine your predicted last breath turned out to be only one of thousands more to come. That would be shocking to anyone. She's only sixteen. There's no reason to push her. Like you said, the oldest age in her school is usually seventeen. Why can't she stay there until her next birthday, which by all medical predictions will be unlikely to occur, so she can continue to receive the treatment we as a society have agreed to grant to those with such a low LP?"

Norm launched himself into the conversation again. "What happens after her birthday though? I think that's the point we're trying to make. Just because she is alive doesn't mean she can just choose to do whatever she wants. There's a reason we have the system we do. To place individuals into society where they can contribute in a meaningful way, we assess their anticipated life span at an early age to determine which career tracks they're eligible for. Individuals follow the track they're qualified for until it can be narrowed to a more specific career education and training curriculum. For individuals who wish to become part of a career track their age does not justify, they are allowed to apply and are admitted on a case-by-case basis. We have found there is a place for everyone, and while people have choices, they are limited by their capabilities and lifespan. It has been proven time and time again through ample data collection that this is the most efficient way to create a functional society and a satisfied population without overextending our resources. This system has allowed us to efficiently use what we have to make us better. Now, where Lucy Hanson fits into that puzzle is up for debate. We have removed the known variable from the equation—her lifespan. A metaphorical wrench has been thrown into the technology we have been so dependent on to organize our society. The more important question we should be trying to answer is why did this happen and what is the risk for it to continue? I think—"

Wide Mouth touched her ear to indicate she was getting a feed from outside the discussion. "I hate to interrupt," she clearly lied, "but there is a breaking news development. I have just been given word that a devastating accident has occurred on the outskirts of the suburb of Stratsvold. The commuter Amway train has suffered a mechanical failure, causing several cars to derail and crash onto the street below."

Twisted metal, smoke, and small fires suddenly replaced the three correspondents on the screen. The road that had once been a quiet suburban thoroughfare was hardly distinguishable from the wreckage of the train cars. Flashing lights from emergency vehicles and people rushing around in fireproof jackets went in and out of the camera's view. A few stretchers were seen rushing past, carrying soot-covered people with breathing apparatuses held to their faces.

"I'm told this tragedy has fortunately occurred near the end of the commuter train's route, meaning fewer passengers were aboard when the failure occurred. The estimated deaths currently are reported as four and counting as emergency personnel continue to clear the wreckage in search of trapped passengers."

The camera continued to pan the scene with the reporter speaking in the background for several minutes, detailing the supposed cause of the accident by experts on the scene.

"It's always a tragic day when an accident causes people to lose their lives before their time." The screen showed the reporter touching the earpiece again, her mouth pursed in a lipsticked pout, undoubtedly her "empathetic" face. "While we have found ways to treat harmful genetic conditions, cure cancer and medically prevent death before our natural time comes, there continue to be risks we can only partially mitigate. Though the risk of danger is small, and train travel is one of the safest types of transportation, accidents still happen. Let us keep the families and friends of the injured and deceased in our thoughts and prayers, and hope that a thorough investigation can find a way to prevent this type of disaster from occurring again."

The footage continued to display the ashy ruins of the train, and engineering experts were soon brought on camera to speculate on what the cause had been.

"Did you want anything besides coffee, babe?" a waitress with lashes too long to be real asked with hand on hip.

Evergreen tore her eyes away from the wreckage of the train crash on the wall-mounted flat screen. The lone waitress of the late-night diner held a steaming coffee pot in one manicured hand, her eyes blinking more frequently than necessary. Evergreen recognized this as Arizona's trick to make someone notice when she had refreshed her lash extensions. Placing her palm over the ceramic cup to prevent a refill, feeling the steam condense on her skin, she said, "Just coffee, thanks. I'm waiting for someone."

"I'll be just over there if you need me." The waitress turned on her heel and sat behind the counter, pulling up a puzzle game on her phone. Evergreen was one of the only customers in the small eatery. One other table had a couple of teenage boys leaning in together, looking at a tablet screen while engaged in a quiet debate. Brief snippets of their conversation and a few friendly exclamations told her they were discussing a new video game and watching active player feeds.

The door of the place opened with a tinkling bell denoting Axon's arrival. Hearing the noise, the waitress slowly got to her feet while still leaning over her phone, looking at the screen. She glanced up briefly in his direction and back to her phone, doing a double-take after seeing his face. He smiled broadly at her, noticing her recognition. Evergreen witnessed the small exchange and wondered vaguely if the waitress like Olivia at the gym was taken by Axon's good looks or sudden notoriety.

Axon slid into the booth across from Evergreen, assessing her with eyes that brought a blush to her freckled cheeks and made her unconsciously tug on the end of the thick blond braid that hung over her shoulder, the end wrapped tightly in red satin.

"You came," she said, feeling relieved and weary, hoping it didn't show in her cat-like green eyes.

The waitress sashayed over to their table holding an empty cup and her pot of coffee, making a show of wagging her hips. Though Axon hadn't asked, she set the cup down and poured. "Thanks," he said with a glance upwards at her fast-blinking eyes.

"Did you want to order any food?" she asked hopefully.

"I'm good, thanks."

"I'm there if you need anything." She gestured to her nook behind the countertop with a glittery pointed fingernail. Axon acknowledged with a nod. Before retreating, she refilled Evergreen's undefended cup.

"So, I'm here. What have you got?" Axon wrapped his palms around the warm mug in front of him. He hadn't removed his leather jacket, which was left unzipped despite the chill outside, his wine-colored V-neck shirt clinging to his chest beneath it. Between his clearly defined pectorals hung a silver beaded chain. Imitation dog tags hung on the end of the chain, clinking together softly, their embossed words indistinguishable from the other side of the table where Evergreen sat.

"It's hard to explain," she began.

"That's the start to your big pitch? I thought you'd have graphs and laminated charts or something." He talked with his hands, mimicking grandeur and sarcastic expectation.

"I saved those for the board meeting," Evergreen said straight-faced.

"Hah," he chuckled. "Well, go ahead. Explain away." He made a sweeping gesture.

"Have you ever read a scientific journal article? Like something published with references cited at the end?"

"Articles besides those about science use sources too . . . but yes." He nodded.

"Anyway, I saw Lucy Hanson on TV and just knew there had to be something there." She put her hand up to stop Axon from interjecting. "And I know that doctors have examined her and say everything is normal and what have you," she declared all in one excited breath. "But I had a hunch there was something remarkable about Lucy. I should have prefaced this with saying that working for a company like Virionics allows me to access every single relevant piece of scientific research mankind has to offer. So, I started digging through what research I could find from the Virionics server to verify if there was any evidence that Lucy isn't the first person in the history of differentiator technology to surpass her LP. As you might expect, nothing stood out. There were plenty of clinical research trials using people of particular LPs, census data, and records of LP distribution nationwide, but there was nothing to suggest that Lucy was anything but an anomaly."

She sipped the coffee she hadn't wanted more of before continuing, "So I decided to challenge the most basic of the data: the census. Turns out, the government only keeps a record of the data every three years."

"Don't we answer mandatory questionnaires every year?" Axon interjected.

"Yes. We do. But the weird thing is, the data is only compiled into a report every three years using the most recent year of collection."

"So why are we wasting our time with it every year?" he asked with a bored shrug.

"I'd assume the data collected annually is useful, even if it isn't put into a report. But the odd thing is, I was able to find several census documents that didn't fit this pattern. In the sense that they were compiled more than just once every three years."

"So?"

"Seems like it isn't a big deal, right? Maybe there was a reason to put the data together in particular years? But the part I thought was interesting was that I found these documents only because they had some sort of error in how they were saved and made searchable inside the Virionics database."

"Meaning?"

"Well, meaning that maybe they were meant to be saved in another way but someone made a mistake. A mistake like, they meant to save it as private but saved it as public instead. I know the company keeps all sorts of data from different studies and it doesn't necessarily publish everything in a public scientific journal. That's pretty common. Not all studies lead to discoveries of something miraculous, but Virionics wants to keep a record of everything they do, all projects their scientists are a part of. My theory is the census data is always configured into a readable report, however it isn't always published publicly, even in the Virionics database. Anyway, I found some anomalies within the census data that appeared to be accidentally made public to all users within the database." She went on to explain her findings and showed Axon examples of the math.

Much to Axon's smug delight, she *had* brought printed tables, though they were not laminated. She showed him the small discrepancies in population count year over year.

"They must have made a mistake. It has to be easy to do when you're dealing with such large numbers," he said, clearly unimpressed.

"That's what I thought at first too," she said with a slight lowering of her voice. "But it doesn't make sense. Why would there be an error each and every time, by such a small number?"

"Well what else would it be?"

"Glad you asked," she said brightly.

Axon rolled his eyes. "This is where I get the conspiracy theory, no doubt."

She continued undaunted, "I think the discrepant numbers represent people. People like Lucy who lived past their LP."

"Like I was saying . . ." Axon muttered in another direction while he rubbed his palm against his face.

"I did some investigative work into each year I found the discrepancies, to see what kind of accidental deaths had happened. I thought at first that these would somehow explain the discrepancies, like someone had died unexpectedly but they weren't counted in the deaths for that year. I was able to find enough obituaries to correlate with the published number of unexpected deaths each year I looked. Accidental deaths aren't common, so these were easy to find. The interesting part is that when I was able to get census data two years in a row, and I assume the few discrepant data points are people, I can tell which LP age they should have come from. When you're able to see two years of data in a row, it's more obvious which age group the accidental deaths should have come from."

Axon stared at her, looking skeptical. "You lost me."

She pursed her lips, contemplating, then nodded. "Okay. I'll give you an example. One of the obituaries of the accidental deaths I looked into was for a thirty-eight-year-old woman named Mariam Olds who ran a self-sustaining farm that mostly produced soybeans for wholesale. Her husband had already died the previous year but their young daughter survived them both. Her obituary says she died in a farming accident at age thirty-eight. When I looked at the census for the year prior to her death, one of my missing deaths should have come from someone who was meant to die at thirty-seven. So, when the following year's census came up, she was thirty-eight, and she accounted for one of the documented accidental deaths that year." She showed Axon how the numbers worked out for her example, as well as a copy of Mariam's published death notification.

"So, you're saying this woman, Mariam Olds, was supposed to die at thirty-seven—you think, anyway. And she doesn't. Instead, she dies in an accident at age thirty-eight. If she lived past her LP, why wouldn't we know about it?" Axon asked.

"Well for one thing, she lived in a pretty isolated farming region. And like I said, her husband was already dead and she had a young daughter with a high LP who was away at school. There wouldn't have been the same kind of media attention if she were to just keep living. Probably nobody knew. And then she dies within a year because of a freak accident. Don't you think that's odd?"

"I mean, sure, it's odd. But you have no proof of this little story you've constructed. This is total speculation," he said, reaching to stretch his arms behind his head. Catching a glimpse of Evergreen's intense expression, he sighed. "Is this the only example you have?"

Eyes lighting up, Evergreen dug into her bag to pull out a thin stack of documents and handed them to Axon. "I have five more. Here. Look for yourself."

Chapter 15

A KNOCK SOUNDED TENTATIVELY on what at first glance might appear to be an ordinary wall painted a designer shade of eggshell white. The crown molding outlining the hidden door was also white, but with a subtle blue hue only detectable upon close inspection. Adorning the wall was an acrylic-on-canvas portrait of a hunting party on horseback, surrounded by keen dogs darting near the horses' hooves. Magnus might have missed the knock, it was so quiet, but he preferred to work in silence without music or open doors, so any deviation from the pin-drop silence was obvious.

"Enter," he boomed. Whoever was behind the door was meant to feel intimidated by the two-man security detail waiting outside, the solidness of the door, and his beckoning call. He preferred to begin all conversations with the upper hand, even if his office automatically conferred this.

The wall opened slowly, its weight obvious.

"Sorry to disturb you, Mr. President," the man said as he entered, his brown shoes clashing with his black pants. Other than that detail, he was unremarkable. Average height, brown eyes and skin tone of indeterminate ethnicity allowed him to easily go unnoticed in a crowd. His slightly receding hairline made his forehead look larger than it probably had been when he was young, and though he had worked for Stryker for over a decade, Magnus could not recall his colleague ever looking any more youthful than he appeared today. The shape of his face was square, but an excess of about thirty pounds made his cheeks doughy and his chin appear weak. Despite his physical shortcomings, Elbert Maletich had always been a problem-solver—a handy trait which had kept him employed and well-compensated throughout his mid-LP career. A little less than four years remained of Elbert's employable days before he could resign and live out his remaining time enjoying a hobby he had never bothered to develop.

"What is it, Maletich?" Magnus said, returning his attention to his screen.

"It's done," Maletich replied with finality.

"And?" Stryker looked up from his desk with a penetrating gaze that revealed nothing of his anticipation.

Maletich, his facial expression unchanging, replied, "She took it well. Won't say another word about it, the nondisclosure made sure of that. Though . . ."

"That sounds like a 'but.' But what?" Stryker's eyes narrowed slightly.

"I had to offer her more than was pre-approved."

"How much more?"

"Ten percent."

Much more and those reviewing the budget were sure to ask some questions about his very expensive bedroom renovation. Only having actually purchased a new mattress and had the walls painted a soothing eucalyptus, there was a limit to how much a few throw pillows could add to the perceived expense of the "new" room. Stryker waved his hand dismissively. "Fine. Glad it's done." He would never visibly reveal relief that the issue was wrapped up.

Even a minute scandal could inch the polls out of his favor. And without the party's nomination secured, Magnus was at risk for losing his position as commander in chief in the upcoming election. The political maneuverings he'd been forced to make to obtain his seat had been demanding. He was unwilling to lose it after only one term; there was still so much more he wanted to accomplish. If someone else in the party was nominated to run, or even worse, if the opposition was elected, his many projects would be squashed immediately.

Stryker had been frequently criticized for being too aggressive with spending on what others might call "welfare programs." Increasing low-LP school funding, mid-LP career assistance programs, an expansion of scientific mentorships for those on track to become the next great scientific minds of tomorrow, and a collect-and-counsel program for those whose ambition to be a contributing member of society had waned, were some of his more infamous initiatives. Unfortunately for the latter policy, the public had come to know it as the "Degenerate Round-up," complete with a Western theme in the opposition campaign art. It hadn't taken hold like Stryker had wanted. He was certain another term could give him time to fix the program's image.

Conservatives often argued about spending money on programs which only benefited those at the lowest productivity rung in society: the low and mid-LPs. Running the government like a business was a common mindset among his counterparts, but Magnus had always prided himself on being more altruistic. Investing in certain programs promoted trust in the government, a much-needed pacifier for the opinionated public. He was continually surprised at the lack of interest in these policies shown by other politicians who claimed to be "for the people." Take his mentorship initiative for young scientists as an example. The program gave funding to companies to take on student interns and allow them to get a taste of their professional lives ahead while supporting the cost of expensive reagents and materials, which could potentially be wasted by inexperienced hands. Some argued that this program sounded like a great idea in theory, but they disagreed with the way funds were monitored and with the so-called benefits given to the students. Historically, there had already been many scientific advances without added "hand-holding" provided by the government to its already hugely funded education programs for the high LPs with aptitude. "Did the return on investment really make sense?" they argued.

His most controversial program by far helped individuals whose LP did not allow them a place in a career they desired, so they chose to do nothing as a form of passive dissent. In order to maintain a nation where people were still free to do as they pleased within reason, nobody could be forced to work, and the minimum stipend granted to those under a certain LP age allowed them to live without societal contribution. Those who disagreed with Stryker's program to counsel and rehabilitate individuals who dropped out of the workforce had always pushed for harsher punishments toward those choosing to be inactive members of society.

He had indirectly cleared the pathway for his continued position as president. His assistant Chereeza had "little mice," as she called them, everywhere, filling her in on the latest gossip among the political crowd. Through her information, he was able to find out that another candidate, Devon Ramsey, had been having an illicit affair with his daughter's nineteen-year-old babysitter right under his wife's oblivious nose. Ramsey doted on his eight-year-old daughter Nina and would surely be devastated if his wife were to take full custody out of spite during the last two years of Nina's life. That is, if she found out about her husband's fun new toy. Adding fuel to the fire, it was never looked highly upon to get involved with young women living out the last few months of their lives, as his teenage mistress was. Tactless as this was of him, he wouldn't be able to have his cake and eat it too. His wife would surely win any custody battle, and his reputation would plummet.

Magnus had considered the possibility of going the route of exposure, but holding this kind of leverage could also be useful. Maletich had arranged for the babysitter to receive funds that would secure her a work-free last few months, a hearty pension for her surviving parents, and an opportunity to check off some of the expensive items on her bucket list—which included, much to his thinly veiled amusement, becoming a boudoir model and skydiving naked.

In return for her silence, Ramsey would support Stryker's nomination for another term and would rally support with others on the fence. Though his judgement in bedmates was questionable, his popularity and persuasiveness had in the past allowed him to influence the views of others in the party.

While nothing was guaranteed, Magnus was one step closer to holding onto his seat, something that was unequivocally in the best interest of the public.

Chapter 16

LUCY'S PARENTS WERE out for the evening at the wake of an acquaintance, and the house was blissfully peaceful without their constant nervous energy. Axon Davis was relieved of his reporter duties for the evening but had yet to return to the spare bedroom he'd occupied since her own wake's unexpected ending. Lucy appreciated that Axon lacked an overly serious attitude, but she could tell that leaving her side for the evening gave him some anxiety, which she thought was adorable. Somehow, he was able to imply mild disinterest in his job while still doing it effectively. She was fairly convinced that he only showed this relaxed side of himself in front of her in conversations when they were alone, her parents elsewhere.

Nobody official had told her to return to school, and since she didn't want to subject herself to the flurry of reporters who still camped outside her driveway, Lucy barely left the house. Lucy's lack of confidants had worn on her since Colton's death, but she'd been feeling an even more intense heaviness in the past weeks since her wake. Axon was the only non-family member available for conversation. While her parents tended to focus on the same few topics—How was she feeling? Had she eaten? Was she sleeping okay?—Axon usually skipped past the small talk and told Lucy stories of his own mid-LP school days and some of the crazier wakes he had attended. His life sounded so exciting and full of fun. Undoubtedly he was popular; his stories evoked a rich social life.

Sometimes, before she fell into another night's fitful sleep, Lucy passed the time playing out imaginary scenes where she attended wakes acting as Axon's assistant. While Axon would glean drunken nuggets of information from girls in revealing dresses with confetti in their hair, Lucy would stick to the edges of the dance floor where she knew a goldmine of stories lived in those who chose to hover just on the edge of the excitement. That's where she would always hang

out whenever she had attended wakes. Her strategy would undoubtedly win her over in Axon's eyes for her ingenuity.

Meanwhile, she imagined *his* interactions would usually go a bit
differently:

"So how do you know so-and-so," he'd shout over the music.

"Oh, he's like my totally global cousin. I'm going to miss him
sooo much," Confetti Hair would say, trying to dredge up some fake
tears, hoping to get a cameo for his video.

Lucy knew girls like that. They tended to be the pretty ones
who'd teased their so-called "global" cousin for wearing glasses as a
kid and talked behind his back about how pathetic he was. Now that
he was dying, they'd have been best friends all their lives. The irony
was that those girls usually had an upcoming LP date themselves, so
in the end they all would end up the same as their pathetic cousins:
dead.

Her imagined scenario would either end with Colton arriving to
hold her and slow dance out of time to the music, or Axon himself
would declare that he "had all he needed, why don't we rage this party?" and grab her by the arm, dragging her to the dance floor.

Usually, the playful imaginings would turn sad if she allowed
Colton to show up and metaphorically sweep her off her feet. Lucy's
thoughts of Colton would sometimes provoke a kind of simmering
anger in her, though oftentimes she just felt numb to it all. It was almost like she lived in a kind of emotional fog most of the time. Axon's presence provided a small distraction from her dwelling.

Lucy found some comfort in thinking of happier times during
her childhood. As a kid, she'd loved strawberry ice cream, but her
mother, ever the frugal parent, refused to buy a carton of only strawberry, knowing it would get freezer burn and become inedible long
before Lucy could finish it. To please everyone, Nadine would buy
the Neapolitan ice cream containing separate strips of vanilla, chocolate and strawberry. Lucy would always finish her section long before

her parents, leaving a huge empty chunk with uneven edges right in the middle between the chocolate and vanilla, which would get freezer burn before they were eaten. The irony never seemed to occur to her mother. The image of her depleted ice cream section crossed her mind a lot lately.

She heard a knock at the front door. Her parents refused to give Axon his own key to the house, so he had to come and go at the mercy of their pleasure to admit him, despite the contract. Lucy checked the peephole before considering releasing the chain and deadbolt her father had reminded her to put up when they left for the party. It wasn't as if her neighborhood was riddled with crime to warrant extra security measures, but the concern that a reporter might decide to get a little ahead of themselves had caused her father to install additional locks on the doors and windows of the house. What she saw when looking through the peephole was that Axon had not returned alone.

Lucy opened the door slowly while keeping her body in the space between the door and the frame. "Who's she?" she asked with mild accusation. Was this Axon's girlfriend? He had never brought up the existence of one, but that didn't rule out the possibility.

"Lucy, this is Evergreen Mason," Axon said with his casual smile, as if bringing a stranger to Lucy's house was an everyday occurrence.

"Hi Lucy, it's great to meet you," Evergreen said, her tone excited.

Lucy's stance remained unchanged, holding her position as gatekeeper to the house. "Hi," she said shortly.

"Evergreen is a scientist at The Virionics Institute," Axon said when she continued to stand in the doorway. "Can we come in?" he asked, his light laughter enough to remove Lucy's hesitation.

Lucy knew that Axon's job was to be an objective observer, so bringing a scientist to her front door was surely breaking his work protocol. Evergreen wasn't even that pretty. Except she did have nice hair: thick and blond, her braid resting heavily over her shoulder.

Evergreen also had colorful eyes, which regrettably Lucy did not. Hers had always been a boring brown, while the scientist had a bright green. She supposed some guys focused on this kind of feature. Lucy was taller and had a more hourglass-proportioned figure. She tried reminding herself that having larger breasts like this stranger did could lead to back problems, and they tended to sag with age. That's what her mother had always told her when she'd complain about her own unexceptional chest. Nadine had said she'd grow into them, but that never did happen.

"I guess so," she replied after a pause, stepping aside to allow them entry.

An awkward silence fell as the three of them stood in the foyer and Lucy closed the door, locking it back up with a metallic click.

"So, Lucy," Evergreen began brightly before Axon cut her off.

"Why don't we go sit in the kitchen?" he said over the scientist.

Lucy shrugged and led the way, noticing how they lagged behind and exchanged quick whispers. How annoying.

Lucy took a seat at the kitchen table and began picking at her cuticles, unsure about what she was supposed to do. "Are you here to poke and prod me or something?" she asked, trying to sound indifferent. Fortunately for her, apathy had become her new specialty.

"Well, no," Evergreen said, trying to catch Lucy's eye. "At least not without your consent, and not today."

"Evergreen wanted to come and talk with you, Lucy. She has done some research on LP and . . ."

Evergreen cut *him* off this time. "A lot of research. I've spent the last weeks since . . ." She paused, clearly trying to find a delicate way to put it.

"Since I didn't die?" Lucy offered bluntly, still picking at her nails.

"Um. Yes," Evergreen said cautiously. "I've been researching LP and the history of how it works, how the population fluctuates, and pretty much looking at as many scientific publications relating to the topic as I can get my hands on."

"And?" Axon prodded her along.

"Right. And I think I've found some pretty interesting evidence that you're not alone here," Evergreen said excitedly. As if this news was supposed to be an immense pleasure to Lucy. "Of course, I still need to keep researching. I've submitted a research proposal to my boss so I can get access to some raw data that wasn't published in the Virionics database. I'm sure I'll have more answers in a week or so, once my application goes through the proper channels." She spoke quickly, enunciating every syllable, irritating Lucy with her correctness.

Lucy drew patterns with her fingertips on the tabletop. "Cool. Good for you." What exactly did *not alone* mean anyway?

"Lucy," Evergreen began as she looked over at Axon.

He stood up and walked over to the coffee maker. "Anyone want some?"

"No thanks, I'm okay," Evergreen muttered, shaking her head while she dug through her bag and pulled out a notebook and purple pen.

"Lucy-Bella? Need some caffeine in your veins?" Axon asked, using the nickname he had adopted for her a couple weeks back. Lucy could feel herself softening. She liked when he called her that, though she had been unable to come up with anything that sounded cool enough to call him in return. Colton would have invented a name like "Ax-on-off" and made it sound global. Lucy knew saying it would only make her look stupid and immature.

"Sure. I'll take some." She needed to take her nightly anxiety medication anyhow. While coffee was probably not the best choice to wash it down with, she was never told *not* to take it with caffeine.

Axon made the coffee noisily, making a big deal of taking out the coffee beans, grinding them, and taking out cups, milk, and sugar for himself and Lucy. Evergreen sat silently, facing Lucy with her hands folded on the dark wood of the table. The machine finished its rapid-brew, and Axon brought two steaming cups to the table, passing one to Lucy.

"Thanks," she said.

"I think Evergreen's discovery is really important," he said. "She thinks that there might be other people who lived past their LP like you did."

Lucy's mind began racing. But wasn't she the special one? Everyone on the news seemed to think so. There had been protesters outside her house for over a week chanting her name! "How come I've never heard of anyone else, then?" she asked accusingly.

"Well," Evergreen said, "I think it's possible that the reason you became more of a high-profile news story has a lot to do with where you live, your parents' socioeconomic status, and the coverage surrounding your wake. Living close to a city and having a large wake party isn't as much the norm in other parts of the country. There are plenty of people who choose to celebrate quietly, with a more intimate audience."

Lucy bristled. She only celebrated her wake the way everyone else did. Certainly, she hadn't exaggerated her importance like it sounded Evergreen was implying. "So, people didn't die when they were supposed to. *Just like me.*" She shrugged, trying to seem indifferent.

Axon put his hand on Lucy's forearm. "So maybe before we thought you were a once-in-a-lifetime occurrence, but come to find out you're one in a million. Most people are still dying when they're expecting to. You didn't. That's still really special."

Lucy's skin prickled pleasantly at his touch, and she relaxed a little. "What happened to all of these people you're talking about?" Lucy asked, reaching for her medication on the countertop behind Axon.

"Well," Evergreen hesitated for a moment, "that part is not entirely clear. There seem to be some cases where the LP sorted itself out naturally." Lucy could feel Evergreen's green eyes on her as she twisted off the child-proof cap, pulling a pill from the bottle and swallowing it with a gulp of her milky coffee. Evergreen continued, "Some people died sometime between one year's census and the next, it appears."

Lucy glared at her, skeptical. "So . . . they're all dead?"

Evergreen backtracked, ignoring Lucy's blunt question. "But that doesn't mean *you're* going to die! I don't have all of the data and not all of the numbers are one hundred percent accounted for. There's no telling how much longer you will live. It could be a year, it could be a hundred, for all I know," she added quickly. "What I'd like to do is to continue to look into this and figure out what makes you different on a biological level."

"Tell her when the poking and prodding happens," Axon said jokingly, clearly trying to lighten the tense mood.

"It may not happen at all. But I need to decide what experiments might be useful to help determine what makes the people who live past their LP special. I think right now having access to some of your medical records would be the most helpful."

"Sure, I guess." Lucy shrugged. She knew that Evergreen must need written consent for Axon to share this information with her. Everything medical lately seemed to require signature after signature.

Evergreen's eyes lit up with eagerness. "Really? I mean, thank you Lucy. That's really great of you to share. I really appreciate it. Axon?" Evergreen looked over at Axon.

"Huh?" he said.

"The consent?" She raised her eyebrows expectantly.

"Right, let me get it." He pushed the chair back and left the room.

Evergreen eyed the pill bottle on the table. "Um, so, how are you coping?" she asked Lucy.

"Fine," Lucy said, grabbing the plastic bottle in front of her and scraping at the label with her fingernail. "These help," she added.

"Do you mind me asking what you've been prescribed?" Evergreen asked.

Lucy showed her the label displaying the long, unpronounceable name of the medication, whose dose her pharmacist had increased after her wake. Evergreen looked at the bottle and jotted down some notes with her purple pen.

"I promise I'll keep you in the loop with whatever I find," Evergreen said as Axon returned with the documents for Lucy to sign on his tablet.

Chapter 17

"WHAT IS THIS PLACE?" Evergreen asked as she ran an index finger across a dusty bookshelf. It was clear the basement of Axon's workplace was unloved. That, or they needed a better cleaning person. She had to admit, she was surprised this was what Axon had meant by summoning her to the nondescript building owned by the *Times* to "do some book learning." She'd almost expected it to be some sort of code for a hookup—a proposition she'd planned to turn down. At least that was what she'd told herself as she'd dressed, putting on a favorite pair of panties with separating elastic in lieu of something more inviting, just to make sure she wasn't tempted.

"We keep all of our past publications here in hard copy, along with volumes of works published by investigative journalists from years past, old obits, notices to county residents, et cetera," Axon said as he pulled heavy volumes from the shelves, seemingly at random. "This is the best place for history, anyway. Not just dry scientific documents that start with an abstract—interesting topics in layman's terms about the world we live in."

Evergreen bristled. "What do *you* know about abstracts?"

"I read?" Axon said with a shrug.

Scientific documents which followed a specified format—Abstract, Introduction, Results, Discussion, Conclusion—were Evergreen's bread and butter. She supposed it made sense for Axon to be more comfortable with a journalistic approach—one that digested discoveries and made them readable for the general non-scientific public—but she was surprised to hear he was familiar with things from her world.

"What exactly are we looking for?" she asked, leafing through a bound copy of *The Oracle: Weekly and Relevant News Publications Volume 223*. "Not that I don't enjoy a good dive into the public pool of obscure press releases," Evergreen added sarcastically. "What do you expect to find?"

"Not sure yet. Did you know what you were looking for when you started digging through the census archives?" Axon asked, kneeling, head awkwardly tilted to the side reading titles from a bottom shelf.

"Well . . . no. Not exactly. I suspected there was something to find, but I didn't know where to find it."

"Precisely. Scientist and journalist. Not so different," he noted, seeming to only be half-paying attention to her.

"I guess not. What's with your obsession with comparing my profession to yours anyhow? It's not as if I think I'm better than you or something."

Axon sighed heavily, his annoyance with her obvious. "You said it, not me."

"Well, I don't think it," Evergreen argued.

"You have a high LP. It's been implied to you since you were born how much more important you are than people like me." He paused, appearing to hold back before saying simply, "Look, we don't have to talk."

"I don't think I'm more important than you!" Evergreen retorted, a little louder than she intended.

"Shhh. This is a library," he said, putting a patronizing finger to his lips. Not another soul was present besides the two of them among the dusty pages. Despite this, Evergreen's cheeks still flushed. "Like I said, we don't have to talk. Why don't you make yourself useful and start looking through some of these?" He indicated the growing stack he had dropped onto a nearby table.

"But you can't just say something like that and expect me not to respond. Just because I was born with the LP I have doesn't mean I think the way *you* expect me to. I happen to believe that everyone in society—"

Axon cut her off. "—has a place and a function to serve. Is that what you were going to say?"

Evergreen stopped short.

"I already told you, I know how the high LPs think," Axon stated, pointing at his head for emphasis before handing her a heavy stack of bound articles.

She struggled to take the books from him without appearing as if she needed help with their unexpected weight. Evergreen huffed in annoyance and sat down in a nearby chair to thumb through the pages, keeping her eyes open for something interesting relating to LP.

"And what makes you the expert, exactly?" she asked after several moments of dusty silence.

Axon closed a heavy volume with a thud and slid it across the desk, creating his own discard pile that she suspected he wouldn't put back in the correct order on the shelves. "Just that I've attended enough of their wakes, or at least their kids' wakes, to get a good idea of where they think they fall in the pecking order. The high-LP parents whose kids die young are the worst. You can tell their kid's existence had been this huge disappointment for them."

"How do you mean?"

"Their kid never got the chance to *be* anyone. They would never have a career like their parents, and they would never create anything useful or good. It's almost a relief for some of the parents when they go. At least if the kid is young enough, the parents can try again for an offspring that will bring them more pride."

Evergreen stared at him in disbelief.

"I'm not saying they didn't love their child. It's just different. It's as if they lost some sense of accomplishment of what could have been. The wakes I've been to where it's an older person who has lived a long life in their high-LP world have had more of a bittersweet feel. If they had kids, they're adults by the time the wake happens, and the adult children are well-prepared to see their parent off. The person has lived their life. They've met their goals. They're done."

She digested this for a minute before replying quietly, "It's funny what having a finite timeline does to meeting your goals." Though she had been young when her mother died, she remembered seeing the scores of lists that were posted on the refrigerator, bathroom mirrors, and the glass dresser top in her parents' bedroom. Evergreen had started learning to read nearly two years prior and had reached a phase where she wanted to read out loud every written word she found. The scattered lists became slowly dictated mantras which she recited over and over again every time she wandered into the kitchen for a snack, or washed her hands at the bathroom sink, or studied her mother's jewelry and perfume bottles.

Anna Karenina
Pride and Prejudice
Moby Dick
Oliver Twist
Dante's Inferno

"What's an inferno?" she had asked her mother once, after recalling the names on the coffee table notepad.

"It's a really hot place where bad people go," her mother had told the seven-year-old. Nightmares about being trapped in a fireplace for forgetting to brush her teeth had persisted for weeks afterwards.

It wasn't until later that Evergreen realized what purpose the lists had served for her mother. Her father, lacking the strength to remove the slips of paper from all of his wife's reminder places, left them as relics of her motivations. Since then, Evergreen found herself creating her own lists of things to achieve before she died. Though she wasn't meant to die for many years, it made perfect sense to her to use time wisely.

She and Axon sat in relative silence, the only noise the turning of pages and scribbling of a pen. Evergreen found articles discussing the history of innovative cancer treatments and humankind's consistent search for prolonged life. Over generations, the human race had advanced science enough to combat and cure any diseases, until only death by natural (or accidental) causes was possible. No longer was a parasite, virus, mutated stem cell or bacterial infection strong enough to challenge mankind and all of their advances. If there hadn't been such clear step-by-step progression of scientific discovery, marked by setbacks and death, it would almost be laughable when nature inevitably tried to push back. A mutated virus here, an antibiotic resistance there. Nature made a valiant effort. Fortunately, humans were now equipped to handle nature's most resilient defenses. A new strain of influenza might mutate enough to dramatically improve its transmissibility, but today's scientists were one step ahead. Vaccinations were created by Virionics scientists as fast as the viruses themselves mutated. In fact, vaccinations were developed knowing precisely *how* a virus might mutate, thanks to humanity's deep understanding of genetics. Pandemics had gone the way of an extinct species, as had untreatable bacterial infection. Easy mapping of genomes allowed scientists the ability to pinpoint precisely where genetic developmental decisions were made, in either the single-stranded RNA of most viruses, or the double-stranded DNA of mammals and other organisms. Having this kind of control over life was the major triumph of humanity.

Death was now controlled and prevented from environmental causes, so individual humans were now able to live the full period their genetics allowed and die naturally. It was an easy next step for scientists to identify that exact moment when a person's genetic code initiated body-wide apoptosis, or natural cell death. Thus, the Lifetime Potential, or LP, technology was created. The testing technology was put into use either as part of prenatal care or shortly after birth, analyzing genetic makeup to provide a person's exact life expectancy.

Though Evergreen knew that Lucy's genes had been reanalyzed as part of the examination she underwent after her wake, the LP result remained the same sixteen years as it had been on the day of her birth. The real mystery was why. What interested Evergreen most when looking back at past discoveries was how people lived before science had essentially conquered death. Perhaps the past would give a clue to the present.

She and Axon dutifully riffled through many records of public health initiatives, some of which provided primary care support to the population, the only way to detect a lurking cancerous cell and treat it promptly. Like tending a garden, consistent and active care of human life was the only way to keep nature from taking over.

"So, do you have any goals you'd like to accomplish before your LP is up?" she asked conversationally after a long period of quiet.

"You might have time for that, but I don't," Axon said dismissively.

Evergreen pushed past his reluctance for discussion. "Well, maybe that's exactly why you should have them?" she said, trying to be encouraging. "Come on, what's one thing you'd like to make sure you did in your life, or one experience you want to make sure you have?"

"I don't think you understand. People like me don't have the luxury of time to think about what we want. I'm in that awkward middle age between those whose LP is so low that they get to do literally whatever they want until they die, and those whose LP is high enough that they get to have an actual meaningful life. I'm stuck knowing that society expects something from me, but I'm not meant to expect anything from society. So, what does that leave for me?" he asked.

"I . . ." Evergreen began, realizing she had never considered goal setting from the perspective of someone with his low-mid LP.

"Apathy," he said, answering his own question. "And struggling to figure out how to live my life the best I can live it day by day. I can't afford to think long-term."

"You never wanted to do some thrill-seeking, like bungee jumping or skydiving?" she tried.

"Not today, I don't. Tomorrow I might wake up and decide that cliff diving sounds global, so I'd head out and try it. If there's something I want to do, I just do it. Why plan for a future I don't have?" He shrugged as if he had never considered an alternative.

It had never occurred to Evergreen to think this way. And why would it? Making plans and setting goals had been the method by which she had always lived her life. If she didn't get around to taking those ballroom dancing classes this year, next year was just as doable. Time was a convenience she could afford to take for granted.

"If your philosophy on life is to take it day by day, why are we here doing this?" She motioned toward the books in front of her.

"Well, for one thing, I still don't have a choice on whether or not to do my job. And while normally I might not expend so much effort, I happen to think you might be onto something."

Evergreen looked up from her page with narrowed eyes, suspecting he was joking. "You do?"

"What can I say? You've convinced me using *science*," he said with an ironic lift of his eyebrows.

"And there's the joke," she said under her breath.

"I think there's something to be found here. And maybe, just maybe, we'll find something to explain why Lucy is still alive, which might be the key to extending the lives of others."

"Others . . . like you?" Evergreen asked tentatively, beginning to understand his interest.

"Maybe," he said without further elaboration. "Also, Lucy is a pretty cool kid—maybe this helps her get a grip on where she's headed and what to do next."

Evergreen had gotten the sense that his concern for Lucy's well-being was a rarity in his relationships. Their own first interaction had been emotionally surface-level, though physically they had been intimate. Fortunately, they had reached a silent consensus to not even bring it up. Though she had only met Lucy briefly, the teenager's defensive act was clearly a shield created to insulate her from everything that was currently out of her control. Unless Evergreen and Axon could find definitive answers, Lucy's life would continue without structure. Everything in society was determined by how long someone was anticipated to live. What you studied, where you worked, if you were permitted to reproduce, and though unintended, it also limited which social circles you could belong to. Lucy's life depended on knowing the answer to the question: If she didn't die when science dictated her death, then when would she?

Evergreen was resolved to find out.

Chapter 18

EVERGREEN HAD A SET morning routine. She would begrudgingly get out of bed after several taps of the snooze button, shower and go through her ablutions, get dressed in the clothes she had laid out the previous night—which were *usually* clean—and head to the Virionics Institute in a state of only mild alertness. Caffeine would be her first stop, but since her desk was not in a "clean area" of the lab, she usually forced herself to tab through her email and jot down to-do notes before rewarding herself with that first cup of eye-opening coffee.

On this Monday morning, Evergreen had gone through her usual steps and arrived at work with five minutes to spare before the more senior scientists arrived. Skimming her inbox, she came upon an email from her boss, Susanne Abdul, which was unusual given the hierarchy at Virionics. Technically, Susanne was her boss's boss's boss. Evergreen reported to the lead scientists, who reported to the laboratory manager, Evan Yearling, who reported to Susanne. Usually when day-to-day issues arose, the leads would inform Evergreen either through brief exchanges (when they weren't concentrating on their own projects) or via curt email messages. Evan had his own projects and initiatives, and she only saw him once or twice a week, where their conversations were either polite, brief, and superficial or nonexistent. Susanne had not reached out to Evergreen since she was hired, and she couldn't tell if this was a good or a bad thing.

Evergreen,
Please come by my office at 9:15 this morning.
Best,
Susanne Abdul

Well, that's cryptic, Evergreen thought as her still decaffeinated heart accelerated nervously. What could Susanne want with her on a Monday morning? She'd heard that people would typically be let go on a Friday, so maybe that meant she was safe from such a fate? Evergreen racked her brain to pinpoint what she could have done wrong. Nothing big enough to warrant losing her job came to mind. But maybe it was something she didn't even know she'd done? Why had Evan been so dismissive of giving her feedback? Maybe she could have avoided this attention from his superior. "You're doing fine" was all she ever heard him say. And maybe if he was around more often, instead of off in meetings to accomplish who knows what, she would be more aware if something about her performance needed to change. No, the rational part of her brain stepped in. It wasn't fair to blame him. Whatever reason Susanne had for the meeting, it was Evergreen's responsibility to own what she had done wrong.

For the next hour and ten minutes, Evergreen nervously chipped away at her daily tasks. A constant buzz of anxiety flowed through her body, nearly causing the destruction of several pieces of expensive lab glassware. Time passed slower as she alternated between glances at the incorrectly set wall clock and her own personal wristwatch. The two-minute discrepancy between the two was like having an itch on her brain.

Finally, it was time. Evergreen removed her nitrile gloves as she was trained to, rolling one glove up into the other, and hung her white lab coat on the wall hook. Her hands shook as she washed them briskly in the porcelain sink. Making her way to Susanne's office, she stared at her feet and tried to take calming breaths. The door was shut when she approached, so she rapped softly.

"Come in."

Recognizing Susanne's voice, Evergreen opened the door.

"Have a seat, Evergreen." Susanne looked up from the desk and smiled.

Evergreen closed the door behind her and obediently sat.

"Well, first of all, you aren't in trouble," Susanne said, clearly sensing Evergreen's trepidation.

Evergreen exhaled a sigh of relief, not realizing she had been suppressing her breathing. "Well, that's good," she said.

"In fact, I have good news for you." Susanne pressed her manicured fingertips together. "I'd like to offer you a job opportunity. A promotion, really. I've noticed the work you've been doing and appreciate all of your efforts thus far in your early career at Virionics."

"Thank you," Evergreen said with sincerity. She didn't think anyone had noticed how hard she worked.

Susanne nodded. "Yes. You've been contributing well here, so I'd like to offer you the chance to shift your focus to a smaller team, innovating annual vaccination updates. I believe I remember from your interview that this would be a step in the right direction to work with the Disease Prevention and Monitoring Department, like you wanted?"

Evergreen couldn't believe her luck. She had only been in her new job for six months, and already she was being offered the opportunity to start working for the elite team that developed the annual vaccines. In order to work with the more dangerous and exotic diseases, it was critical for her to have experience in the vaccine development area of the Pharmacological Development Department. She was one step closer—in record time—and she couldn't help but grin. "Yes, absolutely! I'd be thrilled to work with the vaccination team."

"Excellent. So, you're accepting the role, of which your title would be Research Technologist Level II?"

"Yes! Yes, I'm so excited," Evergreen said, trying to rein in her instinct to jump up and down with her arms in the air.

"I'm glad to hear it," Susanne said. She slid a manila folder toward Evergreen along with a pen. "Here is the paperwork for your promotion and transfer to the other lab. You'll want to read through everything and sign where the yellow tabs are." She opened the folder and indicated with the tip of the black pen where to sign. "It's a pretty standard transfer agreement, but since this is your first one here at the Institute, I want to make sure you're aware of a few things. There is an expectation that you are to leave all of your former work and any projects behind in your old lab to make room for new assignments and focuses."

Evergreen nodded and flipped through the paperwork. Something occurred to her, and she looked back up at Susanne. "So, my research data access request?"

"Has been denied," Susanne responded curtly.

"Oh." It was hard not to be a little disappointed.

Susanne continued, "You will be moving on to bigger and better things which will require one-hundred percent of your attention."

Having spent a significant amount of time investigating LP over the past several weeks, Evergreen was reluctant to let it go unfinished. What about Lucy? And Axon Davis? She had finally made contact with the two of them and felt they were making headway. She considered if it was worth pursuing the subject with Susanne. What if her promotion was revoked? Maybe Susanne didn't realize the chance Evergreen had of making a scientific breakthrough, however small that may be? Virionics strove to be at the cutting edge, so why wouldn't they want her to continue?

"What if I just worked on the project in my spare time, outside of my hours here at Virionics?" she asked tentatively.

Susanne shook her head. "No, Evergreen. That's not how this works. In order to further our department-specific initiatives, we need you putting in your best man-hours toward your new laboratory."

Evergreen bit her tongue to keep from arguing, knowing that nothing she said would change Susanne's mind.

"I realize you're disappointed. But trust me, this is also for your own protection. I understand that you've reached out to a member of the press?"

Nervous butterflies filled Evergreen's stomach, and blood rushed to her cheeks. She hadn't realized anyone knew about her contact with Axon, or that it might be a problem. "Well, I've been in contact with Axon Davis, the wake reporter," she said, hoping to downplay her faux pas by failing to mention his connection with Lucy Hanson's media blitz.

"I know, and maybe you didn't realize—you're still so new to the professional world, after all," Susanne said with a patronizing look that made Evergreen shrink minutely in her chair. "But it never looks good to consort with the media without written consent from the company. There is a process we follow here."

"I'm sorry," Evergreen said, feeling the telltale tension behind her eyes start to build. She willed herself not to cry in front of this woman. "I didn't realize I'd done something against the rules."

"Yes, well, now you know. I know you didn't mean any harm, but you're leaving yourself vulnerable to misperception, which may affect future career opportunities," she added pointedly.

Evergreen tried to take long even breaths, fighting back the welling tears. "Okay, I understand," she said quietly. "Thank you for telling me. I won't do it again. And I appreciate that you're giving me the chance to take on this new role."

"I think you'll be a good fit with this team," Susanne stated matter-of-factly. She stood behind her desk and extended her hand. "You're moving forward now. Congratulations."

Evergreen shook it. "Thank you, Susanne. I am really grateful. I promise I will work really hard."

"I'm sure you will. Now submit your signed paperwork to the Human Resources Department. You start your new role tomorrow.

Take the rest of the day to wrap up any loose ends in your current lab, and take your personal belongings with you."

Evergreen smiled. "Okay. Thank you so much," she said, clutching the manila folder to her chest as she backed toward the door.

Outside of Susanne's office, Evergreen let out a long exhale. A promotion! Her hands were shaking, her legs restless. She needed to walk to get some of the energy out, and she needed to share the news. Tapping buttons on her wristwatch, she called her father. As expected, he already knew about her promotion—being such a respected scientist at the company had its advantages.

"I'm so proud of you, Evergreen dear," he said in his gentle voice. "You have truly arrived in your career. This will only be the beginning for you."

"Mom would be proud too," Evergreen blurted, her excitement overriding the usual restraint she showed when broaching the subject of her mother.

He paused momentarily. "Yes, I suppose she would have been."

They made plans to meet for lunch later in the week, once she was somewhat settled in her new laboratory. Evergreen ended the call and hastily contacted Arizona, seeking the instant gratification of clinking glasses with her best friend after work.

"Lady, I am so happy for you. You totally earned this," Arizona said with her usual aura of confidence. "But I'm really sorry, I'm too swamped this week to get together for a booze-a-thon," she said, sounding as disappointed as Evergreen was to hear it. She elaborated, "I've got projects coming out my eyeballs, and I'm working fourteen-hour days lately. I'd basically face-plant into my margarita after one sip, I'm so wiped. But I absolutely promise we'll do something to celebrate soon."

Having worked the same long days as Arizona, Evergreen could hardly be surprised her friend was unavailable. "It's okay, I understand. We can do something in a week or two when things at work let up a bit. I'm not sure what to expect the hours to be like in this new role anyhow."

They made tentative plans for a future evening and scheduled them into their respective calendars. They weren't students anymore, and perhaps gone were the days they could go out to bars on the regular. This transition into real adult responsibility was just a part of growing up and learning to contribute new innovations using all of the training they had received. Their education was an investment, they were always told. Now it was time to pay back what was given.

Evergreen's phone beeped lightly in her ear. Another call was coming through. Glancing at the screen and seeing Axon's name made her stomach drop several feet. She had already filled Arizona in on what her boss had made clear about contact with the reporter.

"He's calling. What do I do?" Evergreen asked, hearing the slight panic in her own voice as if she didn't already know the answer to her own question.

"Ignore it, stupid," said Arizona. "You heard what Susanne told you. I know he's totally global and you're into him, but it sounds like his status is now off-limits."

"I am *not* 'into him,'" Evergreen retorted, miming air quotes despite the fact that Arizona couldn't see her. "We slept together *once*. And once was enough. He's arrogant, and he seems to hate intellectuals like us. I just needed his help with my research project, and that's it. My interest is purely professional and not at all personal."

"Wonder why he hates intellectuals," Arizona asked sarcastically.

"What?"

"Nothing, just me being purely professional and not at all personal. It's better you don't associate with him anymore. Sounds like the company is onto you, and you don't want anything to jeopardize your career. Just try not to get in your own way, and keep your foot out of your mouth."

"Look who's talking!" Evergreen jabbed back. Arizona had never been great at discretion, a fact her friend was well aware of.

"Mmmh-mmmh-mmmh," Arizona muffled her voice into the phone.

"What was that?" Evergreen said sharply. Another soft beep sounded in her ear—Axon had left a voicemail.

"Oh, sorry. Had to pull my foot out of my mouth again."

"Ha-ha. Very funny." Evergreen allowed her voice to drip with sarcasm.

They said their goodbyes and reiterated the proposed date of their next get-together. She really had missed her friend's humor, despite the nuggets of brutal honesty it sometimes held. She hung up the phone and looked at the screen displaying the voicemail alert. Her index finger hovered over the shatterproof surface to *Listen* or *Delete*. Hesitating for only a moment, she pressed the button on the screen. *Deleted.* It was better this way.

Chapter 19

FOUR UNRETURNED PHONE calls and two voicemails later, Axon was ready to give up. He hated looking weak in front of girls, and calling multiple times without a pickup from Evergreen made him look like a needy chump, even if it was work-related. Sort of. He and Evergreen had hooked up once, and the probability of it reoccurring felt low. She was so focused on her work; it was even having an effect on his.

He had never tried so hard to do additional legwork on a case before. His boss had heavily suggested he wasn't living up to his own potential, but to be fair, they had been naked and post-coital at that point. She could have just been talking, though it seemed unlikely—the feedback resonated. It was his goal to maximize fun, and putting forth the least possible amount of effort into his job was the best way to do this. Either way, the female influences in his life seemed to be making a positive effect on his work ethic, even if it did make him feel like he had lost some autonomy.

Having taken several volumes from the *Times* basement archives, he pored over them at the Hansons' vacant dining room table. They rarely used the room, usually taking their meals at the round kitchen table. Besides, they could generally care less what he was up to. The Hansons fulfilled their part of the contract by letting him stay in the guest room but otherwise ignored him in the not-so-subtle hope that he would get bored of the story and go away on his own. Lucy would sometimes keep him company and kept the secret that he was conducting research on her behalf with the help of a Virionics scientist. The adult Hansons would not appreciate further non-familial interference in their daughter's life. It was traumatic enough for them to see her oscillate with her moods, one minute grateful and jubilant that she had survived past her LP, the next sullen and forlorn about her predicament. Her up-and-down emotions were exhausting for her parents in particular.

She tended to be on better behavior when around Axon. Lucy would usually sit at the table and absently flip through the pages of old publications with a vacant expression, only occasionally asking questions or striking up conversation, which was fine by Axon.

Axon skimmed through the historical timeline of healthcare and medical development Evergreen had put together in her background investigation. Throughout history, humans had always been subject to natural killers, such as viruses that brought death to thousands of children or turned into pandemics, killing millions. History was cyclical when it came to major health events. Smaller outbreaks of diseases like Ebola, smallpox, measles, typhoid, and SARS were noted in her timeline, indicating that nature had always been a threatening presence in human existence, even if the cases were not widespread. Then there were the more deadly and pervasive diseases, such as the one caused by the bite of an infected flea carrying *Yersinia pestis*, otherwise known as the Black Death, during the Middle Ages. The influenza pandemic of 1918, the 2019 coronavirus and the 2080 super flu all killed millions worldwide, as the earth had become a much more interconnected place, giving opportunity for viruses to increase their rate of infection.

Medicine had improved the lives of millions, growing in leaps and bounds since the turn of the twentieth century. Up until a couple centuries before, medicine was limited in its treatment and cure of disease. Since then, science had found ways to treat nearly all acute and chronic conditions, drastically decreasing human mortality from everything but natural death. Unfortunately, not all of the world's population had the opportunity or access to be treated for even the most chronic causes of human fragility. Vaccines, while available, were not distributed appropriately, and small pockets of infections once considered cured cropped up in various places around the globe. Interconnected communities, economies, and trade, along with the boom of population centers internationally, added gasoline to the fire, causing the last pandemic nearly two centuries prior. Because the pandemic had decreased the global population so dramatically, science was able to get ahead of humanity and the incidence of preventable deaths dropped to nearly zero. Fewer humans meant less dependency on the earth's resources, including water, energy, and farmable land meant for food production. Wars started before the drop in population over contentious land and water use stopped in their tracks. Greenhouse gases plummeted. Hunger was no longer pervasive, and the median lifespan increased by eight years within a decade. To say that the pandemic solved some of humanity's most complex problems would be an oversimplification, but despite the high death rate, it provided a brighter future for the survivors.

Whether Evergreen returned his phone call was up to her, but he had found an interesting article which he thought she would know what to do with. A publication from *The Oracle: Weekly and Relevant News Publications*, dating to the period just before the last pandemic, reviewed a scientific paper originally published in the *Socio and Anthropologic Journal* entitled "Population Density: Ratio for Future Sustainment." He was sure Evergreen had opinions about these kinds of summary articles, supposedly full of bias and dumbed down for the average reader. Axon had attended enough wakes to hear these arguments from the smarter, longer-living part of the population. This article reviewed the research conducted by an A. A. Morse, PhD, whose in-depth analysis of population growth, economic development, and life-sustaining resource sharing could be simplified into a mathematical formula. This formula had taken all relevant resources into consideration and suggested that population sustainability for future generations relied on a ratio of 1.0003-to-1 of births to deaths. Why wasn't it a perfect one death for every one birth? The ratio, Morse claimed, allowed for 0.03% growth in resource development annually, predicting that human ingenuity had not yet reached its peak. Based on extensive anthropological research, Morse was able to show how many other civilizations had sustained their populations for generations, holding relatively steady and unchanging standards of living. "Is this a model for the future of the world as we know it?" the article asked. Morse had apparently reached a level of notoriety within the scientific community at the time the review was published. She had been the keynote speaker at several prestigious academic society conferences, relaying her ideas and the importance of population balance. She was also a proponent of widespread vaccination, and as a government researcher, was able to contribute to global programs improving at-risk population access to life-saving medicine. The article had been published about five years before the world's last viral pandemic, occurring nearly two hundred years ago. When Axon tried to find out more about Morse, he discovered that she had survived the pandemic but had committed suicide a few years after the world restabilized.

His phone rang. Glancing at the screen on his wrist, he saw that Veronica was calling. He tapped to accept. "Hel—"

"Listen, Axe, I've got a contact for you to look into."

"Okay . . ."

"Her name is Regina Park, and she works for the Oval Office as a member of the President's administrative team. She has access to recordings in the office and I hear she might be interested in sharing, for a price. Another source confirmed it's legit, that the Stryker administration has bugs in the office, put in place by the last administration's party. Park is part of the team who installed and monitors them, but is having a change of heart about keeping them to herself. The President is apparently unaware. This is big stuff."

"Seriously? That's insane. How do you even know this?"

"Don't worry about that. When can you meet her?" Veronica asked.

"So, you want me to change gears on this story?" Axon asked, confused.

"No, absolutely not. You're doing terrific work," she said quickly, "like I reiterated last night," she lowered her voice, alluding to their most recent hook-up. "The Hanson story has been buzzing for weeks without a peep from Stryker. Don't you want to know how he really feels about the situation?"

Knowing what Stryker was doing in relation to Lucy could explode the story and add further prime airtime to his portfolio, which had huge potential for his career. As an added bonus, he could score some points with the Hansons by possibly giving direction to Lucy's next steps. Nobody knew what she should do next, whether it was to go back to low-LP school, begin a more mid-level education or career, or just sit around and wait to die. Leaked words from Magnus Stryker's own office could provide support for one of these options.

"Yeah. That sounds global. Is it legal?" he asked with only slight hesitation before adding, "Nah, I don't care."

"Maybe not. But if the *Times* can get the recordings, we can use them. *You* can use them. Everyone wins," she added.

"How do we know this Regina Park will be feeling so generous?"

Veronica paused. "She owes me a favor. But she might need some convincing on your end." Her tone implied a raised eyebrow.

"What does that mean?"

"You know what it means, Axon."

"Ah, now I see why you're asking me to play fetch. You're studding me out!" He was only half-joking.

"Come on, she's a *fan*. Specifically asked to meet with you."

He paused for a long moment, leaving silence between them.

Veronica sighed. "She's atomically hot."

"I'll think about it," he said. "Text me her info."

• • • •

ATOMICALLY NOT, was all Axon could think when Regina Park walked through the door to the Irish pub. It could be nobody else but her, arriving promptly on time, wearing the red-caped jacket as described in her message. The Little Red Riding Hood style was hardly popular. Her curly dishwater-blond hair was pixie-cut, doing nothing to hide ears which appeared too large for her head. She had thin lips and a pug nose, slightly upturned and bulbous on the end. Fortunately for her, she was in decent shape, but her face was distracting enough to make him curse Veronica for her fib. He silently thanked the Irish for their contribution to alcohol and apologized in advance to his internal organs. He was committed now.

Quickly adjusting his face to appear unperturbed, he made eye contact as she gave a subtle wave and took a seat on the wooden bench opposite him. She removed her coat and hung it between the booths on a metal hook which curved at the end into the shape of a Celtic knot.

Ordering drinks as they got through the pleasantries, Axon waited until his double whiskey neat was in need of a refill before broaching the subject at hand. "So, what's it like working for the President?" In his experience, open-ended questions usually worked best to get people talking.

Regina rolled her eyes. "Ugh, it's terrible." She took a large gulp of her drink and continued, "He's always glancing down the tops of the admins and complimenting us *heavily* when we wear anything hemmed above the knees. It creates this sort of unspoken dress code in the office. Low top, short skirt, or he won't give you the time of day."

Axon nodded and motioned for the waitress's attention.

"I refuse to give into his misogyny," she said with conviction. "I force him to pay attention to me for my work, because I have ethics."

"Of course."

"I tried to, anyway," she added coyly from behind the rim of her glass. Regina was clearly eager to have an audience in Axon but wasn't going to dive right in. To his irritation, she apparently wanted to savor the attention and unravel her story slowly. It was going to be an interesting night.

"I'll take another," she said to the waitress who had appeared at their side without breaking eye contact with Axon.

Axon leaned in. "What did you try doing?"

"Well, I'd just make sure to be the first one in, last one out, you know. Stand out as the high achiever."

"With or without the short skirt?"

She giggled at this. "Well, like I said, I have *morals*. And anyway, I had made a big thing of it in front of the other girls, so I didn't want to be taken as a hypocrite." She shook her head and smiled, her hand extending across the table to briefly touch the top of his. "Well, uh, I couldn't just give in. I had to be subtle. Not only was I there like, whenever he was, I'd make a big deal of picking something up when things were dropped. Which, let me tell you, happened a lot more often when he was behind me, if you know what I mean." She sipped her second drink. "I'm told I have a nice ass," she said with obvious pride.

Though she hadn't exactly walked in backwards for him to be able to confirm, Axon knew flattery would get him farther and faster. "True."

Regina smirked. "So anyway, he starts to notice me and even compliments me on all of the hard work I've been doing. Trust me, the girls were just green with jealousy at that one. I know I'm not the most atomic in the office . . ." She trailed off, dangling the lure.

This was his cue. "Why would you think that?" he asked with convincing confusion. "We've already determined your ass is presidential."

Laughter pealed from her throat as she simultaneously threw her head back and reached again for the top of his hand. "You're so funny!"

"Part of my charm." Axon winked.

"Anyhow, most girls get sick of the game and leave after a few months. It's a revolving door, really. Personally, I think it's fun to watch, so I stuck around. About two years ago, he promoted me to lead admin assistant because of my work ethic."

"And not because of your nice ass?"

She erupted into giggles again. "That might definitely have been part of it. Anyhow, he's a total pig, but the pay is decent as a lead, way better than I could make elsewhere, especially considering my LP." Axon guessed that, like him, she was low-mid LP. Being promoted to her current role was about as high as she could expect to go.

"So, after I'm in this lead position for about eight months, I'm approached by some high-ranking members of the New Republican Party who are looking for ways to win back the presidency in the next election. It's all covert and shit how they even approach me in the first place. I was at the grocery store buying bread and bananas, and this guy comes up next to me as I'm scoping out the wine section. He goes, 'If you're looking to capitalize on your role in this administration, give me a call,'" she said, mimicking a falsely deep voice, "and he just hands me his business card."

"Huh." Axon tilted his head, going for empathetic confusion.

"Naturally, I'm curious, so I get in contact—and long story short—they're completely legitimate, and they want me to help out with bugging the President's office. Crazy right? The office is checked quarterly for listening devices, so I schedule the inspections as part of my duties. They must have known I'd be the best person to coordinate this," Regina said proudly.

"Sure." Axon nodded in agreement.

"Anyway, I think about it and decide I've got a good thing going, just being promoted and all, making a decent salary, weekends off, and the like. The risk was just too great. So, I turn them down. Work goes along as usual until about two weeks later when one of the other girls quits. Something about inappropriate groping when she went to deliver copies. She had had enough, apparently. So, the administration hires this new girl, Joy Anna, to replace her." She made a face, clearly unimpressed with this person as she finished her drink and called for another. Axon followed suit, starting to feel the effects of the alcohol. Had her eyes always been green? He hadn't noticed before. They reminded him of someone whose face escaped him, and he smiled pleasantly.

"So, little Joy comes in with her long legs, big titties, and perfect fucking everything and ruins all of it. Not only is she a cocktease, but she just *loved* the attention Stryker would throw her way. She relished it, really. Joy Anna, the princess, becomes his favorite pretty quickly because it turns out that shockingly she has a brain! She starts to mimic everything I've done to get ahead. She comes in early, she stays late, she doesn't even *need* to drop things to get his attention. She already has it. Soon enough, she's being asked to take over duties I've been assigned, with the nonsensical excuse that I'm too overwhelmed. Overwhelmed my ass! I was thriving before she came around. I didn't need her stupid help," she simmered with flushed cheeks. Her foot rubbed the side of Axon's leg underneath the table.

"Stryker wound up basically giving this girl all of my leadership duties, and when she eventually pointed this out to him, she was promoted. Well, it wouldn't do to have two lead assistants, now would it? Joy then apparently uses her slutty skills, if you know what I mean," she mimed a stroking motion and puckered her thin lips, "to convince some guy who works in Human Resources to demote me back to a regular assistant. Something about 'a pattern of decreasing responsibility due to my mental state' was cited when he emailed me the update."

"I'd be pissed!" Axon exclaimed as her foot rubbed against his leg with decreasing subtlety.

"Well yeah!"

"What'd you do about it?"

"I decided that I didn't even care what happened. This was bullshit, and I deserved better."

"Cheers to that." Axon clinked his glass to hers.

"Cheers." She sipped. "Obviously, I decided to help the other party's guy. Why not, right?" Axon could think of a few reasons, mostly those involving loss of freedom or life, but restrained his quick tongue.

"I get back in touch with my contact at the New Republican Party and tell him I'm ready to help do some gardening." She laughed at her own joke. "You know, *plant* some bugs."

Axon released a forced chuckle.

"So, this techie group teaches me how to work the software to collect the data from the bugs. The way the office is rigged, there's no way to send the data out remotely. It has to be downloaded from the physical devices after a period of time. They offered me a heap of money to help them with this. I'd be able to quit my job if I wanted and just live how I pleased for the rest of my short life. There was enough to retire and all that." Her mouth betrayed a hint of bitterness as she took a swig of her cocktail, licking her lips.

"I go ahead and help these guys get in and install the devices in his office when I know they'll be safe for a few months until the next sweep. All under that cunt Joy Anna's nose." She smiled.

"And did it work?"

"The recording devices? Oh yeah, they worked. That brings us to last week. I downloaded them on Friday after everyone went home for the weekend. And trust me, I timed this well. I knew Miss Perfect had evening plans with some guy she'd met on a dating app and need-ed to leave on time, so I'd be alone. Want to know how I knew that?" Her smile was mischievous as she looked across the table at Axon.

"How?"

"Some guy," she said, directing a thumb at her own chest.

"What?" Axon said, confused.

"I catfished her." She laughed. "You know, where you pretend to be someone online that you're not? I needed to make sure she was gone when I needed her to be. She has this annoying habit of wait-ing until I leave before she does, even if I work several extra hours. It's practically a competitive sport with her," she said, scoffing.

"So, you pretend to be some guy to lure her out of the office early so you can collect the audio recordings of your boss, who happens to be the President of this nation," he summarized.

She nodded.

"Wow." Axon bobbed his head. "That's badass."

"That and *smart*," added Regina. "Not only did I collect the recordings and give them over to the New Republican Party for the agreed-upon fee, but I made copies."

"Copies, huh?" Axon stirred his nearly empty drink with a straw, acting as if this weren't the exact reason he was here.

Regina pulled a yellow flash drive patterned with emoji smiley faces from her purse and waved it in front of him.

Chapter 20

LUCY'S SHEETS TANGLED around her legs, evidence of her hours-long effort to find a comfortable position for sleep. Some nights she felt like there wasn't enough time in the day to sate her tired body, on others insomnia plagued her for most of the night and she spent the next day in a fog of exhaustion. It had been nearly half an hour since she'd heard the telltale creak of the front door she had left unlocked for Axon and the footsteps downstairs cease. Lucy unwrapped herself from the twisted bedding and crept out of her room. Ed and Nadine had long since gone to bed, and the sound of soft snoring as she passed their bedroom door told Lucy they wouldn't be easily disturbed by her nighttime wanderings.

Intending to have a look through the kitchen for a snack—not because she was especially hungry but because she couldn't think of anything better to do—Lucy made her way downstairs. Walking through the dining room where Axon's many papers had been spread out across one end of the long hardwood table, she spotted his tablet atypically left behind, something she hadn't noticed before she went upstairs for the night. He must have dropped it off when he returned from his evening; whatever that included, he hadn't shared with Lucy. A yellow flash drive with a rubbery smiley face lay on top of his device along with a crumpled receipt from a taxi. Lucy placed them carefully to the side as she turned on the screen.

She knew Axon had taken plenty of video footage during both her and Colton's wakes, and her frustrated attempt at sleep had fueled her nostalgia. The first thing that popped up on the screen was Axon's email program. Looking through his video files of her own boyfriend's wake was one thing, but reading his email was a whole other level of invasion into Axon's personal life. Guiltily, she moved the cursor to minimize the window while she hastily scanned the headers on his messages, convincing herself that hardly counted as *re-*

ally reading his correspondence. She couldn't help it when an email with the subject "Lucy Hanson Internship" caught her eye. Lucy had discussed with her parents and Axon on several occasions what she should do next with her life. The only thing that really interested her was the idea of doing Axon's job, thus being able to spend even more time by his side, learning the tricks of the trade. Her father had helped compile a formal message telling of her interest in working with the *Times* and in what capacity. She didn't need to be paid, it stated, just shadow until she could prove herself valuable. Axon had assisted in finding the right point of contact within his organization, a favor she could tell Ed appreciated. She'd even heard him mumble a small "thank you," the most positive interaction the two of them had had for weeks. That was several days ago, and the response she was eagerly anticipating appeared to be right at her fingertips. What harm could it do to learn a day early? Axon was sure to tell her tomorrow morning. She clicked on the message.

From: Veronica Miles (vmiles@timesnews.org)

Subject: FWD: Lucy Hanson Internship

Hi Axon,

Remember, we're in unknown territory with the contract at this point. Nobody's ever been able to utilize the clause in the contract that permits a Times *rep to continue their relationship with the client after a wake is unsuccessful. After the wake, the timeline in which you can continue keeping close tabs on the subject is ill-defined in print, which could make it difficult to continue without her support. We managed to convince the Hansons in the beginning, but that won't fly forever. I'm only reiterating what you already know, so keep up the good work and stay on her good side.*

P.S. Seems like legal agreed with your assessment of Ms. Hanson. Good luck breaking the internship news to the kid. See below.

Veronica Miles

Editor, Wake Reporting Division

From: Robert Randall (rrandall@timesnews.org)

Subject: Lucy Hanson Internship

Dear Ms. Miles,

After reviewing the request for Lucy Hanson to join our organization in a volunteer capacity with the appropriate parties, unfortunately it has been decided that we cannot commit to this endeavor at this time. While much of the media is still focused on Lucy's case, the legal team believes that her presence at the wakes of others would create too much of a distraction from the guest of honor. It is also clear that many people have varied, and oftentimes extreme, viewpoints on whether the Hanson girl should be allowed to insert herself into a career of her choosing while the limits of her lifetime are yet unknown. Because the wake reporting part of our business generates such a large percentage of our income, it is believed that any threat to this income could jeopardize other important branches of our media division's financial solubility. It is our sincere hope that Lucy Hanson is able to find something else to fill her remaining time, however much that may be.

Best,

Robert Randall, JD

Cris Gonzalez, Executive Vice President of Marketing

Maria Jung, Director of Human Resources

The disappointment of not being able to work with Axon, mingled with the sting of rejection she felt that he had not necessarily supported her pursuit, caused her eyes to water. What did Veronica mean when she implied that Axon's assessment of her had been correct? What had he said? She sniffed loudly. Why wouldn't he have wanted her on his team wholeheartedly? Didn't they get along? Wasn't she helpful and not in the way? She started to feel less remorseful about snooping in his personal files, and clicked hard to search for videos of Colton's wake. Her keyword search proved fruitful, and several video files came up right away. She clicked the first one and watched as Colton's father gave a toast describing the wonderful life his son had lived his whole sixteen years. He was both encouraging to the other parents of low-LP kids and emotional as he recounted his own experience as a father. Lucy smiled as the camera panned over to Colton, his face radiant with pride and love for his dad.

"*Colton expected nothing and gave everything to those he loved,*" his father reminisced.

Lucy could agree with that. Colton had been the shining light of her life, always there to make her feel better when reality felt morose and heavy. He'd lived life as if he preferred the path he was given, the path determined by his Lifetime Potential, instead of the route he might have carved out for himself in a world where he had infinite time. Lucy's wake counselor, Tess, commented frequently that Lucy had a tendency to dwell on the negative instead of accepting what she was given. Lucy argued that had she been able to choose to be low LP, the proffered years of relaxation without purpose might have been more appealing. Instead, being forced to live a life without future or function, she was frequently frustrated.

Lucy double-clicked through the files, immersing herself in memories of Colton's final hours. She saw herself in many of the clips, her face a mixture of emotions beneath perfect makeup worn to cover stress-induced blemishes. About halfway through the video files, she came across a scene she didn't recognize. Maybe this was when she had gone to the bathroom and then got stuck talking to Mary Haskell, the girl who was always called just after her during attendance all throughout their childhood. Mary was a talker whose own wake had occurred just two weeks after Colton's. Lucy had been cornered by her slightly-tipsy classmate in front of the bathroom mirrors while minutes of Colton's life ticked away. Mary spent a precious five minutes prodding Lucy's memory to recall a former classmate, Ross Stooderman, whom evidently Mary had had a crush on and never told. Being a good sport, considering Mary's wake was so near, Lucy tried in vain to conjure Ross's face and managed to only nod along as Mary chattered. When Lucy had finally managed to escape from Mary's attention, she went back to the party to sit with her parents while she reluctantly gave Colton some space to socialize in the crowded room.

The shot started shakily, as if Axon had picked up the camera abruptly in order to catch something unexpected. Two girls in formalwear shouted at each other about ten feet from where the camera recorded. The jumble of other voices muffled the first bits of heated conversation and made it difficult to decipher from the crowd.

"You are such a sociopathic bitch, Kathy! You should be ashamed of the person you've become, you piece-of-shit friend," Girl Number One spat angrily at her dowdier opponent.

Girl Number Two's response was engulfed in the shuffle and growing roar of the crowd gathering semi-circle around the bickering girls. The demands of "Fight!" grew ever louder as the girls continued to hurl insults at the other, edging closer to one another, a preamble to physical contact. The camera zoomed out to get the whole of the scrum forming near the edge of the lacquered dance floor. The angle in which the footage was taken showed one of the corridors leading toward the outdoor garden area.

Two people stood far away from the onlookers to the fight, nearly out of view from the camera, but Lucy recognized one of them right away. It was the way he held himself—she would know it anywhere, even from a distance. While the other guests were occupied watching the girls, Colton stood in front of someone she didn't know in a dark suit and appeared to be consoling them by gently rubbing their upper arm with the palm of his hand. The camera zoomed in, trying to catch Colton in a candid moment to broadcast in the final clips, but Lucy had watched his memorial video dozens of times and didn't remember this.

The person in the dark suit appeared to be another boy around Colton's age, though Lucy did not recognize him. Was he a cousin? A kid from another school? Colton had invited guests from the all-boys summer camp he'd attended for three weeks a year, maybe this person was from there? Lucy thought she knew all of Colton's friends. She watched as Colton continued to rub the boy's arm. Suddenly, the boy leaned into Colton's chest and kissed him full on the mouth. Without so much as a flinch, Colton moved a fraction of an inch closer and lifted his other hand to the boy's face, kissing him back. Lucy stared in horror as her stomach sank like a stone to the floor.

Lucy spluttered unintelligible expletives. No words seemed adequate for her shock. The tablet she had been holding thudded onto the table as if it had suddenly become white hot in her hands. Covering her mouth with her palms, she let out a muffled "FUCK!" while she struggled to inhale normally.

Releasing a moaning scream, Lucy swiped the contents of Axon's project space off the table. Papers, folders, books, and electronics tumbled to the floor, carpeting the dining room. She clawed the remaining papers from the table, crumpling documents in her haste to remove every item from the surface, to wipe it clean.

Not caring whether she roused the entire neighborhood in her rage, she stomped through the house half-screaming, half-growling, "WHAT THE FUCK?!" Storming to the guest room Axon had been staying in, she began pounding on the door. "AXON DAVIS, GET YOUR FUCKING LYING ASS OUT HERE RIGHT NOW!" Her fist banged heavily enough to rattle the hollow door in the frame.

"What's going on?" Ed Hanson shouted from the landing of the staircase behind Lucy.

Unperturbed by her father's presence, Lucy continued to slam her fist into the wood and scream. "AXON, I SWEAR, YOU HAD BETTER GET OUT HERE RIGHT—"

The door opened to a slightly disheveled Axon, his dark hair messy and his T-shirt on backwards.

"What the hell, Lucy?! What is your problem?" was all he could retort before Lucy came at him like a swarm of bees, her fists pummeling his upper body. Lifting an arm to shield his face, he used the other to grab one of her wrists. "Stop! Lucy! Knock it off!"

"LET GO OF ME, YOU FUCKING TRAITOR!" Her free fist continued to throw punches at his gut. Movement caught her eye, and she looked past Axon into his room. The sheets on his bed were tangled, and a girl with dirty blond hair was hastily buttoning her top and reaching for her scattered heels.

"Who the *fuck* is *she*?!" Lucy tried to slap the side of Axon's head but was blocked by his raised forearm.

"You know I'm bigger than you. Don't make me hurt you! Stop punching me! Tell me what the hell is wrong!" he shouted between punches. "Regina! Leave!" Axon exclaimed, giving the girl space to slip past him. She had given up on re-strapping her complicated leather shoes and hurried out holding them by their fastenings, only one arm inside a jacket sleeve. Within a few seconds, Lucy heard the front door slam behind her.

Lucy was not running out of steam anytime soon. Axon grabbed her other wrist and pushed her up against the wall in an effort to reduce her opportunity to use her legs as a weapon. His legs pinned hers firmly as he held her wrists in both hands, trapping her helplessly against the wall. Trapping her only fueled the anger chewing at her insides like gasoline on a fire. "Let go of me, you fucking fuck bastard, FUCK!"

Sometime during the struggle, Ed had made his way down the stairs and now stood in the doorway to the bedroom. "Let go of my daughter!" he roared upon seeing Axon's controlling stance, stepping forward and then hesitating, probably realizing for the first time how much smaller than Axon he was.

"Ed, I'm just keeping her from hurting herself!" Axon shouted over his shoulder as Ed began to half-heartedly pull Axon away from his daughter.

Shrugging Ed off, Axon reestablished his hold on the tornado that was Lucy, to show she had nowhere to go. "Lucy! You've got to stop! Tell me what's wrong?!"

Ed stepped back, clearly torn on how to help his only child.

Lucy's face was streaked with angry tears that dribbled past her chin. "Why didn't you tell me?" she said, shaking her head and grimacing.

"Tell you what?" he asked, relieved that she had at least stopped shrieking.

"Colton!" she said. "You never told me about Colton." Tears ran down her face, and she sobbed open-mouthed, red-faced and snotty.

He waited until she caught her breath. "The videos. I saw his wake video with the . . . that guy."

"What's she talking about?" Ed interjected.

"You watched the wake videos?" Axon asked.

A fresh wave of humiliation washed over Lucy. "Yes, I saw them! I saw him making out with a boy," the last word came out as a fresh sob, nearly unintelligible.

"Oh Lucy, I'm so sorry." Axon sensed any danger of her flinging limbs had passed and released her from his grip.

"Sorry? You're sorry?!" Lucy pushed him away from her with all the force she could. "I trusted you! You should have told me! I thought we were *friends*." She snarled the last word. "You couldn't even support me enough to get an internship! I saw your email from *Veronica*," as if his boss's name was in air quotes. "And it turns out, I can make you leave whenever the fuck I want. And I WANT you to LEAVE. NOW."

"Lucy," Axon started, cautiously stepping toward her with an outstretched hand.

"No!" She slapped away his hand. "Pack up your shit and leave my house. I can't trust you and I hate you!" Lucy pushed past him into his room and began to toss his belongings onto his bed, forming a pile. Ed stood in the doorway, immobilized and bewildered, saying nothing. Grabbing a nearby duffel bag, she shoved it into Axon's hands. "Pack up! I said GET OUT!" she screamed into his face, his confounded expression giving her a small victorious pleasure.

Glancing toward Ed's unhelpful face, Axon began to grab his belongings and shove them into the bag. Lucy's mother strode into the room carrying a banker's box of the papers, books, and electronics Lucy recognized as having shoved from the dining room table. Lucy hadn't even heard her come downstairs but couldn't be surprised she had woken. She felt a small surge of pride as her mother handed the box to Axon, her face expressionless.

"You heard her," Nadine said softly.

Chapter 21

SUSANNE ABDUL HAD NOT exaggerated how much more work the vaccine team would entail. Evergreen was somehow kept even busier than she had been with her previous position and extracurricular research. Early morning hours combined with late evenings in the lab, and working twelve-to-fourteen-hour days meant she was so exhausted when finally returning to her apartment that there was hardly any time to consider her former project. It was nearly two weeks into her new role when she was finally able to celebrate with Arizona, arriving late for an evening happy hour after a grueling day mastering a viral dilution procedure.

"Better late than never," Arizona said with a sing-song inflection when Evergreen slid onto the barstool next to her.

"That expression is so cliché," Evergreen complained. The half-priced tequila shots they ordered slopped over the polished copper bar.

"Your *life* is a cliché, Ev," Arizona quipped as the bartender deposited a salt shaker and a small bowl of lime wedges in front of their drinks. Expertly, Arizona licked the top of her hand and shook the salt until it stuck. Tossing back the amber liquid with one hand, she grabbed a lime wedge with the other and sucked it hard, making a sour face. "Wooooo! Feel that burn. I mean, cheers, Evergreen," she added, lifting her empty shot glass in salute.

"And how is my life a cliché exactly?" Evergreen asked before mimicking Arizona's motions with the tequila. "Ugh, I hate limes. Why can't the etiquette be with lemons or oranges or something?"

"It's a time-honored tradition to use limes, that's why. They complement the tequila or something. And how are you not a cliché?" Arizona asked with an exaggerated eye roll. "Let's see, high-LP girl with a renowned scientist dad," she began counting with her fingers, "graduates her rigorous scientific program at the top of the class, lands her dream job right out of the gate, and gets promoted within a few months. She's going straight to the top, ladies and gentlemen!" Arizona shouted the last part to the Friday night patrons scattered among the mismatched bar stools and booths.

Evergreen's cheeks flushed as she rolled her eyes. "Always the drama queen."

"So how *is* the dream job treating you?" Arizona asked.

Evergreen gave her friend the most recent update on her training and project plans for the coming months. Ordering a second round, the girls chatted about the other graduates of their program, ranking their classmates according to success. Both agreed to tie for second place and determined that the first-place winner was their former class president, Richie Neman. Richie had been newly appointed the deputy to the head of the Department of Lifetime Potential and Health when his boss, Gordon Hayes, was selected for the role. The former official had been the late Arnie Hamilton, who had met his unfortunate early demise in a train derailment several weeks before, thus creating the vacancy. Richie was well-liked in their graduate class, and his luck at having been placed within reach of the Oval Office, his ultimate ambition, was an achievement worth first place.

Inevitably, the conversation led back to boys. Who they were dating, interested in, or otherwise pining for—at least in Arizona's case. While she was able to lay out her latest trysts like a casino card dealer, Arizona rolled her eyes when Evergreen had nothing new to share since her last escapade with the recently noteworthy Axon Davis. Evergreen argued that she had no time for romance or meeting men, reminding her that the two of them had taken two weeks to align their schedules due to their career demands. According to Arizona, "There's always time for sex," and Evergreen's excuses for staying out of the dating game were unreasonable. She wondered how Arizona found the time to work, have sex, and manage to sleep at some point. Evergreen imagined there wasn't much sleeping. Arizona had always survived on a precarious balance of caffeine, alcohol, and boyfriends.

"What you need is some inspiration. When you look good, you feel good, and all the men will come running. That is, if you make yourself the slightest bit available. But step one is the look."

"Are you saying I look bad?" Evergreen asked incredulously.

"No, no, never my friend. You are gorgeous. Cream of the crop. An atomic babe." Arizona waved her hand in defense. "But . . ." She dug something out of her purse. "Try this," she said, thrusting a small jar of white cream into Evergreen's hand. "Latest and greatest beauty product, designed with the assistance of yours truly."

"Why am I always your guinea pig?" Evergreen asked, though she loved the free samples. It was much easier than buying her own makeup. "I liked the lipstick, by the way. Perfect shade every time. So, what's this one for?"

"Let me show you," Arizona said, taking back the jar and dabbing a bit of the cream onto the lids of both Evergreen's eyes, gently rubbing it in. She pulled out a compact mirror from her purse. "Ta-da!" she exclaimed. "Perfect smoky eye."

Evergreen inspected herself in the mirror, closing one eye and then the other to see the difference. Indeed, the white cream had changed to several shades of brown and gray, complimenting her green eyes. "Huh. Nice. How does it work exactly?"

"Ah, trade secrets, my dear," Arizona said with an index finger to her lips. "But notice how the color gets darker as it goes from your lid to the supraorbital ridge—you know, the bone under your eyebrow. It really brings out the eye color and brings that traditional smokiness," she said with a wink.

"Global. I like it, thanks." Evergreen capped the jar and tucked it into her jacket pocket. Her fingers touched a slip of folded paper, which she pulled out to examine. *Phynmynd 45 mg*, the note said. Evergreen squinted as she tried to remember where it had come from. "Oh!" she started, suddenly recalling the paper's origin. "Arizona, do you recognize this drug?"

Arizona took the scrap of paper and glanced at it. "Sure. Why? Are you using it for something at work?"

"No." Evergreen began to explain how she had jotted down the name of the prescription Lucy Hanson had been taking when she first met the medical anomaly.

"Wait, she's actually taking this dose?" Arizona asked, bewildered. "This is *not* a safe medication."

"What do you mean?"

"I mean, in small doses it's used for the treatment of depression, with the bonus side effect of clearing up that pesky acne. Which was why it used to be so popular with the teenage crowd. But as kids started to take higher doses of it to give themselves clearer skin, the depression it was initially meant to treat would boomerang and get noticeably worse. There were a lot of Code Preterm cases, as I recall," Arizona said, using the nickname for the rare and unfortunate case of attempted suicide. "If this is really the dose she's taking, Lucy is well beyond any therapeutic range and is at risk for violent mood swings, extreme depression, and possible suicide attempts. Are you sure you wrote the dose down right?"

Evergreen nodded, though her confidence was waning. "I mean, I think so . . ." She trailed off, her gut dropping nervously.

"She needs to get off this pronto. I know you said you couldn't work on your investigation anymore because of the new job, but you at least ought to contact that Davis guy and give him a heads-up. This could get serious." Flippant Arizona was nowhere to be seen as she stared seriously at Evergreen.

"What, you mean now?" Evergreen asked, thinking of the dozen or so ignored calls from Axon. Would he even answer if she tried to return them now? Could she get fired for even calling him? How would Virionics know?

"Wouldn't you want to know if it was you?"

Evergreen tapped on her wrist to call Axon. He answered after two rings.

"Well, well, well. Looks like Scientist Girl has regained her interest and decided to get back into play. I guess that's the magic of news coverage," Axon said with a sarcastic ring to his voice.

"Nothing stays relevant for long, unfortunately," Evergreen said.

Axon was silent for a beat before saying, "Wait, have you not seen the latest?"

"Huh? What do you mean?" Evergreen asked.

"Isn't that why you called me?"

"No, I called to tell you about the meds Lucy Hanson is on. They're dangerous."

"No shit," he said with mock surprise. "I guess that explains her recent episode. The docs don't know what to call it exactly. Code Preterm doesn't seem to fit, seeing as she was supposed to meet her term weeks ago."

"What did you say?" Evergreen practically leapt off of her bar stool, staring at Arizona and cupping her ear implant as if the usual crystal-clear sound had come in fuzzy.

There was a heavy sigh from Axon's end of the line. "Would you turn on your damned TV already?"

Chapter 22

EVERYTHING WAS SO LOUD. Lucy's eyes opened slowly, feeling crusty and unused. A monitor beeped, the sound reverberating through her ears like a drum. The television mounted across from her bed blared.

An angry female voice shouted, "But does she even deserve to live now?" Her husky tone indicated a predilection for smoking.

"Deserve or not, she's still alive," a man said.

"At this point, what could this girl possibly offer to society? She'd been primed for an early death her entire existence, pampered and given a golden life. Then it turns out something went wrong, and this ungrateful child lives past her LP. And how does this girl thank her lucky stars? She tries to go lights-out on her own terms. That's not how this works! I say she and her parents ought to pay, like everyone else whose next of kin tries to pull this crap." Her tone was vehement.

The man's voice stayed even and calm. "It's true, the girl hardly thought of the consequences of her actions. Her parents will likely never be allowed to have another child, not with this on their record. When she inevitably does pass naturally—soon, if her LP is any indication—this will all be for naught. However, the Code Preterm law applies specifically to those whose LP has yet to pass. Technically, she hasn't broken the law. It's not like she will end up in Leydig for this," he said, referring to the well-known and feared maximum security prison.

"I completely disagree. The law implies that if a person attempts to end their life outside their designated day of death that their next of kin, and themselves if they survive, will pay the penalty. However, there is no precedent for someone like Lucy Hanson. The law was predicated on the idea that everyone's lives are valuable until the very end. Just because she was the exception to her LP doesn't mean she should be excepted from the written law. She did, in fact, attempt suicide at a date and time outside of her designated LP. She should be punished. And so should the parents."

"But that's not how the law is *stated,*" he retorted.

"Well, I suppose we will have to see what the courts decide," she said with resolve.

"Turn that off, Ed." Her mother's voice came from somewhere near the right side of Lucy's head.

A buzzing silence punctuated only by mechanical beeping filled the room. Lucy's eyelashes fluttered as she drifted back into sleep.

The smell of flowers filled her nostrils before she saw them. Dozens of bouquets covered the few surfaces of her otherwise sterile room. In-and-out of consciousness for hours—or perhaps days, it was hard to tell—Lucy heard her parents describe finding her bleeding from her arms and inner thighs, self-inflicted wounds she remembered creating. It was clear this wasn't the primary reason she had been brought here, though. The words "superficial wounds" were used often, as was the phrase "prescription overdose," which was the part that had her most confused. She had only ever taken medication as prescribed, having been instilled at a young age with both a trust and fear of the power of medicine. Enough medication and she would get better, but too much and she could get hurt. Nadine had been afraid of raising a low-LP child with tendencies toward overindulgence in mind-altering drugs, like many of Lucy's peers, and this lesson stuck.

"So, what's dripping into her arm now, then? And what are those tubes for?" Lucy heard her father ask accusingly, glaring at the empty tubes meant for his daughter's blood. Her head felt too heavy to turn and look in the direction of his voice.

"It's just fluids to keep her hydrated, sir. Her doctor wants to let her body reset without meds for now. And I need to take a blood sample to send to Virionics. She's due for her annual vaccination," the nurse said.

I wonder if that scientist lady will look at my blood? Lucy thought through the haze of fatigue, remembering Evergreen and the way she had described her job at Virionics.

"That's good, I guess," Ed mumbled quietly enough that Lucy was sure the nurse hadn't heard.

"It's unfortunate that the previous prescription was filled incorrectly," the woman added.

"Unfortunate?" Ed steamed, irritation flushing his face. "Unfortunate is when you scrape the car door against a wall, not when the medication that was supposed to be *helping* your daughter was wrong and almost killed her. She nearly died," he reiterated.

"I understand. I'm really sorry this happened. Lucy is lucky to have you."

Lucy heard him give a noncommittal grunt and smiled inwardly at the familiarity of the sound.

"I can assure you, Mr. Hanson, we are doing everything we can to support your daughter's health. In the meantime, her body needs rest, and it looks like you may need some too. Why don't you go home and sleep in your own bed tonight?" the nurse asked, her compassion evident.

Lucy heard the shuffling of feet and the rummaging of belongings, quickly shutting her eyes so her dad wouldn't see she'd woken up. Several minutes passed before the room was devoid of his small noises and Lucy knew he had gone. But she wasn't alone.

"I know you're awake," the nurse said, and Lucy felt the slight tug of her IV line as it was adjusted. She opened her eyes. "How are you feeling?"

Lucy attempted to speak, but only a rasp came out. Clearing her throat, she tried again. "Fine. Tired."

"I'm sure you are. Well, you gave your parents quite a scare. Taking a fistful of antidepressants will usually bring you here, but in your case it was worse, the dose being incorrect and all. That med has a build-up effect—take too many pills at that dose for too long, and your organs start to go toxic. You're lucky to be alive."

"I guess," Lucy managed to say.

The nurse sat on the edge of the bed facing Lucy. Her hair was pulled back in a short ponytail, low on the back of her head, and the slightly greasy strands not long enough to be tied back framed her round face. She had a weak dimpled chin that gradually became neck without much distinction. Her hospital identification badge read, "Neva J, RN" with a picture of her smiling, the excitement of starting a new job still sparkling in her eye. Now she just looked weary, and Lucy deduced that perhaps she was near the end of her shift. She reached into the pocket of her hospital issue scrub-top and pulled out a miniature hard drive. "This is from a friend. He wanted you to know the truth," she said slowly, deliberate with each word while looking upwards as if trying to recite from memory.

Lucy furrowed her brow. "All of my friends are dead."

Neva J, RN, sighed heavily. "Look, I promised that I'd make sure you have this. He said you had to watch the video, that it would explain why he didn't tell you. Or something like that," she added with a flip of her hand. She handed the small drive to Lucy, who stared at her. "He said he knew you, and I know he does. I've seen him on TV."

Lucy pursed her lips. Of course.

"I told him you'd watch, so I'm going to set this up," the nurse said as she stood and plucked Lucy's tablet from a nearby shelf. Setting up the video from the file, Neva placed the device firmly in Lucy's right hand and raised the bed to a relaxed sitting position. "Here." She paused, looking at her patient for confirmation.

Lucy sighed. "What else am I going to do," she said, resigned.

Nurse Neva nodded. "Good." She strode out of the room.

Lucy glanced over to where her nurse had retreated, the countertop of the nurses' station visible from her bed. She watched as Neva sat down with a squeak of her chair and began sipping from a paper coffee cup decorated with a drawing of a heart and the digits of a phone number—no doubt her reward for helping Axon. Lucy exhaled loudly and turned her attention back to the screen, holding her heavy finger over the play button in contemplation. She let it tap the screen.

Colton appeared, sitting in a high-backed floral-patterned chair Lucy recognized as belonging to the office in his parents' house. He swiveled nervously from side to side in his seat, the desk his father sometimes used and a closed door visible behind him.

"Shall we continue?" the voice of Axon Davis asked from behind the camera.

Colton nodded. "Sure," he said, his voice cracking slightly.

"So, we left off where I explained how I like to ask my clients if there are things they wish to get off their chest before the wake."

Another nod.

"Anything you say is confidential. Some people find that this makes the transition easier." Axon paused, giving Colton another moment of contemplation. "You don't have to say anything. It's up to you."

"No, I want to." Colton took a deep breath. "I need to say it out loud."

"Say what?" Axon coaxed gently.

Colton hung his head, bracing himself before looking up into the camera. "I might be gay."

There was silence, and Lucy imagined Axon nodding his head, allowing Colton to continue.

Colton released a long breath. "Or bi. Something. I am . . . I don't know." He lifted his arms, lacing his fingers together behind his head, elbows stretching forward. "I just . . . I don't know," he said, looking up at the ceiling as if the script was there to be read. He looked back at Axon in frustration.

"Well? Are you attracted to boys?"

Colton nodded.

"Girls?"

"I have a girlfriend," Colton stated.

"But are you attracted to girls?" Axon pushed.

"She's beautiful," he said with a sigh.

"That doesn't answer the question. She may be—"

"Lucy," interjected Colton.

"Right. Lucy. She might be objectively beautiful, but are you sexually attracted to her?"

"Sometimes?" Colton answered, his face quizzical.

"So, why don't you have a boyfriend if you're, it sounds like, more attracted to boys?"

Shrugging, Colton ran a hand through his hair. "I don't know."

"You know that nobody cares if you're gay, right? I mean, it's nothing to be ashamed of."

"I know that. I just . . ." He trailed off, fiddling with his hands.

"Lucy. You have Lucy."

"Exactly!" Colton exclaimed. "She's like, my best friend. We've known each other since we were little kids and . . . and things just sort of happened, and we turned into a couple. Don't get me wrong, I like it. I like being with her."

"Have you been with anybody else?"

His eyes flicked between the camera and his interviewer, and he rested his mouth on the knuckles of his hand. He gave a slight bob of his head. "A couple of times."

"Does Lucy know?"

He shook his head violently, letting loose a sarcastic laugh. "Of course not!"

"Would she disapprove?"

Incredulous, Colton asked, "Of me cheating on her?"

"All couples are different. I thought maybe you had an arrangement of some sort."

"No," Colton said with an ironic smile. "No. She's special, you know? If I told her I wanted to be with guys instead of her, it would crush her. I couldn't do that to her. She means way too much to me."

"Instead, you did it in secret."

"I kind of had to. I mean, only one life to live right? And an abbreviated one at that. I had a couple of opportunities to explore this side of myself, and I took them. But I don't want her to know. It would change how she feels about us, and what we have *is* real."

"Maybe."

"What do you mean, 'maybe?'" Colton asked.

Axon crossed one leg over the other. "It's not real if you're lying to her. Lying to yourself."

Colton raised an eyebrow. "What are you, my therapist?"

"Just my opinion. I'm only saying, you could have come clean. Only one life to live, right? Might as well live it honestly."

"No. That wasn't an option. Look, she has about as much time left as I do. If I told her, it would be this whole thing that would ruin what we have, and we would never have time to repair it before our wakes. I don't want her dying thinking I wasn't anything but her faithful and loving boyfriend. That's what she deserves."

"Even if only half of that is true?"

"I do love her."

"So, yes."

"I suppose." Colton crossed his arms. "What would you have done?"

"Me?" Axon asked. "Well, I wouldn't have had a girlfriend to begin with, so . . ."

Laughing, Colton's usual bright smile finally making an appearance, he said, "Yeah, I can see that about you. So, I guess tough shit, huh? Sucks to be me!"

They both laughed. "Yeah, pretty much," Axon said before asking knowingly, "Feel better now, don't you?"

"Yeah, actually." Colton brightened, then shrugged. "It is what it is right?"

"Such is life."

"Short, sweet, and complicated," Colton said with a final grin before the video ended.

Lucy set the tablet down on her lap, brushing away the tears that had leaked from her eyes. Leaning back against her pillows, she sighed heavily, not knowing what to feel. Her eyelids felt weighted, and she let them close, welcoming the wave of exhaustion so she wouldn't have to think.

Chapter 23

WIPING HER MOUTH WITH the white linen napkin, the ones her father insisted on using whenever she came over as if she were special company, Evergreen said, "Thanks for dinner, Dad." She carefully placed the silver utensils back onto her empty plate.

"You ordered the food, dear," Doctor Mason gently corrected. "So, thank *you*."

"Right. Well, thanks for accepting a non-home-cooked meal. You know how skilled I am in that arena."

He chuckled. "I appreciate your company, even if your visits are few and far between."

"Ugh, I'm sorry. Work, I—"

Nodding, he stopped her with a wave of his hand. "Yes, I know. And from the sound of it, you're doing just brilliantly."

"I come from good genes." Evergreen grinned.

"Not sure where those came from," he joked, standing to clear the dishes and the leftover takeout containers from the table, hand pressing on his lower back. "Just hope you didn't get my back problems."

"Dad, I'll take care of that," she said, reaching across the table, attempting to grab the dishes from his hands. "Just go lie down if your back is bugging you. I swear I've got this!" she said, prying the dishes from his hands and shooing him away with a nod of her head. "I'm cooking *and* cleaning tonight."

"Alright, alright." He yielded the duties to her and shuffled away toward the next room. Her father, always keen on one-liners, muttered, "Not sure if ordering takeout counts as cooking, though."

"Heard that," Evergreen said.

"You were meant to!" Gerald shouted from the other room before giving a slight "*oomph*" as he eased himself onto the living room couch. Repetitive motion in the lab over the years and a less-than-

169

ideally-ergonomic chair had caused a tightening of his lower back muscles.

"Bring me the clear bottle from the kitchen, will you?" he hollered again from the other room. The only thing that helped provide relief when a spasm hit was a muscle relaxer, which Evergreen knew he refused to take unless the pain was really horrible. She promptly brought him the bottle along with a glass of water.

"Thank you," he said, his voice low, before tossing back a white pill and taking a gulp of water. He would be asleep within fifteen minutes, as soon as the magic of modern medicine kicked in.

Evergreen continued to clear the dishes, loaded the plates and utensils into the dishwasher, and put the leftovers into her father's refrigerator, making a mental note to grab them before she left in the morning. She hated grocery shopping, and leftovers allowed for a break from the convenient-yet-overpriced Virionics cafeteria food. Her father lived outside the city limits in a suburb that provided privacy and some land, a contrast to her tiny apartment a five-minute walk from work. It had been a great place to grow up, surrounded by woods with a nearby creek, apple trees to climb, and a backyard fort she had helped build as a kid. Most other high LPs she knew who weren't fortunate enough to have been a twin or triplet shared a feeling of loneliness growing up as the only child. Without another sibling to play with, they were left with the company of adults, neighborhood children, or their own imaginations. Since her parents had opted to live so far outside of the city, there'd been few neighbors nearby, let alone children Evergreen's age.

There had been only one neighborhood girl she remembered from her childhood—Nancy Grey. The two of them had invented imaginary games they played after school. Though they hadn't attended the same school, Nancy being of low LP and Evergreen high, the girls got along famously. Once, upon returning from a business trip, Evergreen's father had brought home a small bag of colorful multi-sized marbles. The duo decided the marbles were unexplored planets that only they, the brave astronauts, would venture to. The largest marble in the bag was a swirl of white and orange glass which, after some debate, they agreed was a fire planet with only one hour of breathable air each day. They planned their mission accordingly and voyaged to the planet to collect precious gems only found on months that ended in "ber." The mission was successful until Nancy fell down into a hidden crevice as they were approaching the spaceship. In a dramatic rescue mission, Evergreen was able to bring life-saving oxygen to her suffocating friend and pull her out of the pit in time to return to Earth with their excavations. Nancy had died, she remembered, not on the unlivable planet but of a natural death before Evergreen's ninth birthday party. She had been so disappointed that her only neighborhood friend was unable to attend her space-themed party.

Evergreen stared out the kitchen window, absently drying her hands on a dish towel with a picture of a rooster on it. Laying the towel flat next to the sink, Evergreen opened the fridge and pulled out the re-corked bottle of white wine leftover from dinner and re-filled her empty glass. She started to return the bottle but thought better of it, shutting the fridge door and taking it with her out of the kitchen. The sound of her father's snoring was enough indication that the rest of the evening would be spent entertaining herself. She started up the stairs, treading lightly even though she knew that once he fell asleep almost nothing could rouse him. Intending to get some work done, she grabbed her computer and went into the office across the hall from her bedroom, which hadn't changed much in the years since she had moved out.

She clicked open her internet home page and was greeted with the latest news headline. "Hanson Girl Attempts Suicide: Still Alive." She sighed. The news outlets loved to exaggerate the facts. Axon had shared with Evergreen that Lucy's "suicide attempt" had been a misunderstanding stemming from an incorrect prescription dose taken over too long a period. Lucy had been discovered passed out with several actively bleeding razor blade cuts on her inner thighs, but this had been a coincidence the reporters sunk their teeth into with vigor. True, it looked bad, but Axon insisted it wasn't the girl's fault. Evergreen couldn't help but wonder if he was going soft professionally. Wasn't it a reporter's job to sensationalize the facts? As a scientist, she was trained to be objective. Facts were important, and she judged any of those in her field who would approach the world otherwise.

If only she had been able to continue her research, maybe she could have warned Lucy before the teenager succumbed to the effects of her erroneous prescription. Evergreen had worked hard at Virionics in the last couple weeks, trying to prove herself worthy of a promotion so early in her career. It suddenly struck her as entirely unfair to not be able to pursue her former project. Why couldn't she meet the requirements of her new role and take on the research she wanted to in her spare time? She knew that the intention was probably to deter her from spending time she would otherwise have used for new projects, but she wasn't doing anything *right now.* How could extracurricular learning be viewed as a bad thing? In fact, maybe Susanne would even be impressed if she was able to meet, or even exceed, expectations in her new job and continue pursuing her own interest in her spare time, even if she hadn't officially sanctioned it. Susanne didn't own her, after all. Evergreen still had time away from work—why not dedicate some of that to additional learning? It was all purely academic, really. It was what her professors in school would expect from her, right?

She began to poke around in her notes to refresh herself on where she had left off and quickly realized that without the ability to see publications using the Virionics server and access to her previously requested census data, she couldn't do much to move forward. And yet her father with his higher rank in the company had access to a remote server from his home and probably had no restrictions on what publications *he* might be able to see. Evergreen refilled her wine glass with the remains of the bottle and stared at his closed laptop on the desk, the faint green light indicating a full charge blinking back at her. What harm could it do to use his? She was on her own time and just needed to take a peek.

Evergreen made up her mind and opened the computer. *Password,* the screen stated. A hard stop. She tried to think of what her father might use as a login password. Based on her own password requirements, she knew his would require at least one symbol, a capital letter, and a number, which meant the possibilities were endless. Trying a few things without success, she searched around the desk, looking for clues. Prying open the drawers and shuffling through the contents, she didn't even know exactly what she was looking for. Would he even keep a password written down somewhere? The only note she found was a Post-it stuck to the hard wood of the desktop with the words:

Work hard and Believe in success

The word "success" was underlined three times. She stared at the wall behind the desk for a moment, thinking. Her high-functioning brain, trained to solve puzzles and think critically from a very young age, suddenly clicked the pieces into place and she typed into the password box, "Wh&Bis3." It authenticated and she was in.

His computer loaded a desktop image she recognized, one of herself and her parents looking happy on a sandy beach. A younger Evergreen stared into the camera, the green of her eyes obscured by dark sunglasses, but her smile, bright and beaming, was hard to miss. Her mother wore a white dress with buttons down the front, the fabric casually clinging to her thin frame. A floppy sun hat shaded her face, beautiful and vibrant with life. Her father stood next to her mother with his arm around her waist, gazing at his wife instead of the camera. Though Evergreen didn't recall the details of the beach day, or even who had snapped the photo, she did remember feeling content.

Pulling out the notes of her most recent research queries and the list of publications she had requested access to prior to her promotion, Evergreen set to work searching the database. The first article she set out to find had been referenced as a source in several other publications she had read through. "Genetic Mutations: Suppression of the *HG580* Gene" published in the *Journal for Genetic Advances* by James, K; Wilson, H; Proctor, M, came up right away in her search. *Thanks Dad,* she thought, her gut panging with slight guilt at having abused his trust. She skimmed through the article, reading first the Abstract section before moving on to the finer details in the Methods and Discussion sections. According to the publication, the study had sought a way to prevent the activation of the *HG580* gene in carrier patients, though it was unclear what the gene function was. What was important about the *HG580* gene? And why would there be a need to suppress it? The Background section of the paper detailed only that there was an interest in determining if scientists could prevent the gene's activation through a series of injectable hormones during fetal development in mice. Details regarding other genes which had been successfully suppressed using a similar approach were discussed, but surprisingly the document was vague regarding the scientific application. Perhaps this was why it wasn't publicly available? Evergreen was unsure. Conclusions on what she was reading would certainly come later—now was the time to snag what she data could and get out before her conscience got the better of her.

Evergreen riffled through her computer bag until she produced a small white miniature hard drive and plugged it into the laptop. Saving a copy of any relevant documents she found would be the best way to move quickly and review later. Evergreen glanced through the sources listed at the end of the *HG580* article before moving on to the next search on her list. A footnote at the end of the article caught her eye, which read: "This study was funded by Project Hourglass, Virionics Research Division. No other potential conflict of interest was reported by the authors."

Though Virionics was a large company, and Evergreen had only been with the Research Division for less than a year, she had never heard of Project Hourglass. Knowing that there were probably many disciplines she had yet to discover within her new job, and how limited her own exposure had been thus far, she figured this was just one of many. Unable to completely tether her curiosity and spurred on by the three glasses of wine she had consumed, she typed "Project Hourglass" into the database search function.

A verbatim match appeared as a folder icon, indicating that there were many documents within it relating to this project. She double-clicked, and a long list of other file folders appeared within it. Her eyes slid down the alphabetical list, trying to determine which to open first. Among them were: Agenda Items; Archives; Census; Legal; Meeting Minutes; Policies; Political; Research. Wanting to prevent herself from going down the proverbial rabbit hole until later, she selected all, hit "copy" and pasted the folder in its entirety onto her personal hard drive.

PING!

Evergreen jumped, banging her knee on the underside of the desk in the process. She hadn't realized how high the volume was set on the computer, and the chime of the instant message popping up in the lower right corner was startling. She felt like she had been administered a shot of adrenaline, her accelerated heartbeat thumped so wildly in her chest. Rubbing the top of her soon-to-be-bruised kneecap, she looked at the message.

"*What are you up to, Gerald*?" it read, from a sender whose name she didn't recognize.

The creeping sensation of fear at being caught went up her spine, and she felt her palms begin to sweat. How could she have forgotten to turn off the messenger function? Hastily, she unplugged her flash drive and slapped the computer shut—the risk of being caught by someone had suddenly become too great. No more. Picking up the scattered evidence of her intrusion, Evergreen retreated toward the familiar sameness of her old bedroom. The sound of her father's snores still carried up the stairs as she clicked the office door shut behind her.

The next morning, Evergreen slept later than usual, relishing her time away from work. The project she was working on in the lab required her to return in the late afternoon to check on culture samples, and the hours of freedom stretched ahead of her luxuriously. She yawned and stretched, reaching for a bottle of water to quench her dry mouth—undoubtedly a result of finishing the wine she had drank the night before. Wine always dehydrated her. Still in her pajamas, she threw on a hooded sweatshirt and walked downstairs, her fuzzy socks softening her descent on the wooden stairs.

"Ev? Is that you?" her father shouted from some rooms away.

Who else would it be? She thought, rolling her eyes and smiling. "Yeah, Dad. Still me."

"Can you bring me my computer? It's in the office upstairs—if I try to go up, I might not come back down," he hollered with strained laughter in his voice.

Evergreen followed the noise and found her dad in the same spot she'd left him the night before. "Back still out?"

"Yep," he said, pain crossing his face as he tried to sit up and swing his feet to the floor. "Help your old man out, would you? I've got to use the bathroom. At least there's no stairs involved!"

Evergreen grabbed his outstretched hands and hoisted him upwards as he groaned painfully. "Do you want me to stick around, Dad? I can get someone to cover me this afternoon if you need my help." She half-hoped he wouldn't say yes. Ten minutes since waking, and she was already itching to get back to the lab.

Waving Evergreen off as he hobbled to the bathroom he said, "No, no. Just get my computer, and I can let work know I'll be staying put today. I'll take my pills and get some rest. They know the deal. This has happened before."

"Are you sure?" She tried not to sound relieved.

"Yes, yes. I'll be fine, honey." He shut the bathroom door.

Dutifully, Evergreen ran upstairs to grab his work computer, unhooking it carefully from the charging port while she swallowed the wave of guilt, having returned to the scene of the crime. Knowing that her father would likely be asleep again soon and not good company, she collected her things and readied herself to go back to the city early.

Chapter 24

"HOW ARE YOU FEELING, Luce?" Ed Hanson asked, rubbing his daughter's shoulder affectionately. "Ready to go home?"

"Yeah. I feel alright. Definitely ready to leave this place," she said, glaring around the hospital room with displeasure. Having spent the better part of four days recovering from what everyone around her subtly referred to as her "incident," Lucy was sick of the hospital. She knew exactly how many speckled ceiling tiles hung above her head, what each type of ding from the nursing station meant, and the latest gossip from the nearby staff. Nurse Pamela's blind date had gone horribly wrong; the guy turned out to look nothing like his photo and had lied about his height. Another nurse's toddler had recently visited their grandparents and had come home full of new curse words, much to mom's chagrin. Grandma apparently had a filthy mouth. All of the staff seemed to like their boss but detested Barb, the manager of the maternity ward one floor above. Staff complained of her extreme unpleasantness and propensity to make snide remarks about how much harder her floor was to work on. Barb looked down on the nurses of Lucy's unit who cared for the "physically stable, mentally unfit" patients, unlike Barb's, whose bodies were literally torn apart from the inside in order to push out a human life. Considering the hospital only had three wards—Emergency, Mental Health, and Obstetrics—the chatter involved relatively limited stories, so often the same ones circulated through the shifts until they grew stale or took on new details.

One of the day-shift nurses strode into the room carrying a small plastic tray. "Meds for you," she sang, flipping her red hair over one shoulder.

"What now, Erica?" Lucy asked, exasperated.

"What did I tell you about being a pain in my ass?" Erica said fondly, picking up a small plastic cup, which contained a single white pill, from her tray and handing it to Lucy.

"To keep it up," Lucy said with a smirk as she tipped the cup back into her mouth and took a small sip of water.

"Brat," Erica said as she ripped open an alcohol swab and gingerly rolled up Lucy's sleeve to expose the muscle in her upper arm. She made quick work of cleansing a small area of skin and prepped a needle with a vial of clear liquid, dispensing a tiny amount to release any air bubbles. "Small poke," she said as she plunged the shot into her patient's arm.

Lucy made a face and looked away as the needle penetrated her skin. At this point, she should be used to the poking and prodding of her body, but needles were still stressful. Having finished, Erica nudged the protective cap over the sharp needle on the edge of Lucy's bedside table and discarded it in a nearby plastic sharps bin. "All done. What a good girl you are," she patronizingly mocked, patting Lucy's head.

Lucy sighed. "And what was the reason for my latest trauma?" she asked, in dramatic reference to the shot.

"Just your annual vaccination, hot off the presses and personalized for your body," Erica said, the last part a reiteration of something Lucy already knew. During an annual check-up, blood was drawn and used to create an updated vaccine to protect against the latest developments in viruses and provide a boost of immunity. To make it easy to remember, the vaccine was usually administered around the patient's birthday. Though Lucy's was in only two weeks, it made sense to get it out of the way while she was in the hospital.

"Are you ready to get out of here?" Nurse Erica asked, sitting down on the edge of Lucy's bed with a conspiratorial expression.

"I can go home?" Lucy tried but failed to keep her I of indifference, eager to leave this place.

"Later today," Erica said, smiling. "The doctor gave you a clean bill of health."

"Yeah, but have they figured out how much longer I'm supposed to be around before I kick it?" Lucy asked.

Erica furrowed her brow. "Well . . . We don't know for certain. Your LP reading has kept steady at the date you grew up knowing. So really, you should be dead already, which makes you like a ghost or something." Erica widened her eyes in mock realization.

"I prefer zombie."

"Arguably less zombie-like today than when you were admitted. You've made progress, girl." Erica lifted her hand, anticipating Lucy's high-five. "In terms of your lifetime, I can tell you that the doctor says she's confident you will live a long and healthy life. So long as you keep up the progress with your therapy," she added with a wink.

Ed carefully pulled the family car into the driveway, slow enough to give the cluster of reporters still camped out at the end of their property time to dodge the tires. An intense wave of anxiety and frustration washed over Lucy. She was back where she'd started: home, with no plans for the future and nothing to look forward to.

"Looks like you have a visitor." Ed nodded toward the front porch where Axon Davis waited on the wooden two-seat swing, rocking slightly from heel to toe. "Want me to get rid of him?" Lucy sensed her father's resignation had been replaced or at least maintained co-existence with displeasure. Unlike the other media outlets circling like vultures, Axon's honest report on Lucy's hospitalization had marginally altered Ed's view.

"No. It's okay, Dad," she said quietly. Shutting the car door behind her, Lucy made her way to where Axon sat while Ed trailed a little ways behind, giving her space. She took a seat next to Axon on the swing as Ed walked past and through the front door. "I saw the video."

"I'm sorry," Axon said, his voice sincere.

"Why didn't you tell me earlier?" Lucy's voice cracked a little as a tear slipped past her eyelashes and down her cheek. Hastily, she wiped it away, willing herself not to get upset.

"He asked me not to," Axon said simply.

Lucy took a deep breath and exhaled loudly, blinking upwards to prevent more tears. "Of course he did."

"Colton didn't want to hurt you. He cared deeply for you. And none of what he said should change anything about the memories you have of him."

Lucy tried to imagine this version of Colton. The one who kept secrets from her, who cheated on her with guys, who had betrayed the version of him she had been holding onto.

"What are you going to do now?" Axon asked.

"With my life, you mean?" Lucy said, scratching absently over her leggings where the residual scab of her last cut of release hid. She hadn't felt the urge to hurt herself for over a week, nearly the entire time she was hospitalized. Axon's question was really hard to answer. There were only so many options for a formerly low-LP teenager. Even though she and her family had been assured by the doctors that it was unlikely she would die anytime soon, without the familiar ticking clock who could really be certain?

"Yeah. Have you thought about what you'll do with all your newfound free time?" Axon inquired lightly.

"I really don't know," Lucy said honestly. "I haven't really given it much thought."

Axon nodded.

"I mean, it's not like I can go to a high-LP school now, or anything. They start that track so early, I'm behind by like ten years. I would never be able to make it up." The kind of school Lucy went to only focused on structured fun, independent learning, and unrestrained impulses. Want to learn about owls? By all means, here are books and videos and a place to schedule time touching an actual owl. Was ice cream your favorite food? Have whichever flavor sounded best, and would you also like to learn how to make your own delicious snack? Low-LP kids were meant to enjoy every minute of life without much expectation in the way of achievement. Lucy hadn't taken any formal classes like people in mid- or high-LP academies but had merely covered the basics of reading, math, and science to have a rudimentary understanding of the world around her. Low-LP kids were given the tools they needed to learn more, if they wanted. Most didn't. Lucy had always been interested in learning new things, but she was never taught any of the discipline it took to learn something in a finite period of time, especially if it didn't intrigue her.

"Maybe. It depends what you want to do."

"I like the idea of doing something that will help people." She thought of her favorite nurse. Erica was so smart. She'd taken really good care of Lucy and seemed to like her job.

"Like a social worker?"

"No . . . Do you know if there's an LP requirement to be a nurse?"

"It's likely. It's a somewhat physical job, requires education . . . I don't know, maybe need to be high-mid?"

Lucy sighed. "That makes sense." Maybe there were other ways to help people that would be more available to her. They sat in silence for a moment, the swing rocking gently beneath them. "So, why are you here?"

"I wanted to make sure you were okay," he said with concern.

"Well, I'm not. And I probably won't be." She clenched her teeth together as she added, "What else do you want?"

"I'm missing an important flash drive. I think it's somewhere in your parents' dining room. I couldn't find it in the box your mom packed up."

Looking over at Axon, Lucy asked, "What's so important about it?"

"It's just work stuff."

His vagueness irritated her. "You're going to have to tell me more if you want my help. Does it have anything to do with my LP?"

He hesitated. "Sort of."

"What's on it?"

"I don't know yet, exactly, but . . . Look, this has to stay between me and you, okay? I could get in a lot of trouble for even having a copy of this."

"I can keep a secret."

Axon glared at her.

"Who exactly am I going to tell?" she quipped.

Contemplating for a moment, he gave in. "Okay."

Axon found the yellow smiley-face flash drive. It was, in fact, in the Hansons' dining room, having fallen behind the polished hutch that Nadine used for storing special occasion dishware and her mother's collection of silver teapots and serving platters. Lucy's mother would take the silver out once a year and give it a good polish; otherwise, it would go mostly unused in between cleanings. Birthdays, holidays, and annual countdown days—the day of each year that marked precisely one year closer to completing a lifetime—were the only times Lucy's mother permItted its use. Instead of passing it on to Lucy, Nadine would have to bequeath it to a niece or cousin, unless she was permitted to have another child whose own LP outstripped her own.

"Gotcha!" Axon said, victorious, fingering the flash drive. Scooting back a chair, he heaved his work bag onto the table and removed his tablet from an internal pocket. With his thumb, he pushed off the rubbery cap of the drive and inserted it into his tablet. Lucy took a seat next to him, leaning in with elbows on the table.

A prompt came up on the screen, and Axon clicked to display a long series of audio files. "Regina told me the bugs were smart. That they'd only record if they detected human voices. That way the audio should be pretty easy to sort through—they're all conversations."

"Who's Regina?" Lucy asked.

"She's the girl you so unceremoniously kicked out along with yours truly." He pointed a thumb toward his chest. "She's the one who gave me this drive. She works for Magnus Stryker."

"The President?" Lucy said, aghast.

"Yep. And sounds like Stryker's got himself some competition for the next election. I guess that's why the New Republican Party wanted her to bug him."

Lucy's eyes widened. "Wait, what?"

Axon explained what Regina Park had told him and why knowing what Stryker thought about Lucy's situation would be really helpful to determine what she should do next with her extra time.

"Why would the President care about me?"

"Well, to be honest, he might not. But my editor thought it was worth a shot, to see if we could use a reaction from him to stir the news about you."

Lucy nodded, understanding. "Ratings," she said morosely. "That's what I am to you?"

"How many times do we have to do this, Luce? Don't you see the value in having a front-row seat to the President's private dialogue during a time of social questioning of the Lifetime Potential system? This is about you, but it's also bigger than you. What if more people start living past their LP? This will tell us how he will react, what policies he might put into place regarding what to do with people like yourself."

"But I'm a medical anomaly!"

He laughed. "Yes, you are. But what if you're just the first of *many*?"

Did he seem hopeful? If he was, she wasn't sure why. She took a shot and tried to seem casual. "So, you think *you're* gonna be one?"

Axon dragged his finger with purpose across the touch-screen, scrolling through the numerous files. He grunted in response. "Probably not."

"But you never know," Lucy added.

He didn't reply and instead double-tapped on the first audio file and hit the play button.

"No sugar, and fill it half with milk," the voice of Magnus Stryker said. *"And one of those cheese danishes too,"* he added after a pause.

"Right away, sir," a female voice responded.

The faint noise of Stryker rearranging items on his desk or hitting the keyboard sounded, and the audio file ended.

"This is going to take a while," Axon sighed.

Lucy and Axon spent the better part of two hours listening to mostly one-sided conversations over the phone, straight from the President's mouth, covering issues anywhere from the price of natural gas in Asia to the reaction of another senator to proposed legislation Lucy hardly understood. It wasn't until they had skimmed through the audio of over a week's worth of chatter that a topic of interest arose.

"Sir, you asked for an update on the commuter train incident?"

"What's the death toll?" Stryker asked.

"Five."

The sound of papers shuffling came before his response. *"Looks like we will need a new head of the Department for Lifetime Potential and Health, Hamilton was one of the unlucky few."*

"Sir, I also have a status update from Captain Norman's team, who are performing the accident investigation. They think—" he began before Magnus cut him off.

"Accidents happen, Justin. Tell Norman to get on with it."

"This report is only preliminary, the team estimates it will take at least another week to determine the safety implications—"

Cutting him off again, Magnus said, "*I read the preliminary report. Faulty brakes and high speed over a curve in the tracks. Tell them the investigation is over. They have better things to do.*"

There was a pause where it seemed likely the other speaker was contemplating his words carefully. "*Sir,*" he began slowly before being interrupted for a third time.

"*That's a direct order, I don't want any excuses. Pass it on and get out of my office,*" Magnus said sharply.

There was the simultaneous sound of the door clicking shut and the tapping of fingers on keys starting up before Magnus spoke again. "*Kingsley. I saw the report. Job well done. Now I can get someone in who can actually control and prevent another situation like Hanson.*"

Momentary silence filled the audio as the speaker on the other end of the line replied.

"*I like to reward my people for their dedication, Kingsley. How does a ten percent bump sound to you?*" Pause. "*Uh-huh. Great.*" Pause. "*Yes, you too.*" The phone was set down with the familiar tap of plastic on plastic, and the audio ended.

Lucy stared, eyes widening. "Do you think when he said 'Hanson' he meant me?"

Axon leaned back in his chair, crossing his arms. He whistled an exhale and stared at the monitor.

"Axon?" Lucy tried again.

"Yeah," he said softly, a look of deep concentration on his face. "I think he meant you, Hanson."

Chapter 25

YAWNING, DAVID ARRIVED early to the IT department at Virionics, like he did most mornings. His internal clock ran perpetually fifteen minutes earlier than anyone else on his staff, so he was usually the first to arrive in the office. He liked it that way. It allowed him to get a start on any leftover tasks from the day before, dive back into his email, and set up the coffee. He had worked for Virionics for the past eleven years, the last three-and-a-half of which had been as the IT Director. Working hard came second nature to him; he loved to become completely absorbed in a task without interruption. Most people thought him a workhorse, introverted and lacking in other topics of conversation besides his work. He didn't watch the news, play any team sports, or read much. But he was an excellent programmer and problem-solver. David preferred the solitude of single-player video games and creating code for his personal 3D printer. There were countless plastic gadgets cluttering his small apartment that he had printed himself. He had been a little surprised when he was offered the new role upon the retirement of his old boss—there were more extroverted leaders among the team. But he was flattered all the same and worked hard to fight his instinct for solitude when a problem arose that required his intervention with the staff.

The soft beep of his badge rang through the quiet entryway as he stepped into the frigidly air-conditioned room which was the company's central IT hub. The first thing he noticed was though the room's overhead fluorescent lights were at their usual half-dim setting prior to the arrival of his staff, his office light was mysteriously bright. Had he forgotten to switch it off the night before? Walking closer, adjusting the weight of his backpack in order to swing it around his shoulder and rummage for the office keys, he noticed that the door stood slightly ajar. His stomach lurched. *Not again.*

The special requests usually came with unexpected visits from a large, troll-like man with a bulbous nose and a belly hanging over his belt. The man never introduced himself and David never asked. Nudging open the office door, David saw the familiar black trench coat, the man's buzz-cut head facing away from the door. Hearing David enter, the man turned around with a swivel of the chair.

He lifted a large envelope in his hands. "Something new for you."

David nodded and took the parcel. It was the second one in the past month, a little unusual compared to the typical once or twice a year he expected to see the man. "When do you need it by?"

"As soon as possible. The code needs to be activated for 10:53 this morning. It's all in here." His deep voice sent prickles down David's spine. "We expect you can make it happen."

"Yes. I'll get it done." David sat in his desk chair and busied himself booting up the computer, hoping the nameless man would consider his job done and leave. It worked, and he found himself alone in the small office with the envelope. Tearing it open, he found similar documents to those he had seen on other occasions the man visited. When he was promoted to IT Director for Virionics, David had signed a complicated non-disclosure agreement implying more than just monetary consequences if he were to speak of any special requests such as these to anyone else. "You'll be dead in five seconds flat if you violate the agreement," were the exact words of warning he remembered receiving when he took on the new role.

It wasn't clear what exactly the purpose of these little hacking projects was. All David knew was that he was meant to log into a portal using a password given in the envelopes delivered to him. The portal was generic-looking and did little to reveal its functionality. The only distinguishing feature of the login page was a small image of an hourglass in the upper-left corner above the space to enter a password. It was obvious to David that asking questions would not be tolerated, so he didn't dare. His job was relatively simple: log into the portal with the newly provided password, search the database for the account number, also provided, and modify the back end of the application. The ask was easy; he could practically generate the code in his sleep and would have loved to be able to copy and paste it from an external document and change only the specifics from the request, but unfortunately that was against the rules. Under no circumstances was there to be any evidence on his computer of the programming involved to complete this task, so with each instance he needed to start from scratch. After he edited the script and entered the appropriate date for the application's execution, he did a quick debug before exiting the system. The envelope's purpose served, it was promptly shredded in the machine within reach of his desk.

Though he was uncertain what the special requests were for, completing them always made him feel uneasy. He felt a griminess on his insides as if he had eaten something rotten as he wiped clammy palms on his blue jeans. Leaning down to reach the bottom drawer of the desk, he pulled out the flask kept for emergencies, stashed behind spare office supplies. David unscrewed the metal cap shakily and downed two swallows of its contents. The sounds of his first employees starting to arrive in the cool office caused him to hastily recap the container and quickly stash it back in its hiding place.

He hoped this would be the last special request to be given for a while.

Chapter 26

"SO, HOW DOES THIS WORK?" Magnus Stryker spoke into the phone.

"Have you ever asked a butcher how they cut up a cow to get the prime cut of filet?" the female voice questioned flatly.

"No," Stryker said. "Why would I?"

"You don't need to know this either." She paused a moment. "The serum will be delivered to your office via Postal Express tomorrow afternoon. There's a video demonstrating how to safely inject it yourself, into the intramuscular tissue of your upper arm. It's just like the annual vaccination. I'm sure you get the picture."

Stryker refused to admit that he almost never watched the needle puncture his skin—it seemed to hurt more when he did look. Needles made him a little queasy, but he wasn't about to reveal that to her. "I've got it."

"If you have questions, you can reach out to me."

"And what about my transition to Leydig? How does that work?"

"In a few years, depending on the outcome of the next election, you'll remove yourself from the public spotlight and simply fade into history. If you do win the next election, obviously you'll wait until after you've served your final term."

His impolite habit of interrupting took over. "*When* I win the next election."

"Sure," she said, sounding unconvinced. "When you win the next election, you will simply work through the term and wait at least eighteen months before your transition. How old are you now?"

The fact that she didn't seem to know annoyed Magnus. He was a highly public figure. "Sixty and four months," he said, his voice gruff.

"So, you'll be sixty-five after a second term," she said. "That works."

He could feel her nodding through the phone, irritated by the idea that this might be the first time she had assessed his age for the matter at hand. Though he was satisfied that she didn't repeat the word "if." "Well, it had better!" He barely kept himself from shouting. "This is my right as an elected president."

"It is precedent," she agreed.

His annoyance with her grew. "Can you guarantee my privacy?" he asked, changing gears.

"One hundred percent. Like I said, it's precedent. You aren't the first," she said, as though explaining why a five-year-old must wait to eat the cookies from the oven until they are cool. Clearly, she had not voted for him three-and-a-half years ago. He wondered vaguely if other sitting presidents had gotten the same attitude. Too bad he couldn't just replace her position. Separation of governmental branches created its own set of limitations.

"I know what *precedent* means," he said through halfway-gritted teeth as his fists clenched on the table. "What's the story to the public?"

"That you wish to spend your final days with family and close friends out of the public eye," she said automatically. "Of course, the others that have gone before you have set the stage in your favor. Tradition allows the former President to go quietly into the night after years of the intense watchful eye of the public and news stations. I would start plugging that idea now. Most standing presidents do."

"Easily done." Magnus immediately started thinking about how best to insert this idea into his next public statement. Luckily, subtlety was usually his strength when addressing the masses.

"Of course, there's the non-disclosure to sign."

"I assumed. What are the terms?"

"What you'd expect. Once you enter Leydig, you don't leave. You have limited contact with the outside world until a certain point."

She paused before saying sharply, "You'll need to keep up the appropriate appearances, of course."

"Obviously."

"So, we understand each other?"

"Yes. Send me the documents." Stryker was eager to get this conversation over with and get back to work. There were too many problems at hand to deal with.

Chapter 27

THE VIBRATION ON HER wrist informed Evergreen of a new incoming message. Dragging her arm out from underneath the pillow, she rolled over to see who had disturbed her sleep. She glanced at the nearby digital clock which showed a full ten minutes before her alarm was due to go off.

"Goddammit," she muttered, frustrated at the loss of those precious minutes of sleep. "This had better be good." Bringing her wrist up close to her face, she read through bleary eyes, *"Something is up with the President. Think he offed the Director of LP on purpose."* Blinking slowly, trying to refocus, she tapped to respond to Axon Davis.

"The President? Of what?" Evergreen typed back.

The text vibrated. *"THE President. Of our nation. I have proof."*

Evergreen was not awake enough for this mind-bender. *"Journalist proof or scientist proof?"* she typed, feeling snarky. She had really needed those last ten minutes of sleep.

"What's the difference?"

"'He said, she said,' versus 'it did and I observed it.'"

The phone rang, "Axe on Damien" showing on the caller ID. Evergreen had yet to correct his name. She ignored the call, not having enough time to hash out whatever it was he'd found and get to work at a reasonable time.

While it was unfortunate that Lucy's wrongly prescribed depression medication had nearly killed her, philosophical arguments about the girl's prolonged life aside, Evergreen was ever the rational thinker and refused to jump to conclusions about coincidence. Evergreen wasn't a medical doctor, and though Arizona had gone on at length about the improbability of a trained pharmacist prescribing the dose Lucy was taking, she was reluctant to believe in a conspiracy. Comforted by the fact that Arizona tended to add color and hyperbole to life, especially when Arizona knew that her best friend was keen on developments from Lucy Hanson, it was easy to dismiss foul play. Evergreen distinctly remembered an occasion where Arizona had very seriously informed her that it was likely she was about to undergo some complicated health issues, only to discover that Arizona had merely kissed a boy in their class who had been diagnosed with mono. The boy was quickly treated and recovered from his illness, and Arizona never experienced symptoms. This hadn't stopped Arizona from being entirely convinced that she had participated in a life-threateningly risky activity, if only for love. Or at least the love of the week. In a way, Arizona was oddly proud of her "close encounter with death," telling Evergreen how she might have been a goner had she kissed him just a day later when his viral load spiked. Evergreen knew better than to take everything she said at face value. Fortunately, when it came to more important matters, such as school, their grades, and future opportunities, Arizona was far more focused and grounded in reality.

Evergreen removed her bio-watch, setting it atop her bedside table, and readied herself for a shower. She heard the angry insect-like buzz of another incoming message against the tabletop but ignored it. She needed to be at work in forty-five minutes and didn't have time to text back. After coming home from her father's house the previous day, she had been called straight into work and only dragged herself away to get a few hours of sleep. Her patience for extra distractions was limited. This was her third week of processing small sections of DNA, altering pieces of the code with a predetermined sequence and realigning it back into an enzyme solution patented by Virionics. The enzyme solution acted as a vector to alter the rest of the DNA in the sample. A small aliquot of the solution was primed and pipetted into an electrified agarose gel matrix to determine if the targeted portion of DNA taken from the solution as a whole matched with the template sequence. Evergreen had been praised for her technique and ability to produce work free of contamination on her first try. New orders to create targeted DNA alterations came in every day to her department, and Evergreen was proud of the production she was able to contribute to the company.

Hours of DNA extraction later, Evergreen ripped off her gloves to jot some notes onto her desk computer when the familiar ping of an interoffice messaging rang through the small speakers. A window popped up in the corner of her screen from Dr. Ryan Delaney, a long-time colleague of her father's whom Evergreen had known nearly her entire life.

"Hey there! Have you heard from your dad today?" the message said.

She glanced at her wrist automatically, looking for a message from her father, and realized it was bare. *"No. But I left my bio-watch at home,"* she typed.

"I know he was out sick yesterday with his bad back, but he never misses the department meeting, even if he has to video chat in."

"His meds knock him out pretty hard, maybe he slept in and didn't realize the meeting was today?" Evergreen wrote.

"Maybe. If I don't hear from him in the next couple of hours, I think I'll go check and see if he's okay."

"Yeah, that sounds like a good idea. Should I be worried? Maybe I can go head over there and check on him myself."

"I'm sure he's fine. Sorry if I alarmed you. I'll keep you posted."

"Okay. Thanks."

Missing work the day before was uncommon enough for her father, but two days was concerning. He must have just fallen asleep and not realized what time it was, forgetting to call in. With work to distract her, Evergreen was able to keep her anxiety in check, but the longer she waited to hear back from Dr. Delaney the heavier the weight of apprehension grew in her gut. A few hours went by without any word, so she decided to send another message to Dr. Delaney.

"Heard anything?"

Ten minutes passed without a reply.

Evergreen glanced up at the wall clock, which read thirteen minutes past four in the afternoon. She could get away with leaving a little earlier than usual; her immediate workload was complete, and if all was well, she could easily return to the lab that evening. Everything would be fine, she was sure of it. *How sure are you?* A nasty voice from the dark side of her mind challenged. Hastily, she packed up her work bag and set off to check on her father.

Rush-hour traffic crept along at a glacial rate, and Evergreen tapped her heel in frustration. "Come on," she said with gritted teeth. "The light is green! Green means go!" she shouted, gesturing wildly at the car ahead of her, even though she knew they couldn't do anything about it. Cars were backed up from the intersection two streets ahead, and there was nowhere for the person in front to go. Finally, Evergreen moved far enough to make a swift right turn onto a side street, deciding to maneuver the backroads instead of the stop-and-go to the main thoroughfare. It might take longer, but at least she was moving.

Thirty minutes later, she made the turn onto her childhood street and into the long driveway of her father's home. His little car was parked in its usual spot, a dusting of pollen from a nearby tree covering the front windshield. Three other vehicles were parked behind his, one of which she recognized as the sporty SUV Dr. Delaney preferred, another an indistinctive black SUV. The third, she observed with a drop of her stomach, was an emergency vehicle, a white van with familiar blue and red stripes down the side.

Hurrying to park her car and nearly forgetting to shut the door behind her, Evergreen raced through the front door of the house.

"Dad?" Her anxious voice rang through the empty front room of her childhood home.

"In here," Dr. Delaney responded from several rooms away.

Evergreen sprinted toward his voice, into the living room where she had last seen her father resting on the couch. Three men stood with their backs to her as she rushed in. "What happened?!" Ryan Delaney and two men she didn't know turned around slowly, obstructing her view. One was wearing the official white button-down with the insignia of an emergency responder, the others in more formal suits, indistinguishable from each other except by the color of their ties: one red, one blue.

"The daughter," one of the men murmured to the other, who nodded.

"Evergreen," Ryan said slowly, his desire not to alarm her apparent.

"Let me see him!" Evergreen said, hearing the shrill panic in her own voice. She pushed past the bodies blocking her path to lay eyes on her father. There he was, in the same spot she had seen him last, eyes closed, only instead of the rhythmic breathing of a sleeping man, he wasn't moving.

"Dad?" Her voice cracked. "Daddy?" Evergreen's knees hit the floor next to the couch without her realizing she had moved. She touched his face gently. She felt the roughness of his cool, unshaved cheek and knew he was gone.

"It wasn't his time!" she shouted, glaring accusingly at the men she didn't know standing on the periphery. Feeling the wetness on her face before she realized she was sobbing, Evergreen pressed her head against her father's lifeless shoulder.

Ryan's hand rested gently on her back, and he kneeled next to her. "I know, honey."

"Well then, what happened?!" demanded Evergreen.

"Overdose of prescription painkiller," said Blue-Tie Man. "Was he suicidal the last time you saw him?" he asked.

Evergreen bristled. "No. He was *not*."

"Did he ever talk about ending his life before meeting his LP?" the man with the blue tie said in monotone, reading off an official-looking clipboard in his hands.

"No!" she exclaimed. "He would never have done this on purpose!"

"Just making sure. Please calm down, ma'am."

"Calm down?" Evergreen prickled, her voice low and dangerous, teetering on the edge of violence toward these ignorant men.

The suit continued, unperturbed. "This is the standard line of questioning whenever a suspicious death occurs. We haven't ruled out the possibility that this was an accident."

"He was such a careful man. I don't understand how this happened," Ryan said, emotion in his voice.

Was such a careful man? The implication of the past tense hit Evergreen like a ton of bricks. Fresh tears poured from her eyes. How could her father be dead? He was supposed to have nearly fifteen more years. He was supposed to retire, watch Evergreen's career blossom, and maybe even hold his first grandchild someday. None of this would happen now.

"These are powerful drugs sir, it's very possible he forgot the timing of his last dose and took too much too soon," the emergency tech said softly, as if trying to lessen the blow. "We will need to do an official examination to know for certain, but that's what it appears to be. For now, we need to move him," he said as another emergency official entered the room pushing a sterile-looking gurney.

"And I'll need to complete my own investigation," Blue Tie said seriously. "If this turns out to be a suicide, there are legal ramifications." He nodded pointedly toward Evergreen.

"He didn't kill himself!" Evergreen shouted, her anger rising like bile in her throat.

"There does not appear to be any foul play at hand here," the official in the red tie stated without making eye contact as he pulled out a camera to take photos of the room. "Whether it was accidental or not, it appears he did do this to himself. Any evidence of planning, such as a suicide note, will allow us to determine which it was."

The two emergency technicians in white uniform shirts began to position her father on the stretcher and prepared to wheel him to the van parked out front. Holding a clipboard, Red Tie continued to speak and ask questions to which she could only merely nod or shake her head in response. As if in slow motion, she watched as her father was pushed out of the room, out of the home she had grown up with him in. Fatherless. She was fatherless now. Without a father. Her mother was gone, now her father too, long before she was ready to live without him. Without his familiar teasing and cajoling when Evergreen was feeling overwhelmed. Without his mentoring and support. There was so much more she needed from him and now . . . everything was different. Those years were taken from her as much as they were taken from him.

Rage started to bubble under the surface. Why hadn't he been more careful with his medication? Why hadn't she kept a better eye on things? She should have stayed another night and helped him. Why hadn't he asked her to stay? Instead, she had been so absorbed in her own world, her own problems, that she couldn't see he needed her help. And he was too prideful, too concerned he'd interrupt her career trajectory to force her to pay attention.

A wave of intense sadness muddled with guilt washed through her body as she thought of how much he had loved her. She could barely breathe. All of that was gone, his candle blown out, leaving behind the faint trail of hot smoke and residual burning in the center of her chest.

Chapter 28

AXON HAD TOLD HER A few times already that the audio files collected from the President's office would be analyzed and probably used by other journalists at the *Times*, but Lucy didn't let that stop her from going full speed ahead in coming to her own conclusions. She constantly came up with new theories and explanations for things they were hearing. While they ranged from reasonable to outlandish, Axon had kept his promise and humored her with tasks related to the files. For days, Lucy had been cataloging the audio files into labeled bytes for consumption by other writers. She felt like part of the process. Part of something. Her mind had more clarity than ever; the break from her medication was invigorating and filled her with purpose. So, she was rejected from shadowing Axon's role as a wake journalist? Whatever. She could find something else. The *Times* had been concerned about publicity with her working there, so she could take on a research role or even publish under a pseudonym. Lots of people did it. Why not her?

As she daydreamed about the possibilities of a life doing investigative journalism, she heard Axon's now-familiar knock on her parents' front door. Nadine had forbidden the reissue of the journalist's house key and only tentatively agreed to his persistent presence in her home. Lucy had her suspicions of what her parents must use as rationale for allowing Axon back into the Hanson house. She figured that if she, Nadine's maybe (probably not, but maybe) soon-to-be-dead daughter, wanted Axon to be around, then her mother would reluctantly allow it. Whatever the reason, she didn't know, but Ed and Nadine had been hovering more than usual lately, constantly asking if she was doing okay, whether she wanted some pancakes, ice cream, etc. You name the guilty pleasure food, they offered it. Lucy's relationship with mortality made them uncomfortable. Using food as a coping mechanism, not so much.

Axon rapped on the heavy door again as Lucy worked the latches to unlock it.

"Coming, I'm coming!" She undid the final latch. "Hey. Where've you been all day?" she asked, opening the door to him.

"Lunch wake," Axon said.

"Ugh, I hate those," Lucy said, distracted as she craned her neck to see if any residual journalists or protesters remained posted at the end of her driveway despite the quickly approaching darkness. The street was empty.

"Too late in the day to have stayed up all night in anticipation, too early in the day to really get people in a partying mood." Axon shrugged off his bag onto a nearby chair in the Hansons' dining room.

"How old?" Lucy asked as Axon started to unpack the contents of his bag.

"Eighty-one," Axon said before adding, "It was pretty sterile."

Lucy giggled.

"How many files did you get done today?" Axon asked.

"Umm . . . some?" Lucy bit her lip and turned the computer screen around to show him her progress. She had gone down a diversionary path searching for articles on herself, of which there were several, and reading through the thousands of comments posted by mostly anonymous users. To balance the emotions provoked, ranging from elation at finding something extremely positive to anger and frustration that people *just didn't understand her,* she'd found respite in music videos and looking at animal pictures. Unsurprisingly, she hadn't catalogued too many audio files.

Axon glanced at her completed work and nodded. "Okay. Looks good," he said, though Lucy sensed his disappointment.

"I worked all day!" Lucy declared, though she knew this was a distortion of the truth of how she had spent the afternoon.

"Trust me, my colleagues at the *Times* will appreciate it," Axon said. "We'll just keep at it tonight so I can send them off tomorrow."

"I can make coffee," Lucy said eagerly, dashing toward the kitchen. Spending more time working with Axon that evening would keep her on task. And since he didn't seem upset with her, she must be doing a good job proving she was capable of handling more projects. "How do you want it?" she hollered from the adjacent room as she fiddled with the coffee maker.

"Black," Axon said, more than loud enough for her to hear.

Carefully, she walked heel-to-toe to bring out the steaming coffee cups, filled slightly too full and dribbling onto her mother's clean floors. "Coffee!" she said, using overenthusiasm to quiet the slight guilt for not accomplishing more for him.

Axon nodded. "Thanks."

They sat in relative silence long enough to finish second cups of coffee and eat a snack before the caffeine seemed to take enough effect to perk Axon up. "Oh, yeah. Guess what *I've* got for you?" he said coyly.

"What?" Lucy asked, plopping back down into her chair, having returned the dishes to the kitchen.

Axon pulled a gilded envelope from his computer bag and waved it in front of her. In fancy calligraphy, the front of the envelope was addressed to her, though being hand-delivered it bore no postage stamp.

"What is it?" she asked, swiping it and curbing the urge to tear into the letter like a child at their fifth birthday party.

"Open it," he said.

The outside of the envelope glimmered faintly in the dim light of the house as Lucy carefully slit the top of the thick paper, trying hard not to rip the contents. Maybe this was the *Times'* retraction of their refusal of her internship idea? Did job offers come in such decorative packages? She didn't know. She'd had never had one.

"*Dear Lucy Hanson,*" it said in loopy script. "*You are cordially invited to the annual Virionics gala fundraiser, which supports the continued research and fight for disease prevention, done every day by our talented scientists. We would like to welcome you as the guest of honor and give you an opportunity to share your story with our scientific community. We believe that your experience will bring hope to many individuals and their families living with low Lifetime Potential. We sincerely hope you consider our offer.*" The letter went on to give details of the event and was signed with sincerest regards from people whom Lucy had never heard of but assumed must be important.

"Virionics wants me to be the guest of honor at their next *gala*," Lucy said, practically dancing in her seat with excitement. She hadn't been to any sort of party or event since her own wake, and had certainly never been the guest of honor somewhere she didn't know just about everybody in the room.

"I know," Axon said with a conspiratorial lift of his eyebrows. "Excited?"

"I mean, yeah!" Lucy said. "What . . . How?" She was at a loss for words. "How did this happen? Where did you get this invitation from?"

"From Virionics, duh," Axon said, rolling his eyes.

"You know what I mean!" Lucy shouted, exasperated.

"Calm down, calm down. Your parents will think you're kicking me out again."

Her face reddened, guilt at his reminder rising hot into her cheeks. "Tell me!" she begged.

"I had to pull some strings!" Axon said, arms up in surrender.

"Really?!" Lucy beamed.

"Well. My boss did," Axon added, prompting Lucy to playfully smack his arm.

"Why?"

To Lucy's irritation, Axon shrugged. "She thought you should make yourself into a more positive figure in the media. Maybe that would—"

"What do you mean by *more positive*?" Lucy asked sharply.

"I mean," Axon said, hesitating for a moment. "Even the President thinks the media attention is out of control, probably because there is such a debate whether or not you should live and what you should do next."

"Then why didn't your work let me intern?" Lucy mumbled.

"What?"

"Nothing. Go on."

"Look, Lucy, this is just the start of a new direction you'll be able to take. And the more you stay relevant, the more leverage you have to create your own path. Lay your claim on the future. Do your own thing."

Lucy nodded as the fantasies of how her life could unfold started to become less fuzzy and more solid. Maybe the *Times* was wrong—she could take on a journalistic role in the public eye. If this fundraiser went well, maybe other people would be interested in what she had to say. Her experience was unique. As the only girl to live past her LP, she could inspire so many people. People would be so impressed by her willingness to donate her time and body to science, just for the purpose of unraveling the mystery of her survival. She was basically starting a revolution. Just think of how many doors would be opened to her! And what would she wear?

"Yeah," she said dreamily. "I totally could."

"We should work on what you're going to say. A lot of people will be there. Important people. And you'll need to come across as polished but still in need of sympathy."

"What should I wear?" Lucy said over him before processing what he had said. "Wait, sympathy?"

"We can figure that out later." Axon rolled his eyes. "And yes, sympathy is really important."

"So, basically you want people to feel bad for me?"

"Not exactly," he said slowly. "The most effective message would make people feel something. Hope would be best. Everyone who has a low LP wants more time, especially parents of children like you. So, if they see you as this shiny beacon of hope and possibility for their own children, they are much more likely to be supportive of things you may do in the future."

"Some of my classmates' parents wouldn't agree," she muttered.

"That's because the opportunity to use your experience has passed for them. Most of your classmates are dead."

Lucy cringed at the truth. "Exactly, so they're all just mad that I'm the special one who outlived them all. All they're going to feel is jealousy."

"Maybe." Axon paused thoughtfully. "I think the possibility of using your life extension as a starting point for finding a way to extend the lives of future children will strike an altruistic chord for them. Even if it won't affect their own child, it could help others. So long as you walk the straight and narrow, cooperating with researchers and acting with humility about your luck in being the first," he said, the implied message of *behave* clear to Lucy. "You *are* special, but you can't act like you think that way. People won't respond to that."

Lucy crossed her arms with a pout. "I don't act that way," she said, hoping to get Axon to agree with her aloud. Instead, his attention appeared to be elsewhere, responding to a text message.

"Yeah, of course not," he said distractedly. Axon began to collect his belongings and shove them into his bag. "Hey Lucy-Bella, I've got to get going," he said, still looking down at his screen.

"Why?" Lucy asked, wondering if this new urgent matter had to do with her, and hoping he'd divulge.

"Don't worry about it," Axon said.

"But doesn't this have to be done by tomorrow to send out to people at the *Times?*" she asked, changing tactics.

"It's fine. You've got this, don't you?" He looked up at her with confidence she didn't feel.

"You want me to finish by myself?"

"Yeah. You can do it, Hanson. I'll check in again tomorrow, okay?" he said, standing up and pulling on his leather jacket.

"Um, ok. Yeah. I'll keep working on it. Where are you going, though?" she asked again, but Axon was already at the front door.

"Just let the caffeine be your guide!" he shouted over his shoulder without answering her question. Lucy sighed with irritation and disappointment at being left out of the loop and went to make more coffee.

Chapter 29

RYAN DELANEY HAD BEEN Evergreen's father's close friend and coworker for nearly three decades, a fact which he had used to finally convince Evergreen to let him host Gerald Mason's wake at his home. The tidy carriage house located over the three-car garage far back from Delaney's grand city house would serve as her private space in which to seclude herself in her time of grief. Evergreen had taken a week off work with the understanding that she could take more if necessary. Her father had been well-respected at the company to which he had dedicated all of his working years, if Evergreen's email account was any indicator. The vast number of people she didn't know who'd reached out with their condolences and best wishes was overwhelming. She hadn't realized how far her father's reach had gone until she recognized the CEO and members of the executive board in the wake crowd, happily enjoying the party.

The house had several large downstairs rooms where people gathered to talk in small groups, danced in larger ones, and found privacy in the dimly lit garden between the back of the building and the carriage house. Laughter, music, and the familiar loud voices of jovial party guests filled the house with all the evidence of a traditional wake, save for one detail: the guest of honor was already dead.

After a couple of hours, the crush of the noisy rooms, and the repetitive conversations Evergreen held with what seemed like each and every person who crossed the threshold combined with the pain of high-heeled shoes she had stupidly chosen for the occasion finally defeated her. The numerous cocktails she had siphoned dry from tiny straws in crystal tumblers had numbed her brain enough to comment honestly on another woman's dress, calling it "A more disappointing impression of a garbage bag than the off-brand kind bought from the gas station on the corner." The woman's horrified expression at Evergreen's lack of buffer between thought and speech was a sure-fire sign she needed to retreat from blameless guests.

Evergreen stumbled on even flooring in her foreign-feeling heels but quickly regained her balance, reminding herself that she was surrounded by all of her bosses. *How inconvenient.* Making her way into one of the cozier rooms, with high windows and squishy furniture artfully distributed, she spotted Arizona sharing a love seat with a man she didn't recognize. Arizona gestured with her hands and leaned in flirtatiously while her crossed knees rested subtly against her companion's leg.

"Ev!" she shouted, suddenly spotting her friend and gesturing wildly for her to come and join them in the cozy nook.

Evergreen made her way over, using the backs of chairs as support for her aching feet, pretending she didn't also need the crutch to counteract the alcohol she had consumed. "Hey," she said, sitting down heavily in the chair opposite the couple.

"Evergreen, this is . . ." Arizona hesitated, obviously forgetting his name but attempting to make it seem as if she were just allowing him to introduce himself.

"Jordan," the man said, his smile showing a narrow gap between his front teeth which Evergreen immediately found endearing. His hand hovered outstretched for several seconds before she realized what he was waiting for and returned his handshake.

"Evergreen," she said, pointing to herself. She imagined Arizona's new friend might need help remembering his companion's name too and half-shouted over the cacophony of conversations and jazzy music playing from invisible speakers, "And this is Arizona." Jordan nodded, smiling his gap-toothed grin again.

"Who are you? This is my party, and I don't know . . . Who invited you?" she asked, an almost imperceptible slur to her words, not caring whether her question was rude.

"Dr. Delaney is my boss. I've met your father on a few occasions. I am sorry to hear that he died so unexpectedly," Jordan said with what appeared to be sincerity.

Evergreen's solemn nod almost felt sarcastic. Every conversation that night had felt like déjà vu, and it was becoming irritating. Arizona, sensing danger, chimed in sweetly, "Jordan, can you get my friend and I a couple of drinks?"

"Sure," he said, pushing himself off the couch and simultaneously resting his palm atop Arizona's bare knees. "What do you both want?" he asked.

"Champagne," Arizona said quickly. "And bring the whole bottle," she added as he started to walk away.

"And rench fries!" Evergreen hollered after his retreating figure, giggling. "Champagne, huh? What are we celebrating?" she asked, her eyes focusing back on Arizona.

"It's the only thing I know Delaney has run out of already. That'll keep him a few minutes," she said, smiling impishly. "Come," she gestured, patting the empty couch cushion Jordan had just vacated. "Sit with me, babe."

Evergreen obeyed and shuffled over next to her friend. "My feet hurt," she whined.

"Do you want me to take your shoes off?"

Evergreen nodded childishly, a mock pout crossing her face. "Hurt."

Arizona sighed and unstrapped the shoes from Evergreen's feet, dropping them with a clacking noise to the flagstone floor. "How you doing, honey?" she asked, putting her arm around Evergreen's shoulders. Evergreen rested her head on Arizona's shoulder.

"I told some lady she looked like a garbage bag," Evergreen admitted after a few moments. A sheepish grin crept across her face, causing the girls to burst into laughter.

"Oh my gosh, you're going to make me pee!" Arizona said, clutching her side, trying to regain control.

"I think she was my boss's wife," Evergreen added between gasps of breath, tears of mirth beading from her eyes. "Pretty sure that was a bad idea, even if it was true."

"*In vino veritas*," Arizona said with mock wisdom. "You get a free pass tonight, don't worry about it. And if it's the lady I think you're referring to, you are one hundred percent accurate in your assessment of her fashion choices."

The laughter felt good, a kind distraction from the present situation. "Yes, well, I'm very wise," said Evergreen.

"Is there anything I can do to make you feel better?" Arizona asked, changing gears.

Evergreen shrugged and crossed her legs, hands in her lap.

"You know what makes *me* feel better?"

"Huh?" Evergreen grunted.

"I always think of it as steps for the whole 'mind, body, soul.' And not necessarily in that order," she said to a confused-looking Evergreen. "Well, first there's the look," Arizona began seriously, "and I'd say you nailed that," she added, appraising Evergreen with approval. Apart from the uncomfortable, albeit stylish shoes, Evergreen had selected a form-fitting mid-length black dress with long lace sleeves, a conservative neckline, and a low back.

"Thanks," Evergreen smirked. "Is that the 'body' part?"

"Oh no. That's for your soul. When you look good, you feel good."

"That a tagline from one of your products?"

"Maybe . . ." Arizona said with mock slyness. "The next part is the mind, and it appears you're already on your way there." She tapped Evergreen's nearly empty tumbler. "Something to lift you up, let go a little bit. It helps."

Evergreen nodded and sucked down the rest of the drink with the airy slurping noises of an empty glass. "Mmmhmm. And what's 'body'?"

"Find someone to worship it for the night," Arizona said coyly as Evergreen burst out in a fit of laughter.

"And I suppose that's what Jordan is for?" Evergreen asked after regaining her composure.

"For me, yes."

Evergreen rolled her eyes.

"What? I'm sad too! And besides, these are my rules. I need to set an example for you."

Just then, Jordan returned carrying a bottle of red wine, three goblets clutched precariously by their stems, and a plate of snacks. "Sorry, ladies, I looked around but there was no champagne left anywhere. Hope this will quench your thirst," he said, plopping down on the chair Evergreen had recently vacated and removing the half-out cork with a small *pop*. He served three generous pours, handing the glasses around.

"Cheers," Arizona said solemnly. "To Gerald Mason, scientist, colleague, friend, and father."

"Amen," Evergreen said with a hiccup. "I always get hiccups when I drink red wine," she said by way of explanation.

"It's true," Arizona agreed, snagging some of the appetizers Jordan had brought and eating them in two bites. "Eat something, Ev," she instructed her friend.

Mutely, Evergreen assisted Arizona in gobbling down the food. She hadn't realized how hungry she was. Jordan and Arizona picked up their banter where they'd left off when Evergreen arrived while she slouched back into the cushions and sipped idly from the wine glass. Maybe Arizona was right. She needed to do what felt good. The last few days had flown by in a blur of faces and a flurry of decisions she had to make. Despite the unexpected timing, her father's friends had turned out in droves. He had been well respected. Sensing that Arizona and Jordan would be happier occupying the dark corner of Dr. Delaney's house alone, Evergreen plucked up the straps of her heels and set down the half-drunk glass of wine. She gave a small wave to Arizona, who returned it with a wink as she slipped out the back door of the house.

The grass was cool and liberating on her bare feet, still damp from the rain the previous evening. She relished the feeling, walking slowly toward the carriage house where she could be apart from the crush of the party. The day had been hot, and the wide-open windows carried the music and the lull of conversation across the lawn. She reached the heavy wooden door of the guest house, pushing it open with a creak of the hinges. The internal motion-sensing lights slowly turned on to a dim evening glow in greeting. She shut the door behind her with a thud and was overwhelmed with the abrupt silence. A wave of emotion swelled in her chest at the thought of being completely alone, existing in a world where her father did not. She hadn't been ready for this. Evergreen could feel the tears returning to her eyes, the sob building in her throat, and forced herself to swallow it. Hastily, she went to fling open every single window in the small house, filling the vacuum with the noise of the party carrying across the lawn.

She sat down on the couch, hunching over to rest her chin on her hands, feeling less alone. Maybe Arizona was right and she needed to give into things that made her feel good. Her mind wandered to Zane for the first time in weeks, and she found the jilted feeling she'd once held had dissipated. Sex was one of the benefits of relationships, particularly with her ex-boyfriend, whose talent in that area had surprised her. The latest rumor among her former classmates was that he and Silver Bennett had broken up. She contemplated sending him a message. Just for a night—what harm would that be? Evergreen had no intention of reattaching herself, but at least it would be familiar comfort. She scanned her memories of their months together, re-calling pleasurable moments they had shared and fantasizing about how nice it would be to repeat some of them. Realizing that she was reminiscing about a guy whom she herself had described as arrogant, self-absorbed, and immature, she scoffed and ran her fingers through her hair in frustration. She was a mess. Arizona might be right about feeling good, but she certainly didn't need to crawl back to her ex to achieve it. Standing up, Evergreen went to turn out the lights in the room to set the mood for what she had in mind. Just as she turned down the dimmer, there was a soft knock at the door.

Tentatively, she went to answer it, opening the door with a groan of the hinges. Axon Davis stood at her doorway, hands in the pockets of his dark leather jacket, the light of the half-moon reflecting subtly off his sleek black hair.

He smiled at her. "Hey."

Before Evergreen even processed what she was doing, her arms were around his neck and she was kissing him. Feeling Axon's initial surprise at her embrace wane and his hunger to explore her heighten, she gave in to the instincts of her body and guided him to the nearby bedroom where she didn't need to think.

Chapter 30

THE LIGHTS REMAINED off, which would make it difficult to locate his clothing, scattered hastily as it was around the room. Instead, they lay there trying to catch their breath. Evergreen made eye contact with Axon, provoking laughter from them both, equivalent to a resigned shoulder-shrug.

"Well, that was unexpected," he said, staring upwards at the ceiling and grinning.

"Yeah. Sorry about that." Evergreen, not sounding sorry, rolled onto her side to face him, her warm arm stretching across his chest.

"Apology accepted." Axon stretched with a groan and a crack from his back as Evergreen chuckled in amusement.

"How did you even know where I was?" she asked.

"Your friend Arizona messaged me, told me what happened, and said you needed me to come here." Axon rolled toward Evergreen, sweeping her blond hair, tangled beneath both of them, out of the way of his supporting elbow. In his experience, girls didn't like when their hair was pulled, unless it was on purpose.

"*Of course,* she did." Evergreen rolled her eyes in exasperation. "That girl," she added with a frustrated sigh.

"I couldn't even get my condolences out before *someone* jumped my bones."

"I thought I was already forgiven!" she said with mock outrage.

"Mmhmm . . ." Axon said, brushing her lower lip with his thumb. She smiled and turned her face into his chest as he wrapped his arms around her and her thick blond hair. They lay in silence for a few minutes before Axon said softly, "I am sorry to hear about your dad, though." A pleasant breeze blew through the open windows.

Evergreen shrugged in his arms and said quietly, "Thanks."

Sensing it was best to leave it at that, Axon relaxed, feeling her breath become even and her arm grow heavy on his chest. Just as he began to drift off too, the distinct mutter of low conversation and swish of shuffling feet through the grass roused him. Listening hard, he could tell the speakers were both men, whose voices he did not recognize, yet one of them had a distinctive lisp. Their conversation grew louder as they approached the back of the house, probably assuming privacy from eavesdroppers.

"Well, do you think he intended to go public?" one of the men asked, his voice clear through the open window above the bed where Axon and Evergreen lay.

"None of us are certain, but he could have," the other man said, his pronunciation of "certain" coming out as "*thurtan*." "He knew the rules," he continued. "No logging in outside of the open forum window."

"It doesn't seem like he acted on whatever it was he thought he was doing."

"He attempted to download files. That seems obvious enough to me that he was up to something. The system's in place for a reason: to deal with snitches like him."

"Even if we didn't necessarily have proof of his intention?"

"Like I said, Gerald Mason knew what he agreed to when he joined Hourglass. But he always thought he was special, somehow above the rules just because of his status in the company."

"Still, shouldn't we continue to investigate? What if it was triggered by mistake?"

"What's done is done. And why might that worry you?" he said with an air of authority, making it clear he was responding to a subordinate.

"Oh, no reason, no reason," the other man said quickly. "I just wonder what the old man was up to."

The man with the lisp grunted in agreement, apparently satisfied. "Doesn't matter what he was up to, it's been taken care of. The old man was a relic who needed to be voted out of the committee long ago anyway. His altruistic opinions always got in the way of reasonable progress. Always going on about equal distribution among classes, what a crock of shit. It's a privilege to die on time. He got what was coming."

Trying not to make a sound, Axon shifted himself to glance down at Evergreen. His pupils having adjusted to the semi-darkness of the room, he saw that her eyes were wide open as she twisted her body slowly to stare up at him. Her expression was difficult to discern, but he could assume a mirroring of his own look of confusion mixed with disbelief. It was obvious she understood it would be a bad idea to alert the men to their presence on the other side of the wall. They waited quietly while the two men continued to discuss vague office politics and an upcoming corporate event. Slowly, their voices became less audible as they made their way back to the main house. It wasn't until then that Axon sucked in a breath, not realizing he had been breathing so shallowly.

"Wow," was all he could whisper. Axon was certain he'd heard them walk away, but the gravity of their discussion warranted a certain amount of caution. "Did he . . . ?"

"Yep," Evergreen said deadpan.

"So, your dad . . . He works for Virionics, right?" Evergreen turned her face toward him. "Worked, I mean," Axon corrected.

Evergreen grimaced slightly, as if the use of past tense to describe her father was physically painful. "He was one of their chief scientists, had been for years."

"Did you recognize either of those guys' voices?"

"No. But they clearly work for the company too."

"Yeah." Axon paused. "Wait, how do you know that?"

"Project Hourglass," she murmured before untangling herself from the bed sheets and stumbling to get her balance. She stood and started rummaging in a duffel bag on the floor nearby.

"What are you looking for?" Axon sat up in bed.

"The files. I know it's in here," she muttered to herself, shifting belongings around in the bag. The sound of unzipping preceded a small cry of jubilation. "Yes. Found it." She gripped something small in her hand.

"What?" Axon asked again. "Evergreen, you know what this means, right?"

"Of course, I know what it means," she snapped, grabbing a computer from on top of the white dresser and returning to sit on the edge of the bed. Producing a flash drive, Evergreen struggled to insert it into the computer port, trying one way and then the other, attempting to make it fit. "Stupid thing," she griped before securing it into place. The light of her screen shone dimly in the bedroom, and Axon caught a quick glimpse of her desktop background, a younger Evergreen and her parents at the beach. A new window popped up, obscuring the image, and Evergreen searched through the drive with a series of clicks and rapid typing.

"Here it is," she said finally.

Axon moved closer to her so he could see better. Her mouse hovered over a file marked *Project Hourglass* and she double-clicked.

A pop-up appeared. "Corrupt File. No access," it read.

"Huh?" Evergreen said.

"What is it?"

"It . . . it won't open," she said, clicking the OK button on the pop-up, making it disappear. She tried again with the same result. "Why won't it open?!" she asked, voice rising in anger and frustration, clicking and double-clicking the file, yielding the same result. Axon watched patiently as she tried troubleshooting, growing visibly more agitated, clicking different options, resetting the drive, restarting her computer. Nothing worked. "WHAT THE FUCK!" she finally shouted, her frustration climaxing. Slamming the computer screen shut and holding her head in her hands, she started sobbing.

Surprised and confused, Axon could think of nothing else to do but slide himself slowly nearer to put an arm around her shoulders in comfort. He sat in silence, rubbing Evergreen's back gently, allowing her to regain composure.

"It's my fault," she moaned.

Still having no idea what she meant, Axon said, "Of course it's not."

"Yes, it is!" she declared angrily and stood up, her abruptness causing the computer to clatter to the floor. Bending to pick it up and walking it back to the dresser-top, she grabbed the box of tissues sitting nearby and blew her leaking nose.

"Evergreen, I don't know how any of this could be your fault. People die," he said with as much kindness as he could. "Though rarely unexpectedly," he conceded, "it's just part of life."

She shook her head. "No. No. You don't get it. You're not getting it."

Her exasperation with him was beginning to get irritating. "Okay, so tell me," he said slowly, trying not to show his mounting frustration. "Why don't you sit down," he suggested as she started pacing back and forth across the small bedroom.

Ignoring the suggestion, she began to share all about how she had been looking for access to the articles they'd wanted in the Virionics database on her father's computer. How she had been interrupted when trying to copy the files from a folder marked "Project Hourglass" and had hastily ended the process. "And those men. They said my father 'got what he deserved,' and that 'not everyone gets the privilege of a timely death,' or some shit. Don't you see?!"

"So, you're saying you think his death wasn't an accident?"

"That's exactly what I'm saying. And it's because of me." She tapped her fingers against her chest.

"I'm still not seeing how this is your fault."

"Because *I* tried to open the Hourglass files," she snapped.

"So, you opening the files somehow made it so your father gets murdered? That's insane," Axon said.

"I know! But it seems too perfect to be a coincidence. I access some files that I'm not supposed to on his computer. They think he did it, and for whatever reason, he's not supposed to either. So, they kill him."

"Evergreen," Axon began as patiently as he could. "There would have been a medical evaluation of your father's body. It was deemed an overdose."

"Maybe one of them poisoned him in his sleep!" She threw her hands up. "I don't know! I just know that they are responsible. Whoever they are. Someone inside Virionics wanted him dead."

"You really think the company he worked for his entire career, the company you work for, the company that helps the entire country stay healthy, somehow has gone against everything they stand for and set out to murder your father?"

"There's only one way to prove it," Evergreen said pensively, as if an idea had just occurred to her.

"And what's that?"

"We need to examine his body ourselves."

"We?" Axon asked, exasperated. "We should not be doing that." He paused in mock deliberation. "Nope. *We* are not doing that."

"Come on, Axon! I need your help with this!"

"Why?" He sighed. "Why do you need my help with this?"

"I thought we were a team! Look, this is the next piece of the puzzle."

"What, about Lucy Hanson? How?"

She groaned. "The files, remember? I was looking to find files we wanted, somehow opened something classified on my father's computer, and he died. It's logical."

"It's far-fetched." Axon shook his head.

"Is that a 'no,' you won't help me?" Evergreen asked.

With a deep sigh, he looked up at her desperate face. Her green eyes were rimmed in red, making them starker against her pale freckled skin. Despite the tears, her beauty was unquestionable, and Axon felt his insides soften. "So, how exactly do we do this?"

"*We* need to go to the morgue."

Chapter 31

"HOW DO YOU EXIST WITH so much junk in your car?" Evergreen commented as she daintily picked up a dirty-looking pair of gym shorts from the front seat of Axon's car. Tossing them over the headrest into the backseat, she pushed paper bags, receipts, water bottles, and other spare items aside with her foot to create space for her legs. The back seat was covered in clothing, folders, and stacks of papers haphazardly thrown into piles that inevitably shifted around while on the road.

He shrugged. "I'm never home."

Evergreen thought of the neatly stacked personal items in her desk drawers at work and found she couldn't relate to his haphazard organizational scheme. Her toiletries were tidily arranged in order of use, with everyday items such as mints and dental floss toward the front, feminine products and a change of clothing at the back. Office supplies were kept in the top drawer only, where pens were aligned in the same direction, extra staples lived in their box, and her minute orange pencil sharpener was always emptied after use. The state of chaos Axon's vehicle existed in gave her anxiety.

Still wearing the black dress from the party, Evergreen attempted to cross her legs but was constricted by the limited space of the front seat. Sliding the chair backwards was not an option due to the excessive collection of Axon's belongings. Settling for pushing her knees together so as not to appear indecent, Evergreen gazed out the window as the dark houses of Dr. Delaney's neighborhood passed by. Axon had brought her out of her state of numbness for at least a little while. Now she was fueled by a shaky, exhilarating, and terrifying desire to find evidence to support her new theory. Her father couldn't have just *died*. That didn't happen. Gerald Mason was a smart man with accolades and degrees to prove it. He had dedicated his lifetime to supporting the health and wellness of the community around him—who would even want to hurt him? The question danced around her brain, feeling more wide-awake than she had for days. She wasn't even completely certain what they'd find, but her gut told her this was a good place to start.

"You could have let me drive," she added. "My car is much more comfortable."

"No driving for you." Axon mimed drinking from a bottle with a *glug-glug* sound effect. "Now quit complaining, I'm a reluctant chauffeur as it is."

Twenty minutes later, they pulled up to the county morgue where her father's body was supposed to be. The parking lot was dimly lit and nearly empty as they pulled right into a front spot. Evergreen exited the car as gracefully as possible, the flat sneakers she had put on making it far easier than her previous footwear to gain balance.

"Now, look sad," Axon instructed, holding open the front door of the building for her.

Tugging down the bunched hem of her dress with a wiggle, Evergreen glared at him for a moment before walking through the door.

A lone employee sat at the front desk looking half asleep. Seeing them, he ran a hand through his curly red hair and rubbed his eyes, attempting to look more alert. "How can I help you?"

"We've just come from a wake," Axon began with a solemn voice.

The man behind the desk nodded with understanding. "A relative?"

"My father. Gerald Mason?" Evergreen chimed in, stepping closer to the high counter. She could feel her hands shaking and shoved them into the pockets of her light jacket, not wanting to give anything away.

"I'm assuming you want to see him?"

She nodded, and he began to flip through some papers on a nearby clipboard before looking up with a smile.

"You're in luck. Hasn't been cremated yet," he said before quickly correcting, his smile fading, "I mean. Not luck. I'm sorry. Sorry for your loss." He sighed, looking up at them in apology. "I'm not usually covering nights. Mr. Mason is still here. I'll take you back. But first . . ." He turned to face the wall of cubbies behind him and grabbed a clear plastic bag of items, which he handed to Evergreen. "His personal effects. Everything he was admitted with. Except his bio-watch, of course."

"Why not?" Axon asked.

"Biohazard," Evergreen and the attendant said at the same time. The miniscule port on the side of everyone's watch, meant for a pinprick of the user's blood, meant it was considered biohazardous. The blood samples were periodically used as a calibration or internal check against the circulating bio-trackers that fed consistent biological metrics of the user's bodily functions. This feedback loop allowed users to understand when there were impending health risks and to seek treatment. Gerald's watch would have beeped aggressively as the levels of medication became more and more toxic to his internal organs. Obviously, he didn't hear it, or couldn't intervene to save himself.

"Right," said Axon.

Axon and Evergreen followed the attendant back through a secured door and a long hallway with blank white walls. Large black numbers were painted on the doors they passed. "We're going to five," he said, pointing toward the door halfway down the sterile hallway. He unlocked number five with his keycard and held it open for them to enter. The chill of the room immediately brought goosebumps to Evergreen's bare arms. Three metal gurneys holding covered bodies were spaced evenly across the length of the room, with privacy curtains neatly tucked away against the walls. Most visitors came during the day, and there were none at this late hour. There'd be no need to separate the mourners from each other. The attendant flipped through his clipboard again and strode toward the middle gurney. "He's here," he said as he gently pulled back the white sheet to expose the familiar face of Evergreen's father, looking pale and lifeless. Evergreen hadn't seen his face since the day he'd died. She stood, as motionless and stone-like as her father, her mind a blank. He was really dead. She hadn't just imagined that day. He'd died and he wasn't coming back.

Axon pulled a chair from against the wall and slid it beside Gerald Mason's head. Guiding Evergreen by the small of her back, he helped her take a seat.

"I'll leave you two alone," the morgue worker said before backing up slowly from the room and shutting the door behind him.

The faint buzz of fluorescent lights rang in Evergreen's ears. "Hi Dad." She reached to touch his face, but pulled back before making contact, not wanting to feel how cold she knew he would be. A few tears rolled down her face as she stared at him. "I'm sorry," she whispered as more tears fell.

Needing to look away, Evergreen opened the heavy-duty plastic bag containing her father's personal effects and documents from his medical record. Among the clothes he was discovered in were the contents of his pockets: a scrap of paper, lip balm, a folded stack of tissues. Evergreen fingered the yellow-gold wedding ring he had never removed after her mother's death, until someone, likely the coroner, removed it for him. Reaching behind her neck, she unclasped her simple necklace with the heart-shaped pendant, a gift from her father on her eighteenth birthday. She slid the ring, much too large for her own fingers, onto the chain next to the heart and secured the necklace around her neck again. Her mother's red ribbon was wrapped around her wrist and tied in a bow. Now she could carry them both with her.

Axon wandered around the room, silently giving her space as she began to thumb through the medical paperwork. The small stack of documents contained his admission report, a thorough description of how he was found, a few photographs she barely remembered being taken, and some diagnostic test results confirming his overdose. She sighed loudly.

"Not what you expected to find?" Axon asked as he innocuously lifted a corner of the white sheet covering the body nearest the wall. He made an agreeable face and nodded.

"Ew," Evergreen said.

"What?" He shrugged. "She had a pretty hot body."

"You're disgusting," she scolded, but smiled in spite of herself, knowing that in his own way, he was trying to divert her attention from the macabre situation.

"I was so sure the labs would tell me *something*. There was no evidence that someone had broken into the house. It was totally secure. The only way to explain his level of medication is that he took too much."

"Did you expect to find a smoking gun?"

"I mean . . . yeah."

Axon looked thoughtful for a moment before saying, "Have you considered that if someone was trying to get away with something like murder, they'd be smart enough to make sure the lab results looked right?"

Evergreen narrowed her eyes. "I saw them take the blood sample."

"I heard the same conversation you did less than an hour ago. You begged me to come down here because you thought you'd find the evidence in the test results that your father had been murdered. Come on, Evergreen, you're not thinking like a criminal."

"And you can?"

Ignoring her question, Axon gently lifted the sheet covering most of her father's body to expose his left wrist. "I know it's biohazardous or whatever and supposed to be destroyed with his body, but why don't we take his bio-watch? It's pretty hard to get rid of all traces of electronic records—there might be something on it."

"And you know how to do that?" She pursed her lips.

"No, not exactly. But I'm willing to bet *you* know someone who does." Axon unlatched the watch from her father's wrist. Bringing it closer to Evergreen, he turned the device over in his hand and rubbed his thumb purposely over the embossed logo on the inside of the band. *Manufactured by Virionics.*

Chapter 32

TODD MACKEY WAS A GADGET guy with a sweet tooth. Evergreen had never seen him pass up a dessert bar, breakfast pastry, or chocolate fountain and it showed. Todd was well-suited to his chosen sedentary career behind cubicle walls, in front of a top-of-the-line computer and multiple monitors at Virionics, surrounded by the newest toys in the industry. His LP was a decade or so lower than hers, but they had taken some computer courses together in school where they had occasionally partnered on projects. Programming had never been her favorite subject, but his obvious attraction to her had made it easy to get the leg-up she needed to ace the classes.

With her father's bio-watch safely tucked away in her purse, bearing a box of donuts in one arm and a tray of coffees in the other, Evergreen strode carefully to the door of the IT department, trying to avoid creating a sugary, brown mess on the clean floors. As she approached, she saw through the clear glass of the door a beefy man with a large nose and closely cut hair walk purposefully toward it. He pushed the door open from the inside as Evergreen stepped up, expecting him to notice her full hands and hold it open. Instead, he pushed it open just enough to slide through the doorway, his dark trench coat barely clearing the frame before the heavy door clicked shut behind him. Evergreen stared at him and cleared her throat, but he kept walking, his steely eyes set at a point above her head. Something about his face gave her an uneasy feeling.

"Hey!" she exclaimed with an exasperated breath, though she felt a small sense of relief as the man kept walking. "Rude," she said to herself as she tried to adjust the items in her hands enough to attempt a knock on the door. Fortunately, a man with khaki pants and a half-tucked-in shirt entered her line of sight, and she was able to wave awkwardly enough to get his attention.

"Can I help?" he said, poking his balding head out the door to look at Evergreen.

"Hey, I'm just here to see Todd," Evergreen explained, motioning her head toward her hip where she hoped her Virionics badge clipped on the waistband of her pants would give her an air of credibility, as if she couldn't have made it this far into the labyrinthine building without it.

Eyeing her ID, the man propped open the door. "Oh sure. Come on in."

She stood for a moment just past the entrance. "Um." She hesitated.

"His desk is down over that way," he said, noting her confusion, and gestured to the maze of cubicles. "Last one on the left after the bathroom doors."

"Thanks!" Evergreen said brightly, grateful that some people were still polite.

She maneuvered her way through the cubicles in the direction her guide had pointed. Rounding a corner, she spotted Todd, his chair swiveling with a creak side to side, his back to the entry of his small work space. Posters covered the half-walls, held up by push-pins: bands Evergreen had heard of but never listened to herself, movies she knew of but had never watched. Todd was into popular subculture, something Evergreen had never devoted much time to unless otherwise prompted by a peer.

"Knock, knock." She mimed her elbow tapping on the fabric covered wall. "Hi Todd," she said as he swiveled around.

"Oh, hey Evergreen! What are you doing here?" he said, clearly excited to see her. His gaze fell on the box of donuts in her arms.

"Just in the neighborhood. Brought you breakfast." She gestured to the white box of pastries before setting it down on the desktop cluttered with papers, devices peeled open to expose colorful wires, sleek electronics whose function Evergreen hadn't the slightest inkling of, and nearly empty beverages. "Some coffee? I wasn't sure how you took it, so I asked for three creams, three sugars like mine," she fibbed, already knowing his preference for coffee that tasted more like hot chocolate while she drank it black.

"Perfect, thanks Ev." Todd reached for the coffee cup with eagerness. "So, what can I do for you? Another project for Programming 202?" He laughed at his comment, and she obliged him with an appreciative chuckle.

"No, I have a small favor to ask," she began, cutting out the small talk as he moved to clear a space for her to sit on a nearby chair. "Thanks." Making herself comfortable, she sipped her black coffee and brought her leather purse to her lap.

"Sure, whatever you need. I hear you're in R&D now?"

"Vaccination development, in the Disease Prevention Division, but yeah, sort of."

"Oh right," he said, turning his chair around again to face his computer screen. "I was just watching the latest company announcement video. You know how they like to pump up their annual gala. More money, right?" He performed a series of clicks to bring up a video screen and hit play.

"We've had a wonderful year here at Virionics. Our company has been blessed with the gift of innovative talent and scientific discovery . . ." the man on the video said, pronouncing "discovery" as *"dithcovery."* Evergreen felt the color drain from her face. She knew where she had heard his voice before. It was the man from the wake. The one who'd taken pleasure in hearing her father had died. The one who made her believe his death was suspicious in the first place. At the bottom of the screen, his name was listed as Evan Indigo, Chief Public Relations Officer. She had heard of him but had never listened to him speak before to make the connection to her father's wake. Tuning out the rest of his plug for donations and attendance at the gala, Ever-

green tried to shake the feeling of dread before Todd turned back around, hoping her face wouldn't betray her.

"Ev?" Todd said. "Evergreen?" He sat facing her once again, looking at her with a furrowed brow. "You alright?"

"Oh," she said, failing to sufficiently regain her composure. "Just a little too much caffeine, not enough to eat yet today," she said, her hands shaking slightly as she lifted the coffee cup to her mouth again and took a large sip.

"Well, then stop drinking," he said calmly, "and have one of these, why don't you?" He offered the box of donuts with one hand, grabbing another donut for himself with the other. She took one and held it in her hand. She had no intention of eating it. "Alright?" he asked, concerned.

"Yeah," she said, clearing her throat. "Yeah. I'm fine." She shook her head and rolled her shoulders to banish the feeling of dread. Despite herself, she bit into the sugary donut, chewing slowly. The chocolate frosting melted in her mouth, fueling a wave of nausea. She may as well have eaten paint. It would have had the same effect.

"So, do you think you'll be there?" Todd asked, giving her a moment to chew.

"Huh?" She swallowed, her mouth salivating excessively. She was worried she'd throw up and looked around for a garbage can handy enough to suffice, just in case.

"Do you think you'll go to the gala? It's a bit of a pricey admission, but employees get fifty percent off."

"Oh yeah. Sure. Maybe. I haven't decided," she said. "Do you have any water?"

"Uh, yes. I have some here." Todd reached into the bottom of a drawer and tore into a plastic-wrapped pallet of water, handing her one.

"Thanks." She sipped gratefully, the water helping wash the chocolate-paint taste from her mouth. "Are you going to the gala, then?" she asked. Frankly she hadn't given her own attendance much thought between her promotion, her father's death and her complicated relationship with Axon.

"Heck yes, I am. If you end up going, maybe I'll see you there? It's always super fun. They have the best food, and there's usually a global band that plays. Last year it was The Exploding Ions. It was amazing," he said, enthusiastically pointing to a small band poster on the wall of his cubicle.

"Oh. Global," she said, trying to sound interested but knowing she was failing. "I'm wondering if you could take a look at something for me?" she asked, trying to shift his focus back to her original intent. With still-shaky fingers, she undid the clasp on her purse and removed her father's bio-watch, which she had wrapped in a linen handkerchief.

Todd looked down at the item. "That your old man's?" he said awkwardly.

She nodded.

"Don't they usually incinerate those?"

"Yeah. I just . . ." She paused and realized that by explaining the real reason, she could be implicating her old school friend in something serious. Thinking quickly, she continued, "I wanted to get some closure, you know, about his last hours? I was wondering if you could download the Health Log for me to have?"

His expression sympathetic, he nodded and reached for the watch. "Of course," he said softly. "Listen," he said, moving his chair closer to her so their knees were just barely touching, the contact so slight that Evergreen was unsure if it was done on purpose or not. "I'm really sorry about your dad. He accomplished a lot in his life. A real legend around here, especially." He rested his hand on her knee for a moment, long enough for her to wonder if it was more than just a friendly gesture.

Todd scooted back to face his desk without further action, and she breathed a small sigh of relief. Thankfully there wouldn't be *that* weirdness to deal with. "So, you can do it?"

"Yeah. No problem," he said with a touch of pride. "I'll email it to you, okay? I can have it to you this afternoon."

She nodded. "Thanks Todd," she said with genuine gratitude.

"Did you want this back?" he asked, holding up the watch with a raised eyebrow.

Thinking for a moment, she nodded again. "Yeah. Can you send it to my work mailbox?"

"Sure thing. That all?" he asked.

"Yeah. Thank you so much, Todd. I owe you one, really, but I'm afraid I have to get back to the lab. I'm glad we got to catch up," she said.

"Yeah, it was great seeing you, Ev. You should stop by again sometime," he added, his mouth half-full of donut, the powdered sugar coating the edges of his lips. "Come to the gala!" he said as she backed away from his work space.

Evergreen tossed him the most dazzling smile she could manage despite the unease she still felt in her legs as she began to walk away and out of the department. She was still on bereavement leave and didn't need to return to work just yet. Learning the identity of that voice had disturbed her enough to make her want to curl back up in bed.

Something told her that this was bigger than she'd first thought. If the Chief Public Relations Officer was involved, or at least aware that her father's death was no accident, then this likely went all the way to the top. *What were you involved in, Dad?* She wondered, knowing it was futile to speculate without being able to see the Hourglass files themselves. The files she had tried and failed to copy. The reason she suspected he was dead.

Chapter 33

"WHAT DO YOU THINK THEIR LP is going to be?" asked the young woman with large, purely decorative eyeglasses Lucy had just met.

Lucy pretended to contemplate. "Hmm. Fifty-two. A solid mid." She smiled and played along with the most common party game, if a single speculative question could be considered a game. She had been feeling better lately. Her body, having detoxed from the mood-altering medication, had adjusted to a more regular rhythm. No longer did she lay awake all night, only falling asleep as her room started to brighten with early morning light. She'd been drinking hot tea to ease her into sleep before midnight, refraining from sleeping past noon, and had begun a regular exercise and eating routine. Despite her uncertain situation, she felt up to attending social events, such as this birth announcement party. The happy and exhausted parents of newborn children hosted an event soon after the birth, with the purpose of revealing the gender and lifespan of their new bundle of joy to friends and family. Guests were encouraged to take guesses on what sorts of career paths the child might take, what sort of school they'd attend, and how long they would live. The parents typically were told just after the birth of the child, but some preferred to wait for a "big reveal." The risk with this method, of course, was the possibility of disappointment. Lucy had attended one reveal-style announcement party a couple years back where the parents heard the disappointing news that their child would only enjoy nineteen months of life. The father had attempted a stoic and falsely happy look, but the mother, Nadine's cousin, had sobbed. Though the purpose of these events was to inspire confidence that, at any LP, there was hope of a successful and happy life, extremely low results were almost always a downer for those present.

"I'm saying sixty-four. I like even numbers too," the woman whispered the last part conspiratorially and winked. The prize for guessing the closest to the actual age was a large basket of goodies including fresh fruit, wine, candies, and bath products. This was a particularly good haul for the winner, due to the fact that the new babies were triplets of yet-unrevealed gender. Whoever guessed closest would be winning three at once.

Lucy helped herself to punch, the latest batch of which had been spiked by the neighborhood twins, Ashleigh and Renna, from across the street. While she didn't know the family well, her mother had socialized with them on many occasions, whether out of convenience of being in the same neighborhood or real friendship, Lucy was unsure. The mother, whom Lucy only knew as Mrs. Fallon, cooed along with several other women over the three infants, who slept peacefully through the chatter of small talk permeating the new mother's living room. Mr. Fallon was nowhere to be seen, likely posted in the backyard near the barbeque and the rest of the men, who in typical fashion only tolerated the swooning women and the inevitable talk of child-rearing in small doses.

Having children outside of the designated rules was possible, but not encouraged. Couples could apply to counteract the waterborne birth control, taking a fertility drug prescribed only by certain providers. The process was expensive, cumbersome, and considered a social taboo for irresponsibly contributing to the gene pool. Most parents opted for the traditional route, qualifying for children based on how many they currently had and any previous offspring's LP. Lucy's parents, having one child with an LP of sixteen-and-a-half, had missed the first cut-off bracket for having another child before Lucy's time ran out. The Hansons didn't have the means to go the non-traditional route and apply specially for another birth. If Lucy lived another five years, the process became even more expensive. Ten more and it became impossible, both from the perspective of finance and that of Nadine's biology. Her mother's own LP was set to expire in less than eleven years, not quite enough time to start and complete the process of birthing another child if she had to wait those ten years. Most would-be parents banked on having multiple children in a single birth, the most convenient option to achieve a big family.

Lucy walked into the kitchen with her half-full glass of punch, looking for something to do. She spotted the twins giggling as they leaned against the faux-marble countertop and stared at the screen of a tablet. They were a year or so younger than Lucy and were bound for mid-level careers, which meant they attended a different school than Lucy had been enrolled in. She only knew them in passing but found they demonstrated an air of haughtiness she had come to expect from kids with higher LPs.

"What are you watching?" she asked, more out of boredom than out of true interest.

The girls giggled conspiratorially again, their red curls bouncing slightly on their shoulders. Their eyes looked up at her with a wink of menace above their short, pointed noses, too small for their identical faces. "Wanna see?" one of them asked. Lucy couldn't distinguish which one.

Lucy approached the duo and took the tablet in her hands. Ashleigh or Renna wound the video back with a drag of her finger and pressed play. The first scene looked like a typical teenage party with lots of close dancing, exaggerated drunkenness and overly excited girls.

"Guys, I'm ready!" a boy yelled, flipping his straight blond hair triumphantly. The small crowd cheered as the video panned out to show a banner which read, "Farewell Tyler." The boy, who Lucy assumed to be Tyler, strutted to the center of the floor as the other kids fanned out around him. "Are you ready for me to die?!" he shouted, cupping his hands over his mouth like a megaphone. The others cheered in response.

The music suddenly changed to a song Lucy recognized. It was the song she had meticulously chosen for herself, years prior to her own wake, back before Colton died and she stopped caring what came next. The song was meant to be played in the final minute of her life; a melody to die to. Furrowing her brow, she watched as the boy in the center of the circle was embraced from behind by a pretty girl with dark hair and an ironic smirk. The crowd began to count down from five as Tyler swayed with an exaggerated movement of his shoulders. The girls in the circle screwed up their faces as if real tears were forthcoming, their distraught expressions almost convincing.

"Three, two, one!" Tyler relaxed, trust-fall-like, into the girl's arms as she sank with him to the floor. The crowd cheered as they danced around the pair.

"My baby!" the girl who'd held him as he went limp declared loudly. The circle of teenagers cheered and moaned in exaggerated despair.

"My baby!" several of the male teens echoed while putting their hands to their faces in a show of desperation.

Opening his eyes one after the other, Tyler looked around at his friends with wide eyes. "Am I alive?!" he half-shouted over the pulse of the music.

"He's alive!" a boy from his left declared, raising Tyler's hand in his own in a gesture of victory.

The crowd cheered.

"He pulled a Hansonnnnn!" the boy to his left shouted again.

The video changed to a beat-skipping remix showing footage from Lucy's own wake alongside Tyler's party. She thrust the tablet back into one of the twin's hands. "Funny," she added dryly.

"They're *so stupid*, right?" one of the girls asked with a malicious grin.

"Doesn't that make you *so mad?*" the other asked, obviously attempting to get a rise out of Lucy.

Lucy shrugged. "Like you said, *so stupid,*" she said, mimicking their tone and affecting nonchalance, something she had learned from watching Axon.

The girls exchanged sinister looks, one of them raising a blond, nearly transparent eyebrow. "The comments are the best part, really."

"Yeah," the other began. "Here's a good one, 'Lucy Hanson makes fake death look so pathetic. She should just off herself already . . . Oh wait, she already tried!'" The girl paused and threw on a fake affronted look. "I know, so mean. But that's what it says!"

"Did you really fake your wake?" the other twin asked curiously. Her sister elbowed her in the ribs and muttered, "*Ashleigh.*" Undeterred, Ashleigh continued, "Well, did you?"

"Why exactly would I do that?" Lucy asked.

"Attention whore," Renna said with a snort of laughter under her breath.

"I don't know, Lucy, that's what we're asking?" Ashleigh said as she passed the device back to Lucy. "People deserve to know. Look what they're saying."

Lucy took the tablet back and scanned through the comments.

"I heard she tried to off herself for real, but she couldn't even do that right."

"That bitch should really just die already. Why should she get a free pass on the clock?"

"My sister's friend was at her actual wake. This is a totally legit replica. Just die already, Lucy."

"Her real LP is twenty-seven or something. She's obviously just a lazy waste of space who pretended to have a low LP so she wouldn't have to go to actual school. Definitely just avoiding the janitor track her loser father is on. I bet he helped her."

"Lucy Hanson was the biggest slut in her LP school, no wonder she faked her death."

The comments continued in this vein infinitely down the page as Lucy scrolled. A familiar nervous pit began to expand quickly in her gut as she tried to digest what she was reading. She willed herself not to cry in front of these girls. What did these anonymous people on the internet know, anyway? She knew what they were saying wasn't true. Lucy mentally ticked through the people who actually mattered in her life. The few living friends she had remaining would be dead soon anyway. Colton was gone, and Axon certainly could care less. So why did this even matter? The black pit in her stomach contracted to a manageable size and she was able to swallow the lump in her throat.

"Guess I'm just infamous." She shrugged, handing back the tablet once more to the girls. Their masks of glee slipped momentarily, showing the unflattering ugliness hiding just beneath the surface. Suddenly, the twins didn't seem as cute and unflinchingly confident as they had minutes before. Lucy flipped her long dark hair over one shoulder and walked away, resisting the urge to look back at their confused, haughty faces.

Approaching her mother, who was gathered around the sleeping babies and the happy-looking couple with arms around each other, Lucy tapped her on the shoulder from behind. "Mom, I'm ready to go."

"Oh, okay, honey. They're just about to announce the LPs. Hang on one second."

The room quieted as the couple prepared their big reveal. "Everyone ready?" the mother asked with excitement.

The small crowd cheered jovially.

She and her husband pulled a string attached to a paper balloon secured above their heads, releasing blue confetti and helium-filled balloons with the numbers 5 and 2. "Fifty-two!" the couple cried happily in unison. A few balloons and a smattering of colored paper could tell a lot. In this case, identical boys, meant to live until middle age. The group cheered and raised their glasses to the infant boys who were just starting to stir.

Lucy touched her mother's arm gently and led her away from the living room and toward the front door, passing the woman with large glasses she had chatted with. "Called it," Lucy said as she walked out the door before the smiling woman could force the house prize on her. Lucy hadn't actually voted fifty-two. Instead, she had leaned on her newly acquired strength—hope. With these three babies, beautiful and perfect with their smattering of dark hair, she'd imagined their future, with long lives ahead, and optimistically submitted her bid at ninety-seven.

Dusk had fallen while Lucy and Nadine were at the party. It was a short walk through the neighborhood back to the Hanson house, and they walked slowly, enjoying the warm evening and the purpling sky. Nadine put a tentative arm around Lucy's shoulder. Her mother was never big on physical contact, so this small gesture was unusual. Lucy found she couldn't look at Nadine's face, fearing she might just burst into tears in response.

"Lucy?" Nadine stopped their meandering approach back home.

"Yeah, Mom?" Lucy turned her head to catch a glimpse of her mother's face.

Nadine's eyes welled with tears. "I'm . . . I'm sorry," she said, exhaling the words. "I'm sorry, I'm so sorry, honey." Lucy looked away, not wanting to encourage the beginnings of a trembling chin—her mother's emotion would be contagious. "Your father and I really wanted a child. And I had to . . . to . . . bury both my parents and my sister at a young age. I just couldn't do it again. When we found out we'd only get a short time with you, I guess I just . . ."

It was too much to stay stoic. Lucy turned her body and wrapped her arms around her mother.

"I just disconnected," Nadine sobbed onto Lucy's shoulder.

Lucy's tears leaked silently onto the pavement beneath them as she held her mother long enough for Nadine to release nearly seventeen years' worth of guilt.

"I guess I always kept a little distant to protect myself. I didn't want to be so hurt when you inevitably . . . you know." She trailed off.

"Died?" Lucy offered.

"Yes," Nadine said quietly, prompting a new wave of tears.

Nadine broke their hug and added, wiping her eyes, "I thought another child could fix that. But I don't really want another child . . . I just want you." This admission caused fresh sobs for them both. It was everything Lucy had ever suspected. She felt validated, she felt relief—her mother really did want her around. Nadine put her soft hands on Lucy's cheeks, framing her face. "I love you, Lucy."

"I love you too, Mom." Lucy smiled as a few warm tears rolled down her face. Nadine wiped them away gently.

"Now, maybe we should get all the way home. The neighbors are going to start thinking we are crazy or something."

Nadine gave a chuckle of laughter as mother and daughter looped arms around each other's waists and made their way home.

Chapter 34

AXON SAT AT THE SQUARE kitchen table in Evergreen's small, tidy downtown apartment—the most convenient location, they'd concluded, where privacy was guaranteed. After their late-night visit to the morgue, Evergreen had dropped off goodies for her friend Todd and called Axon on her way back, sounding shaken. He'd come over and she explained what happened. After that, it seemed that just his presence was enough to placate her anxiety. A low ping broke their hour-long silence, causing Evergreen to click the trackpad of her keyboard frantically.

"Here it is," she said with excitement. They had been waiting all afternoon for a response from Evergreen's IT contact to see what evidence the bio-watch might provide. Axon watched her eyes dart from side to side, getting wider as she read whatever her friend had sent.

"Well?" he prompted as she finally unglued herself from the screen, leaning back in her chair with a loud exhale.

"Wow," she practically whispered.

Axon raised his brows, watching her face as she processed what she'd read. She pushed the screen toward him so he could see the evidence that Todd had converted into a readable file.

The watch recorded vital signs every ten seconds with a timestamp, and the compiled log started with the final entries of Gerald Mason's life. Axon scrolled through the readings, which included crucial vitals along with the countdown toward Gerald's predicted LP. Right away it was clear something was wrong. The countdown of the LP clock started at zero on the most recent entry, as if the time of Mason's death was in sync with the original predicted moment of death. If he had truly died of an accidental overdose, as indicated by the medical examination, his LP clock would still be consistent with the time and date of death he had known all his life.

"Look at the timestamp from 9:12 a.m." Evergreen said, her eyes steely.

Axon dragged the bio-watch data until he found the time. Between 9:11 a.m. and 9:12 a.m., the LP countdown dramatically skipped. Data from before 9:11 a.m. showed the LP countdown at 10 years, 11 months, 5 days, 4 hours and 50 seconds, whereas *after* this time, the countdown showed mere minutes. "Holy shit. It changed."

Evergreen nodded. "I didn't think it was possible."

"Wait, maybe it changed when his body started to process the medication and couldn't keep up. The sensor realized it was a toxic level?" Axon suggested.

"No. That isn't possible."

"How do you know?"

"Because that isn't how it works. When someone commits suicide or dies in an accident, their LP doesn't change. That's what makes it an unexpected death. Their LP clock is still ticking away, but they're gone. That didn't happen with my dad. But that *is* what happened with Lucy Hanson. Her LP reading never changed, even though it still said her time was up."

"Okay. Let's just lay out everything we know at this point. Because this is starting to get really fucked up."

"Okay, good idea," Evergreen said as she began to sift through her stack of papers.

"So, let's start with your dad. His LP was *changed*."

"Right."

"That means *someone changed it*."

Evergreen nodded.

Axon snapped his fingers. "That guy!" he exclaimed. "That guy we heard last night, he—"

"Works for Virionics," Evergreen finished.

"Seriously?"

"Yes. His name is Evan Indigo. He's the Chief Public Relations Officer. I heard him this morning on a company-wide promotion, encouraging attendance at the annual fundraiser."

"Do you think *he* changed your dad's LP?"

"No," she said thoughtfully. "I don't even know *how* someone would change an LP, and this guy is more of a figurehead. You know, like the face of the company. He also made it sound like accessing those files was what somehow triggered my dad's death. He knows something, but it doesn't fit that he actually did it. But we do know that the Hourglass files must be important."

Axon shook his head incredulously. "Important enough to incite murder, apparently."

"And the files can only be accessed by certain people, including my father and this Evan guy. He made it sound like there was some sort of meeting or committee that opened the files together."

"Okay, so we know that something weird is going on at Virionics. You work there. Anything ever seem off to you?"

"No," Evergreen began defensively. "It's a really prestigious place to work. They exist to keep people alive and healthy."

"Not from where I'm sitting," Axon said. "You sound like a corporate drone."

"I'm not a corporate drone!"

Axon laughed as Evergreen glared at him. "Okay, so you get this really important job, with your dream company. How long does it take most people to move up after they start fresh out of school?"

Evergreen's cheeks flushed pink. "A few years, usually."

"And you managed to get promoted in what? A couple of months?"

"Yeah . . ."

She's smart, Axon thought, *but has some serious blind spots.* "Look, I'm sure you're good at your job, but that *is* just a little bit odd, right?"

Evergreen thought for a moment. "I mean, it is a little unusual. I just got lucky, though."

Axon could feel a twinge of irritation and worked to suppress it. "Luck started at birth for you." Evergreen opened her mouth to retort, but Axon kept going. "You were born as a high-LP to a renowned scientist father. You were given the best educational opportunities because of your long lifetime. You were an investment the system could bank on paying off."

Evergreen tried to interject again, but Axon waved her off. "Let me finish. Sure, you work hard to graduate, and when you do, you move into your very first job at a prestigious company, one you say you've always wanted to work for. Your father happens to work at this same company and is important enough to be included in what sounds like some sort of top-secret committee with deadly consequences for breaking the rules. Lucy Hanson doesn't die, and you get interested in her story. Just as you start to make headway with the investigation and are asking for more information and access, you get promoted. By the same company your father works for. The same company that it seems like your father died for. You don't think that's a little suspicious? And that maybe you shouldn't be so keen to jump to Virionics' defense?"

"You're saying that the intention of my promotion was to distract me."

"I know you work hard, Evergreen. I'm sure you also deserve to be where you are. But I do think there's a chance this was no coincidence. Because what happened after you were promoted?" He paused for a moment as she sat with pursed lips. "You stopped asking questions."

Evergreen waved her hand dismissively. "Fine. Maybe it's true. What else do we have? What about Lucy?" she asked, shifting the focus of the conversation.

"Well, the recording I was able to get implies that the President is unhappy about the situation, and he may have even retaliated against a department head."

"Wait, you never told me that!"

"I did. Sort of. I was going to tell you more but then, your dad died..."

"Oh," was all she mustered in response.

Axon then explained the recordings, how he got them, and how he overheard the President asking for someone to "take care of" Arnie Hamilton, the Director of LP.

"But why would he do that?" Evergreen asked.

"Set someone up to make it look like an accident?"

"Yeah, other than being 'unhappy' about it." Evergreen mimed air-quotes. "He needs a better motive to resort to murder, if that's really what happened. Maybe this Hamilton guy knew something?"

"Virionics is a government-funded company, right?"

"Yes," Evergreen said. "Do you think maybe he's a part of this secret Hourglass committee?"

"It's possible." Axon shrugged. "What else do we know about Hourglass?"

"Oh!" Evergreen exclaimed as if she suddenly remembered something. She shuffled through a manila folder of printouts from journals. "One of the reasons I was looking into my dad's files in the first place was to find some particular documents I didn't have access to. There were a few I found before I sort of got lost in the system and freaked out that I'd get caught." Evergreen explained how a message had appeared on the screen while she was snooping, asking what she, or supposedly Gerald, was doing. "One of the articles refers to Project Hourglass as the source of funding, which I still don't quite understand, but it's something."

"What's the article about?" Axon asked, reaching for the document she had pulled onto the top of her stack.

"It was a gene suppression study for gene *HG580.*"

Axon shook his head and looked at her blankly. "Why would anyone want to suppress genes?"

"Well," Evergreen began, reminding Axon of his former teachers when they started on a topic they were really passionate about. Her face lit up with excitement, obviously ready to share this knowledge with anyone who asked. "There are some genes that turn on and signal to the body to start producing particular hormones, amino acids, all kinds of things. Sometimes this is good for the body, a natural process. Other times this can cause problems, such as degenerative diseases like Parkinson's, or certain types of cancer. Scientists like to study these so-called 'bad genes' and learn how to switch them off so the person with the gene never develops the disease it codes for."

Axon nodded. "Okay, I'm following."

"The techniques applied to these studies are used in my everyday work. I help create the annual vaccinations which are personalized for individuals. This is the best way to administer suppressions to any genes that may cause people to develop diseases and not reach their full LP." She smiled, obviously proud.

"Haven't we supposedly conquered diseases at this point?"

Evergreen thought for a moment, pressing her lips together, then said, "Yes . . . and no. As humans continue to have children and mix their genes, genetic diversity expands. We also start to see mutations over time, especially as humans age. As normal cells die and new ones are made, sometimes the DNA doesn't quite match up and a nucleotide is missed. Which means there is a small mistake in the DNA of the new cell. This DNA is replicated again and again from normal cell growth processes, and soon enough there is a large enough population of this mutated DNA to cause a problem in the human body."

"Okay, you lost me."

Taking a deep breath, as if slowing down her brain was physically painful, Evergreen started again. "Do you know what DNA is?"

"Sure," Axon said confidently. "Building blocks of life."

"Right. And DNA lives inside the nucleus of the cell, where in the process of growing new cells it has to replicate itself, so any new cells have the same information as the parent cell. Make sense?"

"Okay. Yes."

"So sometimes, when the DNA is replicating itself, it makes a mistake. Human DNA is enormous, and even one error can spark a negative change somewhere down the line." She acknowledged Axon's confused face and quickly added, "But not every change is malevolent. Lots of changes do nothing."

"But why *HG580* gene suppression? What does that gene do?" Axon asked.

"I'm not sure," Evergreen said with a shrug. "But it must be important if Project Hourglass was supporting it."

"Okay, let's table that for now," Axon said, stifling a yawn. "Do you want to hear what research *I* found?"

"You found something good?"

"Uh-huh. Here." He pulled a stapled copy of A. A. Morse's economic paper (regarding the population ratios necessary for a stable society of shared resources) out of his bag and showed it to Evergreen. She grabbed it and read quickly, her eyes moving rapidly back and forth across the page. She finished, slapping it down onto the tabletop, and began typing furiously into her computer without a word. After several silent minutes, Axon asked, "So . . . What do you think?"

"Hang on. I'm checking something," Evergreen said, still distracted.

"Alrighty." Axon crossed his arms and willed himself to be patient.

Finally, she glanced up from the screen, looking delighted. "It matches."

"What matches?"

"The ratio of annual births to deaths that A. A. Morse proposed!" she nearly shouted in excitement.

"What do you mean?" Axon said before his brain clicked into gear. "Wait. Did you compare her hypothetical ratio to our current population census?"

"Yep. It fits." Evergreen leaned back in her chair. "My heart is beating so fast right now," she said, pressing a palm across the left side of her chest and breathing deeply.

"This is huge," Axon said. "This is so huge. Either Morse was some sort of prophetic genius, or something really fucked up is happening right now."

"I'd never even *heard* of this person before reading the publication. Had you?" Evergreen asked.

"No," Axon said. "We need more information."

"I agree."

"We need to see those files."

"The Hourglass files?" she asked, her face flushed.

"Yes," Axon said. "We have to see what's in those files. Think about it, Ev." Axon placed a hand on top of hers. "They have to tell us something useful, otherwise why protect them so intensely?"

Evergreen stared at him incredulously. "And how exactly do you propose we do that? The last time I tried to open them, my father died." Her eyes glistened with barely contained tears.

"Evan Indigo," Axon said simply.

"What?"

"Evan Indigo. He has access. We use his."

"You make that sound so simple!" she said.

"It is. We just need to get access to his login credentials and—"

"And then what?! Get him killed too?"

"Maybe. But what do you care? He clearly had it out for your dad."

"Doesn't mean I want to sentence him to death!"

Axon nodded minutely and reached out to tap her shoulder gently. "Okay, maybe we can do both."

"Meaning?" Evergreen said with angrily condensed brows.

"Meaning we still open the files from his login, but we do it when there can be no question that he wasn't the person who accessed them. Therefore, whoever might be responsible for offing non-compliant members of this death committee can't possibly believe he was the one to do it. We'd have to be careful, but there are ways to hide your tracks electronically. We could make it look like an external hack."

Evergreen's hesitation was palpable. "How do we ensure this?" she asked, her skepticism apparent.

"Indigo is the Public Relations Officer, right?"

"Yes," she said slowly, as if not quite understanding.

"Hacking the files has to happen when he's in the public spotlight," Axon explained.

She cocked her head. "Okay . . ."

"Say, the Virionics annual gala?" He shrugged nonchalantly, giving her time to ponder the idea.

After a long moment, Evergreen bobbed her head resolutely. "How do we do this?"

Chapter 35

LUCY'S ALARM WENT OFF with a melodious twinkle, dragging her brain into consciousness. The first thing she saw was the deep blue floor-length dress hanging from the top of the closet door, its color stark against the white paint. She had convinced her mother to alter the length to accommodate flat shoes. One of the resolutions Lucy had made after surviving her wake was to never wear stilettos again.

Today a small team of hair and makeup artists would arrive at her parents' house, paid for by Virionics, to prepare for her presentation as the guest of honor at their annual gala. She had been coached on the short speech she was expected to make and had rehearsed with a Public Relations representative from the company. The company had also set her up with an educational consultant to explore options for her future. Lucy may have had an unpredictable lifespan, but as Virionics' new "Face of Hope," as they were now calling her, she was free to pursue career options previously made inaccessible by her LP. While she wasn't sure yet what she would choose, the prospect of choice was both daunting and thrilling. Lucy did know what she'd be doing in the next year at least, and she was excited to have the chance to announce it tonight. She'd finally figured out a way to help others, even with her unknown LP.

Rolling over in bed, Lucy opened her nightstand drawer to pull out the small handheld device Axon had given her the night before. He and the scientist—Evergreen, that was her name—had explained the plethora of evidence they had compiled regarding suspicious activities within both the government and Virionics, most of which went right over Lucy's head. All she could conclude was that she was an important part of their plan moving forward, to uncover further information that would allegedly confirm their wild theories. Lucy would have done anything Axon needed of her regardless, so when they asked if she had any questions, she merely attempted what she hoped was a nonchalant shrug, implying everything made perfect sense, even though it hadn't quite. Axon once commented on how much smarter she was than her LP indicated, and she saw no need to prove him wrong.

Lucy rubbed a thumb along the smooth plastic edge of the tool, its round button slightly concave. Their ask had been simple: Lucy would put the electronic remote into her small clutch and follow the Virionics itinerary, which had her scheduled to meet and greet Evan Indigo, the Chief Public Relations Officer, at the start of the gala. After waiting for the right moment, she would discreetly press the button. Lucy would need to ensure that she and Evan had at least enough distance from others with company keycards to enclose just the two of them within the invisible sphere of the scan the device would perform. The scan would then pick up the electronic markers on Evan's keycard and clone his coded access onto a blank card, also in Lucy's purse, provided by Evergreen.

The way internal computers and doors at Virionics worked, Evergreen had explained, was that all staff members were provided with individualized permissions to the areas in the buildings they needed to access. The card also allowed for a convenient tap-and-go function on office computers, coding the user's specific password series with the wave of the card over a nearby sensor. Once the card was "tapped," the computer would log into all interfaces the user had permission to access, including the file folders Axon and Evergreen so badly wanted to see. Afterwards, Lucy would pass the access card to Axon, so he and Evergreen could duck out of the gala while everyone was distracted by Evan Indigo's introduction of the speakers and the commencement of the auction. Lucy badly wanted Axon to be back in time for her own introduction and speech, and made him promise to do so. She was looking forward to showing him how comfortable she could be in front of an audience, a trait she imagined he valued, considering his own professional skills.

A knock sounded on the door of Lucy's bedroom, and Nadine poked her head in. "I made breakfast, if you want some," she said with a smile. "Big day today, the crew is set to be here in a couple of hours. You ready?"

Lucy propped herself up in bed, a few joints cracking in protest. "I'm ready."

The little black drawstring bag that hung from Lucy's wrist felt heavy, even though the contents were minimal and lightweight. She kept checking nervously that the mouth of the bag stayed closely puckered shut as she wound through the high-ceilinged ballroom gradually filling with gala guests. Two separate bar areas, decorated with tall vases holding floating candles, bookended the low stage. A lone podium with a microphone was positioned in the middle of the stage, dressed up with a Virionics banner and patiently awaiting the first speaker. Lucy counted three ice sculptures in various corners of the airy room, featuring designs incorporating test tubes, beakers, and pipettes, reminiscent of the science occurring behind the scenes. A six-piece orchestra was positioned along one wall, playing quiet, sanguine music blending nicely into the sophisticated atmosphere, undoubtedly by design. A table near the front double-doors was covered in a silver tablecloth and rectangular place cards affixed with the Virionics logo—a wiggly "V" with one side of the letter suggestive of double-strands of DNA. Two attendants sat behind the long table, checking in guests and handing out numbered auction paddles to those planning to participate in the later activity. Lucy's parents were already seated at one of the long guest tables, the dark grain of the wood complementing the silver candlesticks, which were minimally draped in clear glass beads, refracting the flames into fragmented rainbows across the room. Her father was socializing animatedly with the bored-looking couple seated adjacent to them while her mother sat statuesque, her black hair braided into a complicated updo, a half-smile glued to her face. Lucy waved from across the room where she stood awaiting further instruction from her guide, the Public Relations representative Aurora Birch. Her father waved back with a broad swing of his arm while her mother infinitesimally bobbed her head in Lucy's direction.

Aurora Birch spoke rapidly into her headset, which was placed discreetly in her right ear and partially covered by her bluntly cut auburn hair, which hung pin-straight above the top of her shoulders. Aurora's makeup, done to create a monotone color across her entire face, including masking any natural pinks in her lips and darkness in her eyebrows, had originally been off-putting to Lucy, but the look was starting to grow on her. She began to appreciate the correlation between her representative's look and her company role, one of blending into the background to make things run smoothly.

"Okay, Lucy, he's ready for you," Aurora said, her voice clipped and businesslike.

"Okay," Lucy said as she was led in the direction of a small cluster of people, shaking hands and sipping cocktails near one of the bars. She recognized Evan Indigo in the center of the group, all of his white teeth visible as he smiled, nodding along pleasantly to the conversation. *How am I supposed to get him away from everyone else?* She thought with a pang of anxiety.

As Lucy walked across the polished floor, she tried not to look down at the ground where the hem of her dark dress floated just millimeters above the tops of her toes. Spotting Axon looking glamorous in a black tuxedo, Lucy lifted her wrist in a small wave of nervous greeting. He winked as she passed, and she felt her cheeks color in response.

"Mr. Indigo," Aurora began as they approached the group, her hand prodding gently at Lucy's lower back. "Lucy Hanson, your guest of honor tonight." The small cluster of adults stepped back to admit them into their circle of chatter.

"Ah yes," Evan said, his smile never wavering. "Miss Hanson, it's a pleasure to finally meet you." He extended a large hand for her to shake. "We were just discussing how inspiring you are to all of those with a low LP."

"Um. Global!" Lucy's voice squeaked, and she immediately regretted her overenthusiasm. She cleared her throat and added, "It's been a strange couple of months."

Evan laughed in appreciation, and the others quickly joined in. "Well, we're glad you're here, Lucy. Looking forward to hearing you speak," he said in dismissal as he turned his attention back to the others around him, who began to close the circle they had opened like a door moments ago. Their conversation picked up where it had left off.

That was it? She wondered, her mind racing in a panic. Lucy glanced back at Aurora, who had stepped several paces away and was chatting expressionlessly into her headset again. Clutching the little drawstring bag, Lucy stepped boldly back into the narrow space between the others, elbowing her way into Evan's view. "Mr. Indigo?" she asked timidly. The others kept talking. "Mr. Indigo?" Lucy said again, her voice this time loud and unmistakable over the conversation.

Evan looked up with a smile perfectly positioned to convey surprise and delight that she stood there addressing him. "Yes, Miss Hanson?"

She thought fleetingly of Axon, his confidence always in such stark contrast to how she felt, and took a deep breath. "Mr. Indigo .. . Evan," she said, hoping the use of his first name would make her almost a credible peer. "I'd like to speak with you alone for a moment. Your speeches are always so powerful and well-presented. I was hoping you could share some of your wisdom with me?" Without waiting for a response, she placed her hand on his forearm and began to guide him away from the group, her boldness surprising even herself.

He laughed, his smile sparkling. "Looks like Miss Hanson is hoping to steal some of my genius! If you all will excuse me." He stepped away from the others, Lucy's hand still on the soft fabric of his jacket. As soon as they were several paces away, he pulled his arm back from Lucy and made to adjust his already perfectly knotted tie. "Well, aren't you an insistent one, Lucy Hanson. What can I do for you?" His smile had fallen, hiding his teeth.

"I . . ." Lucy cleared her throat again. This was her chance to distract him long enough to activate the signal—she couldn't blow it. "I was just hoping to hear about how *you* prepare for giving speeches in front of large audiences. You . . . you just have so much more experience than me, I thought I could learn something." Butterflies fluttered in her stomach as she hoped flattery would get him going long enough to complete her job.

"A little nervous, are we?" he asked with a tilt of his head and a wink. "How can I say no to such a request?"

She had him, Lucy thought. Evan began talking about his methods, starting with preparatory stretching of his mouth, as he called it, by reciting a series of tongue twisters he was more than willing to share. Lucy fiddled with her purse, trying to open it and find the small button on the device while maintaining eye contact as she did so. Her freshly manicured fingernails with their half inch of false length made it difficult to maneuver.

"Oh, no need to write this down," he said, misinterpreting and reaching a hand to stop her wrist as she dug in her bag, her finger finally resting on the button.

"Can you email those to me?" she asked, hoping she looked innocent enough as she pressed the button, feeling the faint click.

"Certainly, certainly," he said, withdrawing his hand as she closed her bag with a pull of the drawstrings. "As I was saying . . ." Evan continued his train of thought as Lucy nodded to look interested, though her mind kept spinning elsewhere. She had done it. That wasn't so hard.

Her reverie was soon interrupted by Aurora, who had noticed their side conversation and came to intervene. "I'm sorry, Mr. Indigo, I need to pull Lucy away from you now. She's got people to meet. Special night, after all," she explained, placing a firm hand on Lucy's shoulder and moving her away.

"Of course. Best of luck to you tonight, Miss Hanson," Evan said with a nod and a now-familiar flash of brilliant white teeth.

"Thank you, Mr. Indigo," Lucy said as she stepped away with her guide, relieved to be walking away from him.

"I said meet and greet," Aurora chastised under her breath, her jaw clenched.

Lucy shrugged. "Sorry, I just thought he could help me prepare for later."

"Go over there and talk to some less important people. I'll find you again in a little while," Aurora said harshly as she gave Lucy a little nudge in the direction of the room's center, which had filled with people. Waiters with silver trays glided in and out of the crowd, bearing appetizers and fizzing glasses of champagne. Lucy was suddenly starving. The last part of her role was easy by comparison, and she felt victorious. All she had to do was discreetly hand off the electronically loaded card from her purse to Axon. She undid her purse and reached for the white card inside, cupping it in the palm of her hand. Spotting Axon a little ways away, she paused next to a waiter and grabbed two of the miniature puff pastries with white napkins and popped one into her mouth as she walked.

Axon caught her eye as she approached, his expression questioning. Lucy nodded and he smiled, seeming pleased. Striding over to him and the two young men he was talking with, Lucy sandwiched the card between the two napkins in her hand and arranged the appetizer atop. "Hello," she said brightly.

"Lucy! How's it going?" Axon said familiarly. "Lucy, these two gentlemen here are Justin Kindle and Harley Fellow, they work in Virionics' . . ." He trailed off, seemingly unsure of their titles.

"Packaging and Distribution," the one Axon had indicated as Justin answered.

"Right," Axon said, patting Justin on the arm. "Sorry! This is Lucy Hanson, this evening's guest of honor," he finished and gestured toward Lucy.

She reached out a hand and shook Justin's clammy one before reaching for Harley's. "It's nice to meet you both," she said, looking up to make eye contact with Harley. Her insides immediately melted as if she had poured hot water over ice. Harley's eyes were a light brown with flecks of gray, and she was entranced by them as her arm rocked mechanically within the grasp of his warm hand.

"How long have you two worked at this grand company?" Axon asked as Lucy dropped her hand, a flush creeping across her cheeks.

"Well, I've been here five years," Justin began, "but Harley here just graduated and started last month. I'm mentoring him. Making sure his career gets off to a good start," he said proudly, patting Harley on the back.

Harley glanced quickly over at his coworker with a tight smile, breaking eye contact with Lucy, and ran a hand through his brown hair. "Yeah. Justin's been really great."

Remembering what she was supposed to do next, Lucy said dreamily, "I took one of these," she gestured at the puff appetizer atop the napkins and hidden card in her left hand, "but I didn't realize they had salmon in them. I'm allergic."

"I'll take it," Harley said, reaching over to take the food, though not quite fast enough. Axon swiped the napkins and salmon puff and rapidly popped it into his mouth.

"Mmmm, sorry, man," he said to Harley. "Lucy knows how addicted to salmon puffs I am, right, Luce?" he asked, his mouth full as he glared at her. Lucy looked over long enough to see him put the card securely into his jacket pocket and begin to mouth something at her before she turned back to gaze at Harley, whose brow furrowed in a moment's confusion before he fixed his eyes back on Lucy.

"So, you're giving a speech tonight? Are you nervous?" Harley asked, stepping a fraction of an inch closer to her.

"A little," Lucy admitted. "I've been preparing awhile."

"I'd be freaking out if I were you. I hate giving presentations. That's pretty brave of you."

Nobody had called her brave before. She smiled. "Thanks." Her feet were glued to the floor, exactly where she wanted to be.

"How do you like working here?" she asked.

"It's pretty cool, I guess."

Justin interjected, "I hear *you* get to choose a career path soon. Think you'll end up at Virionics? We have an open position in my department. You and Harley could partner up." Justin elbowed his coworker.

"Yeah maybe." Lucy smirked, thinking it was cute how Harley's ears reddened from the attention.

"If you'll excuse me, I see someone else I know," Axon said distractedly, backing away from the conversation as the orchestra struck up a familiar tune.

"Me too, catch you later, buddy," Justin said with a knowing look and a pat on Harley's back as he strode toward the nearest bar.

"Do you dance?" Harley asked as he tugged at the end of his jacket sleeve, adjusting the length.

"Not really," Lucy said, looking down at her feet sheepishly.

"Me neither." He shrugged. There was an awkward silence as the music reached the chorus Lucy knew well. "Want to anyway?" Harley asked, extending a hand as Lucy looked up from her feet.

"Okay." Lucy pursed her lips and placed her hand into his.

Chapter 36

EVERGREEN SMOOTHED the emerald satin fabric of the long dress over her hips with the palm of her hand. She glanced into one of the full-length mirrors as she passed through the gilded doorway, the same one she had walked through on the day of her first interview at the Virionics Institute. *Good enough for a thief,* she mused at her reflection with a smirk of her red-painted lips. Her eyes looked tired—she hadn't slept much the past couple of nights—but the rest of her reflection betrayed nothing else. Her blond hair was perfectly coiffed, wound heavily on the side of her head, her mother's ribbon hidden carefully inside the folds of her hair so as not to clash with her dress. Axon had told her that the perfect cover for stealing anything was one where the thief was both invited in and could hide in plain sight. She saw that she would fit in perfectly as she passed small clusters of well-dressed scientists, administrators, and donors to the institute snapping selfies in front of the grand entrance with their friends and colleagues. Most of the women wore floor-length dresses like hers, though many also had the embellished jewelry of the elite hanging from their earlobes and wrists, purchases she had yet to prioritize with her modest budget.

A small part of her felt regret for not being able to attend the gala with more pure intentions, to simply be in the presence of other brilliant minds, socializing and networking with those who could propel her career to the top. She hadn't made this decision lightly. If it ended badly, she most certainly was throwing a grenade at her career. But justice was paramount. She felt in her bones that there was something very wrong with this company, which she had previously admired so much. Evergreen had enough evidence to convince herself that Gerald Mason's death had not been an accident and high-ranking Virionics officials were somehow involved, but it wasn't enough to make public or convince anyone else. She hadn't even shared this with Arizona, afraid that if her and Axon's plans went badly, her friend could be in danger. Plausible deniability would be better for Arizona.

Evergreen had always thought of Virionics as this noble, unimpeachable beacon of science that worked for the people. The past few weeks had changed that. Maybe if she could prove there were a few bad apples in the bunch, causing a stain on the institution she had held in esteem for so long, Evergreen could go back to working for something she believed in.

Pushing away her anxiety was proving more challenging than she had thought as she entered the grand room, highly decorated and morphed into a winter fantasy land. Despite herself, her insides welled up with emotion and giddiness for just being here. Being invited to the most prestigious scientific social gathering of the year, among the brightest minds of her generation—and she was considered one of them. The guilt of attending with ulterior motives temporarily permeated her façade, and she grabbed hastily at a glass of champagne carried by a bow-tied waiter and drank deeply. She forced herself to call up the determination she had felt upon discovering the truth.

"Well, don't you look lovely," Axon interrupted her thoughts, appearing out of thin air with a half-full champagne flute. "As ever," he added wistfully, bringing the glass to his lips.

His charm was just what she needed to snap out of her reverie of self-doubt and focus on the goal. "Thanks," she said tartly. "Do you have the card?"

Axon pulled the white electronic keycard from an inner pocket, showing Evergreen discreetly.

"Good," she said, hands trembling. Evergreen sipped from her flute, hoping to steady them.

"Slow down! Don't want to be incapacitated when you brush elbows with the scientific princes, just to snatch their wallet right out of their pocket."

She glared at him and let her eyes roam purposefully between his slowly bubbling glass and his face. He shrugged nonchalantly and leaned close to her. "Not my first rodeo, babe," he half-whispered in her ear, sending goosebumps down her neck.

Color filled her cheeks, and she reminded herself quickly that he probably spoke like this to every girl he met who looked remotely decent in a dress. Hoping he wouldn't notice, she quipped, "And, you've led a life of crime for how long?"

"Well, I can't say it's my first time using my press pass for no good." He winked and a smile blazed across his dark face.

"This isn't exactly the same kind of criminal act as luring distraught girls back to your apartment after their cousin died."

"Hey, it's not a crime. They are always willing participants. And they play their part too." He shrugged. "Being distraught is all part of the act."

Evergreen gave him a look full of judgement.

He continued, "See, there's usually two scenarios. In the first, and most common I might add." He pointed a finger in the air for emphasis. "They either didn't know the deceased very well or didn't really like them. But they play the grieving friend or distant relative so they can use the excuse of melancholy to go home with someone they just met—me, as it so happens. They get to be easy for the night, and nobody judges them or calls them a slut behind their back." He shrugged again, smirking slightly. "Admit it, you've seen this done. You've probably done this before, yourself."

She shook her head disapprovingly.

"Mmmmm," Axon murmured, unconvinced. "Girls like to take calculated social risks. I'm math they can handle." He chuckled and sipped his drink.

She tutted at his bad joke and eyed the crowd around them, scanning for anyone she knew who might get in the way of their exit. "So, what's the second scenario?"

"Ah. Well, I have to be in a certain mood."

"And what mood is that?"

"A generous one."

She cocked an eyebrow. "You never struck me as the type."

"Short-term memory loss, I see," he said sarcastically before continuing. "In scenario two, the girls are actually sad. They knew the person who died pretty well, or at least well enough to feel bad about it. I have to actually comfort them, make them feel better. Lavish attention, make them forget."

"Again, you don't seem like the 'lavish attention on anyone' type."

"What? You don't think I'm up for a challenge every now and then?" Axon asked before adding the caveat, "If they're atomic."

"You're like a predator." She channeled judgement into her eyes as she glared at him.

"Judge all you want." He angled his head sassily. "They always leave smiling. You did," he added.

"That was different," she said, suppressing the urge to smile, not wanting to encourage him.

Her glass was empty, and Axon smoothly swapped it for a full flute from a passing tray. His fingers grazed hers, and she felt the reflexive need to pull back, as if touching a hot surface. He flashed a dazzling smile and brushed a strand of her hair behind her ear slowly, standing a fraction of an inch nearer without her realizing, so she could feel his breath on her cheek. "Don't drink this one, just hold it for appearances," Axon advised before adding, "You think you're immune?" His voice was soft and husky.

Her self-control unaffected by his proximity, she mimicked the tone of his voice seductively, looking directly into his eyes. "Immune to you?" Her face was inches from his when she stepped back decisively and snapped, "I'm vaccinated." Forcing her face to remain serious she added, "We have a job to do."

Axon laughed out loud. "It's always work with you, Miss Mason . . ."

Whatever he said next was abruptly drowned out by the sound of the loudspeaker projecting a voice identifying themselves as the Chief Administrative Officer in charge of developing technologies at Virionics.

". . . and I'm very honored to be able to introduce our President and Chief Scientific Officer, Doctor Emmanuel Covent." Applause sounded throughout the now-crowded room. There was a shuffle near the microphone as Doctor Covent took the podium.

"I am so pleased to see such a turnout of our scientific staff and generous donors," he began, like a salesman at the height of their pitch, with muted excitement and self-assurance that he would close the deal. Evergreen couldn't help but be drawn into the charisma which had propelled his career from a mere research assistant like her, through the ranks until he was sitting president of the company. Inspiration and drive burned through her veins as he began to speak about the accomplishments of the company and their ambitions for the future. A future she had so badly wanted to be a part of until recently. *Maybe I could still—*

Axon interrupted her thoughts with a warm hand on her exposed back. "This is probably where we make our exit, Ev," he murmured into her ear. "Like you said, we have a job to do."

That was the plan, to shuffle out while everyone was distracted. She nodded and reluctantly began to make her way through the crowd diagonally toward the hallway on the left side of the great room. Axon followed slightly behind her, brushing between attendees whose rapt attention to the speaker allowed him to pass unnoticed.

The long hallway off of the main ballroom was a pass-through to the labyrinth of buildings on the Virionics campus. Evergreen knew their route well and wound them through a series of hallways to the main administrative part of the building where she knew Evan Indigo's office would be. When they reached the office, the darkness through the rectangular window made it clear nobody was inside. The card reader on the outside of the door showed a solid red circle of light, indicating its locked status.

"Moment of truth," Evergreen said dramatically, taking a big breath. She tapped the card Lucy had given to Axon against the little black box. An audible *beep* sounded, and the circle of light turned green as the door clicked open. "It worked." She breathed a sigh of relief and pulled the handle to admit herself and Axon into Evan's office, flipping on half the lights and dimming them with a twist of her fingers.

The desktop computer was in sleep mode, the separate electronic lock glowing faintly red much like the door. She tapped the card again, and the computer beeped to life, quickly logging into Evan's desktop and programs. Evergreen sat down in Evan's wheeled desk chair with a faint squeak of the springs while Axon leaned against the dark wood desk. Evergreen navigated her way through the files until she found the folder labeled "Project Hourglass."

Because of her discovery that the files saved from her father's computer were corrupted, Evergreen suspected any documents they found couldn't be transferred to an external drive. They would need to read what was of interest quickly and print the rest. Her apartment was so close to campus, she was able to pick up the newly enhanced signal of her home printer and send documents there to sift through and determine next steps. "Here it is," she said, looking over at Axon.

"Open it," he replied.

She double-clicked.

An excerpt from The Hourglass Files:

Hourglass Committee Emergency Meeting Minutes (dated from two weeks prior)

Meeting commences on-time at 17:00

Agenda:

Determine next steps for committee member Gerald Mason's infringement on committee rules

Discussion:

Committee members agree to follow through with Bylaw #23 Section C which states:

> *Any member attempting to access sensitive committee files outside of routine committee meeting work times shall be assumed to be violating the trust of Virionics and will be outside the protections of the government. Due to the sensitive nature of these documents, unapproved access assumes the user is attempting to break confidentiality and intends to make all documents accessible, leading to possible panic and civil mutiny. Consequences of breaking this agreement include but are not limited to imprisonment in the Leydig facility, house arrest, dismemberment, or termination of predetermined Lifetime Potential clock. Punishment will be determined via majority vote at an emergency committee meeting without the presence of the violator.*

Per his request, it is noted that Dr. Ryan Delaney disagrees with taking any serious action against Dr. Mason and votes to imprison him in Leydig indefinitely.

Decision:

Majority rules 14:1 in favor of alteration of Gerald Mason's internal clock. His Lifetime Potential will be reduced to zero within the next 72 hours.

Meeting adjourned at 17:32.

Chapter 37

AXON'S NECK WAS BEGINNING to ache from staring down at the computer screen over Evergreen's shoulder. Evergreen, always methodical, insisted they needed to open every subfolder to determine what might be important. Thus far, they had skimmed through the official charter of the Hourglass Committee, which included members they already knew of, such as Evan Indigo and Evergreen's late father, Gerald Mason. Others were high-ranking scientists and administrators from both Virionics and the government, including the heads of the Department of Lifetime Potential, Department of Finance, and Department of Homeland Security. They found meeting minutes that dated back decades and decided to only print the last five years, during which it appeared the committee gathered monthly. The bylaws were discovered and printed, confirming their worst suspicions. Gerald's death had been no accident.

"Go back to the 'Articles of Support' folder." Axon pointed at the screen impatiently, not overly interested in reading the blow-by-blow account of the committee's last meeting.

"Fine," Evergreen said, clearly exasperated. She clicked back to the main file tree and found the folder he wanted. Dozens of documents were available to open, with titles they both recognized as articles they had recovered during long research hours. A. A. Morse and her thesis on population sustainability, *HG580* gene suppression, a folder containing census documents that spanned decades, and many others they didn't have time to dive into. One document caught Axon's eye as Evergreen slowly dragged the sidebar: Hourglass Manifesto.

"That! Click on that!" Axon tapped the computer screen with his index finger, overriding her mouse and opening the document with his touch. "Hourglass Manifesto" filled the screen and they read. By the end, Axon felt the need to sit down properly and dragged the chair opposite the desk next to Evergreen, who sat with her mouth agape. "Did you hit print?" he asked shakily, his throat dry.

"Yep."

"I think we need to be done, Ev," Axon said softly. "We have enough to bring this to the public. Everyone deserves to know."

"I thought the pandemic of '93 was caused by a flu," she whispered, ignoring him. "How could they?"

"It *was* flu," Axon confirmed.

"It was . . ." She stared at the computer screen, willing the truth to be different. "Until it wasn't. This is what we learned in school," she said, affronted. "But they manipulated the outbreak. Controlled it enough to cause panic, chaos, and death to meet their quotas. Axon, they *wanted* it to kill people."

"I know."

"All to hit a fucking 'reset' button because humans were living too long?" Evergreen massaged her forehead, leaning her elbow on the desk.

Axon let her sit in silence for a moment while he contemplated. "It all makes sense, though. Get the population back to a controllable level and then keep growth at a sustainable rate. That paper. A. A. Morse's paper on sustainable population growth rates."

Evergreen shook her head in disbelief.

"She killed herself a few years later, you know," Axon added.

"Good," Evergreen said solemnly. "The blood of all those people was on her hands. Millions of them."

"Generations of them," Axon corrected. "Lifetime Potential is all bullshit. All those kids who died young, people who lived to be middle-aged that could have lived until they were eighty."

Axon thought about how the government had not only created the disease that wiped out millions, but had wielded it like a tool to achieve population control. Every day, newborn babies were brought into this world and their parents were fed a lie about how long their child would live for. Out of the laughable consideration of "fairness," the government had decided to randomize children's lifespans in order to maintain the correct population density over time. Disease had all but been cured, so what else could they do, the manifesto argued. Population was bound to grow unchecked until all sustainable resources were depleted, leaving the world in a state of chaos, facing the extinction of the human race.

Axon had to admit, they were creative. Leading scientists had developed micrometer-sized synthetic cells to be programmed with the exact moment of individualized death and injected into the bloodstream shortly after birth. When life's hourglass ran out, specific human cells were triggered to go through the typically natural process of apoptosis, or programmed cell death, all at once. This prompted the body to shut down, appearing as if death were due to natural causes.

"The way the government used the pandemic to institute their health initiatives . . . it just goes against everything . . ." Evergreen hung her face in her hands.

"People will know the truth," Axon said, placing a hand tentatively on her shoulder. "We'll tell them. You and I. And this will all stop."

If the truth of the Lifetime Potential system was unveiled, people could be allowed to live without a ticking clock hanging malevolently above their heads. If he was allowed to die of natural causes, he could be looking at many years more of this life. The thought warmed his insides with hope. There were so many things he would do, so many things he would stop doing. This could mean an actual future. One without so much death, so many shallow relationships.

"You're right. We're doing this. We're committed and seeing this thing through, no matter how ugly it is." Evergreen gritted her teeth and stood. Meticulously, she logged out of the workstation and arranged the office precisely how they had found it. She pointed wordlessly to the chair Axon had dragged from around the desk, and he obligingly moved it back where it belonged.

From his jacket pocket, Axon removed the little squeeze bottle of ethyl alcohol and the cloth Evergreen had given him. Squirting the contents of the bottle onto the cloth, he wiped down the surfaces of the desk, anything they could have touched and left a trace fingerprint or skin cells enough to create a DNA profile. Evergreen watched, an amused look on her face.

"What?" he asked.

"Nothing," she said, smiling.

With an arm around her bare shoulders, Axon walked with Evergreen out of the office, hitting the switch and letting the door shut gently behind them. They walked slowly down the halls back toward the gala, his arm around her satin-wrapped waist, her hands holding up the length of her skirt from dragging on the floor, both staring straight ahead.

Evergreen came to an abrupt stop as they made their way back down the first long corridor used to leave the gala, hearing the noise first. The sound of heavy boots from an adjacent hallway. She gripped his sleeve. "Someone's coming."

Listening hard, Axon could detect the sound of clinking keys. "Security guard?"

"Probably," she said, catching his eye. A glint of something he couldn't quite identify shone there as she suddenly dragged him several feet sideways into the arched doorway of an unlit office. "Just go with it," Evergreen said breathily before he felt his shoulder blades hit the solid wall and she pushed herself close to his chest. Before he could answer or question her intent, Evergreen's mouth was firmly against his. A moment of hesitation passed before Axon returned her kiss, wrapping one hand around the back of her neck, the other around her slim waist. As he breathed her in, Evergreen's body softened against his and Axon pulled gently on her lower lip with his mouth. Everything around them fell away—every thought, every sound, everything. Everything except her. Her mouth on his, her palm on his chest.

"Hey, you two aren't supposed to be over here!" said a gruff voice. The spell was broken. Axon turned his head to see a man with white hair and a closely trimmed beard dressed in a security uniform, glaring at them peevishly.

Evergreen giggled loudly. "I'm sorry, officer!" She backed away with a stumble from Axon's embrace. "We were just . . . just . . ." She lowered her voice to a whisper, placing her fingertips dramatically to her cheek as if telling the man a secret. ". . . looking for someplace more private." She giggled again, bringing her knee up near Axon's hip and letting her body lean against his once more.

Catching on, Axon clutched the side of her knee and looked apologetically at the guard. "I'm so sorry about that, sir, she really insisted." He shrugged as if there weren't anything he could have done about it.

The man's small eyes darted back and forth between them in assessment before barking his verdict. "You two better be gone by the time I make my next round. That's in five minutes!"

"Aye-aye!" Evergreen saluted, laughing while Axon mouthed the word *sorry* to the guard. The man turned with a grunt and walked back around the corner, continuing his patrol.

After he was out of earshot, Evergreen whispered, "Good thinking, huh?"

The green of her eyes was mesmerizing. *Had she meant that kiss?* He wondered. "Yeah."

"Come on, let's get back. Some people need to see that I'm still here before we leave." Evergreen pulled at Axon's wrist gently.

"Wait," Axon said, standing in place. She paused. Before he could think too hard about it, Axon leaned forward, traced his fingers delicately down the side of her jaw, and pressed his lips against hers. For a brief moment he stayed there before pulling away slowly enough to brush her nose with his. He opened his eyes and looked into hers, trying to see past the green hue into the many neurons firing across synapses and understand her feelings.

"Yeah, we should definitely get back," he said as he marched forward, emanating confidence as he dragged her limp arm behind his.

Evergreen smacked his hand jokingly. "You suck. You know that?"

"I don't know what you're talking about," Axon said with false nonchalance, smiling as he walked ahead of her. "I promised the kid I'd watch her speech. You're just trying to make me late," he added flirtatiously, tugging on her hand.

"Yeah?" Evergreen said, jogging slightly to keep up with his stride.

"I stick with my commitments, what can I say?" And in that moment he meant it. He reached for Evergreen's hand and laced his fingers through hers.

"That must be a new thing."

"I'm a committed guy." He shrugged as they re-entered through the doors to the ballroom. The music was in full swing, and the lights had dimmed perceptibly. The auction must have ended, but the speeches had yet to complete, Axon deduced, noting the podium's continued presence.

"I need to mingle," Evergreen said in his ear, her lips brushing against his skin. It *was* prudent for her to be seen by witnesses at various points during the event, to help solidify their alibi, if it ever came up.

"Meet you at your place?" Axon met her eyes.

"Yeah," she said, kissing his cheek quickly and removing her hand from his. Blending seamlessly into the crowd, Axon watched Evergreen walk away and smiled to himself. As if she could feel his gaze, she turned around, catching his eye, and winked at him.

Chapter 38

HARLEY AND LUCY DANCED one song after another, not wanting to break whatever spell was cast when they first began. Lucy could feel the sweat begin to bead on her temple and knew that if she didn't stop soon, her makeup would be a disaster before she had to take the stage. "Should we get a drink?" she asked breathlessly as the tenth song they danced to ended.

"Yeah, sure," Harley said, looking relieved to take a break. Tentatively, he reached for her hand as they walked toward the bar on the right. Lucy smiled and looked down, feeling bashful. It had been so long since the last time she'd had this feeling, this lightness in her stomach.

"What'll you have?" asked the man with the closely trimmed mustache behind the bar.

"Water?" Lucy said.

"Same," Harley said as he leaned casually against the bar with an elbow. "Nothing stronger to calm your nerves before stepping into the spotlight?"

"I'm afraid it'd make me vomit," she said as the butterflies of stage fright began to flutter once more.

"Smart," Harley agreed. "I would definitely vomit."

"So, you're not recommending the front row for the next time you have to speak publicly," Lucy said with a straight face.

"Not even the first three rows, I'd say." Harley shook his head. "You'd definitely be in imminent danger."

"Noted. I think if I stick to water, everyone will be okay."

"Sounds like a risk worth taking, to be nearby when you go up there."

Lucy felt the butterflies somersaulting in her gut. "You'll watch?"

"Of course! How could I miss a speech given by the most global girl I've met here?" Harley said, turning his body toward her again.

"Oh yeah?" This was pleasant news. She threw caution to the wind and asked, "And how many other global girls have you said that to, lately?"

"None. Are you asking me if I'm single?" Harley asked with twinkling eyes.

"I might be," she smiled, trying for flirtatious.

"Might be single too, or might be asking?"

"Both." A blush deepened in her cheeks as she looked away from his gaze.

He nodded and took a drink of the icy water the bartender had placed on the counter in front of him. "Me too," he said finally. "Maybe after this thing we could go somewhere for coffee or something?"

"Yeah," Lucy said. "Okay." The floating sensation that seemed likely to carry her body up to the ceiling was abruptly interrupted by a harsh tap on her shoulder.

Aurora Birch's brows were tense and knotted. "There you are," she said, obviously irritated. "It's almost time to be presented, I've been looking for you everywhere."

"Sorry," Lucy said before Aurora cut her off.

"And your makeup! What have you been doing, letting yourself sweat it all off?"

Lucy blushed again, embarrassed to have attention drawn to her sweat. "Is it wrecked?"

"I think she looks beautiful," Harley said quietly from behind Aurora. Lucy's expression turned smug, catching Harley's eye before looking back at Aurora.

Aurora sneered, ignoring him, and pulled Lucy's elbow aggressively away. Lucy found herself dragged toward a backstage dressing room where two stylists descended upon her in a hurried attempt to "fix her face," as it was sternly put. After much dabbing, blending and reapplying, Lucy was deemed acceptable to await her introduction.

She was instructed to stand quietly in the tiny makeshift alcove of
black curtains near the stage.

Evan Indigo's familiar voice began flowing from the speakers as
he attended to the moderating duties of the night. ". . . and she has
surprised us all by surpassing her LP. We hope to learn something
from her so we might help others live longer lives. Without further
ado, I present Miss Lucy Hanson, Virionics' new Face of Hope."

Applause rang through the ballroom, and Lucy felt a nudge from
behind to approach the stage. Taking a deep breath to steady herself,
she pulled back the heavy curtains and ascended the three steps to
the platform where Evan waited, glancing at his watch before meeting her eyes with a grin. The curtained background of the stage was
lit up with the projected words 'Face of Hope,' and the lights from
the ceiling glared down, causing Lucy to blink several times, trying
to adjust. Evan reached out an arm to help her climb to her place behind the podium. He placed a dry kiss on her cheek before stepping
back, allowing her to take center stage.

Lucy cleared her throat, looking down at the wooden surface
of the podium where a copy of her speech rested, waiting for her.
"Thank you, everyone," she began. "And thank you, Evan, for the
warm introduction," she added, looking back at Evan, who was once
again looking at his watch. He jerked his head up at the mention of
his name with his plastic grin and waved. "And a special thank you
to Virionics for giving me this great honor tonight." She paused for
polite applause.

"I am very lucky to have grown up in a community where such
support was given to those with a low Lifetime Potential like myself.
I was able to spend time with my family, make friends, and pursue
passions and interests I had freely. My informal education allowed
me to learn about things that most struck a chord, such as architecture, ocean ecology, and fantasy novels, to name a few." There was a
tittering of appreciative laughter.

Lucy looked at the crowd, finally having adjusted to the bright lights, and saw Axon, his white smile standing out a few rows back. When she met his eye, he winked and gave a thumbs up. Her eyes darted and spotted Harley a few feet away, his eyes meeting hers, causing an immediate melting sensation. She cleared her throat again, holding his gaze. "When I found out that I wouldn't be dying anytime soon, I have to admit it was a bit of a shock." More laughter.

"While it might not seem at first glance that low LPs have structure to their lives, we do. While there might not have been regimented planning for the future like for many of you, when I didn't die, the day-to-day routine was suddenly broken, and the future became this infinite void I was afraid to approach. It made me realize how many walls were carefully built around my life that had suddenly come crashing down. And without those walls, I had to build my own. I'll admit, it wasn't the easiest transition between attending your own wake and finding out that what you expected to happen wasn't going to. It was like the universe had played this practical joke on me. I have come to realize, though, that this joke was actually a blessing." As she said this, she realized how true it had become. Lucy had a lot to live for. Her parents, her passions, her future. Her speech continued in this same vein for several minutes, the rehearsed words coming easily, the inertia of getting to this moment in time becoming a bittersweet memory.

"My strength was tested when things I had known my whole life changed without notice, but I think I have passed that test. I feel optimistic and excited about my future. I feel honored and privileged to live in a society that can take my experience and learn from it. To be able to help the wonderful and intelligent scientists at Virionics apply new knowledge to extend the lives of others. We still don't know exactly why I've lived so long past my expected date, but I fully appreciate the extra time I have been given."

Her gut churned as she prepared for the announcement she was planning to make. Axon had sparked her to think about what she would do next in her life. While she might not have been a good fit to tag along in his shadow, she could still pursue something that would require some of the same skills.

"I want to help people and use this opportunity life has given me—this platform that I didn't ask for but that I got anyway. I've decided to publish a memoir of my experiences and my journey, and I'm hoping that all of you can commit to purchasing a copy. Because the proceeds will be donated entirely to a non-profit organization, The Lovely Wakers, who provide wake counseling to youths such as myself who face death early on in their lives."

The crowd cheered appreciatively as Lucy scanned the audience again. She saw her parents—Ed, wiping a rogue tear away from his cheek, pride for his only daughter overcoming him with emotion, Nadine wearing a genuine smile. Lucy saw Evergreen Mason standing off in one corner of the room, someone she had recently decided wasn't so bad. Axon and the scientist were better suited for each other than Lucy was, she realized, thinking of Harley. Though she had just met him, their connection felt two-sided and entirely real. Axon may be charming and handsome, but he had only ever been an unattainable crush. Someone to hold the place in her heart while she waited for another love to come her way.

She was going to be okay. She really was. "Thank you everyone for your support. The future is bright and I am full of hope!" She raised her fists in the air as her speech ended, and the crowd cheered. Evan had come up to her side, waiting to take the podium. He looked down at his shining wristwatch again and placed his hands on her shoulders.

He leaned over her to speak into the microphone. "Thank you, Lucy. Let's give it up one more time for Lucy Hanson!" The crowd responded enthusiastically. Lucy beamed and began to walk across the stage in the opposite direction she had come from, waving.

Suddenly, her feet felt like she was walking through sludge. It was hard to move. She stopped mid-stage, still angled toward the audience, feeling confused. Her legs were numb. She couldn't move. *What's happening?* She thought, her panic starting to rise. The lights were suddenly brighter and warmer on her skin, the prickling sensation of sweat building in her armpits and down her back. Before she could understand why, the floor was rapidly approaching her face. *Why is the floor getting closer?* She wondered, feeling oddly like she was suppressing a laugh. Her cheek was resting against something hard—the stage floor, she realized dreamily. How did she get here? Her body was frozen.

Lucy was aware that people had rushed to her side on the stage, the background roar of so many, their voices indistinguishable from each other. She stared off across the room and watched, confused, as the scientist—what was her name? Evergreen. Her brain felt thick. It was difficult to grasp onto any one thought. Why was Evergreen being pulled away from the crowd? The woman's arms were pinned behind her back, and men in dark uniforms had surrounded her. Lucy stared at the green of her dress, the shine of the satin. *Such a nice color*, she thought lazily. Her eyes, no longer in focus, took in the brightness of the lights, the blur of faces, the absence of sound until she saw nothing. Because in death there was nothing left to feel.

Chapter 39
Ten minutes earlier

EVERGREEN SHOULDERED her way through the crowd, having spotted a congregation of other Virionics employees she knew, a smile playing on her face. *That kiss*, she thought, touching her lips. Axon really seemed like he meant it, that he really was interested in starting something with her. Could they even work? They were so different. She was so driven; he was so spontaneous. He probably did this with lots of girls, charming them to the point where they started to imagine a future with him. This felt different, though. This spark had lit a flame deep in Evergreen's chest, and she could feel the pleasant heat washing through her. It had been a long time since she felt this way, and even with Zane . . . This thing with Axon was different somehow. Sure, there was chemistry with her and Zane, but it had been almost a victory to land one of the most popular guys in school. Evergreen had felt confident, sure of herself, smug even. That was then. Evergreen had spent the better part of a year in her new life, with a foot propping open the door to her dream job while the government kept massive secrets, mysteries she was part of and could unravel. She was a grown woman now with principles and scruples. She could decide what she needed. Axon, despite his LP, was smart and witty. He could hold a conversation about more than just himself—an area where Zane demonstrated obvious weakness.

What would it be like to go on an actual date with Axon Davis? Evergreen mused, chancing a glance back to where she'd left Axon in the crowd. She felt a warm flush in her cheeks, realizing he had been watching her walk away. His ivory smile shone through the milling party guests as he gave her a subtle wink. She attempted to mask the gooey feeling that must have been plastered all over her face with a half-smile.

She took another two steps toward her intended destination before crashing into someone's very solid chest. Evergreen turned to apologize for her inattention, and had to crane her neck upwards to meet the eye of the bulky man in front of her. "I'm so sorry, sir," she said, miming regret with a hand to her chest. Without waiting for acknowledgement, Evergreen made to step around him.

"Evergreen Mason," he said, pushing a teapot-sized palm toward her, the obvious symbol for "stop."

Her weight already committed to the step around this rock of a man, Evergreen looked up at his face, trying to meet his eye. "Yes?" Did she know this man?

Expressionless, the man momentarily met her searching gaze before looking away and nodding into the distance. His dark dinner jacket was unremarkable aside from the Virionics logo embroidered above his left lapel. *He must be some high-ranking security guard,* she thought. Evergreen noted that he looked too big and dumb to have a scientific role like hers.

She furrowed her brow, confused at the interaction, and again began to step around the man when she felt strong hands grab her arms on either side.

"Evergreen Mason. You need to come with us," a low voice said in her ear.

"What's going on?" Evergreen asked indignantly, a cold feeling dropping into her gut. *Did they know?* Steel-gripped hands encircled her upper arms on both sides. She could feel the color draining from her face. This must be a mistake. *How could they know?* There was the tiniest prick of something sharp against her bare arm, and Evergreen's knees buckled as a wave of relaxation washed through her body. *Did they just drug me?* She thought incredulously. As her mind dulled, the crowd was focused on listening to the speaker on stage and didn't seem to notice the three men overpowering Evergreen. They started shuffling awkwardly together toward the nearest exit,

Evergreen's feet dragging with every other step, her vision starting to blur as edges became softer. The light of the room was so soft and comforting, she almost smiled.

"You're wanted for questioning," was all one of them would say as she was briskly shepherded to the edge of the room, avoiding the bulk of the gala crowd. Evergreen focused on the clink of ice in glasses and murmured conversation alongside an amplified voice coming from the speaker on stage. Her feet weren't touching the ground anymore.

A couple stood, nursing drinks along the far wall as the men hustled Evergreen out of the ballroom. They stared quizzically and Evergreen felt a flutter of hope. Someone had noticed her predicament. Their faces came into sharp focus as Evergreen concentrated on signaling for help.

"Help me!" she exclaimed, her voice finally cooperating.

"What the hell is going on?" the woman in the long silver dress demanded as her date stepped forward, ready to intervene. Her dress fluttered as if from an invisible wind, cascading down to the floor like a waterfall. Evergreen couldn't help but stare. Her date's muscle mass showed through his fitted tuxedo jacket. Evergreen wondered how he moved in something so form-fitting.

"Get your hands off her," he said evenly, his biceps flexing so hard Evergreen could swear she heard his shirt tear with the pressure.

"Official business," the man holding her left arm spat, welcoming the challenge.

The woman interjected, "I don't care what it's about, she clearly needs help, and you need to get your hands off her before I yell 'fire.'" Evergreen silently cheered her on.

"Whoa, whoa," the men gripping her arms said in unison. "No need to cause a scene." They hastily released Evergreen. She had to stop herself from asking out loud why that actually worked. She was free!

Wait.

She inhaled sharply as her mind rapidly snapped away from an imagined escape and back to the present—reality had much sharper edges. The men were still moving Evergreen through the decorated ballroom, the crowd focused elsewhere. They passed an elegantly dressed woman in a long silver ball gown, her hand casually resting on the forearm of a tuxedoed man. They leaned against the wall of the ballroom, half-empty drinks in their hands, smiling and hardly noticing Evergreen's situation. The woman looked in her direction and made eye contact with Evergreen, an unarticulated question dancing on her face.

"Too much to drink," one of her captors' deep voices barked in gruff response to the onlookers. The silver-dressed woman looked away, satisfied enough with the answer to mind her own business.

Suddenly the guests gave a collective gasp.

Finally, Evergreen thought. Had they finally noticed her being dragged away against her will? Wouldn't someone be coming to help her?

The commotion got louder, but Evergreen wasn't able to turn—if it wasn't her they were ruffled about, then what? The men gripping her arms were too sturdy, pillar-like in their obstruction of her view, and she couldn't see. People had started shouting, and she could feel the tension in the atmosphere despite the fog that was descending on her senses. Something must have happened.

Just before Evergreen was pushed through a side door that led into a windowless hallway, she was able to cast a glance at the crowd. From across the room, she saw a man—*Axon?* She thought—sidestepping the crowd and moving with purpose toward the ballroom's main exit. If that was him, he had eluded detection, or escaped hulking handlers, unlike Evergreen. Her seconds-long view ended as she was forcibly taken through the doorway into the hall. The men marched her along in silence without releasing their grip on her arms. It was starting to hurt.

"Where are you taking me?" She might as well have asked the wall for all the answer she got. Her eyelids grew heavier. They reached the end of the hall and opened a metal door leading to a back alleyway where a black SUV idled. The man at the front of their procession opened the back door of the vehicle so the other two could shove Evergreen in the backseat. She heard the distinctive sound of fabric ripping when she stepped on the hem of her green dress. *Shit.*

Evergreen woke to intense fatigue despite sleeping for longer than she felt she'd ever done. She opened her eyes slowly—the light of the room hurt. She started to roll from her side onto her back and immediately regretted the infinitesimal movement. Her stomach lurched, and bile climbed her esophagus. She steadied herself with a palm pressed to the white sheets of the mattress beneath her. The fabric was rough to the touch, overly washed and bleached with frequent use. The pilling beneath her hand helped steady her brain. She swallowed, willing herself not to throw up until the feeling passed.

"How are you feeling?" a disembodied voice said near her feet.

Evergreen couldn't find the energy to muster a response.

"The sedative they gave you was powerful, made more so if you consumed any alcohol. Based on how you look, I'd say that's what isn't sitting well."

Evergreen remembered the single glass of champagne she'd had at the start of the gala, hours ago. Or days? It was hard to tell. She wanted to respond and set the record straight—she wasn't a lush—but her mouth was powdery dry and she found it challenging to move.

"You've only been here sixteen hours, if that's what you're wondering," said the voice. The details of the room were starting to take shape. Evergreen could make out four walls painted a light gray and a tiled floor, beige with a predictable edged pattern. A woman with a dark buzzcut sat just beyond the foot of her bed, the plastic frames of her glasses reflecting the fluorescent light of the room. Evergreen couldn't see a window from her vantage, but she sensed the room was as enclosed as she felt in spirit. A steel door with wire-reinforced glass in the tiny window faced her bed.

"The nausea will pass. Here, drink some water," the woman said, handing Evergreen a bottle with the lid already unscrewed. Evergreen leaned forward and took the bottle in her hands. It felt heavier than it should. She sipped cautiously, not wanting to aggravate her upset digestive system. Why was she here anyway? What did they want from her? Her brain was slowly waking up, her government-educated mind revving.

"You're probably wondering why you're here, and better yet, where here is." The woman said lightly. Evergreen was already annoyed with her flippancy.

"Who are you?" Evergreen asked, her vocal cords grinding through the silt of her throat.

"Ah. Good question. I'm your Orientation Officer, Lauren."

Evergreen managed to awkwardly roll herself into a position on her back, propped up by her elbows. "Orientation?" Her own voice was starting to become more recognizable. The water was helping.

"Yes," Lauren said simply. "I am here to help you adjust to your new way of life . . . or not," she added ominously.

"And what 'way of life' might that be exactly?" Evergreen asked. She took a gulp of water, emptying most of the plastic bottle and glaring back obstinately. She spotted the Virionics logo embroidered onto the upper breast of Lauren's white collared shirt.

"Well, that's entirely up to you, Evergreen. You have a choice here," Lauren said, scooting her chair forward to sit closer to Evergreen's head and placing a cool hand on her forearm. Evergreen looked down to see a box sitting open in Lauren's lap. Several glass bottles and syringes lay encased in molded foam. Lauren followed her gaze. "Oh, don't worry about those," she cooed. "So long as you do as you're told, they won't come anywhere near you."

"What's in them?" Evergreen asked, though she already suspected the answer. Virionics had a division of palliative care that served the group of people whose loved ones, spouses, and friends passed long before their own life was meant to end. A drug was developed for those who wished to quickly pass the time before their LP was up without resorting to the illegal option of suicide. *SleepPotential* sold well among certain demographics, and although Evergreen had never worked in the area of the company that manufactured it, she knew the effects were heavy. A user was expected to sleep indefinitely, provided a caregiver could administer fresh doses and manage the patient's bodily needs. Without that support, those who took the sleep medication often died of hygiene-related disease, a miserable way to die in a world with such advanced modern medicine. The drug was said to be pain-free and generate only pleasant dreams—that was the wording of the marketing campaign, anyway. Evergreen remembered the backlash *SleepPotential* experienced when first introduced to consumers. Over half the people who tried it had experienced a sort of paralysis where their minds were dull, but alert enough to sense the passing of time as their bodies remained motionless. The hours would tick by and they would remain the same, aware and trapped. It was like a living death.

Lauren held up one of the vials, confirming Evergreen's suspicion. "It won't hurt. Your mind might waste away though," she said sweetly. "Unless you'd rather adhere to the alternative?"

The bile she'd felt upon waking was sitting higher in her gut than moments before. "And what is the alternative?"

"You work for us," Lauren stated simply, the option obvious.

"Who? Virionics?" Evergreen pointed at the logo on Lauren's shirt. "You mean the company responsible for killing millions prematurely, culling the population down to a manageable size, only to keep a level of fear and control over them for generations?"

"Oh, honey," Lauren said patronizingly. "You aren't above this. You helped, after all."

"I did my job, but I didn't perpetuate this . . . this . . ." She struggled to find the words. "This conspiracy. This is inhumane. I don't want to end lives. I want to prolong them. I just helped make annual vaccinations to keep people safe from the *real* diseases, not the fake pathways to death we've all been sold."

Lauren's eyes glittered with satisfaction. "And what, pray tell, do you think those annual vaccinations you tailored for individual people really did? Help people?" she asked with raised eyebrows. "Hm?"

Evergreen stared back at her. Was this a trap?

"Oh no, dear. You didn't know." Lauren frowned empathetically. "It's just, those tailored medications were made for people like that Lucy Hanson, who had developed antibodies *against* their original bio-trackers. It reset the clock, so to speak. They could go back to dying at the time their LP was originally determined to be. Lucy was a new one for us, though. We didn't catch it until after she surpassed her LP. And then when the media coverage made her famous, it made things riskier. New mutations like Lucy's have been cropping up lately that seem to provide some resistance to those internal clocks that tick-tick-tick away until the predicated time. We'd like you to continue the work to help Virionics prevent these minor mutations from causing such a fuss as Lucy's case did. It was really bad for business. Bad for public morale really!" she exclaimed. "Imagine the people who thought that suddenly they might rise up and live longer than the timeline they were assigned at birth? We'd have a plethora of uneducated masses, that's for certain." Lauren sighed again. "So, will you do it?" she asked briskly, hands clapping on her lap as if asking Evergreen whether she wanted to play a game of chess instead of betray her morals and work against the health of the public.

"No?" Evergreen said with a scrunch of her eyes. "I'm not doing that," she said, now with certainty.

"Oh!" Lauren puckered her lips. "Well, I guess I have no choice then! How does two weeks sound, to mull it over?" She reached for the syringe in her lap and Evergreen flinched back toward the wall. "Adam!" Lauren hollered over her shoulder.

A key twisted the lock of the metal door, and the beefy man from the gala pushed his way inside, moving with swifter agility than Evergreen predicted. He put his large hands on the crook of Evergreen's elbows to hold her down. Lauren plunged the needle into the vial, sucking the liquid sleep into the syringe.

"Shh, enjoy your nap."

Evergreen tried to fight back, but they were faster than her tired body, and she quickly became limp, her eyes half open and her body motionless. Adam rolled Evergreen onto her side so she faced the room. Before Lauren left Evergreen alone, she placed a digital clock displaying a countdown from fourteen days. Evergreen stared at the red numbers, unable to move.

"Welcome to Leydig," Lauren said before pulling the door shut with a metallic click.

Thirteen days, twenty-three hours, fifty-nine minutes, and thirty seconds.

Chapter 40

Epilogue

"YOU'RE NEW," A SLENDER man with scrubs commented while setting down his tray next to Evergreen's at the cafeteria table. She had only just started eating outside of her room, becoming more comfortable with her surroundings.

"Yeah. Sort of." Evergreen replied blandly, glancing his way and noting taped eyeglasses over small brown eyes. He had a familiar look she couldn't quite place.

"I'm kidding. I know who you are, Evergreen."

It had been six months since Evergreen was brought to Leydig. Her "little rebellion," as it was delicately referred to by her handler, didn't last long. Lauren had only needed to induce the awareness coma in Evergreen a few times before she gave in. It had felt like years instead of weeks. It took her *days* to regain physical control of her body, requiring rehab to utilize her muscles again properly, and even longer until she felt able to think straight again.

A week or so after she agreed to do whatever they wanted so she could remain undrugged, she was taken to a more comfortable infirmary to recover and then moved to her current living space. Boxes containing her clothing, books, and other personal items showed up shortly after, all having been thoroughly searched before being delivered by two men in dark suits. She wouldn't be getting her computer back. They had issued her a new one. Evergreen had asked that all the papers from her home, evidence from her investigation, be brought to her. They'd be destroyed otherwise, and in here, she and the knowledge could be kept hidden away. The stacks of documents that had been piled up on her dining table in her tiny apartment were filed haphazardly together in one box. When she made mention of the items left on the printer, the men had denied that any existed. It was no matter. She was privy to all of the information she and Axon had uncovered, and more. The entire Virionics database was hers to explore now.

"Hang on, I'm good at this. Let me guess." He squinted, mocking deep thought. "Favorite protein is hemoglobin."

Evergreen smiled. "DNA polymerase." Arizona's favorite science joke involved a sexualized description of how DNA polymerase was the sluttiest because it "unzipped your genes."

Obviously familiar with the joke, his laughter boomed across the cafeteria, disproportional to his small frame.

When she was arrested at the Virionics gala, shortly after Lucy Hanson had collapsed due to her newly programmed death, Evergreen had been naïve. Now she was informed. Not that it made the situation any better. She wasn't allowed to leave. Not ever. But she was given a private dormitory room with its own adjoining bathroom and enough closet space for her shoes—not that she would ever have occasion to wear the fancy strappy stilettos again. It was comfortable enough, considering.

The last time she had seen anyone familiar was the night of the gala. Arizona undoubtedly would have been fed some story of Evergreen's intention to work abroad or for some top-secret government agency, which would be closer to the truth. Axon still hadn't been caught, at least to her knowledge. She thought she had seen him running along the opposite side of the ballroom toward another exit, a lifetime ago. But with so many people sporting indistinguishable black tuxedos, she couldn't be certain.

Chaos had descended quickly when Lucy Hanson collapsed on stage. This had allowed for Evergreen's arrest to go unnoticed and apparently unreported. She was able to connect with the outside world, but the relationship was one-sided. Like one-way glass, she could see everything, but they couldn't see or hear her.

Why hadn't they just killed her like they did her father? Evergreen asked this repeatedly during the breaks between doses of *Sleep-Potential*. The explanation was simple, and from Lauren, patronizing. She was too valuable. Gerald Mason was past his prime and only had so many good years left. The system had invested in her education, her promotion and knowledge. Science needed her to continue its secret side hustle.

Leydig turned out to be different than what she had been led to believe. Instead of being the place where only the worst criminals went, it was a refuge for select scientists, politicians with connections, and a smattering of others who knew the truth of the Lifetime Potential system. It was meant to keep the secret in, to keep the system running.

She knew the full truth now. After the government had orchestrated the pandemic which effectively leveled out the population to a manageable number, it had needed a way to keep the population steady. Using the existing structure for preventative medicine, they were able to inject proteins into the bodies of all citizens, which targeted specific series of DNA and integrated themselves into the genetics of the individual. The new code allowed for algorithm-based control over death, where people were assigned a death date and time immediately following birth. That time was hardwired into an individual's genetic code. The new DNA sequences were adopted by the human host and instructed the body on when to begin a rapid progression of programmed cell death, or apoptosis, throughout all major organs. Death was painless, with the individual barely knowing they were dying before their body stopped working.

Some people, like Lucy, had developed mutations that resisted the binding of DNA from the medication, preventing a change in their genetics and allowing them to die on their own body's terms. Unlike other people, Lucy's particular mutation was new. The research Evergreen had found for *HG580* was one of the first known evolutionary mutations discovered in humans to protect their bodies against foreign protein binding and alteration of their DNA. The specialized vaccination program Evergreen had begun working on at Virionics unknowingly created personalized medicine for those who tested positive for a series of gene mutations, which made them resistant to the government's DNA change. Scientists on her team were told that the genetic anomalies they were creating products to work around were the sneaky tricks of viruses or bacteria, not of human genetics. After all, the proteins of DNA were the same for all organisms with the familiar bases of Adenine, Guanine, Thymine, and Cytosine. They had never thought to question the source but were presented with the genetic resistance as if it were a puzzle, a challenge they needed to overcome to help prevent disease. How wrong they were.

Evergreen's job at Leydig was to search for new genetic mutations, Lucy's now having been added to the list of possibilities to screen for. The government usually took a proactive approach so the Lucy Hansons of this world would be discovered *before* their wakes. In her case, a new mutation hadn't been discovered in decades, and the Hourglass program had proved to be unprepared. The media had tenaciously latched onto the story, making Lucy Hanson difficult to sweep under the rug. Their next failed attempt, to medicate her to a late death, had enraged senior members of the Hourglass committee sufficiently to posit a more dramatic ending for Lucy Hanson.

It had been Evan Indigo's idea, Evergreen was told through the gossip mill at Leydig. Word got around quickly. There wasn't much else to talk about. Most of the other scientists weren't like her, at least not in the sense of having figured out the Lifetime Potential secret like she had. No, they were hand-selected by the Hourglass committee, screened for their talent and, most importantly, their isolation. The no-family-left type were the most popular choice. She wondered vaguely if the man with the glasses, who introduced himself as Max between large bites of pancake, had been recruited straight out of school.

He chatted animatedly about his own lab work. The science talk was comforting, and Evergreen found herself injecting opinions about her own latest developments against mutations.

Initially, she hadn't taken pleasure in the work but still managed to at least be productive. The first two weeks after the gala, she had been kept in a cement-floored cell, alone and devoid of stimulation for her intelligent brain. It had been a little frightening how quickly she began to question her sanity. When the minders had presented her with the choice to continue that life of solitude and gray quiet or to work and contribute, she was more than ready to forget any principles she might have prided herself on having before Leydig.

"What do you think of Leydig?" Max asked curiously.

She contemplated her answer for a moment. Once the initial shock wore off, she had found it easier than she expected to make friends. The food was good, there were social events several times a week, and everyone seemed so impressed by her resourcefulness and the lengths she had gone to in order to unravel the puzzle for herself. They'd respected her immediately. Initially, she hadn't understood why anyone would volunteer for such a life, but she was beginning to see what benefit their work played in society. Wasn't it better to live in an organized place where death was predictable? She'd heard this a lot from encouraging staff while she was still adjusting. Their work was helping people, many argued when Evergreen asked. This way, with this model, the human race would prosper. Evergreen was starting to see what they meant. Though she would never be famous, though her name would never hold notoriety within her field, at least not publicly, she was able to do something cutting edge: use science to help humanity. And wasn't that what she had wanted all along?

"I like it here," she said truthfully.

• • • •

WANT MORE OF *Hourglass?* To receive a free deleted scene from Evergreen and her High LP School days, plus a peek into more about the *Hourglass* world, visit my website to download at:
  www.elizabethmeanswriter.com[1]

---

1. http://www.elizabethmeanswriter.com

Acknowledgements

It's been at least eight years in the making, but I've finally accomplished my dream of publishing a book. Thank you, reader, for picking up a copy of *Hourglass* and taking the time to read it. I truly hope it provided you with entertainment and escape. Without you, it'd just be the small group of my family and friends who saw my work. It only means something if a *stranger* is reading it, after all. I'd love for us to not remain strangers, and if you check out my website and join my mailing list, we can connect. (I'm a really cool person!)

Thank you to my supportive friends and family who have read drafts and maintained interested looks while I explained plot points and my publishing journey. You are the real champions. Special shout-out to my husband, who has been supremely supportive of this whole writing thing, even if my books aren't space-opera enough for him. I still love you. Thank you to my mom and dad and grandfather, who all read drafts and gave critical feedback and encouragement. Thanks to cousins and friends who also read versions and gave encouragement: Tessa, Susie, Tim, Robert, BethAnne, Aaron, Elisabeth, Laurel, Geneva, Uncle Alex, Amy, Aunt Glo. To other supportive friends and family who are eager to read what I've been plodding away at for years, thanks for your pats on the back and your unbridled amazement that I had taken on such a daunting task. I assume if you're reading this section that means you actually bought my book—thank you for putting your money where your mouth is! Thanks to Danielle for her always-objective advice—I am envious of your solid logic.

More than half of this book was written at my favorite local bar. Thank you to the fabulous servers and bartenders at The Lime—Grant, Delilah and Rachel. You kept me in wine and pickle fries, and for that I am grateful. And thanks to Amy, my writing and ballet buddy—having someone to keep me accountable, complain about work to, and power through writing corners with has been immensely helpful throughout this process.

My friend Julia and I came up with our own series when we were nine and seven respectively, called *The Runaways*. We would act out the scenes we wrote to make sure they made sense. It was half make-believe and half actual writing. Other times we would pretend to be Harriet the Spy, after reading the book and seeing the newly released Nickelodeon movie. We'd take notes in our composition notebooks and imagine becoming just like Harriet. Julia writes comedy now, among her many talents—thanks, lady, for the early inspiration.

Thank you to those who also provided inspiration for me to write: Aunt Sarah, Aunt Carrie, Grandma Tess. Also the teachers I had as a kid who helped me along the way: Mrs. Bundas, Mrs. Morris, Mrs. Hale, Mr. Karman. When I was seven, I decided I wanted to be a writer and instead I became a scientist (because that was, I guess, more responsible?). Coming back full circle to that childhood dream is pretty surreal.

Thanks to the Facebook group 20BooksTo50K®—you are a wealth of information for professional independent writers. I wouldn't have done this had I not stumbled upon the group earlier this year when I was in dire need of an energy-consuming project. Thank you to my editors Nia and Lori—after going through my copy edits, I realized why all writers thank their editors. It is otherwise a truly thankless task, like pulling weeds only to have them come back up two weeks later, or paying a doctor's office bill (why did I pay for the insurance, then?). Next time I will do better with commas, I swear.

The person I need to thank the most I can barely put into words my appreciation for. She read countless drafts, and versions of chapters that no longer exist. She developed attachments to my characters and gave advice and input when I got stuck. She cried when I killed off Colton, which made me feel pretty powerful, pushing me to keep going, I don't know how to explain what a muse she has been. This project would not have taken off had it not been for her.

Thank you the most, Cassie.

About the Author

Elizabeth Means is a Medical Laboratory Scientist and currently works in a hospital. She is a novice ballerina, avid reader and has traveled to thirty-one countries. Elizabeth grew up in Dearborn, Michigan but lives in the Pacific Northwest with her husband Mark, and their two rescue dogs Franklin and Henry.

Read more at www.elizabethmeanswriter.com.

Made in the USA
Columbia, SC
19 July 2021